Jill Mansell

rumour has it

headline
review

First published in 2009
by HEADLINE REVIEW
An imprint of HEADLINE PUBLISHING GROUP

First published in paperback in 2009
by HEADLINE REVIEW
An imprint of HEADLINE PUBLISHING GROUP

25

ISBN 978 0 7553 4983 8 (A-format)
ISBN 978 0 7553 2819 2 (B-format)

Typeset in Bembo by Palimpsest Book Production Limited,
Grangemouth, Stirlingshire
Printed and bound in Great Britain by Clays Ltd, Elcograf S.p.A.

Headline's policy is to use papers that are natural, renewable and recyclable
products and made from wood grown in sustainable products. The logging and
manufacturing processes are expected to conform to the environmental
regulations of the country of origin.

HEADLINE PUBLISHING GROUP
An Hachette Livre UK Company
338 Euston Road
London NW1 3BH

www.headline.co.uk
www.hachettelivre.co.uk

To Dad,
with love.

Chapter 1

How weird that you could push open your front door and know in an instant that something was wrong.

Tilly stopped in the doorway, her hand fumbling for the light switch. Back from work at six o'clock on a cold Thursday evening in February, there was no reason to believe that anything should be different.

But it was, she could feel it. She could *tell*.

Flick went the light switch, on came the light. So much for spooky sixth sense; the reason opening the door had felt different was because the hall carpet had gone.

The hall *carpet*? Had Gavin spilled something on it? Mystified, her heels clacking on the bare floorboards, Tilly headed for the living room.

What was going on? She gazed around the room, taking everything – or rather the lack of everything – in. OK, they'd either been targeted by extremely picky burglars or . . .

He'd left the letter propped up on the mantelpiece. Gavin was nothing if not predictable. He had probably consulted some etiquette guru: Dear Miss Prim, I'm planning on leaving my girlfriend without a word of warning – how should I go about explaining to her what I've done?

To which Miss Prim would have replied: Dear Gavin, Oh dear, poor you! In a situation such as this, the correct method is to convey the necessary information in a handwritten letter – not in an email and *please* not in a text message! – and leave it in the centre of the mantelpiece where it can't be missed.

Because, in all honesty, what other reason could there be? Tilly conducted a rapid inventory. Why else would the DVD recorder – hers – still be there, but the TV – his – be missing? Why else would three-quarters of the DVDs be gone (war films, sci-fi and the like), leaving only the slushy make-you-cry films and romantic comedies? Why else would the coffee table given to them by Gavin's mother have vanished while the—

'Tilly? Coo-eee! Only me!'

Damn, she hadn't shut the door properly. And now Babs from across the landing was doing her exaggerated tiptoeing thing as if that made barging into someone else's flat somehow acceptable.

'Hello, Babs.' Tilly turned; maybe Babs had a message for her from Gavin. Or maybe he'd asked her to pop round and check that she was *all right*. 'Did you want to borrow some tea bags?'

'No thanks, petal, I've tea bags coming out of my ears. I just wanted to see how you're doing. Oh, you poor thing, and there was me thinking the two of you were so happy together . . . I had no idea!' Bright green earrings jangled as Babs shook her head, overcome with emotion. 'Love's young dream, that's what Desmond and I used to call you. Bless your heart, and all this time you've been bottling it up. I wish you could've told me, you know I'm always happy to listen.'

Happy to listen? Babs *lived* to listen to other people's woes. Gossip was her middle name, her number one hobby. Then again, you couldn't dislike her; she was a good-hearted, well-meaning soul, in an avid, meddling kind of way.

'I would have told you,' said Tilly. 'If I'd known.'

'Oh my GOOD LORD.' Babs let out a high-pitched shriek of disbelief. 'You mean . . . ?'

'Gavin's done a runner. Well,' Tilly reached for the letter on the mantelpiece, 'either that or he's been kidnapped.'

'Except when I saw him loading his belongings into the rental van this afternoon he didn't have any kidnappers with him.' Her expression sympathetic, Babs said, 'Only his mam and dad.'

The commuter-packed train from Paddington pulled into Roxborough station the following evening. It was Friday, it was seven fifteen and everyone was going home.

Except me, I'm escaping mine.

And there was Erin, waiting on the platform, bundled up against the cold in a bright pink coat and waving madly as she spotted Tilly through the window.

Just the sight of her made Tilly feel better. She couldn't imagine not having Erin as her best friend. Ten years ago when she had been deciding whether to do her degree course at Liverpool or Exeter, she could have chosen Liverpool and it would never have happened. But she'd gone for Exeter instead – something about the seasidey feel to it and possibly the fact that a friend of a friend had happened to mention that there were loads of fit boys at Exeter – and there had been Erin, in the room next to hers in the halls of residence. The two of them had hit it off from day one, the platonic equivalent of love at first sight. It was weird to think that if she'd gone to Liverpool instead – where there would surely have been hordes of equally fit boys – she would have a completely different best

3

friend, a tall skinny triathlete, say, called Monica. God, imagine *that*.

'Oof.' Erin gasped as Tilly's hug knocked the air from her lungs. 'What's this in aid of?'

'I'm glad you aren't a triathlete called Monica.'

'Blimey, you and me both.' Shuddering at the thought, Erin tucked her arm through Tilly's. 'Come on, you. Let's get home. I've made sticky toffee pudding.'

'You see?' Tilly beamed. 'Monica would never say that. She'd say, "Why don't we go out for a nice ten-mile run, that'll cheer us up!"'

Erin's flat, as quirky and higgledy-piggledy as the properties that lined Roxborough's High Street, was a one-bedroomed affair situated on the first floor above the shop she'd been running as a dress exchange for the last seven years. Working in a shop hadn't been her dream career when she'd graduated from Exeter with a first-class degree in French, but Erin's plans to work in Paris as a translator had been dashed the month after her twenty-first birthday when her mother had suffered a stroke. Overnight, Maggie Morrison had been transformed from a bright, bubbly antiques dealer into a fragile, forgetful shadow of her former self. Devastated, Erin had given up the dream job in Paris and moved back to Roxborough to nurse her mother. A complete ignoramus where antiques were concerned, she converted the shop into an upmarket dress exchange and did her best to combine caring for Maggie with keeping the business afloat.

Three years after the first stroke, a second one took Maggie's life. Grief mingled with relief which in turn engendered more guilt-fuelled grief, but this was when the inhabitants of Roxborough had come into their own. Having always intended to move back to Paris once the unthinkable had happened, Erin

4

realised she no longer wanted to. Roxborough, an ancient market town in the centre of the Cotswolds, was a wonderful place to live. The people were caring and supportive, there was real community spirit and the business was doing well. This was where she was happy and loved, so why move away?

And now, almost four years on, Erin had even more reason to be happy with her decision to stay. But she wouldn't tell Tilly yet, not while she was still reeling from Gavin's disappearing act. That would definitely be insensitive.

Although it had to be said, Tilly didn't seem to be reeling too badly. It had come as a shock, of course it had, but discovering that her live-in boyfriend had moved out appeared to have left her surprised rather than distraught.

'I phoned him this afternoon,' Tilly said now, between spoonfuls of sticky toffee pudding. 'Honestly, you wouldn't believe it. He couldn't face telling me in person in case I cried, so doing a bunk was the only thing he could think of. He's moved back in with his parents and he's sorry, but he just didn't feel we were going anywhere. So he left!' She shook her head in disbelief. 'Which leaves me stuck with a flat there's no way I can afford on one salary, and I can't even advertise for a flatmate because there's only one bedroom. I mean, talk about selfish!'

'Would you have cried? If he'd told you face to face?'

'What? God, I don't know. Maybe.'

'*Maybe?* If you're madly in love with someone and they dump you, you're supposed to cry.' Erin licked her spoon and pointed it at Tilly. 'You're supposed to cry buckets.'

Tilly looked defensive. 'Not necessarily. I could be heartbroken on the inside.'

'Buckets,' repeated Erin. 'Which makes me think you're not actually that heartbroken at all. In fact, you might actually be quite

5

relieved Gavin's gone. Because secretly, deep down, you *wanted* him to finish with you because you couldn't bring yourself to do the deed yourself.'

Tilly flushed and said nothing.

'Ha! See? I'm right, aren't I?' Erin let out a crow of delight. 'It's Mickey Nolan all over again. You really liked him to begin with, then it all got a bit boring and you didn't know how to chuck him without hurting his feelings. So you did that whole distancing yourself thing until he realised the relationship had run out of steam. And Darren Shaw,' she suddenly remembered. 'You did the same with him. You feel guilty about finishing with boyfriends so you force them to finish with you. I can't believe I never spotted it before.'

It was a light bulb moment. 'You could be right,' Tilly admitted.

'I *am* right!'

'Did I ever tell you about Jamie Dalston?'

'No. Why, did you do it to him too?'

'No, we went out for a couple of weeks when I was fifteen. Then I realised he was a bit weird so I dumped him.' Tilly paused, gazing into the fire as she dredged up long-forgotten memories. 'That was when it started getting awkward, because Jamie didn't want to be dumped. He used to phone the house all the time, and walk up and down our road. If I went out, he'd follow me. Then, when it was my birthday he sent me some quite expensive jewellery. My mum took it round to his mum's and the police got involved. I don't know exactly what happened but I think he'd stolen the money to buy the jewellery. Anyway, his family moved away a couple of weeks later and I never saw him again, but it frightened the living daylights out of me. And reading in the papers about ex-boyfriends turning into stalkers always creeps me out. I suppose that's why I'd rather let the other person do the dumping. That way, they're less likely to stalk you after-wards.'

'So you are actually quite glad Gavin's gone,' said Erin.

'Well, it wasn't working out. He was so set in his ways. I did feel kind of trapped,' Tilly confessed. 'But his mother kept telling me what a catch he was and I didn't have the heart to say, "Yes, but couldn't he be a bit less boring?"'

'But you moved into the flat with him,' Erin pointed out. 'Was he boring from the word go?'

'That's just it! I don't know! I think he probably was, but he hid it well. He definitely didn't tell me he belonged to a model aeroplane club until after I'd moved in,' said Tilly. 'And he completely forgot to mention the bell-ringing. Oh God, I'm so ashamed. How could I have gone out with someone for six months and not known they were a secret bell-ringer?'

'Come on.' Erin's tone was consoling as she put the empty pudding bowls on the coffee table and stood up. 'It's stopped raining. Let's go to the pub.'

Chapter 2

The joy of living at one end of Roxborough High Street was that the Lazy Fox was situated at the other end of it, far enough away for you not to need earplugs at home if they were having one of their karaoke evenings but close enough to stagger back after a good night. Tilly enjoyed the atmosphere in the pub, the mix of customers and the cheerful staff. She loved the way Declan the landlord, upon hearing her just-been-chucked story from Erin, said easily, 'Fellow must be mad. Come and live in Roxborough. Fresh country air and plenty of cider – that'll put hairs on your chest.'

Tilly grinned. 'Thanks, but I'm a townie.'

'Damn cheek. This is a town!'

'She means London,' said Erin.

'That's a terrible place to live.' Declan shook his head. 'We're much nicer.'

'I've got a job up there,' Tilly explained.

He looked suitably impressed. 'Oh, a *job*. Prime Minister? Director General of the BBC?'

Erin gave his hand a smack. 'Declan, leave her alone.'

'Our newspapers have proper news,' Tilly riposted, entertained by his sarkiness and poking at the copy of the *Roxborough Gazette* he'd been reading between customers. 'What's that on your front page? Cow falls through cattle grid? On your front page!'

'Ah, but isn't it great that we aren't awash with terrorists and murderers?' Declan winked at her. 'That's why I like it here. And I lived in London for thirty years.'

'What happened to the cow anyway?' Tilly leaned across but he whisked the newspaper away.

'Oh no, anyone who laughs at our headlines doesn't get to find out how the stories turn out. Was the cow winched to safety by the fire brigade, lifted up out of the grid like a parachutist on rewind? Or was it left dangling there to die a horrible death? Now that's what I call a *moo*-ving tale . . .'

Declan relented as they were leaving two hours later, folding the *Gazette* and slipping it into Tilly's green and gold leather shoulder bag. 'There you go, you can read the rest yourself. It may not be the *Evening Standard* but our paper has its own charm, you know. In fact in some ways it's *udder*ly compelling.'

The awful thing was, after three pints of cider Tilly secretly found this funny. Somehow she managed to keep a straight face.

'So that's why you were drummed out of London. For making bad puns.'

'Got it in one, girl. And I'm glad they did. In fact,' said Declan, 'I'll be for-heifer grateful.'

Once outside on the street, closing time hunger pangs struck and they were forced to head up the road to the fish and chip shop. While they waited to be served, Tilly unfolded the paper and read that the cow – a pretty black and white Friesian called Mabel – had indeed been winched to safety by the Roxborough fire brigade and reunited with her calf, Ralph. Ahh, well that was good to hear. Better than a lingering death with its legs dangling through the grid and poor baby Ralph mooing piteously . . .

'Oh sorry, one haddock and chips, please, and one cod and chips.'

Back out on the pavement, Tilly greedily unwrapped the steaming hot parcel and tore off her first hunk of batter.

'Mm, *mmm*.'

'I'm going to save mine until we get home,' said Erin.

'You can't! That's what old people do! Fish and chips taste a million times better in the open air.'

'I'm twenty-eight,' Erin said happily. 'I'm knocking on. And so are you.'

'Cheek!' Outraged, Tilly threw a chip at her. 'I'm not old, I'm a spring chicken.'

A couple of teenage boys, crossing the street, snorted and nudged each other. Tilly heard one of them murmur, 'In her dreams.'

'For heaven's sake!' Indignantly Tilly spread her arms. 'Why is everyone having a go at me tonight? Twenty-eight isn't geriatric. I'm in my prime!'

The other boy grinned. 'In two years' time you'll be thirty. *That's* geriatric.'

'I can do anything you can do,' Tilly said heatedly. 'Pipsqueak.'

'Go on then, try peeing up against that wall.'

Damn, she hated smart kids.

'Or do *this*,' called out the first boy, taking a run-up and effort-lessly leapfrogging the fixed, dome-topped litter bin just down from the chip shop.

Oh yes, this was more like it. Peeing up against walls might be problematic but leapfrog was practically her specialist subject. On the minus side she was wearing a fairly short skirt, but on the plus side it was nice and stretchy. Dumping her parcel of fish and chips in Erin's arms, Tilly took a run up and launched herself at the bin.

Vaulting it went without a hitch; she sailed balletically over the top like Olga Korbut. It was when she landed that it all went horribly wrong. Honestly, though, what were the chances of your left foot landing on the very chip you'd earlier thrown at your best friend after she'd called you old?

'EEEEYYYYAAA!' Tilly let out a shriek as her left leg scooted off at an angle and her arms went windmilling through the air. She heard Erin call out in horror, 'Mind the—' a millisecond before she cannoned into the side of the parked car.

Ouch, it might have broken her fall but it still hurt. Splattered against it like a cartoon character, Tilly belatedly noticed that it was an incredibly clean and glossy car.

'Hey!' yelled an unamused male voice from some way up the street.

Well, it had been incredibly clean and glossy up until five seconds ago. Peeling herself away from the car, Tilly saw the marks her fish-and-chip greasy fingers had left on the passenger door, the front wing and the formerly immaculate side window. With the sleeve of her jacket she attempted to clean off the worst of the smears. The male voice behind her, sounding more annoyed than ever, shouted out, 'Have you scratched my paint-work?'

'No I haven't, and you shouldn't have been parked there anyway. It's double yellows.' Glancing over her shoulder and checking he was too far away to catch her, Tilly retrieved her fish and chips from Erin, then did what any self-respecting 28-year-old would do and legged it down the road.

'It's OK,' panted Erin, 'he's not chasing us.'

They slowed to a dawdle and Tilly carried on eating her chips.

11

As they made their way together along the wet pavement she said, 'Lucky there was no one around to take a photo. In a place like this, getting greasy fingers on a clean car could've made the front page of next week's *Gazette*.'

'You know, Declan's right. You'd like it here.' Erin, who was still saving her own chips, pinched one of Tilly's. 'If you wanted to give it a go, you can stay with me for as long as you like.'

Tilly was touched by the offer but knew she couldn't. During the years of nursing her mother, Erin had slept on the sofa in the living room while Maggie occupied the only bedroom. It hadn't been ideal by any means. She knew how claustrophobic Erin had found it. Coming down for the weekend and staying for a couple of nights was fine, but the flat was small and anything more would be unfair.

They'd reached the bottom of the High Street. All they had to do now was cross the road and they'd be home. Still greedily stuffing chips into her mouth, Tilly waited next to Erin for a bus to trundle past, followed by a gleaming black car—

'You sod!' Tilly shrieked as the car splashed through a puddle at the kerbside, sending a great wave of icy water over her skirt and legs. Leaping back – *too late* – she glimpsed a flash of white teeth as the figure in the driver's seat grinned and raised a hand in mock apology before accelerating away.

'It was him, wasn't it?' Shuddering as the icy water soaked through her opaque tights, Tilly hugged her bag of fish and chips for warmth. 'The one who yelled at me.'

'It's the same car,' Erin confirmed. 'Some kind of Jag.'

'Bastard, he did that on purpose.' But she was inwardly impressed. 'Quite clever though.'

Erin gave her an odd look. 'Clever how?'

Tilly pointed at Erin's unsullied cream coat, then at her own soaked-through skirt and tights. 'The way he managed to avoid you and only get me.'

The next morning Tilly woke up on the sofa with a dry mouth, cold legs and the duvet on the floor. It was ten o'clock and Erin had tiptoed past her an hour ago in order to head downstairs and open the shop. Later Tilly would join her for a while before taking off for a wander around Roxborough, but for now she would enjoy being lazy and spend a bit of time wondering what to do with the rest of her life.

Tilly made herself a mug of tea and a plate of toast before hauling the duvet back on to the sofa and crawling under it. Next she switched on the TV, then rummaged through her bag for her phone, to see if there were any messages on it. No, none, not even from Gavin. Which was just as well really, because the last thing she needed was for him to start having second thoughts and regretting his decision.

Plumping up the pillows and taking a sip of tea, Tilly pulled the *Roxborough Gazette* out of her bag and smoothed out the creases where it had been scrunched up. The cow story still made her smile.

She leafed through the paper and learned that two sets of twins had been born to women living in the same street. Now how was that not a front-page newsflash? There was a piece about a tractor auction – be still, my beating heart – and a whole page devoted to a charity bazaar at Roxborough Comprehensive. Tilly flicked past photos of wedding couples, an article about an overhanging tree branch that could be really quite dangerous if it snapped off and landed on someone's head, and another about a bus breaking down in Scarratt's Lane, causing the road to be blocked for – gasp! – three and a half hours. There was even a photograph of the broken-down bus with offloaded passengers standing alongside it looking suitably downcast, apart from one lad of about five who was grinning from ear to ear.

Actually, it was quite sweet. The worst thing that appeared to have happened in Roxborough in the last week was that a man had collapsed and died while digging up potatoes in his allotment, but he'd been ninety-three so what did he expect? Sipping her tea, Tilly turned the page and came across the jobs section. Garage mechanic required, washer-upper needed in a restaurant, bar staff wanted for the Castle Hotel, lollipop lady required for the crossing outside the infants' school. She skimmed through the rest of the list – office work . . . taxi driver . . . cleaner . . . gardener . . . hmm, that could be the widow of the 93-year-old needing the rest of her potatoes dug up.

Tilly's attention was caught by a small box ad at the bottom of the page.

Girl Friday, fun job, country house, £200 pw.

That was it, brief and to the point. Tilly wondered what fun job meant; after all, some people might call Chancellor of the Exchequer a fun job. John McCririck might regard working as his personal slave a fun job. Or it could be something dodgy like entertaining slimy businessmen.

She took a bite of toast, turned over the page and began reading the articles for sale – a size eighteen Pronuptia wedding dress, never worn . . . an acoustic guitar, vgc apart from toothmarks on the bottom . . . fifty-nine-piece dinner service (one plate missing – thrown at lying, double-crossing ex-husband) . . . complete set of *Star Trek* DVDs: reason for sale, getting married to non-Trekkie . . .

Tilly smiled again; even the ads had a quirky charm all their own. Finishing her toast, she scooted through the Lonely Hearts column – male, 63, seeks younger woman, must love sprouts – then the houses for sale, all of them out of her league financially, then the boring sports pages at the back.

She reached the end, then found herself turning back to the page with *that* advert on it.

Almost as if it was beckoning to her, calling her name.

Which was ridiculous, because it didn't even say what the job involved and the money was rubbish, but a quick phone call to find out wouldn't do any harm, would it?

Scooping up her mobile, Tilly pressed out the number and listened to it ringing at the other end.

'Hello,' intoned an automated voice, 'please leave your message after the . . .'

'Tone,' Tilly prompted helpfully, but the voice didn't oblige. All she got was silence, no more voice, no tone, nothing. The answerphone was full.

Oh well, that was that. Whoever had placed the ad had been inundated with calls and was beating potential employees off with a stick. It was probably a vacancy for a topless waitress anyway.

Better get up instead.

Chapter 3

Erin drove Tilly to the station on Sunday afternoon.

'So, any idea what you're going to do?'

Tilly pulled a face, shook her head. 'Not yet. Find somewhere cheaper to live, that's all. What else can I do? Well, apart from persuading my boss to double my salary. Or maybe writing to George Clooney and asking him if he'd mind me moving into his villa on the banks of Lake Como. That's always a possibility.' It was cold out here in the car park; she gave Erin a kiss and said, 'Thanks for the weekend. I'll keep you up to date.'

'You could ask him if he'd like you to be his new girlfriend.' Erin hugged her. 'Sure you don't want me to wait with you?'

'Don't worry, I'm fine. The train'll be here in ten minutes. You get off home.'

Famous last words. Within two minutes of Tilly bagging herself a seat on the platform, the announcement came over the tannoy that the train bound for London Paddington would be delayed by forty minutes.

Everyone on the platform let out a collective groan. Clutching at straws, Tilly looked at the elderly woman next to her. 'Fourteen or forty?'

The woman clicked her tongue in disgust and said, 'Forty.'

The husband of a younger woman, attempting to placate their screaming baby, shook his head and said grumpily, 'This is going to be fun.'

Fun.

Fun job, country house. Picturing the copy of the *Roxborough Gazette* she'd stuffed into Erin's recycling box, Tilly wished she'd tried calling the number again.

Then with a jolt she realised she still had it stored on her phone. All she had to do was press last number redial.

'Hello? It's me. Fucking train's late, so we won't be back before six at the earliest, fucking typical . . .'

Tilly stood up and moved a discreet distance away from Mr Grumpy, now complaining loudly into his mobile that the baby was doing his bloody head in. She pressed her own phone to her ear and listened to it ringing at the other end. No answering machine this time. No answering of any kind, by the sound of things. Eight rings, nine, ten . . .

'Hello?' The voice was young, female and breathless.

'Oh hi, I was calling about the ad in the paper,' began Tilly. 'Could I just ask—'

'Hang on, I'll get Dad. DAAAD?' bellowed the voice.

'Ouch.' Tilly winced as the noise bounced off her left eardrum.

'Whoops, sorry! I've got very strong lungs. OK, he's here now. Dad, it's another one about the job.'

'Oh bloody hell, haven't we got enough to choose from?' The voice was flat, fed up and Liverpudlian. 'Just tell her she's too late, we've given it to someone else.'

Tilly's competitive spirit rose to the surface; until two minutes ago she hadn't even wanted the job. But now, if he was going to try and fob her off . . .

17

'Actually,' she cleared her throat, 'you can tell him I heard that. Could he at least have the decency to speak to me?'

The girl said cheerfully, 'Hang on,' and, 'Ooh, Dad, she's cross with you now.'

Tilly heard the phone being passed over, coupled with fierce whispering.

'Right, sorry.' It was the father's voice, still with that Liverpudlian twang but marginally more friendly than before. 'If you want the truth, this whole thing's been a prize cock-up. We've just got back from holiday to find the answering machine jammed with messages. The ad was meant to go into next week's paper, not last week's. All I want right now is a cup of tea and a bacon sandwich and I'm not getting either of them because the damn phone keeps ringing with more Girl Fridays than I know what to do with. But go ahead,' he said wearily. 'Fire away. Give me your name and number and I'll call you back sometime in the week, fix up a time for the interview.'

'Hang on,' said Tilly, 'I don't even know if I want an interview yet. What does a Girl Friday *do*, exactly?'

'Everything.'

'And you said it was a fun job. What does *that* mean?'

'It means there's an outside chance you might enjoy it for about two per cent of the time. The other ninety-eight per cent will be sheer drudgery.'

'OK, now you're just trying to put me off so you don't have to see me,' Tilly said suspiciously. 'This so-called job. Is it anything to do with porn?'

'Prawns?'

'Porn. Ography. *Sex*.' A collective sharp intake of breath informed Tilly that everyone else on the platform was paying attention now.

'No. Sorry.' He sounded amused. 'Why, was that what you were hoping for?'

'No it was not.' Tilly did her best to sound ladylike but not offputtingly prissy. 'And why are you only paying two hundred a week?'

This time he actually laughed. 'It's a live-in position. Everything else is paid for, including a car.'

OK, this was definitely a good enough reason. Tilly said promptly, 'You know what? I'd be great at this job.'

'Fine, fine. Let me check my diary.' She heard pages being riffled. 'Right, let's start booking appointments. Come over on Thursday afternoon and we'll take a look at each other. Four o'clock suit you?'

'Not really.' Tilly screwed up her face.

'Five, then? Six?'

'Look, are you in Roxborough?'

'No, we're in Mumbai, that's why I advertised in the *Roxborough Gazette*.' There it was again, that laconic deadpan Liverpudlian wit.

'Well, I live in London. But right now I'm on the platform at Roxborough station, waiting to go back there.' Going for broke, Tilly took a deep breath and said, 'So what would be really fantastic would be if I could come over and see you now.'

Silence.

Followed by more silence.

Finally she heard a sigh. 'Did I tell you how bloody knackered I am?'

'While you're interviewing me,' Tilly said innocently, 'I could always make you a fantastic bacon sandwich.'

He gave a snort of amusement. 'You're sharp, aren't you?'

'I'm right here.' Tilly pressed home her minuscule advantage. 'If you can't see me now, I'm going back to London. And you'll have missed your chance.'

'Modest, too.'

'Just think. If I'm perfect, you won't have to interview anyone else.'

Another pause. Then he said, 'Go on then, get yourself over here. We're at Beech House on the Brockley Road, just over the bridge and on the right as you're heading out of town. Do you know it?'

'No but I'll find you, don't worry.' That sounded nice and efficient, didn't it? 'I'll be there in ten minutes.'

Well, she would have been if there'd been a taxi outside the station. But that was wishful thinking, because this was Roxborough station on a wintry February afternoon and any self-respecting taxi driver was at home sleeping off his Sunday lunch. Tilly couldn't bring herself to phone Erin again. How far away could Beech House be, anyway? Surely not more than a mile. She could be there in fifteen minutes on foot . . .

It rained. It was more than a mile. It rained harder and the sky darkened along with Tilly's grey sweatshirt and jeans because of course she didn't have anything so sensible as an umbrella. Her case-on-wheels jiggled and bounced along the pavement as she dragged it behind her. After twenty-five minutes she saw a house up ahead on the right and quickened her pace. There, thank God, was the sign saying Beech House. She turned into the stone-pillared entrance and headed up the gravelled driveway. The Regency-style property was grand, imposing and as welcomingly lit up in the gloom as Harrods at Christmas.

Panting and drenched, Tilly reached the front door and rang the bell. What was she even doing here? The man would probably turn out to be a right weirdo; all she'd need to do was take one look at him to know she wouldn't work for him for all the—

'Bloody hell, kid. Look at the state of you.' Having flung open the door, the right weirdo hauled her inside. 'I thought you'd stood us up. Treat 'em mean, keep 'em keen. Don't tell me you've walked all the way from the station.'

Tilly nodded, the blissful heat causing her teeth to start chattering wildly. 'There weren't any t-taxis.'

'Ah well, that's because the taxi drivers around here are all lazy gits. And you didn't even have a coat.' He looked askance at her drenched sweatshirt. 'If you'd called me again I'd have come and picked you up. If you catch pneumonia and drop dead I'm going to have it on my conscience now, aren't I?'

'I'll sign a disclaimer.' Tilly stuck out her hand and shook his. 'I'm Tilly Cole. Nice to meet you.'

'Nice to meet you too, Tilly Cole. Max Dineen.' He was tall and greyhound thin, aged around forty, with close-cropped wavy blond hair and friendly grey eyes behind steel-rimmed spectacles. 'Come along in and we'll get you dried off. That's what I usually say to Betty,' he added as he led the way into the kitchen.

'Your daughter?'

Max indicated the brown and white terrier curled up on a cushion in one of the window seats. 'Our dog, but it's an easy mistake to make. I get them mixed up myself. Betty's the one with the cold nose,' he went on as a clatter of footsteps heralded his daughter's arrival in the kitchen, 'and the noisy one in the stripy tights is Lou.'

'Hi!' Lou was in her early teens, with mad red hair corkscrewing around her head and an infectious grin. 'It's Louisa actually. Euww, you're all wet.'

'I knew that expensive education would come in useful one day. Lou, this is Tilly. Run upstairs and fetch her the dressing gown from the spare room.' Max turned to Tilly. 'We'll chuck your clothes in the tumble-dryer. How about that then?' He winked.

21

'How many job interviews have you done in a dressing gown, eh?'

The thing was, he wasn't being sleazy or suggestive. He was simply making the suggestion because it made sense. Nevertheless, it would be surreal . . .

'It's OK, I've got something I can change into.' Tilly pointed to her case.

Max said, 'Spoilsport.'

Chapter 4

The house was amazing, decorated with an eye for colour and real flair. Whether Max Dineen was married or divorced, Tilly guessed this was the work of a woman. In the bottle-green and white marble-tiled downstairs cloakroom she stripped off her wet things and changed into the red angora sweater and black trousers she'd worn last night.

Back in the kitchen Max took her jeans and sweatshirt through to the utility room and put them in the tumble-dryer. Then he handed her a cup of coffee and pulled out one of the kitchen chairs.

'Right, let's make a start, shall we? The situation is this. Lou's mum and I split up three years ago. Her mum lives and works in California. For the first couple of years Lou stayed out there with her, but she missed all this . . .' he gestured ironically at the rain-splattered window, 'all this glorious British weather, so last year she decided to move back for good. I tried changing my name and going into hiding but she managed to track me down.'

'Dad, don't say that.' Lou rolled her eyes at him. 'People will think it's true.'

'It *is* true. I was hiding in doorways . . . wearing a false moustache . . . hopeless. It was like being hunted by a bloodhound.'

'Nobody's going to want to work for you if you say stuff like this. OK, here's the thing,' Lou took over. 'I'm thirteen. Dad cut back on work when I first came home, but now he's stepping it up again.'

'It's a question of having to,' said Max. 'You cost a fortune.'

'Anyway,' Louisa ignored him, 'we decided we needed a Girl Friday to help us out, someone to pick me up from school and stuff, do a spot of cooking sometimes, help Dad out with the business – just anything that needs doing, really. We kept it vague, because—'

'We kept it vague,' Max interjected, 'because if we advertised for someone to look after a bad-tempered old git and a whiny teenager, everyone would run a mile.'

'Just keep on ignoring him.' Louisa's eyes sparkled as she snapped the ring on a can of Pepsi Max. 'So. Does that sound like the kind of thing you might like to do?'

Tilly shrugged. 'That rather depends on your dad's business. If he's the town rat-catcher I'm not going to be so keen on helping him out.'

'How about grave-digging?' said Max.

'Dad, will you leave this to me? He's not a grave-digger,' said Louisa, 'he has an interior design company. It's good fun. He's very in demand.' She nodded proudly. 'So that's it. That's what you'd be doing. Now it's your turn to tell us about you.'

Tilly hid a smile, because Louisa was so earnest and sparky and bossy and young, and she, Tilly, was being interviewed by a thirteen-year-old freckly redhead wearing huge hooped earrings, a lime-green sweater-dress and multicoloured stripy tights. She'd also been wrong about the ex-wife being responsible for the way the house looked.

Plus no rats, which had to be a bonus.

'OK, the truth? I live in London, my job's pretty boring and my boyfriend's just done a bunk. Which doesn't upset me, but it means I can't afford to stay on in the flat we shared, which *does*. Then I came down here for the weekend to stay with my friend Erin, and—'

'Erin? Who runs Erin's Beautiful Clothes?' Perkily Louisa said, 'I know her. I used to go in the shop with Mum, and Erin would give me jelly sweets shaped like strawberries. She's cool!'

'I know she's cool. And she'll be thrilled to hear you think so too,' said Tilly. 'We've been best friends since university. Anyway, I saw your advert in the paper and tried to ring you yesterday but your answering machine was full. Then this afternoon my train was delayed and on the off chance I thought I'd give it another go. Erin says this is a really nice place to live. She'd love it if I moved down here. So here I am.'

'Can you cook?' said Max.

'Ish. I'm not Nigella.'

'Don't look so worried, we're not after Nigella.' Max pulled a face. 'All that sticking her finger in her mouth and groaning in ecstasy – put me right off my dinner, that would.'

Phew, relief. 'I'm the queen of the bacon sandwich.'

'That's grand. Food of the gods. Criminal record?'

Shocked, Tilly yelped, 'No!'

'Ever nicked anything from any previous employers?'

'Paperclips.' She concentrated on remembering; honesty was important. 'Envelopes. Pens. Cheap ones,' Tilly added, in case he thought she was talking Mont Blancs. 'Oh, and a loo roll once. But only because we'd run out at home and I didn't have time to stop off at the shop. And *that* was embarrassing, because I was smuggling it out of the building under my coat and the doorman asked me if I was pregnant.'

25

Max nodded gravely. 'I hate it when that happens to me. Clean driving licence?'

'Absolutely.' This time Tilly was able to reply with confidence, chiefly because she didn't own a car and only occasionally borrowed her parents' Ford Focus – and after being owned and driven by them since the day it had come out of the showroom it had never even *learned* how to travel faster than thirty miles an hour.

'Like yellow?'

'Excuse me?'

'Do you like yellow? That's the colour of the room you'd be sleeping in if you came to live here.'

'Depends on what kind of yellow. Not so keen on mustard.'

Max laughed. 'Now she's getting picky.'

'You two. Honestly.' Louisa shook her head.

They went upstairs and Max showed Tilly the room, which was fabulously decorated in shades of pale gold with accents of silver and white. The view from the elongated sash windows was breathtaking, even if the hills rising into the distance were currently wreathed in grey mist. The curtains were sumptuous and glamorously draped. And as for the bed . . .

'Well?' said Max.

Tilly's mouth was dry. Was it wrong to take a job just because you'd fallen in love with a bed?

Except this was so much more than just a bed. It was an actual four-poster, draped in ivory and silver damask, the mattress so high you'd practically need to take a running jump at it, the pillows piled up in true interior-designer style.

This was pure Hollywood, the bed of her dreams, and she wanted to roll around on it like a puppy.

'She hates it,' said Max.

Tilly shook her head. 'I can't believe you've made so much effort for someone who's just going to be working for you.'

'I'm a very generous employer,' Max said modestly.

'Dad, you liar.' Louisa rolled her eyes at Tilly. 'Don't be impressed; the room was like this before he even thought of advertising for someone to move in. This is just our best spare room.'

'Oh. Well, it's still amazing.'

Max said, 'And I could have used one of the others.'

'Except that would have meant sorting them out and basically he couldn't be bothered. Still, it's nice, isn't it?' Louisa surveyed Tilly beadily. 'So? What's the verdict?'

'I want this job,' said Tilly. 'Although I suppose I should talk to Erin first, check out your credentials. You might be the Asbo family from hell.'

'Oh, we're definitely that.' Max nodded. 'And maybe we should give Erin a call too, find out all about you.'

'She'll say nice things, tell you I'm lovely. If she doesn't,' said Tilly, 'she knows I'll give her a Chinese burn.'

Over bacon and egg sandwiches and mugs of tea they carried on getting to know each other.

'So how often would you be nicking the toilet rolls?' said Max, feeding Betty a curl of bacon under the table.

'Not more than once or twice a week, I promise.'

'Are you bright and cheerful when you get up in the morning?'

'I can be.'

'Christ, no, I can't bear people being cheerful in the mornings.'

'He's a grumpy old man,' Louisa said comfortably, 'aren't you, Dad?'

Tilly pointed a teasing finger at her. 'If I came to work here, it'd be like *The Sound of Music*.'

'Minus the singing nuns,' said Max.

'And with a lot less children to look after,' Louisa pointed out.

'I wouldn't make you wear dresses made out of curtains,' Tilly promised.

'And you won't end up marrying Captain Von Trapp,' said Max. Quite bluntly, in fact.

Oh. Right. Not that she wanted to marry him, but still. Tilly guessed it was his way of letting her know right away that she wasn't his type. God, did he think she'd been flirting with him? Because she genuinely hadn't.

Talk about blunt, though.

Across the table she intercepted a look passing between Louisa and Max.

'Oh Dad, don't tell her,' Louisa wailed. 'Can't we just leave it for now? Wait until she moves in?'

'Tell me what?' Tilly sat up, her stomach tightening with apprehension. Just when everything had been going so well, too.

'I have to,' Max said evenly. 'It's not fair otherwise.'

For heaven's sake, were they *vampires*?

'Please, Dad, don't,' begged Louisa.

'Tell me *what*?'

The phone started ringing out in the hall. Max looked at Louisa and tilted his head in the direction of the door. 'Go and get that, will you, Lou?'

For a second she stared back at him, her jaw rigid. Then she scraped back her chair and ran out of the kitchen, red curls bouncing off her shoulders.

'Is this to do with your wife?' Tilly had done *Jane Eyre* at school; had Louisa's mum gone loopy? Had the bit about her going to America been a lie? Was she actually tied up in the attic?

'In a way.' Max nodded and listened to the murmurings as Louisa answered the phone. 'The reason Kaye and I got divorced is because I'm gay.'

Crikey, she hadn't been expecting *that*. Tilly put down her sandwich. Was he serious or was this another joke?

'Really?'

'Really.' Max surveyed her steadily for a moment. 'OK, let me just tell you before Lou comes back. When I was in my twenties it was easier to be heterosexual. I met Kaye and she was great. Then she got pregnant. Not exactly planned, but that was fine too.' His smile was crooked. 'And my mother was thrilled. So anyway, we got married and Lou was born, and I told myself I had to stay straight for their sakes. Well, I lasted nearly ten years. And I never once cheated on Kaye. But in the end I couldn't do it any more. We split up. Poor old Kaye, it wasn't her fault. And Lou's coped brilliantly. She's a star.'

'I can see that,' said Tilly.

'But it's obviously been a lot for her to cope with. I don't have a partner right now, which makes things easier. And it's not as if I'd ever bring home a different man every week.' Max paused, then said, 'The thing is, you have to remember this isn't London, it's Roxborough. Before we advertised in the paper, I spoke to a woman who runs an employment agency and she said I shouldn't mention the gay thing at all. Apparently a lot of potential employees would be put off, especially if half the reason for taking the job was because they fancied their chances with a wealthy single father.' He half smiled before adding drily, 'And then you came out with your *Sound of Music* comment.'

'I didn't mean it like that,' Tilly protested.

'Well, that's good news. But according to this woman, some people might just not want to live in a house with a gay man.'

Max shrugged. 'I'm just repeating what she told me. Apparently some people might find it a bit . . . yucky.'

A noise behind them prompted Tilly to swivel round. Louisa was back, standing in the doorway.

'Well?' Louisa looked anxious.

Tilly was incredulous. 'This woman who runs an employment agency. Is she by any chance two hundred and seventy years old?'

Louisa's narrow shoulders sagged with relief. 'Does that mean it isn't a problem? You still want to come and live here?'

Unable to keep a straight face, Tilly said, '*That's* not a problem. But if we're talking yucky, I'm going to need to know exactly what your dad's like when it comes to digging butter knives in the marmalade, dumping tea bags in the sink and leaving the top off the toothpaste.'

Lou pulled a conspiratorial face. 'He's OK most of the time. When he concentrates.'

'That's all right then,' said Tilly. 'So am I.'

Chapter 5

'Tilly, Tilly!' The door to the flat was open and Babs burst in like a rocket. 'It's Gavin, he's here! Oh my word, this is so romantic, he wants you back . . .'

Tilly stopped dead in her tracks. Not again. She finished zipping up the last suitcase and moved over to the open window.

Yes, Gavin was down there. Clutching a bunch of lilies and wearing extremely ironed jeans with knife-sharp creases down the front, courtesy of his mother.

She marvelled at the fact that they'd lived together, yet he still hadn't grasped the fact that lilies were her least favourite flower.

Gazing up at her, Gavin called out, 'Tilly, don't go, I can't bear it. Look, I made a mistake and I'm *sorry*.'

'It's like one of those lovely films with Cary Grant,' Babs sighed, clasping her hands together.

It was nothing of the sort; Cary Grant would *never* have let his mother iron his jeans like that.

'Gavin, don't do this. You left me, remember? It's over.' Since coming to regret his decision, Gavin had been begging her to change her mind about leaving. This was the bit Tilly hated, but at least she was spared the guilt of having been the one to initiate the split.

'But I love you!' In desperation he held up the bunch of lilies as proof.

'Oh Gavin, it's too late. How could I trust you? Every day I'd come home from work and wonder if you were still there.' Whereas in reality she'd been coming home from work and enjoying the fact that he wasn't.

'I made a mistake. I wouldn't do it again, I promise.'

'You say that now. But it's too late anyway. I've left my job.' Hooray! 'I'm leaving London.' Yay! 'In fact . . .' Tilly nodded at the minicab pulling up at the kerb behind him, 'I'm leaving right now.'

Babs helped her drag the suitcases downstairs. Actually having to say goodbye to her was quite emotional; Babs might be the world's nosiest neighbour but she meant well.

Then it was Gavin's turn. Tilly dutifully gave him a hug and a peck on the cheek. 'Bye then.'

'I messed up big-time, didn't I?' He looked utterly dejected. 'I broke your heart and now I'm paying the price.'

Tilly said bravely, 'We'll get over it.'

'Ahem.' As Tilly climbed into the minicab that would take her to Paddington, Babs nudged Gavin and said, 'Aren't you going to give her the lilies?'

Oh God, please no, they smelled awful, like the zoo.

'Well, she probably wouldn't want to have to carry them on the train.' Since his ploy to win her back hadn't worked, Gavin was clearly reluctant to hand them over. 'And they cost twelve pounds fifty.' He took a hasty step back as Babs's eyes lit up in anticipation. 'So I think I'll just take them home and give them to my mum.'

Was this how a shoplifter felt as they made their way around a store stealthily pocketing small items, nerve-janglingly aware that at any moment the tiniest slip-up could lead to them being caught out? Erin did her best to stay relaxed, to keep her breathing steady, but the terror showed no sign of loosening its grip; any minute now she could make that slip, give herself away.

And to add insult to injury she was in her own shop.

Not trusting herself with the portable steamer in case her hands trembled too much, Erin busied herself with the computer and pretended to be engrossed in a spreadsheet. Three feet away from her, riffling through a rail of tops, Stella Welch carried on chatting to her friend Amy through the door of the changing cubicle.

'I saw Fergus again last night, by the way. Bumped into him in the Fox.'

That's because you've been stalking him, thought Erin. You saw him going into the Fox so you followed him inside.

'How's he looking?' Amy's voice floated out of the cubicle above a vigorous rustle of clothes.

'The truth? Pale.'

It's February.

'In fact, I told him he could do with a few sessions on the sunbed.' Stella flicked back her tawny hair, held a pomegranate-pink silk shirt up against herself and surveyed her reflection in the mirror. 'Does this colour suit me? It does, doesn't it?'

'It looks great.' Erin nodded, because the colour was perfect against Stella's permatanned skin.

'I also told him he was a bastard.' Stella seamlessly continued her conversation with Amy. 'I can't believe it's been six months since he left. I mean, why would anyone in their right mind want to leave *me*? What did I ever do wrong? It's not even as if Fergus is amazing looking! I *so* don't deserve to be treated like this. Eleven years of marriage and then he ups and goes, out of the blue. He was lucky to get me in the first place, for God's sake. Some men are just . . . deluded!'

'Did you tell him that?' said Amy.

'Only about a million times. God, he just makes me so mad. I asked him last night if he was seeing someone else but he still says he isn't. He'd better not be, that's all I can say. Oh yes, that's perfect on you.'

The changing room door had opened. Amy did a twirl in the midnight-blue Nicole Farhi dress. 'Not too over the top for a first date? I was wondering if I should play it cool and just wear jeans and a little top, but what if I do that and he thinks it means I don't like him?'

'Can't risk that. Go for it,' Stella pronounced. 'Get the dress.' She turned to Erin and said, 'Amy's being taken out to dinner tonight. By Jack Lucas.'

'Gosh. Lovely.'

'I'm so nervous!' Amy's eyes sparkled as she did an excited twirl in front of the mirror. 'I won't be able to eat a thing! I can't believe it's actually happening!'

Erin couldn't think why she couldn't believe it; when you'd been out with as many girls as Jack Lucas had, it was hard to find someone who *hadn't* been one of his conquests. In fact she, Erin, was practically the only female she knew who hadn't been there, done that. Then again, she'd never been tempted, it was far more entertaining to stand back and let all the other girls do their moths-around-a-flame thing, and to watch them crash and burn.

For the female inhabitants of Roxborough, it was practically their number-one pastime.

'I'll take it,' said Amy, dancing back into the cubicle to change out of the dress.

'See, if Fergus looked like Jack Lucas I could understand him

34

doing what he's done.' Stella shook her head in disbelief as she draped a pale turquoise scarf experimentally around her neck. 'But how does he have the nerve to do it when he looks like Fergus?'

'Maybe he'll change his mind and come crawling back,' Amy offered.

'That's what I've been waiting for! But it's been six months now and he still hasn't! You go to the Fox sometimes, don't you?'

Her skin prickling, Erin realised this question was being directed at her. Unwillingly, she looked up from the computer screen. 'Sometimes.'

'Have you heard any rumours about my husband? Any gossip, any signs that he's seeing another woman?'

Erin's mouth was dry. 'No. No, I don't think so.'

Stella's immaculately shaped eyebrows rose slightly. 'You don't *think* so?'

'I mean no, definitely, no signs, nothing.'

Stella gave a nod of satisfaction. 'He'd better not be. For God's sake, he's trying to ruin my life. I deserve so much more than to be treated like this. Talk about selfish. I mean, how old are you, Erin?'

What? Why? For a moment Erin's own age escaped her.

'Thirty-three?' Stella hazarded. 'Thirty-five?'

Ouch.

'Actually I'm twenty-eight,' said Erin.

'Oh. I thought you were older than that. And I know I look young for my age but I'm thirty-seven. Thirty-*seven*! We were supposed to be starting a family this year, and my husband's had some kind of bizarre mental breakdown and buggered off instead. Meanwhile my fertility is declining. Ooh, it just makes me so *mad*. There should be a law against men being allowed to do this to women.'

'Quick, I didn't realise it was nearly two o'clock.' Bursting out of the cubicle, Amy frantically waved the Nicole Farhi dress at Erin and scrabbled for her credit card. 'I've got an appointment at the hairdresser's in five minutes. Can't meet Jack Lucas tonight without having my roots touched up!'

Two minutes later they were gone. Erin could breathe again. Breathe, but not relax, because the dilemma currently tearing her in two was still inescapably there.

Fergus was the best thing that had happened to her in years; he was the light of her life. Currently he was the first thing she thought of when she woke up in the morning and the last thing she thought of at night.

But nothing was ever simple, was it? Because Fergus had spent the last eleven years being married to Stella and although he was now desperate to put those years behind him and divorce her, Stella was digging her heels in, still unable to grasp the concept that he might not change his mind and go back to her.

The irony was that although she had known them both for years, ever since she'd moved back to Roxborough, in all that time Erin had never, not even once, secretly lusted after Fergus. He'd always been a lovely friendly person and he and Stella had always been generally regarded as something of a mismatched couple, but even the news of their separation hadn't caused Erin's heart to give a secret leap of hope. With his messy, unstyled dark hair, merry eyes, large feet and eternal struggle to dress smartly, Fergus Welch was simply a lovely person to know.

Which had only made it all the more surprising when, just six weeks ago, they had bumped into each other and *whoosh*, out of nowhere the spark had ignited. So completely unexpectedly that it made you wonder who might suddenly become inexplicably irresistible next. John Prescott? Robbie Coltrane? Johnny Vegas?

Oh no, poor Fergus, not that he looked like any of *them*. Erin hastily blocked that thought from her mind. But still, who would have thought that her feelings towards Fergus could have changed so dramatically in the space of . . . crikey, what had it been? A couple of hours?

And just think, if it hadn't been raining that day, it would never have happened.

Although to call it raining was an understatement. It had been a full-on thunderstorm, with rain hammering down like bullets from an iron-grey sky. It was also undoubtedly what had inspired the bored teenagers to run around the car park flipping up the windscreen wipers of an entire row of cars.

Erin's Fiat, sadly, had been the oldest in the row and her windscreen wipers the most fragile. When she emerged from the supermarket on the outskirts of Cirencester and got soaked to the skin unloading her bags of shopping, she didn't immediately realise what had happened. When she leapt into the driver's seat and switched on the ignition and wipers, she couldn't work out why they weren't working. It wasn't until she climbed back out of the car that she found the wipers on the ground. A posh middle-aged woman in a nearby 4x4 unwound her window a couple of inches and bellowed, 'I saw 'em doing it, little sods. Gave 'em an earful and they ran orf. Bloody hoody types. String 'em up, that's what I say. Set the hounds on 'em!'

Which was all well and good but it didn't exactly solve the problem to hand. Erin, her hair plastered to her head and her clothes clinging like papier mâché to her body, gazed in dismay at the snapped-off windscreen wipers. Driving the car would be impossible in this downpour, like wearing a blindfold. She was stuck here ten miles from home until the rain stopped, and in the meantime her three tubs of Marshfield Farm ice cream were going to melt all over the—

'Erin! What happened, did someone superglue your feet to the ground? Stand there for much longer and you might get wet!'

Turning, Erin squinted and saw Fergus Welch hurrying towards her across the car park, holding a half-broken golfing umbrella over his head and waving his key at a dark green Lexus parked not far from hers. Possibly wary of setting off the alarm, the teenagers had left his car alone. As he slowed, Erin held up the amputated wipers. Fixing cars wasn't her forte but maybe Fergus would know some way to tie them back on.

'Oh no.' His forehead creased with concern. 'Vandals?'

'Well, I didn't do it myself.' Rain dripped off Erin's eyelashes and nose. 'And from the look of the sky, I'm going to be stuck here for hours yet. It's Monday, my precious day off – what could be nicer than this?'

'Hey, no problem, I can give you a lift home.' Indicating his car, Fergus said, 'Hop in, I've got an appointment in Tetbury but that won't take long. Then I'm heading straight back to the office.'

'Really?' Erin's shoulders sagged with gratitude. 'I've got a load of food in the boot.'

'Come on then, let's shift it into mine. Then if we get marooned in a flood, we won't starve. And if it stops raining this evening I can drop you back here . . . oh, I say, honeycomb ice cream. That's my all-time favourite.'

They transferred the bags of food and Fergus, struggling to close his half-broken umbrella, completely broke it and ended up chucking it into a nearby bin. Then he held open the passenger door of the Lexus with a flourish.

'Are you sure you want me on your seats?' By this stage Erin couldn't have been wetter if she'd just climbed out of a swimming pool.

'Hey, don't worry. I'll be demanding payment in ice cream.'

And that was how it had started. The rain had brought them together. She'd waited in the car whilst Fergus had shown a client around a house in Tetbury, then he'd driven her back to Roxborough and because it was still raining had helped to carry her bags into the flat. Then Erin had made coffee and they'd shared the entire tub of honeycomb ice cream – semi-melted by now, but still delicious.

They didn't leap on each other, ripping each other's clothes off in an unstoppable frenzy of lust. Of course they didn't do that. But without a word being said, each of them silently acknowledged that . . . well, they'd quite like to.

Stella was a major stumbling block.

'She's spent the last eleven years telling me I don't deserve her, that she's better than me,' said Fergus as Erin made another pot of coffee. 'She told me a million times she was out of my league. I thought she'd be thrilled when I moved out. But she's taking it so badly. I wasn't expecting this to happen at all.'

'Do you think you'll get back together?' Erin did her best to sound impartial.

'No, never. It's over.' Fergus shook his head and sat back, combing his fingers through his unruly, still-damp hair. 'I've put up with Stella's attitude for years. She doesn't love me, she's just outraged that I had the nerve to leave. My nephew's too old for his Teletubbies,' he went on drily, 'but you should have heard the screams when my sister tried to pack them off to the charity shop. He wrestled her for them and yelled that he'd still love the Teletubbies when he was *fifty*.'

Erin hoped Stella wouldn't still be clinging on to Fergus when she was fifty. Then she felt a twinge of guilt because Stella was his wife.

'Maybe she'll meet someone else,' Erin said hopefully.

Fergus nodded in agreement. 'That's what I'm hoping. In fact I'm thinking of writing begging letters to Ewan McGregor and Hugh Grant.'

Fergus had had to head back to the office after that. He worked as a senior negotiator at Thornton and Best, the estate agents at the top of the High Street. Later that evening he'd given Erin a lift back to her car and the evening had ended with her planting a careful thank-you kiss on his cheek. Perfectly chaste and innocent on the surface but seething with longing and less-than-innocent possibilities underneath.

Erin was jolted back to the present by the phone shrilling on the desk in front of her. Since that night she and Fergus had carried on secretly meeting up and the chastity aspect wasn't set to last for much longer; she was besotted with Fergus and, blissfully, he appeared to be just as—

OK, enough, no more daydreaming about lovely Fergus. Answer the phone.

Ooh, it might even *be* Fergus!

'Hello? Erin's Beautiful Clothes.'

'Hey, you!'

It was Tilly's voice. Not quite Fergus, but nearly as good. Erin said happily, 'Hi, how's everything going?'

'Oh, you know. Are you busy or can you talk?'

'It's OK, the shop's empty, I can talk.'

'Great. Hang on a sec.'

Erin's heart sank as the bell jangled above the door, heralding the arrival of another customer just when she'd been about to settle down for a good chat. Then her head jerked up and her mouth fell open because there, standing in the doorway, was . . .

'Tilly! What's going on?'

Tilly flung her arms wide. 'Surprise!'

'Surprise? You nearly gave me a heart attack! I thought you were calling from London! Why didn't you tell me you were coming down?'

'I can see I'm going to have to explain some basic rules about surprises. They kind of work better if they happen without warning.' Her eyes dancing, Tilly said, 'And this isn't a visit.'

'It isn't? What is it, then?' Erin was by this time thoroughly confused; Tilly didn't even have an overnight bag with her.

'You said I'd like it here. Well, you'd better be right,' said Tilly, 'because I've done it, I live here now. As of today.'

'What? Where? Where are you living?'

'Beech House. I'm working as a Girl Friday for Max Dineen.'

Erin sat bolt upright. 'Dineen! Max Dineen who was married to Kaye? Daughter with red hair called . . .'

'Lou. That's right.'

Astonished, Erin said, 'Wow.'

'I know! And we really get on well.' Tilly pulled a face. 'Please don't tell me he's a raving psychopath.'

'Don't worry, everyone likes Max. And Lou's a cutie, she used to come in here with Kaye and eat—'

'Strawberry sweets. She told me about that. And now I'm living here, in their house! Wait until I go to the Fox and tell grumpy Declan. He won't believe it!'

'*I* can't believe it.' Erin shook her head, still in a daze.

'I know, isn't it great? New job, new home, whole new life! And on my evenings off, we'll be able to go out together!'

At that moment the door opened again and more customers drifted in. It occurred to Erin that with its usual unerring sense of timing, fate had managed to get it wrong again. All these years without a relationship and *now* Tilly had turned up. Maybe this

41

was God's way of telling her she wasn't cut out to be a lying, deceitful, husband-stealing bitch.

'What? What's wrong?' said Tilly.

'Nothing.' Erin gave her a hug. 'I'm just glad you're here.' As she said it, the other customers began pulling dresses off the rails and posing in front of each other. It probably wasn't the best time to be confiding in Tilly about her top-secret budding romance with Fergus.

Chapter 6

'Here she is,' Max announced as Tilly, back from her visit to Erin, padded into the kitchen in her socks. 'Here's the girl I was telling you about.'

Tilly turned to greet the visitor and stopped in her tracks. Because there, leaning against the Aga with his arms casually folded in front of him and a devastating grin spreading across his face, was one of the most disconcertingly good-looking men she'd ever seen in real life. Thickly fringed green eyes surveyed her with amusement and glossy dark hair flopped over his forehead. His face was tanned, emphasising the whiteness of his teeth, but the teeth themselves were just imperfect enough not to have been the work of a dentist.

Phew. And he was wearing faded paint-splashed jeans, Timberlands and a pale brown polo shirt beneath a well-worn dusty grey gilet. Pretty spectacular body too.

Max performed the introductions. 'Tilly, this is my . . . *friend*, Jack Lucas. Jack, meet Tilly Cole.'

'OK, let's just make something clear, shall we? From the word go? I'm not Max's . . . *friend*,' said Jack. 'I'm just his friend. No hesitation, no significant emphasis. Max likes to say it that way to try and embarrass me, to make people wonder what he's insinuating. He thinks it's hilarious. Just ignore him.' Hauling himself upright he reached forward and shook hands. 'Hi, Tilly. Good to meet you.'

'You too.' Tilly did her best to behave as if being introduced to knee-tremblingly attractive men was a daily occurrence. His handshake was warm and dry and when she breathed in she smelled a mixture of paint, delicious aftershave and brick dust.

'You know, something about you reminds me of something . . .' Letting go of her hand, Jack circled an index finger as the connection eluded him.

'Oh God, here he goes.' Max shook his head in disgust. 'You don't waste any time, do you? And talk about unoriginal. Watch out, girl,' he told Tilly. 'Next he'll be saying he's sure he's met you before, and you'll believe him and start wondering where.'

'Max, shut up. This isn't a chat-up line, it's the truth.' But Jack Lucas was laughing as he said it, making it impossible for Tilly to know whether he was telling the truth or not.

'I'm from London. We haven't met before.' If she had, Tilly knew she would definitely have remembered.

'Well, you're here now. And Max and I sometimes work together, so I'm sure we'll be seeing more of each other.' The playful glint in his eye told her he was perfectly well aware of the double entendre. But something altogether more impressive was happening, Tilly discovered, at the same time. When he looked at her it felt as if all his attention was focused on her; when he spoke to her it was as if all he cared about was what she might say in return.

Neat trick.

It was also, of course, the sign of a champion seducer. Tilly could just imagine the trail of broken hearts a man like Jack Lucas must leave weeping and wailing in his wake.

At that moment the front door opened and slammed shut, and Louisa erupted into the kitchen in her navy school uniform.

'You're here!' Her eyes lit up and for a moment she hovered just over the threshold, unsure what to do. Then she rushed over and flung her arms around Tilly. 'I'm so glad!'

'Hey, how about me?' Jack was indignant. 'Are you glad I'm here too?'

'Of course I am. I'm always glad to see you.' Louisa hugged him in turn. 'Even if you do smell of paint.'

'So sorry.' He gave one of her coppery plaits a fond tweak. 'Rush job on today and we were two men down. If I'd known you were going to complain, I'd have sat back and let the others get on with the work. Anyway, you can talk,' he added, pulling a face. 'You smell of . . . ugh . . . blackcurrant.'

'Nesh's mum drove us home, she gave us some sweets. It's what kind parents do. Hi, Dad.' Louisa gave Max a kiss, then grinned over at Tilly. 'And kind Girl Fridays too, when it's their turn to pick us up from school.'

'And then you aren't hungry and you don't want your tea,' said Max.

'Dad, that's so not true. I'm hungry now! What are we having? Jack, are you staying for something to eat?'

Erk, Tilly hoped not. If cooking dinner was her job, she didn't need Jack Lucas hanging around and distracting her on her first day in the job.

'Not today. I'm out for dinner this evening.' Jack glanced at his watch. 'In fact I'd better be off, I've got tenants to see in Cheltenham first.' He turned back to Tilly, gave her that thrilling look again. 'What am I missing?'

Tilly didn't have the foggiest; she hadn't even checked the contents of the fridge yet. 'Something fabulous.'

Jack grinned. 'I'm sure. Never mind, some other time.' Raising a hand and moving to the door, he said, 'Right, I'm off. See you soon.'

When he'd left them, Tilly said, 'Well, *he* thinks he's irresistible, doesn't he?'

Max looked amused. 'Jack's all right. He's a good mate. And to be fair, most of the women around here think he's pretty irresistible too.'

'I know that kind,' said Tilly.

'He'll make a play for you, don't worry. It's up to you, but if you go for it, don't go getting your hopes up,' said Max. 'Strictly no-strings, that's Jack. Bedpost? There's been that many notches there's no bedpost left.'

'Euww, Dad! Can we not talk about this?'

Max ruffled his daughter's hair. 'Sorry, pet. I'm just warning Tilly, letting her know the way things are around here.'

As if she would be attracted to Jack Lucas for one moment. Honestly, the very idea. Tilly said bluntly, 'Don't worry, I'm not planning on being anyone's notch, especially someone who uses chat-up lines like—'

The kitchen door swung open and Jack stuck his head round.

'Bloody hell, you're supposed to have gone,' said Max. 'How are we meant to talk about you behind your back if you're going to creep back and eavesdrop?'

'Sorry, sorry.' From the way Jack was grinning it was obvious he'd overheard every word. 'I *was* leaving, then I spotted something interesting out in the hall.' He raised an eyebrow at Tilly. 'Two interesting things, actually.'

Tilly blinked as he reappeared in the kitchen holding the boots she'd kicked off and left by the front door five minutes ago. Were emerald-green leather cowboy boots with customised

46

glittery heels not allowed in Roxborough? Were they against the law, perhaps? A health and safety risk? Might their glitteriness cause herds of cows to take fright and stampede through country lanes?

'I love Tilly's boots.' Louisa leapt loyally to her defence. 'They're cool.'

'I didn't say I didn't like them,' said Jack. 'I think they're very . . . individual. The kind of boots you might wear when you're leapfrogging over litter bins, in fact.' He paused. 'Well, when you're *trying* to leapfrog over a litter bin.'

Tilly's hand was already clapped to her mouth. 'You saw me?'

'Oh, I did more than see you.' His own mouth twitched. 'I shouted at you.'

She let out a squeak of dismay. 'That was your car?'

'My brand new car,' Jack emphasised. 'Only two days out of the showroom. You left grease marks all over the window.'

'I said I was sorry. It was an accident. Unlike you,' Tilly added pointedly, 'splashing me when you drove through that puddle. You did that on purpose.'

'Semi on purpose,' Jack conceded. 'It was only meant to be a little splash. Hey, I'm sorry too. But look on the bright side, at least now you know I wasn't spinning you a line.' His eyes glittered good-humouredly. 'I knew I remembered you from somewhere, I just didn't know it was from the night you ended up spreadeagled across my new car.'

'Come in, come in. Sorry my room's a mess. Dad used to moan and tell me to put things away but now he's given up. I told him there's far more important stuff for us to fight about and being untidy doesn't matter. Anyway, it feels more cosy like this.'

Louisa was sitting up in her double bed wearing purple pyjamas and reading *A History of the Industrial Revolution*. She smelled of soap and toothpaste.

'Like doing your homework,' said Tilly. 'That's more important.'

'I'm doing it now.' Louisa beamed and waggled the school text-book at her. 'Revision. It's really boring . . . oh no, Dad *told* you!'

'Sorry. He's the boss.' Having lifted the pillow next to the one propped up behind Louisa, Tilly located the copy of *Heat* and whisked it out of reach. 'He said if I looked under here I might find one of these.'

Louisa pulled a caught-out face. 'I was only going to glance at it for five minutes. Our history test isn't till next week anyway.' She sat back, her eyes bright. 'So, do you think you're going to like it here?'

'I hope so.' Tilly sat on the edge of the bed, checking out the framed photos on top of the bookcase and deliberately not thinking about Jack Lucas. 'I like that one of you and your mum.'

'That was taken on the beach in Hawaii. We went there on holiday last year. Everyone else was tanned and glamorous.' Louisa grimaced. 'And there was me with my stupid red hair and my spindly white legs, looking like a complete dork.'

'You don't at all.' Reaching for the photo, Tilly surveyed the two of them laughing together into the camera. 'And look at your mum – she's got red hair too.'

'She's covered in fake tan. And factor fifty suncream. I don't know how she stands it out there in LA. I'm more of a cold-weather person. I like living here.'

Carefully Tilly said, 'You must miss her a lot.'

Louisa shrugged. 'Yes, but when I was over there living with Mum, I missed Dad loads too. And I talk to her all the time. She's happy, and work's going really well. She loves her job.'

Who wouldn't? Tilly had discovered over dinner this evening

that Kaye Dineen, mother of Louisa, ex-wife of Max and unsuccessful British stage actress, was in fact well known in America and throughout large parts of the rest of the developed world as Kaye McKenna, one of the stars of the Emmy-garlanded TV drama series *Over the Rainbow*, watched by zillions of viewers each week. One lucky audition, that was all it had taken – and what all aspiring actors dream of. After eight months of rejections and with her spirits at rock bottom, Kaye's car had had a flat tyre on the way to the casting director's office. By the time she'd turned up, her white dress covered in axle grease and her make-up sweated off, she was an hour and a half late. The director, seizing on her air of fragility and near-desperation, had demanded with deliberate brutality, 'Why the fuck should I see you now?' Prompting Kaye, unshed tears shimmering in her eyes, to snap back, 'Because I loved my ex-husband, my ex-husband is now gay, our daughter loves both of us and if I don't deserve a break I don't know who the fuck does.'

Her ferocity, coupled with her cut-crystal English accent, had swung it. All the boxes were ticked and she'd secured the job on the spot. Kaye famously credited that flat tyre with launching her career in the States.

'Here's a good one.' Louisa reached for another photo in a turquoise frame, of a group of cavorting teenagers around an LA pool. 'That's me and some friends after a wedding party. You know the actress Macy Ventura? She's the main star of Mum's show. Anyway, she was getting married for the fifth time to some ancient film producer and she'd never met me but she asked my mum if I'd like to be one of her bridesmaids. So Mum said yes, that'd be cool, and we went along to meet Macy and Macy's people and the wedding coordinator.'

'And?' Tilly was frowning, wondering what the giant pink mushrooms were doing in the swimming pool.

'Oh, it was hysterical. Like when you open a present thinking it's going to be a diamond bracelet and you get a dictionary instead. Macy and the wedding guy took one look at me and started babbling all these excuses. They were horrified! I was too ginger, too pale, too freckly, too tall . . . basically, I was going to wreck the whole wedding, not to mention the magazine deal. The brides-maids were wearing sugar-plum pink. Well, you can guess how I'd look in sugar-plum pink. They ended up offering me five hundred dollars to not be a bridesmaid.'

'Tell me you're joking! That's the most horrible story I ever heard.' Tilly shook her head in disbelief. 'Did you take the money?'

Louisa snorted with laughter. 'Too right I did! I never even wanted to be her bridesmaid in the first place. Especially not if it meant wearing sparkly pale pink. Anyhow, I got chatting to the other bridesmaids at the party afterwards and they were so great. As soon as I told them what Macy had done, they all took off their dresses and chucked them into the pool. I thought that was really nice of them.' Adopting an earnest Californian accent, she said, 'Like, you know, totally supportive?'

'So those are the dresses.' Tilly pointed to the floating mushrooms.

'They were proper designer ones, too. Vera Wang. They cost thousands of dollars.' Louisa giggled. 'Macy was furious.'

'Bloody hell, *you're* the one who should have been furious.' Tilly was outraged on her behalf. 'I can't believe you even went to the wedding after she did that to you.'

'Oh, I don't care. It's all panto. All I did was fail the audition.' Louisa seemed genuinely unperturbed. 'Anyway, it was a Hollywood wedding, not the proper kind. They were only married for six months.'

'Well, if I ever get married,' said Tilly, 'you can definitely be my bridesmaid.'

'Oh thank you! And when I get married you can definitely be mine.' Louisa grinned. 'If you're not too ancient by then.'

Tilly gave her a playful push. 'I've never been a bridesmaid. Never even been asked.'

'I was nearly one once. When I was nine.' Louisa yawned, tiredness catching up with her. 'That was for Jack and Rose's wedding.'

Jack? 'You mean Jack who was here this afternoon?' Ready for gossip, Tilly perked up. 'What happened? Did they cancel it at the last minute?'

'Well, they had to.'

Ooh, lovely. Eagerly Tilly said, 'Why, who finished with who?'

'Nobody. It wasn't anything like that. They would have got married,' Louisa explained, 'except they couldn't. Because Rose died.'

Chapter 7

Downstairs in the living room Max was uncorking a bottle of red wine.

'Here's to the end of your first day.' He clinked his glass against Tilly's. 'You haven't run screaming back to London yet. Cheers. Not too unbearable so far, then?'

'I've hardly done anything. I feel like a fraud.'

'Hey, that's because I haven't started cracking my whip yet. You'll hate the sight of me by the end of the week. Now, I've written a list of things I need you to do tomorrow. I'm off up to Oxford first thing, but any problems and you can give me a ring.' Max showed her the sheet of paper, which said:

8.00a.m. Take Lou to school.
a.m. Drop wallpaper books back to Derwyn's in Cirencester.
Buy food, cook dinner, take Betty for a walk, collect six
    framed prints from Welch & Co. in Roxborough.
Pick up Lou and Nesh from school at 4.10p.m.

'That looks fine.' Tilly was finding it hard to concentrate; the revelation about Jack was rocketing around inside her head and she was longing to ask a million questions. 'Um, what would you like me to cook?'

'Oh, God knows. It does my head in, trying to think about food. The joy of having you here is that now it's your job. But we're not fussy, so don't get your knickers in a twist worrying about it. I'll be home by six,' said Max. 'And the next day you can come out with me, give me a hand with measuring up the next job.'

'Fantastic.' Tilly wondered how soon she could swing the conversation round to Jack.

'Nothing too fancy, just one of Jack's.'

Bingo!

'Actually, Lou and I were—'

'Here, I can show you the details, he left me the brochure earlier.' Max reached for a folder on the table. 'Jack's in buy-to-let, did you know that? Built up quite a portfolio over the years. He picks up properties at auction and renovates them, then I make them look great before he rents them out. Now this one, for instance, is a second-floor flat in a Victorian house in Cheltenham with a south-facing living room and—'

'Lou told me about his girlfriend dying,' Tilly blurted out, no longer able to control herself. 'The week before their wedding. Lou said she drowned.'

Max paused, smiled slightly, drank some wine. Finally he turned to look at her.

'That's right. Oh dear, and now you've joined the club. I can see it in your eyes.'

'What? I don't know what you mean.' But Tilly could feel herself turning red, because deep down she did know.

'The romance of it all. The tragic widower – except he isn't a widower because they didn't quite manage to get married. Sorry.'

Max shook his head, his tone wry. 'Jack's one of my best friends and what happened *was* terrible, but it just amuses me to see the effect it has on the opposite sex. As if he isn't bloody good-looking enough to start with, and smart and successful with it. The moment women hear his history, that's it, they lose all control. It makes them want him all the more. And now it's happened to you.'

'It hasn't,' Tilly protested, redder than ever.

'Don't give me that.' Looking resigned, Max said, 'D'you know what? If Jack seduces you and dumps you and breaks your heart, and you're so distraught as a result that you realise you can't carry on living here any more and you hand in your notice and bugger off leaving me and Lou high and dry, I swear to God, best friend or no best friend, I'm personally going to break the tragic widower's neck.'

Tilly was still longing to hear all the details; having told her the basics, Louisa had been overcome with the urge to sleep. 'I already told you, I'm nobody's notch.'

'Ah, but that was before you knew the whole story.'

Frustration welled up. 'I still don't know the whole story!'

'OK. Ready for a top-up?' Max refilled her glass then stuck his feet up on the coffee table in front of the sofa. 'Get those tissues ready, girl. Jack and Rose were together for three years. She was gorgeous, a year younger than him, the prettiest thing you ever saw. Everyone loved her. They got engaged on Christmas Eve five years ago. The wedding was booked for the following December. It was due to be held at the church in the village in Pembrokeshire where Rose had grown up. Everything was arranged. Then they found out Rose was pregnant, which was the icing on the cake. They couldn't wait to become parents. Rose was crazy about horse-riding but Jack made her give up in case it damaged the baby. Anyhow, the week before the wedding, Rose went on ahead to Wales to stay with her parents and do all that last-minute faffing about. Jack stayed behind here, tying up loose ends to do with the business. On the Sunday morning, Rose took her parents' dog for a walk along the seafront. It was a stormy day, the sea was rough. Basically, the dog was chasing a seagull into the surf and it got into difficulties. This was an animal Rose had practically grown up with. The whole family was besotted with him. Well, people saw Rose yelling to the dog but he couldn't get back to shore. The next moment she'd jumped off the rocks into the sea.'

Tilly's mouth was bone dry; listening to a story like this when you already knew the outcome was unbearable.

'And you know what?' said Max. 'She *did* rescue the dog. God knows how, but she managed to reach him and get him close enough to the rocks to be able to scramble to safety. But she couldn't save herself. A huge wave crashed over her, then the weight of the water dragged her down and the currents swept her away. By the time the lifeboat reached her, it was too late. She was dead.'

'I don't know what to say.' Tilly shook her head, trying and failing to imagine the horror of it. 'Her poor family.'

'It was rough,' Max agreed, taking another glug of wine. 'The parents were devastated. They'd lost their daughter and their grand-child – their whole future, basically. And of course Jack blamed himself. He was convinced that if only he'd gone to Pembrokeshire instead of staying here, it would never have happened.' He paused, exhaled heavily. 'The thing is, of course, he had a point. Anyway, that was it. No more wedding; we had a funeral instead. Rose's family were in pieces. Jack went through the whole thing on autopilot. Afterwards he threw himself into his work. Then, about six months later, he started . . . socialising again.' Drily Max said, 'And he's been socialising ever since, in pretty epic fashion. We're thinking of contacting the *Guinness Book of Records*. Except they'd send some poor innocent girl down here to check him out and we all know what would happen next. Imagine the next year, opening the book and reading: "The world record for seducing women is held by Jack Lucas, aged 33, of Roxborough in the Cotswolds, who *said* he'd phone me, who promised faithfully that I'd see him again, but oh no, he's just a rotten lying bastard who thinks he can get away with treating us women like rubbish . . . I mean, who the hell does he think he *is*?"'

There was a not-so-subtle message in there somewhere. In fact Tilly supposed she should be grateful Max wasn't using a megaphone to bellow the message right in her face.

'Everyone wants to make him better,' Max went on. 'They all think they'll be the one to make a difference, to break through the barriers and make Jack fall in love again. But it's been four years now. Take it from me, he's not interested in any of that lovey-dovey stuff. He'd rather steer clear of commitment and stay single. That way he can't be hurt again. And that,' Max concluded, 'is what makes Jack irresistible. That's the challenge.' He stopped and looked sideways at Tilly, to gauge her reaction.

'What happened to the dog?' said Tilly.

'It died a year later. Nothing dramatic, just old age. Went to sleep and never woke up. Pretty good way to go.' Max held up his glass and said deadpan, 'Although given the choice, I'd prefer a night with Johnny Depp.'

Chapter 8

So far, so good. Tilly was delighted with the way her first proper day was going. She'd dropped Louisa off at school at the appointed time, driven over to Cirencester and taken the wallpaper books back to Derwyn's and called into the butcher's for a three-pack of beef en croute. The potatoes were ready to be roasted, the carrots were chopped – into *batons*, if you please; none of your common old slices – and Betty had enjoyed her walk through Roxborough woods, thankfully not managing to catch any of the rabbits that had come out to taunt her.

Tilly checked her watch. It was two o'clock and all she had to do now was pick up the framed prints. Then she'd have time to call in on Erin before heading back to Harleston to collect Lou and her friend Nesh from school.

Ha, there was even a parking space practically outside Welch and Co., the blue and white bow-fronted shop with the bay trees in matching blue and white tubs flanking the doorway.

Inside, Welch and Co. was the kind of place you go to when you want to buy something nice for your house and you're feeling flush. The walls were covered with assorted paintings and mirrors, there were ornate lamps everywhere, candle holders, stylish vases, ceramic pots, sculptures, real-looking fake flowers – it was one of those shops that everywhere you looked, you saw something that made you say, 'Ooh, *that's* nice,' then go a bit light-headed when you saw the price.

The woman sitting at the back of the shop at a white lacquered table with a stained-glass candelabra on it looked expensive too. Currently chatting on the phone, she was attractive and well-groomed, with long tawny hair that might just be extensions. She was wearing a pink shirt, a white pencil skirt and a lot of make-up.

'. . . OK, but don't get your hopes up. He always says he'll give you a ring, but he never does.'

Designery-looking shoes, Tilly noticed. A glittering diamond tennis bracelet on her left wrist.

'Well, I'm glad you had a nice time. Yes I know, he is, isn't he?'

Sheeny, superfine tights. No wedding ring. Musky, heavy perfume.

'Hang on a sec, Amy. Customer.' Covering the phone with French-manicured nails, the woman looked at Tilly and said charmingly, 'Can I help you, or are you happy to browse?'

Browse. The word always made Tilly want to smile; as a child she'd thought it was something you did with your eyebrows, and that it meant walking round a shop furrowing your forehead as hard as you could while you stared at the items for sale.

But now she was a grown-up and knew that it didn't. Aloud Tilly said, 'Actually I'm here to pick up some prints. For Max Dineen?'

That got the woman's attention. Her eyes widened in recognition and she sat up straighter on her chair. Raising an index finger, she said into the phone, 'Amy, I have to go, someone interesting's just come into the shop.' Pause. 'No, not *him*. God, you're obsessed.'

'Crikey,' said Tilly. 'I didn't know I was going to be interesting. I hope you aren't expecting me to do a tap dance.'

'Not if you don't want to. But you're definitely interesting.' The woman, having put down the phone, was now giving her an unashamed once-over, her confident gaze taking note of Tilly's wind-blown hair, lack of make-up, battered jeans and pink spotted wellies. Evidently having decided that her visitor didn't present any threat – Tilly felt like announcing that she did scrub up well – she said, 'You must be Max's new girl. He told me you were starting this week. He mentioned your name too, but I've forgotten it.'

'Tilly Cole.'

'That's right. Funny name! And I'm Stella, Stella Welch. Pleased to meet you. Aren't you the lucky one, working for Max. I'm quite jealous!'

'Well, I'm enjoying it so far.' Tilly smiled, keen to make a good first impression even if her hair and wellies were letting her down. 'And Lou's great.'

'So what d'you think of him?' Stella leaned forward, her tone conspiratorial. 'Pretty dishy, wouldn't you say?'

Flummoxed, Tilly said, 'Um . . .'

'And so *funny*. I just love that Liverpudlian sense of humour. He cracks me up. I bet you secretly fancy him, don't you?'

OK, getting weird now. Was Max's sexuality not as widely known as she'd assumed? Tilly hesitated, then said, 'I don't secretly fancy him, no.'

'Oh, come on! You must do! I think he's *really* attractive.'

No, they'd talked about it last night; Max had definitely told her everyone knew. 'But he's . . . gay,' said Tilly.

'Oh that.' Stella dismissed the protestation with a shrug. 'Not completely, though. Only semi-gay. He was married to Kaye for

59

long enough. They had a kid together. So it's not as if he only likes men.' Twizzling a ballpoint pen between her fingers, she added blithely, 'There's definite room for manoeuvre.'

'Right. Um, I hadn't realised.' Hastily Tilly said, 'But I still don't fancy him.'

'Why not? Are you gay?'

Blimey.

'No, he's not my type. And I just split up from my boyfriend so I'm taking a bit of a break from all that stuff.'

'Hmm, but it's all right for you. You're younger than me. How old are you?' Stella was alarmingly forthright.

'Twenty-eight.'

'And how old do you think I am?'

Tilly hesitated. 'Um . . .'

'Thirty-seven. I know I don't look it, but I am.' Stella was alarmingly modest too. 'And my husband and I broke up six months ago. He just left me high and dry. At thirty-seven! So it's not as if I have time to take a break. I want babies before it's too late. All those years we were married, we held off having children so we could enjoy ourselves. We always said we'd wait a bit longer, have fun while we still could. The plan was that this year – *this* year,' she pointed emphatically at the table in front of her, 'we'd start trying. Then out of the blue he tells me he's off, that our marriage is over and he wants a divorce. Bam, just like that. Talk about selfish. I mean, this is my whole *life* he's messing around with here. My whole future!'

'Crikey, poor you.' The woman might be scary but, given the circumstances, it was a valid grievance. 'And is he . . .' Tilly wavered; how could she put this tactfully? '. . . seeing someone else now?'

'No, no. Definitely not.' Vigorously Stella shook her head. 'No way. You know, I reckon he had one of those mental crisis thingys, a kind of panic attack at the thought of so much responsibility. I mean, I'm on the prowl for another man just in case it doesn't happen, but I can't help thinking that sooner or later he's going to come to his senses and beg me to take him back.'

'And would you really want that?'

'God, yes, of course I would. He's my husband. I want babies. He'll be a great dad.'

The bell went t-ting above the door and a middle-aged couple wandered into the shop.

'He'll come back. He has to.' With a nod of determination, Stella changed the subject. 'Anyway, let's get you what you came for.'

'Thanks,' said Tilly as Stella helped her load the framed prints into the boot of the car.

'No problem. Give my love to Max. It's nice to meet you.' Stella straightened up. 'We could go out for a drink sometime if you like. I'll introduce you to my friends. Actually, that might not work. You're probably too young. OK, never mind. Well, I'm sure we'll bump into each other again, anyway. I'd better get back inside before that couple start helping themselves from the till.'

'Who? Stella? Oh God,' said Erin.

See? This was the trouble with not knowing people's backgrounds; you never really knew them until you knew them.

'Why? What's up with her?' said Tilly. 'She seemed quite nice. Friendly enough. Quite blunt though. And very confident. I heard all about her husband running off. She's convinced he's going to come crawling back.'

'Oh *God*.'

Tilly experienced a rush of relief that she hadn't arranged to meet Stella for a drink. 'What's wrong? Is she a complete nightmare?'

Carefully, Erin put down the red beaded evening dress she'd been checking over. 'I've been seeing Fergus.'

'Who?' Honestly, this was like twenty questions.

'Stella's husband.' Erin licked her lips. 'I was going to tell you.'

Tilly winced. 'Oh my God. Is that why he left her?'

'No! Nothing like that. They broke up six months ago. We only started seeing each other a few weeks ago.' Fiddling with the shoulder straps of the beaded evening dress, Erin said, 'But obviously no one else knows. Especially not Stella. I don't think she'd take it very well if she found out.'

'I only just met her and I already know that's the understatement of the year.'

'Well, that's why we're not going to tell her.'

'Scary,' said Tilly. 'Is he worth it?'

A dreamy look spread over Erin's face. 'He's the nicest, *nicest* man.'

'Does he know she's waiting for him to go back to her?'

'Of course he knows. She's told everyone in Roxborough!' Defiantly Erin said, 'But it's not going to happen. Sooner or later she'll have to accept that.'

'Crikey,' Tilly marvelled. 'You're really serious about him.'

'I've waited a long time for something like this to happen. And now it has.' Erin was all aglow. 'Fergus is worth being serious about.'

While they were on the subject . . .

'Ooh, guess who I met yesterday? The owner of the car I skidded into when I leapfrogged over that bin the other week!'

'Oh bloody hell, you mean he recognised you? Was he cross?'

'He was pretty good about it, all things considered. It was a brand new car.' Tilly couldn't suppress a squiggle of excitement at the thought of seeing him again tomorrow. 'He seemed quite nice too. His name's Jack.'

Had she secretly been wanting Erin to clap her hands and shriek, 'Of course! My God, you two would be *perfect* for each other!'

Well, secretly, maybe she had.

Instead Erin did a comical double-take. 'Jack? You mean Jack Lucas?' She looked horror-struck. 'Oh no, don't even *think* of going there, that's one man you definitely wouldn't want to get serious about.'

'Why does everyone keep telling me that?' It was like when you were little and your mum warned you that if you waded any deeper into the pond, water was going to slosh into your wellies.

'Trust me, I've seen it happen a million times.' Erin had her pay-attention-now-because-I-mean-it face on. 'I'm saying it because it's true.'

Tilly pretended to examine a long black velvet coat with a turquoise silk lining.

'Tilly. Are you listening to me?'

'Yes. This is nice.'

Let's face it, she never had been able to resist getting her feet wet.

Chapter 9

'See how shiny my car is? That's because I put it through the car wash last night,' said Jack. 'So try not to throw yourself over the bonnet.'

'I'll do my best to control myself.' Tilly emerged from Max's BMW, parked behind the Jag. Jack, waiting for them on the frosty pavement outside his newly acquired flat on Marlow Road, was wearing a faded blue sweatshirt and jeans. If she was tempted to throw herself over anything, it was him.

'Hey, you. Stop flirting with my assistant. And you,' Max addressed Tilly, 'stop encouraging him.'

Tilly spread her arms. 'What did I do?'

'You don't have to do anything, that's the trouble.' Shaking his head, Max said, 'Maybe a burkha would help.'

'It's OK, I'll behave myself.' Jack led the way to the front door. 'Come on, let's show you the flat.'

Tilly swallowed as she followed him up the stairs; they'd only arrived a minute ago and here she was, palpitating already. Long legs, broad shoulders, loose piece of thread stuck to the back of his jeans . . . Tilly dug her fingers into her palms, resisting the tantalising urge to pick it off because touching Jack's bottom clearly wouldn't be a sensible thing to do.

Phew, though, bet it would feel fantastic . . .

'Are you looking at my backside?'

'Oh Jesus, here he goes again,' Max exclaimed. 'Give it a rest, will you? Leave the poor girl alone.'

Tilly looked suitably grateful.

'She was, though,' said Jack. 'I could feel her eyes on me. I can tell.'

Please don't let this be true.

The second-floor flat smelled of fresh plaster and sawdust. The south-facing living room boasted a fine view over the park. 'The plasterers finished last night,' Jack explained to Tilly as Max strode from room to room, taking in every detail and scribbling notes in his Filofax. 'Now it's time for Max to come in and do his thing.'

'I thought property developers just painted everything magnolia.'

'Most do. But first impressions count, and Max knows his stuff. Make the place look a bit special and you'll attract a better class of tenant.'

'Paying a better class of rent,' said Max. 'He doesn't hire me out of the goodness of his heart. It's all about making a profit.'

'Money makes the world go round.'

Tilly opened her mouth to argue that no, *love* made the world go round, then shut it again. Under the circumstances, perhaps she wouldn't say that.

'OK, hold this tape measure. Keep it steady,' Max ordered. 'Let's get to work.'

His mobile rang twenty minutes later as they were finishing measuring up. Max, with his hands full, nodded at the phone on the window sill. 'Can you get that?'

The name flashing up was Kaye.

'It's Kaye,' said Tilly.

'That's all right.' Max grinned. 'You're allowed to speak to her.'

'Hooray,' said a cheery female voice when Tilly answered. 'You must be Tilly – I tried calling the house to see if you were there but no reply. So, what's it like working for the old slave-driver?'

'Fine so far. We're just measuring a place up at the moment.'

'Somewhere glamorous, I hope!'

'It's a flat in Cheltenham, for Jack Lucas.'

'Oh ho! And have you been introduced to Jack yet?'

Aware of Jack's gaze on her, Tilly said, 'Um, actually he's right here.'

'Oh ho *ho*!' Kaye chuckled knowingly. 'Say no more. I get the picture. And how are the two of you getting along?'

Why did people always do that? Why did they say 'say no more' then promptly ask another question? Turning away from Jack – who was evidently telepathic and was grinning broadly – Tilly murmured, 'He seems OK.'

'He is OK. Keep reminding yourself though, he's not to be taken seriously. Jack's for amusement purposes only. Buckets of charm and sex appeal,' Kaye went on, 'but you must never believe a word he says.'

'I know.'

'Excuse me,' Jack drawled. 'Am I being discussed here? What's that dreadful woman saying about me?'

Max, still busy measuring the windows, said, 'The truth, the whole truth and nothing but the truth.'

'Tell them I can hear everything they say.' Kaye sounded amused. 'And tell Jack I'm just issuing the standard Government Health Warning. I rang because I wanted to say hello to Max's new Girl Friday. Lou emailed me last night to tell me how lovely you are.'

'I'm really enjoying myself.' Touched by the endorsement, Tilly said, 'Lou's lovely too. She's a real credit to you.'

'She means the world to me. Oh my baby, I miss her so much. Never mind.' Kaye exhaled and audibly gathered herself. 'I'll be back for a holiday at Easter. Only a few more weeks to go. Now listen, any time you want to call me, don't even hesitate. Any questions, any worries, just give me a ring, d'you promise?'

'Absolutely.'

Max announced, 'Kaye just asked Tilly if I'm the best boss she ever had.'

'No no no.' Jack shook his head. 'She asked her if I was the most fanciable man in Roxborough.'

'Sshh,' said Tilly.

'Tell them I can still hear them. One other thing, has Lou mentioned anything about a boyfriend?'

'No, not at all.'

'Oh right. OK, I just wondered. She's mentioned a boy at school a few times recently, that's all. In a God-I-can't-*stand*-that-idiot kind of way. So of course I'm wondering if she has a bit of a crush on him.'

'I'll keep an ear out.' Tilly felt for Kaye; it must be agonising being so far away while your thirteen-year-old daughter was making her initial foray into the confusing world of boys. As if it got less confusing at any age.

'Thanks . . . oops, I'm going to have to go now, they're calling me into make-up. I'll speak to you again soon,' said Kaye. 'Give my love to everyone.' Cheerfully she added, 'Even Jack.'

Chapter 10

How was it that you could spend weeks, months, years, even, cooking perfectly edible meals without incident, then just when you were desperate for dinner to be perfect it all went pear-shaped?

Erin let out a yelp as the red-hot oven shelf made contact with her inner wrist and went *sssss*. Ow, that *really* hurt.

And it wasn't only the food she was managing to cock up; preparing to have first-time sex with Fergus was turning out to be a dangerous occupation. Normally she could shave her legs without incident in two minutes flat, but tonight – OK, probably because she'd been so determined to get them super-silky-*ultra*-smooth – she'd given herself half a dozen razor cuts and the shower had ended up looking like the one in *Psycho*. Then, having stubbed her toe against the chest of drawers in the bedroom, she'd managed to drop the hairdryer on her other foot.

And now dinner was going tits up too.

Was somebody up there trying to tell her something?

No, she mustn't think like that. Fergus had left his marriage six months ago; she wasn't doing anything wrong. And he was worth it. What were a few cuts and burns compared with the chance to impress the man of your dreams?

Erin collected herself; it was ten to eight and Fergus would be here soon. All she had to do now was concentrate, baste the chicken and slice up the courgettes, preferably without chopping her fingers off.

The doorbell rang at eight on the dot. As she let him into the flat, her heart was hammering against her ribs.

Between kisses, Erin said, 'You didn't stand me up.'

'I'd never stand you up.' Fergus enveloped her in a hug.

And that was the brilliant thing; she knew he wouldn't. God knew, she'd had her share of relationships with tricky, mercurial, hard-to-keep men during her university years; she was over that now. Fergus was someone you could trust and rely on. He was utterly dependable. Maybe when she'd been eighteen it was a quality she might have laughed at, but at twenty-eight dependability had turned into something of an aphrodisiac.

'Come on in.' Erin led him into the flat, still super-aware of her heart hammering away. Did Fergus know that tonight was *the* night? Did the fact that she'd invited him round for the evening and was cooking him a proper dinner imply that the rest would follow? Was he wondering if it might happen or did he know for sure? It was one of those questions you couldn't just blurt out, just as she hadn't been able to say casually to Fergus, 'Oh, and by the way, when you come over for dinner on Thursday we'll have sex afterwards, if that's all right with you.'

If he wanted to.

Yerk, *that* hadn't occurred to her before now. What if it wasn't all right with him? What if he looked horrified and said, 'Actually, would you mind awfully if we didn't?'

Erin swallowed. God, something else to worry about. Although let's face it, she'd never yet met a man who'd said no.

'Fantastic smell.'

'It's roast chicken.'

He shook his head. 'Nope.'

'Oh. Red wine sauce.'

'Not that either. It's you.' Fergus flashed his lopsided boyish smile. 'You're the one who smells fantastic.'

She was wearing her favourite perfume. Jo Malone's Pomegranate Noir. Erin felt all warm inside; wait until she got him into bed and he discovered she'd sprayed it on the sheets.

'That was brilliant.' Finishing his dinner, Fergus pushed his plate to one side and gave her hand a squeeze. 'Clever girl. Thank you.'

'It's a miracle we could eat any of it, the way you kept putting me off.' Erin loved his hearty appetite; it had been hard to concentrate on cooking with Fergus in the kitchen. Distracted, she'd sprinkled sugar instead of salt into the red wine sauce but by happy accident this hadn't done it any harm. And if Gordon Ramsay had been here, he might complain that the courgettes had been fried in butter for too long, but . . . well, that was why she'd invited Fergus for dinner and not the ultra-picky celebrity chef.

'I like putting you off.' Fergus grinned, then pulled a face as his phone burst into life.

'You'd better answer it,' said Erin. 'Might be work.'

'I'm not being dragged out this evening. Not for any client.' Leaning back on his chair and reaching behind him for his discarded jacket, Fergus located the still-ringing mobile. When he saw who was calling, he grimaced again and glanced across at Erin. But he didn't answer it and the next moment the ringing stopped.

'Work?'

'No. No one important.'

'Pudding?' Relieved, Erin collected the plates.

Fergus relaxed. 'Now that's what I call important.'

'Let's hope I didn't put salt in it.' Bee-eep went the phone in Fergus's hand, indicating that a message had been left. He put it down on the table.

'Aren't you going to listen to your message?'

'Nope.' He broke into a smile. 'I told you, it's my evening off. Let me give you a hand with those plates.'

As they were eating their lemon syrup pudding, the phone rang again. This time Fergus switched it off before calmly helping himself to more cream.

'One of your other girlfriends?' Erin meant it jokily but regretted it the moment the words were out of her mouth; not only might Fergus think she was revealing a jealous, possessive side, but she was actually implying that *she* was his girlfriend. Presumptuous or what? She waved her fork apologetically. 'Sorry. Just ignore me.'

'Hey, don't worry. As if I could ignore you anyway.' Fergus shook his head. 'I've loved these last few weeks. You have no idea how much.' He paused, mentally replayed what he'd just said, then blurted out, 'Oh God, now it's my turn. That sounds as if I'm telling you it's all over. I'm not, I promise. In fact, quite the opposite. I think you're fantastic . . . Shit, look at me, getting all flustered and tongue-tied. This never happens at work. Ask me to sell a house and I can do it, no problem. But here with you, trying to tell you how I feel . . . well, I suppose I'm out of practice.'

Erin couldn't eat any more. 'It doesn't matter.'

'It *does*. I really like you.' Fergus hesitated, the tips of his ears going pink. 'A lot.'

For a mad moment Erin wanted to burst into tears of happiness. But that would definitely be enough to scare him off. Gazing into his eyes – blueish grey and fringed with blond-tipped lashes – she said breathlessly, 'Have you finished?'

He looked startled. 'You want me to say more?'

'Actually, I meant the pudding.'

'Oh right, sorry, yes, yes . . .' Fergus shook his head. 'God, sorry, completely losing it now.'

'OK, here's an idea.' Feeling brave by comparison, Erin said, 'How about we both stop saying sorry to each other?'

'Good thinking. Yup. Definitely do that.'

'And how about we make some coffee and go and sit on the sofa?'

Fergus nodded, relieved. 'Coffee. Sofa. Sounds great.'

But when he followed her out to the kitchen seconds later, he stood behind Erin and slid his arms around her. All the little hairs on the back of her neck leapt to attention as he kissed her on the shoulder. And carried on dropping a tantalising trail of kisses along her collarbone until she was squirming with desire. Finally swivelling round in the circle of his arms, Erin said breathlessly, 'Or we could give the whole coffee and sofa thing a miss.'

Fergus stroked her face. 'You know what? That's an even better idea.'

And it was.

Phew, no disasters, what a relief.

'What are you thinking?' Fergus murmured in her ear.

Erin lay in his arms, smiling uncontrollably into the darkness as she slid her left foot lazily up and down his leg. 'I'm thinking I'm so glad I didn't fall out of bed or do anything wrong or say anything stupid. I'm thinking it went . . . very well, considering how nervous we both were beforehand.'

'Ha, you think you were nervous. Trust me, it's fifty times scarier for men.' Fergus paused, then said, 'Unless it isn't, and it's only me

72

who worries about . . . you know, the kind of thing a man might worry about.'

'I bet they all do.'

'Hmm, I'm not so sure. I can't imagine it troubling some people. Like Jack Lucas.' His tone was dry. 'Then again, Jack's had more practice. I've been out of the loop for the last twelve years.'

'It was lovely.' Erin hesitated, wondering if it was too personal a question. 'Am I . . . ?'

'Lovely too? Oh yes.' He hugged her more tightly.

'I didn't mean that.'

'Right, so you were wanting to know if you're the first since Stella?' He'd been teasing her, had known what she was trying to ask. 'That would be another yes.'

Erin's heart expanded; she was glad he wasn't the kind of man who just slept with any woman who happened to cross his path. This way she felt special.

'I'm flattered.' She wiggled her toes playfully against his ankle.

'And seeing as we're being honest, that was Stella trying to call me earlier.'

Oh. Erin's foot stopped wiggling. That put a bit of a dampener on proceedings.

'Sorry. I just thought you should know. She rings me sometimes, asks me to go round to the house for a chat.'

A chat. Right. Erin said, 'Is that a euphemism for something else?'

'No, no! God, no.' Fergus shook his head emphatically. 'And that's the truth. No way. She's just called me up a couple of times to get me over there so she can have a go at trying to change my mind. But that's not going to happen.'

OK, better. Erin breathed more easily. 'Shouldn't you call her back, then? At least let her know you won't be turning up?'

Smiling, Fergus said, 'See? That's the difference between you and Stella. She'd never consider another woman's feelings.'

'I've been out with my share of men who don't bother to return your call. There's nothing worse than sitting at home waiting for the phone to ring.' Magnanimous in victory, Erin ran her hand over his furry teddy-bear chest. 'Give her a quick ring, get it out of the way.'

He leaned over and kissed her. 'You're a nice person.'

Erin gave his chest hair a mischievous tweak. 'I'm not, I just think if you're getting up to fetch your phone, you can bring that bottle of wine back to bed.'

She lay back against the pillows and watched Fergus wrestle with the inside-out arms of her towelling dressing gown. She loved it that he chose to cover himself up rather than strut around the flat naked.

'Sorry.' Catching her watching him, Fergus said, 'You don't mind if I borrow it, do you?'

'Feel free.'

He managed to get it on and wrapped around him, tying the belt with a secure double knot. 'Wouldn't want the sight of my stomach to put you off me.'

Oh, the relief. 'You pretend not to notice my spare tyre,' said Erin happily, 'and I'll pretend not to notice yours.'

Fergus leaned over the bed and gave her another lingering kiss. 'That's my kind of deal. You wouldn't believe the grief Stella used to give me about going to the gym.'

He was lovely. Erin found herself beaming like an idiot when he left the room. Less than a minute later he was back with their two glasses and the half-full bottle of wine.

'You've forgotten something,' said Erin. 'Phone.'

'I'll call her tomorrow morning,' Fergus pleaded.

'No. Do it now. Then we don't have to feel guilty.'

He rolled his eyes good-naturedly. 'I wasn't planning on feeling guilty. OK, you win.'

This time when he came back into the bedroom he was no longer smiling.

'What's wrong?'

'Seven messages.' Fergus stood in the doorway frowning and pressing buttons on his phone. 'In one hour. Hang on . . .'

Chapter 11

Not for the first time, Erin's pulse quickened. While she and Fergus had been romping in bed, had something terrible happened to one of his parents? Filled with fear, she held her breath and watched his face as he listened to the first message. Oh God, what if someone had died and no one had been able to contact him because his phone was switched off because he was busy having sex with—

Fergus looked up, his expression grim. 'Bing's been sick and all the lights have fused in the house.'

Who? *What?*

'Who's Bing?'

'The cat.' Listening to the next message, Fergus said, 'Stella's in a panic. The fuse box must have blown.'

At least no one was dead. Erin said, 'Can't she call out an electrician?'

'You don't know what Stella's like. She's terrified of the dark. And Bing's the love of her life. You have no idea.'

Erin wished she hadn't been quite so nice now. This was what happened; it came back to bite you on the bum. The happy, relaxed atmosphere had gone and Fergus was now visibly on edge. As he listened to the third message they were both able to hear Stella's desperate voice spiralling upwards.

'Call her.'

Fergus nodded and switched off the message. Next second, the phone burst into life in his hand.

'Hi . . . yes, no, I was just about to . . . OK, calm down, no I didn't do it on purpose. I turned it off because I was busy. With *work*, Stella.' As he said this, Fergus turned away slightly, too guilty to meet Erin's gaze. 'Look, have you checked the fuse box?'

The high-pitched shriek at the other end of the phone reached new heights. Erin flinched.

'All right, all right.' Fergus heaved a sigh. 'I'll come over.'

Oh *fantastic*.

'Sorry, I couldn't say no. She's in a terrible state.' Off the phone now, Fergus was dressing hurriedly. 'Bing's thrown up twice now and it's all over the place. Probably only fur balls but she can't be sure. And it's too dark to clear up the mess.'

He'd dressed at record speed. Lifting her face for a last kiss, Erin did her best not to feel resentful towards Stella's vomiting cat.

Fergus stroked her cheek. 'This wasn't how I'd planned on ending this evening.'

'I know. Me neither.' Bloody animal, buggering fuse box. Bravely Erin said, 'Never mind.'

'I do mind. I wish I didn't have to go.' Fergus checked his watch. 'It's only eleven thirty. If it doesn't take long I could come back.'

Erin was touched, but he'd already told her he had to meet a client in Gloucester at eight o'clock in the morning.

'It's all right. I wish you didn't have to go too. But if you're that keen to see me again,' she smiled up at Fergus, secure enough to say it, 'I'm free tomorrow night.'

'OK, just in case you were thinking I have a cushy job, here's the kind of crap I have to put up with.' Max's voice crackled down the phone from Oxford, where he was meeting a new client. 'Robbie and Clive are supposed to be making a start on the Marlow Road flat but they aren't going to be able to let themselves in because, get this, Robbie left the key in the pocket of his denim jacket. And guess what?' He paused for dramatic effect.

Dutifully Tilly said, 'What?'

'Brain of Britain Robbie went out on the lash last night, ended up at some girl's house, woke up late this morning and managed to leave his denim jacket behind, like bloody Cinderella. By the time he realised what he'd done and went back to pick it up, the girl had left for work.'

'So you sacked him,' Tilly guessed.

'I'd love to sack him, silly sod. Except he's a bloody good painter and decorator, so I'd only be shooting myself in the foot. So could you be an angel, get yourself over to Jack's place and pick up the spare key, then take it over to Cheltenham? No rush, they won't get to Marlow Road before midday.'

'OK.' Eek, Jack's place. 'I don't know where Jack lives though. Hang on, let me grab a pen and write down the address.'

'No need. It's the house at the top of Miller's Hill, the one with the black iron gates and the best view over the valley.'

Of course. What else?

Tilly wondered if the iron gates were to keep out the hordes of women who chased after him, or to lock them in. Then she wondered, if she quickly changed out of her old combats and into her far more flattering black jeans, would Jack somehow be able to tell?

The gates were open and the view was as spectacular as Max had said. There was Jack's beloved Jag on the driveway. In addition, parked next to it, was a sporty lime-green Golf. So who did that belong to, then? It was definitely a girlie car.

Really wishing now that she'd changed into the black jeans – because in all honesty how *would* he have known she hadn't put them on when she'd got up this morning? – Tilly approached the L-shaped, ivy-strewn Cotswold stone house. The front door swung open as she reached it.

'Saw you coming.' Jack was grinning at her, his hair wet from the shower and his white T-shirt clinging damply to his torso. His feet were tanned and bare and he was wearing grey jersey jogging bottoms. 'Come on in.'

He could have just met her on the doorstep and handed over the key to the flat. Glad he hadn't, Tilly followed him through the parquet-floored hall and into a long sunny kitchen. It was all very tidy, very clean.

'Got time for a coffee?' Jack was already filling the cafetière.

'Why not?' She perched on a high stool and rested her elbows on the marble-topped central island. 'This is nice.'

He half smiled. 'I know it's nice. If it weren't nice I wouldn't be living here.'

Tilly fell silent. This was the house he and Rose had bought together at auction five and a half years ago; Tilly knew this because Max had told her. They had spent eighteen months restoring it from a shell into their dream home, only properly moving in together a few weeks before the wedding had been due to take place.

OK, don't think about the rest of that now. Sad stories had a way of bringing tears to her eyes.

'Jack?' A female voice, huskily seductive, called down from the top of the stairs. 'Are you finished in the bathroom now? OK if I go in the shower?'

Tilly examined her fingernails and did her best to look as if it made absolutely no difference to her who he had stashed away upstairs.

Not bothering to disguise his amusement – oh dear, was he still able to read her mind? – Jack raised his voice and drawled, 'Feel free, darling. Want me to scrub your back for you?'

His guest had a velvety laugh. 'Thanks, but I think I can manage.'

'I'm sure she can.' Jack winked at Tilly. 'One of the advantages of being double-jointed.'

OK, he was crossing the line now. Being flirtatious was one thing, but this was teetering on the edge of sleaziness. Maybe he wasn't so nice after all.

'Oh dear.' Catching her look of disapproval, Jack said, 'Sorry. Milk and sugar?'

He made the coffee and they talked about Max's plans for the flat in Marlow Road. From upstairs they heard the sound of the shower running and Tilly wondered if his compulsion to sleep with more women than Robbie Williams actually brought him happiness. After ten minutes, as the shower was turned off upstairs, she drained her cup.

'Another one?'

'No thanks.' She didn't particularly want to meet his latest conquest. 'I'm going to pick up some food then head over to Cheltenham.'

'I'll get you the key. Sorry to have put you out. I could have driven over there with it myself but my business manager's due in twenty minutes and we're going to be tied up all morning.' He was taking a third cup down from the cupboard, filling it with coffee as he spoke. 'Give me two minutes and I'll be right back.'

Jack disappeared upstairs, leaving the coffee on the side. He'd probably nipped up there to have super-speedy sex with his super-bendy girlfriend. Left alone in the kitchen, Tilly instantly slid off the stool and sidled out to the hall. One of the other doors, slightly ajar, looked as if it led into the sitting room which might be more interesting.

Oh all right then, it was photos she was looking for. But that was only natural, wasn't it? Curiosity prodded her along like a stick. Double-checking that the coast was clear, Tilly pushed open the oak door.

It was a light sun-filled room with huge squashy sofas, period furniture and, surprisingly, several examples of modern art on the walls. But Tilly's attention was instantly drawn to the photographs in silver frames on the small circular table next to the fireplace. Stealthily she approached the table, focusing on each of the photos in turn: an old black and white one, most likely Jack's parents; one of a small boy – Jack? – racing across a field with a mad-looking black and white dog; a group shot of university-age friends in evening dress cavorting on the steps of a grand country house . . .

Whoops, footsteps on the stairs, approaching at a rate of knots. Caught off guard, Tilly abruptly shot into reverse and half turned, desperate not to be caught snooping in—

'*Ow*.' The heel of her boot caught in the fringed border of the rug behind her, catapulting her to the ground like a felled tree. Pain shot through the hand that had semi-broken her fall. Mortified, she heard a voice behind her exclaim, 'Oh my *word*. Are you all right?'

A husky, sexy female voice, needless to say.

The fall had knocked the air from Tilly's lungs; she gasped for breath and cautiously eased herself into a sitting position.

'Hang on, mind how you go, let me help you up.' A powerful pair of arms hauled her to her feet. Deeply ashamed of herself, Tilly saw that her rescuer was a well-built woman in her mid-fifties with dark hair in a bun, a generous helping of turquoise eyeshadow and an emerald-green nylon housecoat. Behind her, plonked on the coffee table, was a wicker basket bristling with cleaning products.

Blimey, but she was strong though. Had she been using that Mr Muscle or drinking it?

'So, looks like the two of you have met.' From the doorway, Jack said drily, 'Monica, this is Tilly. Tilly, this is my fantastic cleaner Monica.'

'Hi. Thanks.' Tilly clutched her painful left hand. 'Sorry.'

'Poor you, can you move your fingers?' It was actually quite bizarre to hear that sex-kitten voice emerging from such a no-nonsense, less-than-young body.

'Here, let me have a look.' Jack took over. 'I can't imagine how you managed to fall over. Were you leapfrogging the TV?'

Could she lie? Would he believe her? 'My heel got caught in the rug. I was looking for the loo.'

He carried on expertly testing each of her fingers in turn. 'We decided against installing a lavatory in the sitting room. It didn't go with the furniture.'

OK, so he didn't believe her.

'I looked in here to see if it was a bathroom,' Tilly amended. 'Then, when I saw it wasn't, I spotted the photos. And I was . . . interested.' God, why did he have to look at her like that? Lamely she said, 'I like looking at other people's photographs.'

'Funny. Most people do when they come here. Does this hurt?' He began gently rotating her wrist.

'No. It's OK, I'm fine. Nothing broken.' She retrieved her hand, decided to come clean. 'When Max was telling me about Rose he said she was the prettiest girl he'd ever seen. I was curious.'

'I don't keep a photo of Rose on that table.' Jack paused. 'But at least you're honest.'

'Sorry.'

'Right,' Monica announced. 'I'm due a break. Did you pour me a coffee, Jack?'

'I did.' As Monica collected her cleaning basket and bustled out of the room, he said, 'She only likes to drink it lukewarm. Here's the key, by the way.'

'Thanks.' Tilly took it, stuffed it into the front pocket of her combats.

'Is Max still calling me the tragic widower?'

She pulled a face. 'Um . . . yes.'

'Thought so. Well, that's OK. I'll just keep on calling him the Scouse poof.' Jack looked amused. 'Did he also warn you off me?'

'Oh yes.'

'I suppose he would. So how does that make you feel?'

Tilly hesitated. Truthfully, it made her feel like a fifteen-year-old whose mother has told her that hitching up her school skirt by folding over the waistband half a dozen times isn't a flattering look. Just because you hear it, doesn't mean you're going to take a blind bit of notice.

But did he seriously expect her to tell him that?

'I'm sure it's good advice. OK, I'm off. One thing,' said Tilly. 'Was that deliberate? Letting me think you had a woman upstairs?'

Jack grinned as he showed her out. 'I did have a woman upstairs.'

Tilly gave him a look. Ha, she knew she'd been right.

Chapter 12

Erin watched the woman squeeze into the size eighteen Jaeger wool coat with the big faux fur collar.

'I love the shape.' The woman was admiring her reflection in the mirror, turning this way and that. 'What do you think?'

Oh dear, sometimes she really wished she had less of a conscience. Hesitating, Erin had a quick wrestle with her inner cold-hearted businesswoman; the coat had been here for over a fortnight now and this was the first time anyone had shown any interest in it. Furthermore she knew that Barbara, who had brought the coat into the shop, was desperate to raise cash for a much-needed week away in Majorca.

Then the door swung open and her heart leapt into her throat as – *oh God* – Stella came into the shop.

'Don't mind me. Just looking.' Stella, glamorous in a white trouser suit, airily waved a hand and began flicking through the knitwear rail.

'Well?' said the woman in the Jaeger coat.

It was no good, she couldn't do it. 'The shape's really flattering,' said Erin, 'and the colour's good. But I'm wondering if it might be a bit tight across the shoulders.'

Well, that was the polite way of saying it was two sizes too small.

'Really?' The woman's face fell. Tentatively she flexed her back, stretched her arms, sucked in her stomach and generally tried to shrink herself into the coat.

'I think so. After a while you might start to feel a bit constricted. Sorry,' said Erin. 'It's just my opinion.'

The woman shrugged and stretched again, then turned hopefully to Stella. 'Do you think it's too tight?'

'Honestly? Put it this way. If you lost three stone it'd fit you a treat.'

That was the thing about Stella, she wasn't the type to stab you in the back. She stabbed you right there in the front so you could watch all the blood gushing out.

'Tuh.' Stella sniffed as the door swung shut behind the woman. 'If she didn't want my opinion, she shouldn't have asked for it.'

'Mm.' Erin started busily rearranging the handbags on the perspex shelves behind her.

'Then again, you were the one who said the coat was a bit tight. She'd probably have bought it if you hadn't told her that. So that was quite a nice thing to do, wasn't it?' She tilted her head inquiringly. 'You must be a pretty honest person.'

Oh God, where was this leading? Was Stella testing her? And why was she moving closer? Did she have a gun hidden under that white jacket? With a casual shrug, Erin said, 'I just like people to buy clothes that suit them.'

'And that coat definitely didn't suit her.' Stella's tone was dismissive. 'She looked like an overstuffed sausage. Can you pass me that cream leather bag?'

Erin held her breath and handed it over. Stella began examining the various zips and pockets. 'This is quite nice. Good quality leather. You know, I might treat myself.' Pause. 'I deserve a treat after last night.'

'Oh?' *Just sound natural.* 'What happened last night?'

'Oh God, a fuse blew in the house and all the lights went out. Then to cap it all, my cat was sick and I didn't know *where* he'd been sick, so I was worried about him and I *hate* the dark. I'm telling you, it was a nightmare.'

'Sounds awful.' *Keep on sounding natural, just as if someone's telling you about their trip to the dentist.* 'Is . . . is your cat all right now?'

'He's fine.' Stella's eyes narrowed and her nostrils flared as she expertly investigated the bag from every angle.

'And . . . and the lights? You managed to get them back on?'

'In the end. Fergus came over.' Exhaling noisily, Stella said, 'You know, I really think he might be secretly seeing someone behind my back.'

'Do you?' *Oh help, just breathe . . . and breathe again . . .*

Stella gave the handbag a final cursory once-over, then handed it back. 'He'd better not be, that's all I can say. Thanks, I won't bother with this. The buckle on the front looks a bit cheap.'

It was hilarious, watching everyone come streaming out of school. At ten minutes past four the silence was shattered by the bell ringing, and by eleven minutes past four, pupils were spilling on to the steps of Harleston Hall, weighed down with school bags and musical instruments and sports holdalls bulging with games kit.

Tilly, leaning against the car waiting for Lou to emerge, watched as gaggles of girls freed their hair of scrunchies and shook it loose. Groups of boys with deliberately untucked shirts and tousled hair sauntered along. Some pupils were already plugged into their iPods. There was plenty of texting going on. Girls eyed up boys and boys chucked things at girls. A can of Red Bull went flying through the air and hit one of the sycamore trees lining the drive, exploding in a fountain of froth. There were pupils of all shapes and sizes, slouchy boys with bad skin, knowing girls with hiked-up skirts and kohl-lined eyes, confident athletic types, serious studious ones, cheerful jokey ones.

And there, bless her heart, was Lou coming down the stone steps, struggling to simultaneously loop her school scarf round her neck and stuff a pair of trainers into her backpack. Tilly wondered if this was how it felt to be a proud parent; already Lou seemed more vivid, more interesting than everyone else. With her wild red-gold curls and skinny legs in matt black tights and clumpy shoes, she stood out from the rest, maybe not the prettiest girl in the school but surely the one with the sparkiest personality.

Then Tilly straightened up and focused more intently as Lou turned and said something to the boy behind her, clearly replying to some remark he'd just made. The boy, tall and lanky, was grinning and carrying a tennis racquet. As Lou swung round, one of the trainers fell out of her backpack and with lightning reflexes he reached down with his racquet, scooped it up and batted it high into the air. Even from this distance Tilly could see the look Lou shot him as her trainer landed in a hedge. Shaking her head in disgust, she stalked past him and retrieved it. Laughing, the boy said something else and Lou tossed back her hair as she retaliated.

Tilly smiled. It looked like Kaye had been right. Watching Lou's reaction to the boy's attention brought back memories of her own first tentative foray into the scary but thrilling world of boys. Her particular nemesis had been called Lee Jarvis and he'd teased her non-stop, driving her demented. How could one fourteen-year-old boy *be* so annoying? And then somehow, after months of him being the absolute bane of her life, she had mysteriously found herself agreeing to dance with him at the school disco. And somehow he hadn't seemed quite so annoying any more, and somehow Lee had ended up mumbling in her ear, 'You know, I've fancied you for ages,' and to her own amazement she'd found herself realising that, actually, she fancied him too. And right there and then, in the middle of the dance floor in front of *everyone* while George Michael sang 'Careless Whisper', they'd ended up kissing, *with tongues* . . .

And braces, sadly. There'd been a brief uncomfortable clash as metal had scraped against metal, but they'd eventually managed to work around them.

Lost in a nostalgic glow as she remembered that happy summer of clunky metallic kisses, Tilly jumped a mile when Lou appeared in front of her.

'Boo! You were miles away.'

'Sorry, I was just thinking back to my schooldays. Seems like a lifetime ago now.'

'It *was* a lifetime ago. You left school before I was even born.' Interested, Lou said, 'Does that make you feel really old?'

'Thanks, yes, it really does.' As they climbed into the car, Tilly glanced over her shoulder and saw the boy with the tennis racquet loping up behind them. As he drew level he grinned at Lou and waggled his fingers in a kind of half-teasing, half-sarcastic wave.

Lou didn't wave back. Instead she pointedly turned her head away and hissed air out from between her teeth like a radiator being bled.

'Who's he, then?' Tilly said it in a light, casual way.

'A complete idiot.'

'Is he? I saw you chatting as you came out of school.'

'We weren't chatting. I was telling him he's a complete idiot. Or words to that effect.'

'He looks quite nice.' The boy had floppy dark hair, no spots and killer cheekbones. You could imagine girls falling for him; he wouldn't look out of place in a boy band.

'Well, he's not. I hate him. What's for tea?'

Tilly kept a straight face. Oh yes, that was familiar. How many times, when her friends had said Lee fancied her, had she announced that she hated him? Then abruptly changed the subject. She watched out of the corner of her eye as Lou rummaged through her jam-packed rucksack and found a bent Curly Wurly then glanced briefly at the boy she hated before ostentatiously turning away again.

'What's his name?'

'Eddie Marshall-Hicks. What are we having for tea?'

'Fish pie and blackberry crumble.' Tilly mentally squirrelled the name away. Next time she spoke to Kaye on the phone she'd find out if this was the same boy.

'It was weird.' Erin didn't mean to go on about it but her lunchtime visit from Stella had put the wind up her. 'She seemed . . . different. I can't describe the way she was.'

'So don't try. Let's just relax and have fun.' Fergus twirled Erin through from the kitchen and pulled her down with him on to the sofa. 'If Stella knew about us, trust me, *we'd* know about it. She'd come right out and say it. But she hasn't, so that means she doesn't. And I'm not going to let the thought of my ex-wife spoil our evening. We'll cross that bridge when we come to it. In the meantime, did I ever tell you what a difference you're making to my secretary's life?'

'Jeannie? I've never even met her.'

'Ah, but you can still make a difference.' Fergus arranged Erin's legs so they were resting across his lap and ran a hand affectionately over her ankles. 'Thanks to you, I've been in a ridiculously good mood today. When Jeannie double-booked me for meetings with two clients I said, oh well, no problem, I'll just have to squeeze them both in somehow. I'm telling you, she nearly fainted away with the shock. Next I asked for coffee and she brought me tea, and I didn't threaten to sack her. Then I checked a letter I'd dictated for a client and instead of Dear Mr Robertson she'd typed Deaf Mr Robertson. Which could have been tricky, seeing as Mr Robertson is deaf. But I didn't even yell at her.' Fergus shook his head, amazed by his own forbearance. 'I just said she might like to alter the letter before we sent it out.'

Erin didn't believe for a moment that he ever yelled at his secretary, but she smiled anyway. 'And all because of me?'

'All because of you.'

A thought struck her. 'Does Jeannie *know* that? Could she have told Stella?'

'Hey, stop it.' Fergus stroked her arm. 'You're getting paranoid now. For a start, Jeannie may have guessed I'm seeing someone, but she has no idea who. And secondly, if she did know, she wouldn't tell Stella. They never did like each other. Ever since the day Stella came into the office and said, "Jeannie, have you ever thought of writing in to one of those transformation TV shows and asking for a makeover?"'

'Ouch.'

'Well, yes. I thought there'd be bloodshed. Anyway, we're back to talking about Stella. Can we please change the subject again? Could we maybe talk about you for a change? I'd much rather—'

Ddddrrrringgg went the doorbell, causing Erin to catapult upright in fear. 'Oh God, it's her!'

'Don't be daft, of course it isn't. It could be anyone.'

'I suppose it might be Tilly.' Erin began to relax. That would be all right, she could invite Tilly in to meet Fergus.

'Could be someone with a collecting tin. You'd better go and see.'

Cautiously Erin peered out of the window overlooking the High Street, but there was no one there. Leaving the living room, she crossed the hall and ventured halfway down the stairs; the fact that her front door led out into a narrow side alleyway was a bonus when it came to enabling Fergus to enter the flat unobserved, but the downside was that it meant she had no way of peering out and seeing who was on the doorstep.

'Hello?' Please, *please* let her visitor be Tilly.

'Erin? Can you open the door please? It's Stella Welch.'

Chapter 13

Oh God, oh God. Collapsing back on the stair in fright, Erin clutched at the handrail for support. Oh God, Fergus had told her she was being paranoid. It wasn't supposed to actually happen. 'Um . . . I can't come down at the moment . . . I'm not dressed . . .'

'Please, just open the door. I need to see you.'

Erin's heart was banging like a cannon doing a twenty-one-gun salute. 'What about?'

'Well, for a start, the fact that you're refusing to open the door. What's wrong, Erin? What are you afraid of?'

You, you, *you.*

'Nothing.' All the feeling had gone from her legs.

'So why won't you let me in?'

'It just isn't . . . convenient.'

'Oh? And why's that?' demanded Stella. 'Could it possibly be because you have my husband up there with you in your flat?'

How? How could she possibly know? Feeling sick, Erin said, 'I don't, OK? He's not here. Look, I'm not answering the door and I'm going back upstairs now, so please just . . . go away.'

Unbelievably, Fergus hadn't heard any of this. As she stumbled back into the living room, he patted the sofa and said, 'What was it, Jehovah's Witnesses? Come here, I've missed you.'

'It was Stella.' The words felt like ice in her mouth.

His expression abruptly changed. 'You're joking. It can't be.'

They both jumped as a shower of gravel rattled against the window.

'Oh *God*.' Erin's stomach clenched. This was turning into *Fatal Attraction*.

'Come on, Fergus, I know you're in there.' Stella's furious voice sailed up to them; she was outside on the pavement now, in full view of anyone who happened to be passing.

'She's making a scene,' said Erin.

Fergus looked grim. 'She wants to make a scene. Stella's always been a drama queen.'

'Fergus, you cheating BASTARD,' bellowed Stella.

'Oh God.' Erin covered her mouth as Fergus rose to his feet.

'Right, that's it.' He crossed the room and flung open the window.

'Ha! I knew it!' Stella yelled.

'Fine, good for you. But this is exactly why I didn't tell you before.' Fergus shook his head in despair. 'I knew you'd make a fuss.'

'Why wouldn't I make a fuss? You're my husband!'

'Stella, we're not *together* any more. We broke up six months ago. We're getting a divorce.'

'Thanks to *her*,' Stella screeched like a parrot.

Oh no, no, *no*. Leaping up, Erin raced over to the open window. 'Hang on, that's not true, you can't—'

'*You*,' Stella jabbed an accusing finger up at her, 'are a lying, marriage-wrecking bitch!'

'I'm not, I'm really not, I promise. This only just happened.'

'Oh yes, and of course I'm going to believe that.' Shaking her head, Stella said bitterly, 'Of course I'm going to believe everything you say.'

'I swear to God, I'm telling the truth!'

'Really? Just like you did the other day, when I came into the shop and asked you if you thought Fergus was seeing anyone? And you said no, you definitely didn't think he was?'

Erin flinched, closing her eyes for a moment. 'OK, that wasn't completely true. But I promise the other stuff is. I would never have an affair with a married man.'

'You're having an affair with one now!'

'But you're *separated*.'

Below her on the pavement, Stella spread her arms wide. 'And now we know why!'

God, this was a nightmare. Look at them, yelling at each other like a couple of fishwives. People heading along the High Street were turning to stare, stopping to listen.

'Right, that's enough.' It was Fergus's turn to intervene. 'This isn't getting us anywhere. Stella, you're being unfair—'

'*I'm* being unfair? My God, you hypocrite! My life is in tatters thanks to you, and you expect me to just stand here and take it?'

'Everyone's looking at you. You're making a spectacle of yourself.' Exasperated, Fergus said, 'Go home, Stella. We'll talk about this tomorrow when you've calmed down.'

'Hang on.' Erin knew she wouldn't be able to rest until she'd asked the question. 'Look, I'm really sorry you're upset, and I *swear* I've only been seeing Fergus for a few weeks, but how did you know he'd be here tonight? Did someone tell you?'

Stella gazed up at her. 'Like who?'

'Like anyone. Because we haven't told anyone,' said Erin. 'Because we didn't want you to find out and be upset.'

'Well, that worked well, didn't it?'

Erin bit her lip. 'Please.'

She saw Stella hesitate. The temptation not to spill the beans must be huge. Luckily it didn't quite match up to the even greater temptation to do her Miss Marple bit and tell all.

'When Fergus came to the house last night, he smelled different. I thought I recognised the perfume but I couldn't be sure. That's why I came into the shop at lunchtime. And there it was again, on you.' Stella paused. 'Very . . . distinctive. No one else in Roxborough wears that scent.'

This was true. Possibly because there was no Jo Malone shop within fifty miles. Tilly had sent her a bottle of the fabulously exotic perfume for Christmas.

And the moral of the story was, if you don't want people to know you have a secret lover, you're probably better off *not* spraying Pomegranate Noir all over your brand new Egyptian cotton sheets.

The phone rang as Tilly was doing her impression of a chef in the kitchen. Feeling super-efficient, she tucked the cordless phone between ear and shoulder, stirred the frying mushrooms with one hand and whisked the cheese sauce with the other. Oh yes, this cooking malarkey was a piece of cake.

'Hi there.' It was Kaye's voice, cheerful and have-a-nice-dayish. 'How's everything going?'

'Oh, fine. I'm multi-tasking! Just making – *oops.*' Tilly jumped back as the cheese sauce bubbled and spat, causing her to lose control of the phone which slid down her chest, bounced off her right breast and landed in the frying pan on top of the mush-rooms. In a panic she hurriedly scooped it out with the spatula, sending the phone clattering across the stove and slices of mush-room flying through the air like confetti.

Having given the phone a hasty wipe with kitchen towel, Tilly said, 'Hello, are you still there?'

'Just about.' Kaye sounded amused. 'What happened to me?'

'I just dropped you. I'm only a trainee multi-tasker. Sorry about that.' She switched off the gas rings before anything more drastic could happen.

'No problem. Is Lou around?'

'She's upstairs doing her homework, I'll just take the phone up. By the way, I saw her bickering with a boy yesterday as they were coming out of school. Quite good-looking too.'

'Ooh!' Avidly Kaye said, 'Do you think she fancied him?'

'Well, I asked her what he was like and she said he was a complete idiot. Then she changed the subject.'

'Classic. Textbook response. Was his name Eddie?'

Bingo. 'That's the one. Eddie Marshall-Hicks.'

'Bless. My baby's getting interested in her first boy.' Kaye faltered, emotion welling up. 'Oh God, and I'm not there to help her through it.'

'Ah, but did you ask your mum for help when you were thirteen?'

'No, I suppose not.'

'Nor me. Sshh, Betty.' Turning round, Tilly saw that Betty had bounded up on to the window seat and, paws scrabbling against the glass, was barking in indignation at the rooks who had the temerity to be cawing and strutting around the lawn as if they owned the place.

'Oh, Betty! Let me speak to her,' Kaye begged.

OK, slightly weird but never mind. Glad she wasn't the one paying the phone bill, Tilly knelt on the window seat and held the receiver to Betty's ear.

'Betsy-Boo! Hello, Betsy-Boo! It's *meee,*' crooned Kaye.

Betty tilted her head to one side, then returned to gazing intently out of the window.

'Betsy-Boo? Betsy-Boo-Boo-Boo! Hello, is the phone by her ear? Can she hear me?'

'Bark,' Tilly whispered urgently in Betty's other ear. 'Woof, woof, go on, do it.'

'She's not barking. She's never not barked before.' Kaye sounded distraught. 'She doesn't recognise me.' Her voice rose to a wail. 'She's forgotten who I am!'

'She hasn't, she's just distracted.' Now Tilly really felt sorry for her. She gave Betty a nudge, willing her to bark.

'Betty-Betty-Betty,' begged Kaye.

Betty turned her head away, supremely uninterested. Tilly, crouched down next to her, did a doggy-type snuffle into the phone.

'Is that her? Betsy-Boo?'

Tilly closed her eyes and did an experimental high-pitched *yip*. Actually that wasn't bad at all. Who'd have thought she'd be so good at this? Even Betty had turned to look at her in surprise. Encouraged, Tilly took a deep breath and moved closer to the phone. 'Yip, yip-yip, yip . . .'

'Hang on.' Evidently she wasn't the world-class dog mimic she'd imagined. Kaye said slowly, 'That wasn't Betty, was it?'

'Um . . . what?'

'That was you, wasn't it?'

Tilly's heart sank. Oh well, she'd done her best. 'Yes. Sorry.'

'Never mind. Thanks for trying. I'll speak to Lou now.' Drily Kaye said, 'That's if she wants to talk to me.'

Swivelling round, Tilly saw she wasn't the only person in the room. Just inside the doorway were Max and Jack. Honestly, as if yesterday's embarrassing moment in Jack's sitting room hadn't been

97

enough. Keen to retain some dignity, she slid off the window seat and crossed the kitchen. As she passed between them, she waggled the phone and said, 'Call for Lou. I'll just take it up to her.'

Thankfully, Lou had a better memory than Betty. She seized the phone with delight. 'Hey, Mum, I got fifty-eight per cent in French today, and that might not sound brilliant but it really *was*. Euw,' she added, wrinkling her nose. 'This phone smells of mushrooms.'

Back downstairs, Tilly switched the gas rings back on and resumed cooking without looking at either Max or Jack. For several seconds there was silence in the kitchen.

Then, behind her, she heard, 'Woof.'

'Yip-yip.'

'Woof, woof-woof.'

'All right.' Tilly turned to face them. 'It was Kaye on the phone. I was just trying to make her feel better.'

'Does it for me, every time,' said Jack. 'Phew. Being barked at. Nothing beats that.'

'Woof,' said Max.

'Or there's growling.' Jack nodded thoughtfully. 'Maybe a growl beats a bark. I can't decide.'

Max beckoned with both hands. 'Come on, Tilly, give us a growl. We'll see which one we like best.'

'You know how much you hate mustard?' Tilly levelled the spatula at him. 'I could always put mustard in every meal I cook. And pepper in every pudding.'

'Can't mess with this girl.' Grinning, Max searched amongst a pile of papers on the dresser before pulling out a folder. He passed it over to Jack. 'Here's the plan for the Avening conversion. See what you think.'

'Great.' Jack moved towards the door, jangling his keys. 'Coming down to the Fox later?'

Max grimaced. 'What, and spend the evening having to stand there like a spare part while every woman in the place chats you up?'

'They don't.'

'They do. Even the geriatrics. And let me tell you, *that's* not a pretty sight.'

'It's Declan's fiftieth. He asked if you'd be there. Bring Tilly along,' Jack suggested as Lou bounded into the kitchen. 'It'll be a good night.'

'I can't go,' said Tilly. 'Who'd be here to look after Lou?'

'Look after me when?' Lou looked puzzled.

'This evening.'

'Excuse me! I'm thirteen, not *three*. I don't need a babysitter.'

'Fancy it?' Max turned to Tilly. 'Declan's the landlord of the Lazy Fox on the High Street.'

Proudly Tilly said, 'I've been there. With Erin. Declan was really nice.'

'Must've been having an off day.' Jack headed for the door. 'Right, maybe see you later.'

'Maybe.' Tilly returned her attention to the mushrooms and did her best to sound casual. After all, she might decide to stay in and watch TV instead.

Chapter 14

'It's you!' Recognising Tilly, Declan said, 'The one who made fun of our headlines.'

The Fox was busy, crammed with friends and customers helping their favourite grumpy landlord to celebrate his birthday. Silver helium balloons bobbed against the ceiling and the staff behind the bar were all wearing black and white T-shirts with 'Declan – 86 today!' emblazoned across their chests.

'You said I'd like it here,' said Tilly.

'And now she's taken you up on it,' said Max.

'Ha, so you're the one Max has got working for him.'

'All thanks to you. I wouldn't have seen the ad if you hadn't given me that newspaper.'

Declan patted her on the back. 'You'll be fine. We're not so bad. Erin coming along tonight?'

'No, she's not feeling too well.' Tilly had sent a text earlier to ask if she wanted to join them but Erin had texted back saying she had a headache, and that she'd see her another time.

'That's a shame. Anyway, let's get you two a drink.' Declan ushered them over to the bar.

Max was greeting friends, gazing around. 'Jack not here yet?'

'Jack?' Declan sounded surprised. 'He's around somewhere.'

At that moment the crowd shifted and they glimpsed him, surrounded by a gaggle of girls in their twenties. Max, cupping his hands around his mouth, called out, 'Hey, Lucas, never mind them. I'm here now.'

Excusing himself, Jack came over. He grinned at Tilly. 'You made it, then.'

As if there'd ever been any possibility she wouldn't. Tilly shrugged. 'Just for an hour or two.'

'And by the look of things we got here just in time.' Max nodded at the gaggle of girls who were still watching them. 'Once that lot get their claws into you, there's no escape.'

'Scouse poof to the rescue.' Drily Jack said, 'You have your uses.'

Then the door to the pub swung open and Tilly saw Jack register the arrival of someone whose presence didn't fill him with joy. A split second later he raised a hand in greeting, flashed a friendly-but-distant smile and mouthed, 'Hi'.

Turning, Tilly saw a thin blonde who ignored the 'but-distant' part of the message and like a heat-seeking missile determinedly battled her way through the crowds towards them. Except she was being a Jack-seeking missile. With a start Tilly realised she was dragging a friend along in her wake, and that the friend was Erin's chap's ex-wife, the confident one from the upmarket interiors shop – what was her name?

'Amy.' Jack greeted the blonde with a nod. 'Stella.'

Stella, that was it.

'Hi, Jack, how are you? I had such a fantastic time the other night.' Amy gazed up at him, adoration shining from her eyes. 'Wasn't it great?'

What might have become an awkward pause was averted by

101

Stella clutching Max's arm and blurting out, 'Never mind that. Oh Max, wait till you hear what's happened. You will not *believe* this.'

Uh oh. And she wasn't saying it in a good, I've-won-the-lottery kind of way.

'*You.*' Recognising Tilly as Max's assistant, Stella said, 'Remember I told you about my husband? Well, I found out why he left me.' Addressing everyone now, she declared, 'Because he was having an affair! I knew it all along – why else would he move out? And get this, it's not even with someone amazing. Compared with me, she's eugh, not even close. And that just drives me insane because how *dare* she? I mean, how sly is that? And it's my husband she stole!'

Tilly opened her mouth to protest but Amy was already trilling, 'And you'll never guess who it is!'

'Edwina Currie?' said Max. 'Jo Brand? Peg-leg Aggie from the corner shop?'

Hang on.

'Actually, that's not fair,' Tilly blurted out. 'It wasn't a question of stealing him. Nothing happened until *well* after he left you.'

Every head instantly swivelled in her direction. Jack's expression was unreadable. Max exclaimed, 'Fuck me! *You're* having an affair with Fergus? Is that why you were so desperate to move down here?'

Stella's immaculately lipglossed mouth fell open. 'Not you as well! My God, how many women has my husband been shagging behind my back?'

OK, getting out of control now.

'Not me.' Vigorously Tilly shook her head. 'I didn't mean me. I've never even met your husband.' Breaking into a cold sweat, she realised she might have just blown Erin's cover; what if Fergus *had* been multi-tasking, running more than one relationship? 'Sorry, I don't know why I said that. Oh, thanks.' She took the glass of wine Declan was offering her and gratefully dived into it.

'Come on then,' said Max. 'Who's he seeing?'

'OK, put it this way,' Stella announced. 'You know the dress exchange at the bottom of this street? Erin's Beautiful Clothes? Well, from now on I'm going to be calling it Erin's Enormous Nose. Because I asked her if she thought my husband was seeing someone and she *lied* to me. It's her! She's the one! I've been going into her shop and she's been pretending to sympathise with me, and all this time that witch is the reason I was distraught in the first place!'

Tilly swallowed. On the bright side, Fergus hadn't been playing the field. Aware that Max had made the connection, she said, 'Look, Erin's my friend. I didn't know about all this when I met you the other day, but she's told me since. And I promise you, she isn't like that. She'd never steal another woman's husband.'

'You're her friend?' Stella raised an eyebrow. 'Good luck there, then. Keep her well away from any boyfriend *you* might want to hang on to.'

Hyper-aware of Jack standing next to her, Tilly said again, 'She's really not that kind of person. And she told me herself, she only started seeing Fergus a few weeks ago.'

Stella half laughed. 'Well, of course she did. She's always going to *say* that, isn't she?'

'Because it's true!'

'But it's *not* true, is it, because why else would he leave me?' Clearly finding an alternative scenario impossible to comprehend,

Stella stroked the cream fur collar of her coat and flipped back her glossy, straightened, high-maintenance hair.

'Anyway, let's change the subject,' said Max.

'Absolutely.' Declan put an arm round Stella and presented his cheek. 'Happy birthday to me.'

'Sorry, Declan. Happy birthday.' Stella gave him a kiss and Amy did the same.

Then Amy said gaily, 'Ooh, now I just want to kiss *everyone*,' and gave Max a kiss. Realising why, Tilly kept a straight face as Jack neatly turned to greet a friend, just as Amy had been about to launch herself at him. For a moment disappointment flared in her lavishly mascaraed eyes, then the smile was plastered firmly back in place.

'So you're Max's new assistant,' Amy said brightly. 'Stella told me about you. No boyfriend at the moment.'

'That's right.' Was this how Stella and Amy categorised people around here? Tilly felt herself being given a critical once-over by two women who devoted more time in a week to their beauty routine than she had probably done in her entire life.

'Ah, she's doing fine,' said Max. 'Settling in a treat.'

'Making new friends.' Jack, who had rejoined the conversation, said, 'Woof woof.'

Stella's eyebrows lifted. 'What?'

'Sorry.' He grinned. 'Just a joke.'

Evidently keen to demonstrate that she did have a sense of humour, Stella said, 'He's gone barking mad.'

Amy wasn't amused. Her glance flickered suspiciously from Jack to Tilly. At that moment a mobile went off nearby. As it was answered, Jack tilted his head like Betty and said inquiringly, 'Woof?'

'Don't worry,' said Tilly. 'He's just making fun of me.'

Clearly sensing danger, Amy gave Jack's arm a possessive squeeze. 'Jack and I went out to dinner the other night. We had such a great time, didn't we?'

'Of course we did.' Jack's reply was warm; it would be easy to humiliate someone so gushy and over-keen but Tilly sensed he would never do that.

Amy glowed. 'Maybe next time we could try out that new restaurant in Tetbury.' She paused, pretended to think. 'I can't remember, did I give you my mobile number?'

'Yes, yes . . . oh, could you excuse me for a minute?' Across the pub a tall brunette was calling his name, beckoning him over. With a genial smile Jack removed himself, easing his way through the crowds.

'Marianne Tilson.' Amy shot the brunette a look of disdain. 'Honestly, talk about desperate. She's so *obvious*. Jack doesn't even like her.'

'When's that ever stopped any woman throwing herself at him?' Max winked at Tilly as he lit a cigar.

Amy turned back to Tilly. 'Do you fancy Jack?'

There was more than a hint of accusation in her tone. It seemed only sensible to say no. Shaking her head, Tilly said, 'Um . . . no.'

'Oh, come on, of course you do. Everyone does.'

'He's very . . . good-looking,' Tilly conceded. 'But I don't go for men with his kind of track record.'

Amy looked suspicious. 'So if he asked you out, you'd turn him down? You wouldn't even be tempted?'

God, this really mattered to her. 'OK, never say never, because in twenty years' time I might change my mind. But the way things stand at the moment,' said Tilly, 'no, I definitely wouldn't be tempted.'

'Wouldn't be tempted to do what?' Jack's voice behind her made her jump. Had he heard the rest?

'Run the London Marathon.' She turned and looked at him. 'Amy was just saying, she's very keen to do it next year.'

If ever a girl was surgically attached to her spindly four-inch stilettos, it was Amy. Her face was a picture. Jack said, 'Amy, you didn't mention that! Rather you than me, but I'll definitely sponsor you.'

Amy looked like a stunned goldfish. 'Er . . . thanks.'

'You should give it a go too,' Max told Stella. 'Take your mind off other things. It'd do you the world of good.'

'No thanks. God, aren't I already miserable enough?' Stella smartly sidestepped that trap. 'Anyway, exercise is for people who need to lose weight. If anyone should be running marathons it's my husband's new girlfriend.'

'Stella.' Max shook his head at her.

'What? She's fat! Why can't I say that?'

'Because Tilly's here and Erin's her friend.'

'And Erin stole my *husband*, who has to be having some kind of breakdown because he's *never* liked fat girls. I'm sorry, but I'll call her whatever I like.'

Tilly briefly imagined the reaction if she were to chuck her drink in Stella's face. But no, this was Declan's birthday – and he'd supplied the drink, come to that. There would be no public scene. Instead she would do the Shilpa thing and rise above it, meet rudeness with grace and serenity.

And everyone would think she was a lovely person as a result.

'That's fine.' Tilly did her understanding Shilpa smile. 'Stella's bound to feel—'

'Jack! Jack! Oooh, you naughty creature, come here and give me a big kiss!' Tilly, knocked to one side by a slinky-hipped brunette in a silver halter-neck top and tight-fitting designer jeans, spilled her drink over Max's sleeve. So much for not wasting it.

'Bloody hell,' said Max, shaking his arm. 'See what I mean about coming out with him? We should get danger money.'

'Lisa.' Jack allowed the brunette to give him a kiss on each cheek. 'How nice to see you again.'

'If it's nice to see me again, why haven't you been in touch? You promised you would.' Lisa pouted and clung to him. 'I've been waiting for you to call.'

'Sweetheart, I'm sorry. I've been rushed off my feet.'

'Sleeping with Marianne and Amy and God knows who else,' Max murmured in Tilly's ear. 'I'm telling you, this man makes Mick Jagger look like a hopeless amateur.'

Jack turned. 'What was that?'

'Nothing.' Max looked amused. 'I'm just glad I don't fancy you myself.'

Tilly escaped to the ladies and phoned Erin.

'It's me.' She closed the toilet seat and sat down on it, keeping her voice low. 'I'm at the Fox. Stella's here. She *knows.*'

Erin wailed, 'I know she knows! Is she still furious?'

'And outraged. I told her you didn't break up the marriage.'

'So did I. Did she believe you?'

'Not for a second. How did she find out?'

'My Jo Malone scent. Never mind, it was always going to happen sooner or later. I was scared she was going to come into the shop today, make a scene.' Erin heaved a sigh of relief. 'At least that didn't happen. Oh well, who else is there?'

'Loads of people. Me and Max. Stella and her friend Amy.' Tilly paused. 'Jack's here. Women keep coming up and grabbing him.'

'Always fun to watch. So long as you're not tempted to join in.'

'Don't worry, I'm not. The more I see him in action, the easier it becomes to steer clear.' Tilly meant it. Watching the other girls clamouring over Jack made her determined not to join in. She felt powerful and confident and . . . well, whatever the word was for the opposite of a besotted pushover.

'Well, good,' said Erin. 'That's the safest way.'

Chapter 15

Making her way back from the ladies, Tilly met Jack in the white-washed corridor.

He smiled. 'Enjoying yourself?'

'Yes, thanks. I hardly recognised you without all those women clinging to you like barnacles.'

'Sorry about that. I don't ask them to do it. Pretty embarrassing really.' When he did that self-deprecating shruggy thing he looked irresistible. 'Anyhow, you did well with Stella.'

'I did very well.' *Considering I could have ripped out her extensions.* 'In fact I was saintly.'

Jack looked amused. 'She's flirting with Max now.'

'Best of luck with that, then.'

'Actually, you could do me a big favour.' He gazed at her intently. 'I'm being put under a bit of pressure by, um, a couple of people in there.' His head tilted in the direction of the bar.

'A couple? Or maybe three?'

'OK, three.'

Tilly said, 'It must be exhausting, being you.'

'Now you're being sarcastic. Will you do me this favour or not?'

'Come on, you seriously expect me to say yes when you haven't even told me what it is?'

'I've been invited to a charity dinner in Cheltenham and I have to take a guest along with me.' Jack paused, leaning back against the wall. 'The thing is, word's got out and all three of them are angling to be the one I ask. To be honest, it's turning into a bit of a nightmare and I could really do without the hassle. They're all in competition with each other. So I'm thinking the best way round it would be to take you instead.'

Was he serious? Tilly said, 'Are you trying to get me publicly stoned and run out of Roxborough?'

'But you're new. I can tell them you're already involved with the charity, and that the organisers asked me to bring you along. That way, nobody feels snubbed. And I can relax and enjoy myself. We'll have a great evening, I promise. No barnacles, no one thinking they've won and reading too much into it . . .'

'I can't.' Tilly shook her head. 'Amy was quizzing me earlier. She wanted to know if I'd go out with you if you asked me. I said no.'

'God, like a bullet through my heart.' Clutching his chest, Jack said, 'You know how to hurt a man's feelings, don't you?'

'Excuse me. You're the one hurting *their* feelings.'

'But Amy meant would you go out with me if I asked you out on a date. And this wouldn't be a date, would it?' He shrugged. 'It wouldn't be romantic. In any way at all. So I don't see the problem.'

Tilly's stomach was churning. Was he playing some kind of game? Because if he was, it was working.

'Look, it's a straight favour, nothing more.' Jack shook his head, his tone persuasive. 'If I had a sister I'd take her along with me. But I don't, so the next best thing is if I take you instead. Purely platonic.'

Perversely, it rankled to be thought of as the next best thing to a sister. But if she said no, would he think that was what was bothering her? Oh God, now this was starting to get complicated.

'Unless you don't want it to be,' said Jack.

Which didn't help *at all*. Now her stomach was going like a washing machine on spin. He was a nightmare, and if she had an ounce of sense she'd turn him down flat. To make matters worse, her mouth was so dry she could barely swallow.

Having waited, Jack raised his hand. 'I'll take that as a no.'

Nooo! Tilly got that eBay feeling when you see the lot you've been bidding for slip from your grasp.

'When is it?' Her voice came out a bit squeakier than expected. 'I'd have to ask Max, see if he'd give me the night off.'

As they rejoined the others in the bar, Tilly was aware of Amy's eyes on her. Then she glanced briefly to the left and right and saw that she was the focus of Lisa and Marianne's scrutiny too. And this was the kind of attention Jack had to deal with all the time.

Then again, only because he'd slept with them.

'I was looking at some of the websites this afternoon.' Stella, deep in conversation with Max, said, 'It's brilliant. I had no idea! If you want George Clooney you can have him!'

'Well, that would be the answer to all our prayers,' said Max. 'But you can't *really* have him, can you? Because George isn't *really* advertising himself on the internet, is he? Lonely God-like Hollywood superstar seeks anyone at all for long walks and cosy nights in.'

Stella rolled her eyes. 'You haven't been paying a bit of attention, have you? Honestly, Max. I'm not talking about dating websites here!'

'Oh. Sorry, I drifted a bit. But you do go on,' said Max. 'OK, fire away. I'm listening now. Websites to do with . . . ?'

'Donor sperm!'

Spraying wine, Max clapped a hand over his mouth. 'Is this a joke?'

'Do I look as if I'm joking? I want a child.' Stella's back was very straight. 'My husband's buggered off and the thought of having sex with another man makes me feel physically sick. So this seems like the answer.' Defiantly she added, 'If you can think of a better way, please let me know.'

Tilly glanced at Max. Stella certainly sounded as if she meant it.

'But . . .' Amy was perplexed. 'You can't really buy George Clooney's sperm.' She frowned. 'Can you?'

Tilly bit her lip, determined not to smile. God, wouldn't it be great if you could? Imagine the bidding frenzy on eBay for some of *that*. Imagine the millions of little Georges being born all over the world . . .

'Of course you can't buy George Clooney's *actual* sperm.' Stella shot Amy a despairing look. 'I meant if you wanted a sperm donor with his qualities and physical characteristics. They give you this great long list and you tick all the relevant boxes. You get to choose every detail. If George Clooney's your ideal man, those are the boxes you tick.'

'Just don't get him confused with Mickey Rooney,' said Max.

'And how much would it cost?' Amy was clearly concerned.

Stella sipped her drink. 'It's a baby, not a new sofa. You can't put a price on a child.'

'But think how many beautiful shoes you could buy! Jimmy Choos,' Amy said dreamily. 'I'd rather have new shoes than a baby any day.'

'Shoes are better,' Max agreed. 'Shoes don't throw up on your shoulder.'

'Now you're just making fun of me.' Stella mock punched him on the arm. 'And it's no laughing matter. Men don't understand how it feels to have that clock ticking away inside you. I just hate feeling this helpless.' She shook her head. 'All my life I've made plans. I'm the queen of lists. I like to be in control and always know what's happening next. And it's driving me insane that now, thanks to Fergus, everything's changed. It's just *killing* me.'

'Well, don't go rushing off to a sperm bank,' said Jack.

Max grinned and exhaled cigar smoke. 'Jack'll do it for free.'

'Hey, leave her alone.' Putting a friendly arm around Stella's shoulders, Jack gave her a squeeze. 'Give the girl a break. She's had a rough year.'

'Speaking of making plans and knowing what's happening . . .' Amy nodded at Stella, her tone meaningful.

'What? Oh right. Yes.' Prompted by Amy, Stella turned to Jack. 'While you were gone just now, Marianne came over and said something about going with you to the charity ball in Cheltenham. She's so pushy. And I said I wasn't sure but I thought you might be inviting *someone else*.' As she spoke, she subtly tilted her head in Amy's direction while Amy suddenly lost all hearing and gazed into thin air as if communing with the spirits.

Max, observing this too and clearly intent on making mischief, said, 'Hey, girls used to do that when I was at school.' He adopted a high-pitched Liverpudlian voice. 'All right? Me mate wants to know if you want to go out with her, like?'

Amy carried on staring into the distance but her cheeks went pink.

'As a matter of fact, I'm not taking Marianne,' Jack said easily. 'And I am inviting someone else.'

A tiny smile of anticipation tweaked at the corners of Amy's mouth, like a shortlisted awards nominee ignoring the fact that up on the stage her name is being announced.

No, no, Tilly winced inwardly. Not here, not now, not like this.

'I've asked Tilly to come along with me and she's said yes.'

Oh bugger, he said it.

Amy stiffened as if she'd been shot with a tranquilliser dart. Her gaze accusing, she blurted out, '*What?*'

Stella said bluntly, 'You said you wouldn't.'

'It's not a date,' Tilly put in hastily, 'and I haven't said yes either. I said I'd ask Max.'

'Next Friday.' Jack looked over at Max. 'Can you spare her for the evening?'

'Fine by me. No hanky-panky, mind.' Wagging a finger, Max said, 'Behave yourself.'

'What's going on?' Eavesdropping on her way to the bar, Marianne's head snapped round. 'What's happening?'

'Jack's taking *her*.' Amy indicated Tilly.

'*What?*'

'I *know*.'

Oh please, she didn't need this. Tilly took a step back and said, 'This is crazy. Forget it.'

'Don't be daft. I'm inviting Tilly for a reason.' Jack eyed each of the indignant girls in turn. 'She's been raising money for the charity for years. Now she's moved away from London, this is her chance to get to know the fundraisers down here. They were thrilled when I told them about her.' He smiled easily. 'So who else could I take along as my guest?'

Marianne's face fell. Amy looked resigned. Stella said suspiciously, 'Which charity is it?'

This was the question Tilly had been dreading. Honestly, why did people have to be so *nosy*? The really frustrating thing was,

Stella was asking *her* and Jack was waiting for her to give them the answer because he'd told her the name of the charity moments before they'd come back through to the bar.

Except it had gone, slithered away like mercury, and she couldn't remember now for the life of her what it was. And everyone was standing there waiting, gazing expectantly . . . OK, it definitely wasn't anything to do with animals, or dolphins, or restoring buildings, or birds, or gardens, or children or Aids or guide dogs or great crested endangered newts . . . Damn, she really couldn't remember, it had completely slipped her mind—

Ooh!

'Help for Alzheimer's!' Tilly gave a nod of triumph. Phew, just in the nick of time.

Stella, her tone waspish, said, 'For a minute I thought you'd forgotten.'

'I nearly did.' She managed a little laugh. 'I support so many charities!'

'It's a deserving cause,' said Jack.

'And it's not a date,' Tilly reminded them, because there were still some mutinous faces.

'Absolutely not a date.' Jack shook his head in agreement. 'God, I'm not even looking forward to it. Sometimes we just have to do our duty, don't we?' He knocked back his drink and grinned. 'Is it my round?'

Looks of hate were still winging her way as Tilly checked her watch. So this was what happened when you agreed to do someone a favour. If she didn't get run out of town first, she couldn't wait to ask for one in return.

Was it time to go home yet?

Chapter 16

After three years in LA you'd think she'd be used to its funny little Californian ways but the parties still made Kaye smile. This one, thrown by the director of *Over the Rainbow*, was glitzy and lavish in so many aspects, yet it still ended on schedule – like a birthday party for a class of six-year-olds – at five o'clock on the dot. Even more bizarrely, guests were leaving in chauffeur-driven limos because they were too rich, rather than too paralytic, to drive themselves home. Nearly everyone had spent the afternoon sipping iced mineral water. If any recreational drug-taking had been going on, she hadn't seen any evidence of it. Denzil and Charlene Weintraub's house in the Hollywood Hills had been spectacular and the dresses and jewels worn by the female guests had dazzled in the sunlight but in all honesty it wasn't the kind of party you'd remember for the rest of your life. Over here you were expected to network rather than enjoy yourself. Fun was frowned upon and actually eating in this world of size zeros was categorised as a dangerous sport, indulged in only by those fool-hardy enough to completely let themselves go.

Anyway, sod hiring a chauffeur-driven limo for no reason other than to show off. Hitching up her narrow skirt, Kaye slid behind the wheel of her convertible and wondered whether she'd been imagining it or if Charlene's manner towards her this afternoon had been a bit odd. Several times she'd caught Charlene looking over at her in a less than friendly fashion. Out by the pool earlier she'd drawled, 'So, found yourself another man yet, Kaye? One of your own, I mean, rather than somebody else's?'

Which had been a weird thing to say, hadn't it? Then again, the wife of your director wasn't the kind of person you took issue with. Charlene was pampered, prickly and famously indulged by Denzil, whose children from his first marriage were all older than she was. Kaye had heard on the grapevine – well, Macy Ventura, who knew pretty much everything about everyone so was as good as any Hollywood grapevine – that Charlene was secretly battling an addiction to painkillers, so it was best to stay on the right side of her. She could be volatile when crossed.

Putting the car into gear, Kaye reversed out of her parking space and waited for a glossy black stretch limo to manoeuvre its way past her before heading down the drive. Music, music. She pressed play on the CD player and cranked up the volume as Jennifer Hudson launched into 'And I Am Telling You I'm Not Going'. Oh yes, this was her favourite song of all time. She never tired of it and those powerful vocals never failed to send shivers down her spine. In fact this was definitely the song she wanted played at her funeral, with the added bonus that any American mourners would be appalled and the British contingent delighted by the choice of lyrics. Amused, Kaye envisaged the scene, maybe with the music emanating from speakers hidden in the lid of the coffin. Max would find that hilarious. Actually, if he had anything to do with it, he'd arrange for the lid to creak open and a fake hand to slide out as the song rose to a crescendo. Moved by the prospect, Kaye sucked air into her lungs and bellowed along with Jennifer, 'And I am *telling* you . . . I'm not *gooooooinggg—*'

Shit, what was *that*?

In a split second the tiny brown creature had appeared out of nowhere, shooting out from behind a palm tree and disappearing under the front wheels before she even had a chance to react. She stamped on the brakes and let out a shriek of fright as the car slewed to a stop on the drive. Oh God, please don't say she'd hit it, even if it was only a rat. She hated rats but that didn't mean she wanted to kill one. Had it escaped or was it dead? It had looked like a rat but was it a rat? Would she have felt the bump if she'd run over it or was the creature too small to make itself—

'Oh God, oh *no.*' Having stumbled out of the car and dropped to her knees, she saw the sight she'd been most dreading. The little body lay unmoving in the shadows under the car. She'd killed the rat. Screwing up her face, hopelessly squeamish, Kaye knew she had to get it out of the way or she'd crush it beneath the back wheels when she drove off. She had to reach it and drag it towards her. Ugh, rats gave her the creeps, they were—

'Nooooooo!' shrieked a high-pitched voice in the distance as a door slammed and footsteps came racing down the drive.

'No,' Kaye croaked as she pulled the rat out from under the car and saw that it wasn't a rat after all. Oh no, oh no, oh no. She went hot, then ice-cold all over, nauseated and appalled by the sight of the tiny creature, Charlene's pet Chihuahua, on the ground.

'You killed Babylamb! You killed my baby!' Charlene had reached them, panting and distraught. Scooping the little body into her arms, she began rocking to and fro. 'Oh my Babylamb, wake up, wake up . . .'

'I'm so sorry. It was an accident, I'm so sorry.' Dimly aware of more footsteps approaching, Kaye shook her head helplessly. 'It was an accident. He just came out of nowhere, ran straight under the car. There was nothing I could do, I'm so sorry.'

'No you're not! You're lying,' screeched Charlene, eyes ablaze, mouth distorted with hatred. 'You bitch, you did it on purpose!'

Kaye stumbled backwards, stunned by the ferocity of the attack. 'That's not true, I wouldn't do that, it's not *true*!'

'You hate me. You're jealous,' Charlene spat vehemently. 'You want Denzil and you can't bear it that I have him. You're deranged,' she went on. 'You're a bunny boiler and a dog killer and I'm going to get you for this. Denzil's my husband and you're not going to take him away from me. You're nothing but a skinny ginger husband-stealing tart and you ran over my Babylamb on purpose.'

'I didn't, I didn't.'

'Oh, don't lie. Look at the state of you. You're drunk.' Charlene jabbed a bony finger at her. 'And I know you did it on purpose because I saw it happen. I was up there on the balcony and I saw you deliberately swerve to run over him. You wanted to hurt me so you killed my baby.'

This was a nightmare. Kaye couldn't believe it was happening. Guests, security guards and household staff hurried over to see what was going on. Her legs lost their ability to hold her up and she collapsed sideways in the passenger seat of her car, protesting her innocence to anyone who'd listen.

'She's drunk,' Charlene yelled over and over again. 'All through the party she was helping herself to wine. That's when she wasn't eyeing up my husband.'

'I had one glass of wine. *One glass*,' Kaye protested, but it was no use.

'She's a bitter, twisted, murdering bitch and she is *finished* in this town!' screeched Charlene, still cradling the dog's body.

'It was an accident. I'm sorry, I don't know what else I can say.'

Kaye had never felt more alone in her life. Nobody believed her, not one person was on her side. Guilt engulfed her because whether or not the fault had been hers, Babylamb was still dead. Burying her head in her trembling hands, she realised for the first time that her tight skirt had split when she'd been reaching under the car.

'What's going on?' Denzil, the last to reach the crime scene, came lumbering down the drive. Breathing heavily, he slowed to a halt and gazed in horror from Kaye to the tiny bundle in Charlene's skinny arms. 'Ah Jeez, not Babylamb.'

Tears were sliding down Charlene's face, dripping off her recently remodelled chin. 'She m-murdered him, Denny. She did it on purpose.' Between noisy sobs she said, 'C-call the cops. That bitch is going to pay for this.'

There were five customers in the shop when Stella made her entrance.

Erin's heart sank like an anchor. This was what she'd been dreading all week. Anything could happen now.

'What d'you reckon, Barbara? How about this for our Angie's wedding?' A middle-aged woman reverently stroked a pale green matching dress and jacket. 'Lovely material. Here, have a feel. Eighty pounds, but it's Frank Usher. Ooh, I've always wanted an outfit by Frank Usher.'

'Eighty pounds?' Stella clicked her tongue in disbelief. 'I should open a shop like this.' Reaching over to take a closer look at the dress and jacket, she said to the woman, 'It's a pity you didn't try the Oxfam shop on Hill Street yesterday morning. You could have bought it in there for six pounds fifty.'

Erin's heart dropped still further. The middle-aged woman and her friend instinctively took a step back from the outfit and turned to look at her in shocked disbelief.

'That's not true.' Erin shook her head at the two women. 'Just ignore her. It's not true.'

'Oh come on, we all know that's what you do. I gave three bags of clothes to the church jumble last summer and most of that stuff ended up in here too.'

Another outrageous lie, but the prospective customers in her shop weren't to know this. Erin said, 'I keep a record on this computer of everyone who brings clothes into this shop to resell.'

'I'm sure you do. I'd make up a list of names and pretend that's how I got them as well,' Stella said sweetly. 'Otherwise it might look bad, don't you think? By the way, did you ever hear back from that woman who complained about the cardigan she'd bought from you, the one with maggots in the pocket?'

The two women backed out of the shop. The other three glanced at each other before silently following suit, the last one to leave surreptitiously wiping her palms on the side of her coat.

'She's lying,' Erin called out before the door clanged shut behind them.

'Worked, though.' Stella looked pleased with herself. 'Didn't it?'

'You can't do this.'

'Just did.'

'It's not fair.'

'I think it's fair,' said Stella. 'I think you deserve it.'

'I didn't steal Fergus from you.' Erin shook her head; if she said it another fifty thousand times, would Stella believe her?

'Now you're the one who's lying.'

OK, maybe not. She tried another tack. 'The thing is, marching in here like this and causing trouble isn't going to make Fergus want to come back to you.'

'I know that. I'm not *stupid*.' Her chin raised and her shoulders stiff, Stella said, 'Until the other night I thought it might happen, but now I know it won't. Thanks to you, I'm not going to have the life or the family I'd planned to have. Which, funnily enough, I find really upsetting.'

'But I didn't—'

'Oh give it a rest, little Miss Innocent.' Stella's disparaging gaze slid down to Erin's hips. 'Actually, not so little.'

Trembling, Erin said, 'I don't want you coming into this shop again.'

'Don't worry, I won't. But just remember.' Stella paused with her hand gripping the door. 'You've hurt me. And now it's my turn to hurt you.'

Chapter 17

'There's a photographer up a tree across the street.' Clutching the phone, Kaye ducked away from the window before he could get a shot of her. 'And a load more milling around on the sidewalk.'

'Sidewalk,' mimicked Max, six thousand miles away. 'Get you and your fancy Americanisms.'

'Max, shut up.' She knew this was his way of attempting to lighten the mood but it really wasn't working.

'OK, sorry.' After so many years of marriage they understood each other. 'But it'll blow over, won't it? Give them a day or two and people will lose interest, move on to the next bit of gossip.'

'I hope so.' Except she wasn't so sure, and now an outside broadcast truck was pulling up outside. She hadn't been arrested – the police had released her without charge after an excruciating couple of hours down at the station – but she already knew Charlene wasn't going to let it go. Journalists contacted by Charlene had been ringing for her response. And this was Hollywood. The right story happening to the right people at the right time could be picked up and whipped into overdrive; it could spread like wildfire, detonate a media frenzy. And let's face it, who wouldn't love the idea that one of the stars of *Over the Rainbow* – the cute British red-headed one, no less, who seemed so ladylike – was in reality a jealous, man-hungry, puppy-murdering psychopath?

'Hey, you'll be fine,' Max said helpfully. 'Just tell everyone to fuck off.'

'Oh yes, that'll work.' A reporter was standing outside the house wielding a microphone and addressing a camera.

'Threaten to sue the mad bitch.'

'Max, you're starting to get on my nerves now.'

'OK then, come home. Just jump on a plane and get out of there. We'll look after you.'

Kaye's eyes abruptly filled with tears, because what he was suggesting was so tempting and so impossible. If this story took off, running away would be, more than anything, what she'd want to do.

'Except I have this little thing called a job,' she reminded Max. 'And a killer shooting schedule and a contract for next season about to be renewed. And something tells me the studio wouldn't be too thrilled if I did a bunk.'

Above a faint tapping sound, Max said, 'Well, we're here if you need us. Don't let the buggers get you down. If anyone contacts me I'll tell them – bloody hell.'

Oh God, what now? Had an OB truck just pulled up outside the house in Roxborough? Her mouth dry, Kaye said, 'What is it?'

'I've got the laptop here. I've just been Googling you. There's a piece about it on one of the gossip sites.'

'Saying?' She braced herself.

'They're calling you the bunny boiler of Beverly Hills.'

'Poor Mum.' Three days had passed and wildfire wasn't the word for it; the Hollywood gossip machine had gone into meltdown and Kaye was now officially the most reviled woman in America. Clicking on to the next link, Lou was confronted with a photograph of Charlene tearfully hugging a portrait of Babylamb. The accompanying article was headlined: 'I don't know how I'm going to get through the funeral. I just want to *die*.'

Tilly said, 'Stop reading them now.'

'I can't. That's my mum they're talking about. Look, here's a photo of her being carted off to the police station. She had one glass of wine and passed the breathalyser but they're still trying to make out she's got a drink problem. If she didn't have before, she'll end up with one at this rate.'

Tilly peered over Lou's shoulder at the photograph of Kaye, understandably upset and dishevelled and with her skirt torn, taken on the day of the accident; of course they'd used the shot where she'd been blinking so her eyes were half-closed and she looked as if she'd been on a week-long bender.

'Perfect English Rose or Deranged Drunk?' screamed the headline.

'The perils of jealousy,' said the next. 'Kaye McKenna's career is in tatters, thanks to an unrequited crush on her boss and a moment of murderous madness.'

'Denzil Weintraub is in his sixties.' Lou shook her head in disgust. 'Why doesn't it occur to any of them that my mum wouldn't *be* interested in some fat old director with a failed hair transplant and a nose like a potato?'

'Because he's a multimillionaire super-successful fat old director.' Tilly pointed to the relevant line of text.

'My mum isn't like that! She doesn't chase after ugly old men just because they're rich!'

'We know that. Don't worry, she'll get through this. Turn off the computer now, sweetheart.'

125

'Are you by any chance trying to stop me reading the next link?' Amused, Lou tweaked the mouse and said, 'It's OK, I've already seen it. The loopy psychologist claiming that Mum's having a belated breakdown because her husband turned gay on her. It's all rubbish.'

Tilly gave her narrow shoulders a squeeze. 'Of course it is.'

'And I can't turn the computer off yet either. I've got to look up some stuff about Shakespeare. He's so boring.'

'We did *Macbeth* for GCSE.' Tilly pulled a face; she could sympathise with that.

'We're doing *Romeo and Juliet*. Half the time I can't even work out what everyone's trying to say, the dialogue's so twiddly and complicated. I mean, why can't they just talk proper English?'

'My daughter the philistine,' Max announced, coming into the kitchen with a design board. 'If it isn't *Heat* magazine, she's not interested.'

'Thanks for that, Dad. I'll have you know I'm actually *very* intelligent. I just don't happen to like Shakespeare.'

'That's because you haven't seen it being performed. Right, let's do something about it. Shift your backside.' Dumping the design board, Max expertly nudged Lou out of her seat and took her place in front of the laptop. 'Royal Shakespeare Company, Stratford. Here we go. *Richard the Third* . . . maybe not. *Coriolanus*, hmm.' Jabbing at keys, he scrolled through the events diary. '*Twelfth Night*, you'll like that. Right, fetch my wallet, we'll book the tickets now. Tilly, you up for this?'

Startled, Tilly said, 'Are you serious? You really like Shakespeare?'

'Ha, she thinks I'm too common to appreciate the Bard. But I'm not.' Max wagged a finger at her, 'He's bloody brilliant. Just go with the flow and you'll be hooked, I'm telling you. Oh yes, I'll drum a bit of culture into your heads if it kills me. Bugger, I can't do the Wednesday or Thursday, I'm up in London with a client. It'll have to be Friday the twentieth.'

Phew, reprieve.

'I can't make that. It's the night of the charity ball. What a shame,' said Tilly.

'Charity ball?' Lou looked interested.

'In Cheltenham. Jack invited her. I'll just book the two seats then.' Max busied himself inputting his credit card information.

'Jack *invited* you?' Grinning, Lou said, 'Oo-er! I thought you said you weren't interested in becoming another notch on his bedpost.'

'I'm not.' For heaven's sake, now she was being teased by a freckly thirteen-year-old. 'It's not a date, he just asked me along to get him out of a tight corner.'

Lou nodded with the air of someone who knows *sooo* much better. 'You'll have to watch he doesn't get you into one.'

The atmosphere on set hadn't improved. Everywhere she went, Kaye encountered groups of people whispering together then shutting up and melting away the moment she came into view. It wasn't the most welcoming sensation; this was probably how it felt to be a homeless person who really smelled.

She was also aware that the team of writers had been called back and were currently holed up in a Winnebago, working away on last-minute alterations to the script for the final episode of the series.

Hmm, wonder what that could possibly be about? *And* she was still waiting for her contract to be renewed. Funny that.

In the make-up trailer, the only sound came from the TV tuned to one of the entertainment channels.

'. . . And now we move on to the Kaye McKenna affair,' announced the presenter.

Drily Kaye said, 'Just for a change.'

Ellis the make-up girl put down the blusher brush she'd been using on her cheeks. 'Want me to change channels?'

'No, leave it. I don't care any more. Let's see what they're saying today.'

'And this morning we have here in the studio three guests who all have something in common with Charlene Weintraub.' The presenter paused significantly, her mouth pursed like a cat's bottom to indicate that this was *really serious*, before indicating the first woman on the left. 'Paula here says she was walking along the street minding her own business one day last year when a car driven by Kaye McKenna came careering at top speed towards her. If she hadn't leapt out of the way she's convinced she would have been killed, just like Babylamb.'

'Oh my God . . .' breathed Ellis, glancing in horror at Kaye's reflection in the mirror. 'You did *that*?'

'No of course I didn't do that! I've never seen the woman before! I'm a *careful* driver!'

'Next we have Jason, who tells us that Kaye McKenna deliberately tried to run over his pet dog, Brutus.'

'How can they be allowed to go on television and say this?' Kaye demanded.

'And finally we have Maria who says she and her grandmother were verbally abused in the street by a deranged and clearly under the influence red-headed woman whom they now believe to have been Kaye McKenna.'

'I should sue them all! How *dare* they?' bellowed Kaye.

There was a tap at the door, then Denzil entered the trailer. Ellis hurriedly switched off the TV.

'Denzil. You won't believe the things they're saying about me on there.' Kaye indicated the blank screen. 'It's all lies. People are just going on television and making stuff up.'

'Kaye, you know what my lawyer said. I can't discuss any of that with you.' Hovering in the doorway, Denzil said gruffly, 'Can we just get this new scene shot?'

'OK. Sorry.' She saw that he'd come empty-handed. 'Do I get to see the script?'

'No need.' Denzil's chins wobbled as he shook his head. 'You don't have any dialogue.'

Kaye looked steadily at him, her all-too-brief acting career flashing before her eyes. 'Let me guess. Am I going to be floating face down in a swimming pool?'

He couldn't even bring himself to meet her gaze. His tone abrupt, Denzil said, 'Something like that.'

Chapter 18

'No thanks. Just water for me.' Tilly was going to hang on to her faculties tonight if it killed her.

Jack said, 'Hey, the whole point of getting a taxi here was so we didn't have to worry about driving home. We can relax, have a few drinks and enjoy ourselves.'

'You don't say.' Honestly, did he think she wasn't aware of that? It was exactly why she was sticking to water.

'One glass of wine wouldn't hurt, would it?'

A glass of wine would be heaven but she wasn't risking it. Tilly said perkily, 'I don't need alcohol to enjoy myself.'

Yes, *perkily*.

'Bloody hell, I've brought Pollyanna along to the ball.' But he was clearly amused by her attitude; grinning at the waiter with the wine bottle, Jack confided, 'She's scared I'll seduce her.'

The waiter in turn pulled a Graham Norton type face and stage-whispered in Tilly's ear, 'Go for it, darling. Lucky old you.'

Which was a great help.

'I'm not going to,' said Jack. 'I gave my word I wouldn't. And I always keep my promises.'

'Don't worry.' The waiter winked at Tilly. 'I'm sure you can persuade him to change his mind.'

Just the thought of it made her go hot. Tilly grabbed a glass of sparkling water from a passing waitress and gulped it down. Glad of the reprieve as the young waiter minced off and Jack was collared by a couple of florid businessmen, she stood back and surveyed the scene.

The ball was being held at a huge wedding cake of a hotel in Cheltenham; the ballroom was glamorous, vast and high-ceilinged and thronged with people chatting and dancing along to the band. The noise level was impressive and the ages of the guests ranged from twenty upwards; it wasn't, as Tilly had feared, confined to a scrum of oldies with clacking false teeth and walking sticks. It was a colourful, friendly crowd and Jack knew a great many of them. He was also, despite the fact that she wasn't drinking, becoming more attractive by the minute.

OK, stop that, must behave. She wasn't anybody's notch . . .

'Oh, don't you look lovely in that dress!' An older woman resplendent in purple silk came swishing up. 'I've been meaning to come over and say hello! Dorothy Summerskill, from the committee,' she introduced herself. 'And you're Jack's girlfriend.'

'Friend,' said Tilly. 'We're just friends.'

'Oh, right! Probably safer that way!' Dorothy had a jolly laugh. 'Hard to keep up with Jack's social life these days. Then again, who'd begrudge him some fun? We all love him to bits, you know. He's done so much for our charity. One of our greatest supporters here in Cheltenham.'

'Is that because a member of his family had Alzheimer's?'

'Actually, it was through Rose, his fiancée. Darling Rose, we miss her still. Her grandmother was affected, which is how Rose

131

got involved with fundraising for the society. After she died, I have to tell you, we didn't think we'd see Jack again. But he's stayed on board. Wonderful for us. And hopefully we'll see you again after tonight.' Dorothy's eyes sparkled. 'Any friend of Jack's is a friend of ours.'

After dinner the dancing began in earnest. Having been introduced to plenty more people, Tilly spent the next couple of hours being twirled around the dance floor by them, with varying degrees of success. Dorothy's husband Harold was an enthusiastic amateur mountaineer and danced just like one. A cheerful accountant called Mervyn had a gurgling laugh and a penchant for knock-knock jokes. Patrick the farmer looked like an all-in wrestler but danced like Fred Astaire. And their wives and girl-friends were fun too. Great, uncomplicated company. Barely even aware that she still wasn't drinking, Tilly was having a whale of a time.

Then Jack had to come along and spoil it all.

Exhausted after a couple of energetic tangos with Patrick, she was perching on the edge of a table giving her feet a rest when she saw Jack heading towards her.

'What?' said Tilly, because he was checking his watch. 'Is it time to go?' Her heart sank. It was only midnight. They didn't have to leave yet, surely.

'Not unless you want to. Why?' He tilted his head. 'Are you hating every minute?'

'No.' She could smell his aftershave.

'Good. Actually, I was thinking it was time we had a dance.' He paused, watching her reaction. 'Sorry. It's just that people might think it a bit odd if we don't.' Another pause. 'So how about it? Shall we do it now, get it out of the way?'

'OK.' He was right. Reluctantly she slid down from the table.

'It's not the gallows,' said Jack. 'Don't worry, I'll behave myself. Perfect gentleman tonight, just like I promised.' Grinning, he drew her to him as the music restarted. One warm hand rested on her bare shoulder, the other just touched the base of her spine. Then he swung her skilfully out on to the dance floor. The next moment the hand on her spine was all over her bottom and he was pawing like a wild animal at her skirt.

'What are you *doing*?' Horrified, Tilly slapped his arm and wrenched herself free.

'Sorry, your dress was caught up at the back. I was trying to pull the hem down before everyone saw your knickers.'

For heaven's sake, as if dancing with Jack Lucas wasn't palpitation-inducing enough. Now she'd given a couple of hundred people a free flash of her pants.

Oh well, too late now to worry about it. And at least they'd been her best ones.

'Thanks.' Exhaling, she allowed him to resume physical contact. Right, just relax, move in time with the music and keep on moving in time with the music until it ends. Then that's it, job done. And how long would it take, anyway? Three or four minutes, she could manage that. If the going got tough she could break it down, get through one minute at a time, maybe even do it in seconds . . .

OK, one . . . two . . . three . . .

'Are you *counting*?'

'What? Oh, sorry.' Tilly ducked her head, tinglingly aware of the fact that most of the front of her body was touching most of the front of his. The third button of his white evening shirt was exactly level with the neckline of her shell-pink strapless evening dress. His aftershave smelled better than ever; if she completely lost control of herself and reached up on tiptoe she could lick his neck . . . OK, stop that, start counting again, but this time keep it in your head.

'Having fun?' said Jack.

She nodded; he had absolutely no idea how dancing with him was making her feel. 'Everyone's really friendly.'

'They're a good crowd.'

Forcing herself to look into his eyes, because avoiding them was starting to look odd, Tilly said, 'Dorothy was saying nice things about you.'

'Could be because I'm a nice person. Every now and again,' Jack amended with a brief smile. 'When I want to be.'

That smile. At such close quarters it was even more devastating. He was making it hard to concentrate. Tilly closed her eyes for a second and thought about Amy and Marianne and whatever the other one's name had been . . . Lisa, that was it. Because that was the thing about Jack, he bestowed his smiles indiscriminately and left a trail of havoc in his wake. He wasn't remotely interested in any kind of meaningful relationship either. All he cared about was sex. Remember that. And *keep right on remembering it* . . .

'What are you thinking?' His voice broke into her feverish, tangled thoughts.

'Nothing.'

He grinned. 'That means I don't want to know.'

Tilly shrugged and hoped her palms weren't growing damp. She could feel his hips against hers and if that wasn't disconcerting she didn't know what was. And she couldn't *believe* she was wondering if while he'd been tugging her hooked-up dress over her bottom he'd happened to notice how silky and nice her gorgeous new pink and cream knickers from La Senza had felt.

'OK, you can stop now,' murmured Jack.

For a second she thought he meant she could stop wondering if he'd appreciated her knickers. Then she realised the music had ended and she was still swaying from side to side. Collecting herself, Tilly said hastily, 'I thought they'd launch straight into the next song. I was just . . . you know, keeping the momentum going.'

'You want to stay for another dance?' As he moved his hands to her waist, the music started up again.

Now that they were out here on the dance floor it made sense. 'Well . . .'

'We've done our duty, haven't we?' Jack released his hold on her, disappointing all her nerve endings at once. 'Why don't we go and get another drink instead?'

Jack had promised to treat her like a lady and behave like a perfect gentleman but Tilly hadn't actually expected him to do it. All the way back to Roxborough in the back of the taxi she'd been mentally bracing herself, waiting for him to make a move. At the very least, surely, he'd suggest going back to his place for coffee.

But he hadn't. Instead he'd directed the taxi driver to Beech House and now here they were, outside it.

'Right,' said Jack. 'Well, got you back safely. Thanks for coming along tonight. It was good.'

'Yes, it was.' Tilly realised this was it, he wasn't even intending to lean across the seat and plant a polite goodbye kiss on her cheek.

Right. So here they were outside her home and here she was, unkissed, unpropositioned and, frankly, starting to feel just the teeniest bit unattractive.

But he still wasn't moving, so what else could she do but climb out of the car?

'Bye.' Jack nodded.

'Bye.'

Did he find her *ugly*?

Chapter 19

Tilly had got her dates muddled; when Max had been booking the tickets for the RSC she had thought the ball in Cheltenham was being held on the Friday evening. Happily, by the time she'd realised her mistake – the ball was on Thursday – it had been too late for him to book another seat.

Max still thought she'd done it on purpose.

After school on Friday afternoon Lou grumbled, 'I don't know why Dad thinks seeing people prancing around on a stage is going to make me like Shakespeare. I bet I'll still think he's boring.'

Tilly was struggling to tame Lou's wild red curls with serum before making an attempt at a French plait. 'You never know, you might love it.'

'You want to go in my place?'

'That's so generous. But then you'd miss out.'

'We could check the website again; you never know, lots of people might have had to cancel and now there's some tickets left.'

'You are so *sweet* to think of that.' Tilly gave one of her curls a tweak. 'Luckily, I thought of it first and I have my great excuse all ready for you. One of us has to stay at home and look after Betty.'

'Bloody hell,' complained Max, just home from a meeting with a client in Bristol. 'You'd think I was threatening you with a night in a torture chamber having your ribs cracked without anaesthetic.'

'And if I try to fall asleep in the theatre he'll poke me awake.' Lou pulled a face and patted her lap as Betty trotted into the living room at Max's heels. 'Come up here, Betty. How would you like to go to the theatre with Dad tonight?'

Betty bounded on to her lap and licked her face.

'That means yes! Yay, good girl, Betty! You can have my ticket.'

'I'm living with a bunch of ingrates. Right, I'm off for a shower. We'll leave at six.' Shrugging off his jacket, Max said, 'By the way, Jack rang me earlier. You left your pashmina on the floor of the taxi last night. He's got it.'

'Oh brilliant.' Tilly exhaled with relief. 'I thought I'd lost it.'

'He said he can drop it back next time he's passing, or you can call in and pick it up.'

'So what are you going to be doing this evening while we're gone?' said Lou.

'Nice long bath. Chinese takeaway. Three episodes of *Ugly Betty*. Not *you*,' Tilly exclaimed as Betty, sitting up straighter on Lou's lap, shot her a wounded look. 'You're not ugly, sweetheart. You're beautiful. And a Marks and Spencer cappuccino walnut whip.'

'Lucky thing,' Lou sighed.

Tilly said smugly, 'I know. Not an unfunny Shakespearean comedy couplet in sight.'

'Any more sarcasm from your fair lip,' said Max, 'and I shall eat your walnut whip.'

Lou twisted round and gazed mutely up at Tilly.

Tilly gave her shoulder a sympathetic pat. 'See? Still not funny.'

★   ★   ★

They left just after six to drive up to Stratford. Having double-checked her walnut whip was still sitting safely in the fridge, Tilly took Betty for a long run through the woods. When they got home Betty collapsed into her basket and Tilly ran herself a bath. By eight o'clock she was dressed again in her post-bath grey velour tracksuit.

'Betty? Coming in the car?' She jangled her keys enticingly but all Betty did was slowly open one eye then close it again. 'Fine, suit yourself. I won't be long.'

On her way to the only Chinese takeaway in Roxborough it occurred to Tilly that she could pick up her pashmina en route, seeing as she would practically be passing Jack's house. On the minus side, she was wearing her comfy TV-watching velour track-suit and no make-up. On the plus side, at least he'd know she hadn't tarted herself up for the occasion. That's if he was even at home. Let's face it, this was Friday evening; the chances were he'd be out anyway.

Except he didn't seem to be. When she drew up outside the gates his car was parked on the drive and there were plenty of lights on. The alternative scenario, of course, was that he had company.

Tilly hesitated then switched off the ignition and climbed out of the car. All she was doing was knocking on the door and asking for her pashmina back. How long would she be there on the doorstep? Thirty seconds, tops. Whoever was inside the house with Jack would assume he was dispatching an unwanted Jehovah's Witness.

'Hey, you. Quick, come in.' Jack opened the door wider, stood to one side. He was wearing a blue sweatshirt with the sleeves pushed up and a pair of drastically faded jeans.

Tilly hesitated. 'I just came to collect—'

'I know, I know, but my sauce will stick if I don't get back to it. Bit of a crucial moment.'

Tilly followed him through to the kitchen. There was no earthly reason to be impressed just because a man was cooking an actual proper meal rather than poking holes in cellophane, but somehow she couldn't help herself.

And it did smell fantastic. Even if he was probably only doing it in order to show off to some woman.

Who might even *be* here.

'Do you have company?'

'Hmm?' Jack was busy adjusting the flame on the gas ring and stirring the contents of the Le Creuset pan. 'Oh, no, all on my own. Hang on, let me just add something . . .'

A teaspoon of caster sugar, a glug of port and a splash of lemon juice later, he tasted and gave a nod of satisfaction.

'I didn't know you were into all this.' Tilly mentally compared him with Jean-Christophe Novelli; God, imagine if he were to adopt a sexy French accent, think of the chaos *that* could cause.

'I can't cook many things,' Jack admitted, 'but I do a pretty good Bolognese sauce. It's my signature dish.' He paused. 'Actually, it's more or less my only dish.'

'That just means you've had lots of practice at it.' She was longing to try the sauce, see how it tasted, but that wasn't why she was here. 'Thanks for picking up my pashmina, by the way. I thought it was gone forever.'

'You'd dropped it on the floor of the taxi. I only spotted it as I was getting out.' Jack turned to look at her. 'How much of a hurry are you in?'

'For what?'

'The pashmina. Thing is, there were a couple of marks on it from where it had been on the floor. I think you'd had your shoes on it. So I just put it in the wash.' He indicated the half-open door to the utility room, through which Tilly could see a washing machine merrily churning away.

'Oh no.'

'What?'

'My pashmina is one hundred per cent cashmere! It cost two hundred pounds from Harvey Nichols and it's dry clean only!'

Jack had stopped stirring the sauce. 'Shit. Really?'

Yee-ha, got him.

Tilly put him out of his misery. 'No. Polyester, loves washing machines, six pounds fifty, Camden Market.'

The relief was visible on his face. 'That's where I always buy my pashminas too.'

Tilly grinned. 'I really got you.'

'Déjà vu.' Reaching into a drawer, Jack pulled out a corkscrew. 'Managed to get myself into some major trouble once with a white lacy top thing and a load of filthy old rugby kit.'

'I wouldn't have had you down as the white lacy top type.'

He took a bottle of red wine from the rack, expertly opened it and glugged a good couple of glassfuls into the pan. 'I thought Rose was going to explode when she saw what I'd done. It was the first time she'd worn it.' Drily he said, 'And the last. There was me, thinking I was being helpful. Until it came out of the machine.'

Tilly winced. 'Grey.'

'Grey and ruined,' Jack agreed.

She looked worriedly through to the utility room. 'Um . . . what's in there with my pashmina?'

'Don't worry, I learned my lesson the hard way. White wash, wool cycle. Can you pass me the pepper mill?'

She handed it over, watched him put the finishing touches to the sauce he still hadn't asked her to taste. 'How long before the washing machine finishes?'

'Thirty, thirty-five minutes.'

'OK,' said Tilly. 'Well, why don't I go and order my takeaway? Then when I've got it, I'll pop back here and pick up the pashmina on my way home?'

'Is that your plan for the evening?' Jack shrugged. 'You could stay here with me and try my signature dish instead.'

Had he done it on purpose? Was this why he hadn't offered her a taste before now? Because the fact that he hadn't meant she now really *really* wanted to know what his pasta sauce was like.

Plus it smelled fantastic.

'I was going to have Chinese.'

'But I've made loads. And hasn't Max taken Lou to Stratford? You'd be all on your own.'

Amy and Lisa and Marianne would have said yes by now.

'I wouldn't be on my own. I'd have Betty. She's waiting for me to get back with the prawn crackers.'

'But she can't tell the time.'

'I don't want to leave her on her own for too long.'

'A couple of hours wouldn't hurt.' Jack's eyes glittered with amusement. 'You could give her a ring if you like, *yip-yip*. Let her know, *woof*, where you are.'

'Don't make fun of me.'

He broke into a smile. 'I actually thought that was a really sweet thing to do.'

Tilly wasn't sure if she liked the sound of sweet. Was that a good thing to be?

'And if you go home to Betty, I'll be the one left here on my own.' Jack gave her a soulful look. 'Just me and a big vat of Bolognese sauce.'

Which smelled *fantastic*.

Anyone else would have said yes by now, wouldn't they?

'You know you can trust me,' said Jack. 'I proved that last night.'

'OK, OK. I'll stay for a bit.' Tilly put down the keys she'd been clutching; she *had* to know what that sauce tasted like.

'Great.' He sounded genuinely pleased.

'But I'm definitely going to be home by ten.'

Chapter 20

You knew you'd really made it when Jay Leno made jokes about you on his show. That was when it hit you that you were an actual household name.

OK, laughing stock.

As jokes went, it hadn't even been particularly funny. Some sly patter about a rumour that Kaye McKenna was going to be starring as Cruella de Vil in the remake of *101 Dalmatians* . . . cue squealing car tyres . . . oh, sorry, that's one hundred Dalmatians . . . more squealing car tyres . . . whoops, ninety-nine . . .

The studio audience had found that hilarious. They'd practically fallen off their chairs. The drummer had gone ba-boom *chinnggg* and Jay had done his impression of a smug nodding bulldog before moving on to the next victim whose reputation he was about to skewer on a stick.

'Wake up, love. Is this the place?'

Kaye, who hadn't been asleep, opened her eyes. Knowing her luck, she was in John o'Groats. But no, peering out of the taxi she saw that the sat nav had worked its magic and brought her home.

Well, not *home* home. But it had been until three years ago.

And she knew she was welcome, which meant a lot. Actually, it meant everything in the world just now. To be with people who believed her, to be back with her family . . .

OK, don't cry, just pay the taxi driver and get your cases out of the trunk.

Not trunk. Boot. You're back in England now.

Within ten seconds of ringing the doorbell she began to regret sending the driver away. How stupid not to have checked first that someone was at home. Having assumed that the cars were parked in the double garage she now realised they more than likely weren't. This was what jetlag and chronic lack of sleep did for you; it scrambled your brain. Bending down, she pushed open the letterbox and yelled, 'Max? Lou? Anybody there?'

Her hopes soared as a door creaked inside the house, followed by the sound of someone approaching at a fast pace—

'Woof!' Betty let out a volley of barks, bouncing up at the letterbox on the other side of the front door.

'Betty!' Kaye dropped to her knees and felt her eyes fill with tears. 'Betsy-Boo, it's me! Oh sweetheart, *hello!*'

Every time Betty bounced off the floor, Kaye was able to catch a glimpse of her for a split second. It didn't seem to occur to Betty that if she moved back from the door they'd be able to gaze at each other uninterrupted. Then again, she'd never been the brightest of dogs, certainly not the practical kind like Lassie who might with some encouragement and a bit of nifty paw work be persuaded to somehow unlock the door from the inside.

'Woof! Woof!'

'Oh Betty, it's so lovely to see you again. I've missed you so much.' Stuffing her fingers through the letterbox, Kaye felt them being licked by the little dog's dear familiar tongue and almost burst into noisy sobs. Then she accidentally let go of the spring-loaded letterbox with her other hand and gave a yelp of pain instead. This was ridiculous, why on earth hadn't she hung on to her front door key as Max had suggested? But no, at the time she hadn't felt comfortable about keeping a key to her ex-husband's home and had insisted on giving it back.

She shivered; even more ridiculously, she'd forgotten just how cold it could still be in March, so-called *spring*, in this country. OK, what to do next? Phone Max, obviously. She sat down on the mat – less uncomfortable than the stone step but only just – and unearthed her mobile and called his number.

Switched off. *So* typical of Max. *Where was he?*

Next she tried Lou's phone. Oh yes, and this time it was ringing, thank God.

Shit, she could hear it chirruping away from the other end too. Opening the letterbox again, Kaye's heart sank as she recognised the jaunty ringtone. Lou might not be at home but her phone was.

Which wasn't the most useful place for it, given the fact that her bum was going numb, her fingers were freezing and her nose was starting to run.

Kaye McKenna, infamous Hollywood actress, unwitting star of the Jay Leno show, crouching on a darkened doorstep with a runny nose. Couldn't get more glamorous than that.

OK, how about if she went round to the back of the house, smashed open a small window and climbed in? But Max would have set the burglar alarm before going out and she wasn't sure she could remember the code. Plus, it had probably been changed by now. Setting off the alarm and getting arrested for breaking and entering would just about put the tin lid on it.

So much for a happy homecoming.

Right, think. What other choice did she have? Stay here and

hope someone came home before she died of hypothermia. Or leave her cases here and walk into Roxborough.

Oh well, there was bound to be someone she knew in the pub.

How had it come to this? Tilly marvelled at the difference a dropped pashmina could make. It was nine thirty, they'd eaten the meal Jack had cooked and now here she was, sitting on the sofa gazing at a photo of Rose Symonds.

And she hadn't had to creep around the house or rummage furtively through drawers in order to get her hands on it. This time Jack had said, 'Still curious to know what Rose looked like?'

Just like that. And when she'd nodded, he'd said with amusement, 'You could have asked Max. He's got photos. Didn't you think of that?'

Honestly, did he think she was completely clueless?

'Thought of it. Decided not to do it.' *Because Max wouldn't have been able to resist telling you if I had.*

Jack had left the living room at that point, returning a couple of minutes later with the photograph.

Now he resumed his seat on the sofa, watching her. 'I have to say, I don't usually do this. I just keep thinking that if you two had ever met, you'd have really liked each other. You would've got on together really well.'

Tilly carried on taking in every last detail; Max hadn't been exaggerating when he'd talked about Rose. She'd had conker-brown eyes and long, fantastically glossy dark hair. In the photo she was wearing a Comic Relief T-shirt, muddy jeans and wellies, and big silver hoops in her ears. She was standing in the middle of what looked like a building site, laughing into the camera. Love radiated from her eyes. Tilly knew without having to ask that the person taking the photo had been Jack.

147

'I think we'd have got on well together too. She looks . . . fun.'

'She was.' Jack nodded, his expression controlled. Giving nothing away.

'And you took her to all the best places.' Tilly indicated the building site.

'That was here. In the back garden while the extension was being built.'

All those months of work to put together the house of their dreams. Then the dream had been shattered. Tilly wondered how you ever got over something like that. Perhaps by sleeping with hundreds of women and making a point of not getting emotionally involved with any of them.

But did it work? Was that getting over it or getting through it? And was Jack still going to be doing the same thing when he was sixty?

'Thanks.' She handed the photo back. 'She was beautiful.'

'I know.' Jack glanced at it again, smiled briefly. 'She's laughing there because her grandmother's just come out carrying a tray of mugs. We'd asked for coffee, no sugar. We got tea, six sugars. With grapes floating on top.' He paused. 'Does that sound cruel? We weren't laughing *at* her, just making the best of a situation that had its funny side. Rose loved her to bits. We both did.'

'Was she still alive when . . . the accident happened?' For some reason Tilly had thought Rose's granny-with-Alzheimer's had died many years ago.

'Oh yes.' Jack exhaled slowly. 'At the funeral she kept asking who'd died. Then every ten minutes during the service she'd look round the church and say, "Where's Rose, then? Why isn't she here yet? Honestly, that girl would be late for her own funeral." Which I have to say was less funny. And every time someone told her who'd died, it was as if she was hearing it for the first time.

Which was pretty hard to bear.' He stopped, shook his head. 'I can't believe I'm telling you all this. I don't usually.'

If he hadn't just relayed such a heartbreaking story, Tilly might have been tempted to retort that it was probably because he was *usually* far too busy doing other things.

But she obviously couldn't say that now. In fact, seeing as there was a lump in her throat the size of a tennis ball, she wasn't sure she was up to saying anything much at all.

'Actually, that's not true,' Jack amended. 'I think I do know why.' Another pause, then he shook his head. 'Shall we change the subject?'

Tilly nodded, still not trusting herself to speak. All of a sudden, like some kind of weird but unstoppable chemical reaction, her whole body was reacting to his. There was his leg and here was hers, right next to it. Could Jack feel what was happening, could he tell that every nerve ending in her body was jangling and buzzing with an urgency completely beyond her control? She wanted to touch him, hold him, lessen the terrible pain and make him feel better . . . Oh God, this must be the infamous tragic-widower effect, the lethally effective means by which Jack persuaded women to abandon their principles, their free will, their dignity . . .

'Go on then.' He looked at her. 'You choose.'

As he said it, his hand momentarily brushed against hers and Tilly felt the spark of emotional static arc between them. She heard her own breathing quicken. 'Choose what?'

'We're changing the subject. To something happier.'

Happier, *happier*. She swallowed with difficulty. 'How about hand-bags?'

'That's cheating.' Jack slowly shook his head.

'Cricket?'

'Fine, let's talk about cricket.'

'I hate cricket.' Was it her imagination or was he moving closer?

'We could discuss Italy.' OK, his mouth definitely wasn't as far away as it had been twenty seconds ago. 'Ever been to Italy?'

'No.'

'Oh dear. We're running out of things to talk about.' He waited. 'If I told you that I like you, would you think I was spinning you a line?'

Tilly managed a nod.

'Well, I'm not. It's the truth. I really do like you. A lot,' said Jack. 'In fact it almost scares me. I'm not sure I want it to be happening.'

Was this how he did it? Was this the well-spun line? It probably was. She imagined him trotting it out over and over again to an endless parade of gullible females, each of them falling for it and believing they were the one person capable of making that difference and unthawing the tragic widower's frozen heart . . .

Oh God, but what if it *wasn't* a line? What if this was the one time he actually meant it?

'And in case you were wondering,' Jack's voice was low, 'it almost killed me, keeping my promise last night.'

Had it? Really? He looked as if he was telling the truth. He *sounded* believable. And he had the most incredible mouth she'd ever seen. Breathlessly Tilly said, 'I thought you weren't bothered.'

He half smiled with his incredible mouth. 'Oh, I was bothered all right.'

Tilly's stomach was by this time awash with butterflies. 'I wish you didn't have such a reputation.'

'I know. Me too. I'm not proud of some of the things I've done.'

'Like that girl Amy, from the Fox last week. As far as you're concerned, she meant nothing. But you still slept with her. She

150

was boasting about it,' said Tilly. 'She was so thrilled and besotted, because she didn't realise it was just a meaningless one-night stand, and that's so *sad*. You're just making her look stupid.'

Jack surveyed her for a long moment, his expression unreadable. Then he said evenly, 'I don't want to talk about Amy. I never discuss my relationships. Everyone knows that.'

'So is that part of the attraction? They know they can trust you to be discreet?'

A glimmer of amusement. 'I'm sure it helps.'

He was right, of course. Tilly had never forgotten the desperate humiliation of going back to school after breaking up with Ben Thomas, only to discover he had broadcast intimate details of their relationship to everyone they knew. But instead of telling them what a great kisser she was – like he'd told her a *million* times while they'd been seeing each other – he'd delighted in spreading the news that she stuffed tissues in her bra to pad it out, and had once laughed so hard at a video of Mr Bean that she'd accidentally wet herself.

Only a tiny bit, but Ben hadn't said that, had he? To hear him crowing about it, you'd think it had been a bucketful. The jokes she'd had to endure had kept everyone else in Year 12 entertained for months.

So yes, the prospect of a relationship with someone who knew the meaning of discretion definitely had its upside.

'What are you thinking?' The little finger of Jack's left hand brushed against her wrist as he spoke, reminding her that he was still there.

As if she could forget. Tilly's mouth was dry.

What am I thinking? That I could sleep with you and no one would ever know. We could go upstairs and have sex right now and it would stay our secret. All I have to do is be home before

151

midnight, when Max and Lou are due back from Stratford. As far as they're concerned I'll have spent the evening watching DVDs with Betty, because that's the great thing about dogs, they can't raise an eyebrow and coolly announce – à la Hercule Poirot – that actually, Tilly Trollop, that's not quite true, is it, because you were—

Dddddrrrrinnnngggg.

Chapter 21

Doorbell. *Bugger.*

Back to earth with a bump.

'Who's that?' Apart from the most inconsiderate caller of all time, obviously.

Jack shrugged. 'Never did get round to having those CCTV cameras installed.' But he wasn't looking too thrilled. Nor was he moving from the sofa.

'Shouldn't you find out?'

'They might go away.'

It was probably one of his many women, someone who might not take kindly to being turned away on the doorstep, who might even insist on being invited into the house. Maybe Jack's way was best.

Ddddddrrrinngggggg, the bell went again, followed by the sound of the letterbox being pushed open. Tilly held her breath. Perhaps they were posting a note to say they'd been round and could Jack give them a call later when he—

'Jaaa-aaack! Are you there?'

A female voice, surprise surprise. Tilly looked at Jack, who was frowning.

'Who's that?'

'Jack, it's meee! Please open the door, I'm *desperate*.'

Tuh, and not ashamed to admit it.

'Looks like you're going to have to let her in.' Unfolding herself from the sofa, Tilly said, 'If it's someone with a jealous streak, maybe I'll leave by the back door.'

But Jack was already on his feet, his face clearing. 'It's OK, I know who it is. My God, I don't believe it . . .'

He hurried out to the hall, leaving Tilly hovering in the living room like a spare part. The next moment she heard the front door open and mutual exclamations of delight, followed by footsteps hurrying across the parquet flooring, then another door being opened and shut.

Jack returned to the living room, shaking his head and smiling. 'She was desperate for the loo.'

Ha, that old excuse. 'Is it Amy?' It hadn't sounded like Amy.

'You'll see. She'll be through in a minute.'

They heard the flush of a toilet, then the sound of water running in the cloakroom sink. Finally the door opened.

'Thank goodness you were in,' the female voice called out. 'I was going to use the loo in the Fox but it's Declan's night off. I didn't know a soul in there and a group of teenagers recognised me and started making smart remarks so I got out fast. And then of course it just got worse, I was ten times *more* desperate. If you hadn't answered the door I'd have had to wee in your back garden – oh, hello!'

Having finished drying her hands, the mystery visitor materialised at last in the living room. Tilly's mouth dropped open as she realised who it was.

'Oops, am I interrupting something?' Kaye pulled a face. 'Sorry, have I just barged in at completely the wrong moment?'

Yes, yes, *yes*.

'Not at all. Kaye, meet Tilly Cole.' Easily, Jack effected the introductions. 'Tilly, this is Lou's mum, Kaye.'

'Tilly!' Kaye's eyes lit up. 'How lovely to meet you.' She crossed the room, greeted her with a hug and a kiss. 'Although it would have been lovelier if you'd been at home when the taxi dropped me off! No one there but Betty. I've had to walk all the way from Beech House.'

'Max and Lou have gone to Stratford,' said Tilly. So much for no one ever knowing she'd spent the evening here with Jack.

'The RSC!' Kaye smacked the side of her head. 'Lou told me. I didn't realise it was tonight. My memory's gone completely to pot since I became public enemy number one in the States. Oh God, here I go again.' Abruptly her sapphire blue eyes filled with tears and she flapped her hands by way of apology. 'Sorry, sorry, it's been a hell of a week. I just had to get away . . .'

'Hey, sshh, don't cry.' Jack was there in a flash, folding Kaye into his arms and rubbing her back comfortingly.

'Oh God, and I haven't even got a tissue.' Sniffing, Kaye wiped her eyes. 'Everything's just been building up and up.'

Over her head, Jack said, 'There's a box of Kleenex in the kitchen.'

Tilly obediently found them then paused in the doorway on the way back, pierced with envy as she watched Kaye and Jack standing together in the middle of the living room. Which was ridiculous and shameful, because Kaye had been through a horrible time, but the sight of her rocking in Jack's embrace while he murmured words of consolation and kissed the top of her head . . . well, it did look heavenly.

'Tissues,' she said lamely, and Kaye turned, grateful and pink-eyed.

155

'Thanks so much. I'm not usually such a crybaby. I didn't get to sleep on the plane, I suppose I'm just shattered.' Noisily blowing her nose, her face pale and blotchy but somehow still beautiful, she said, 'What time are you going home? Can I hitch a lift?'

'Um . . .'

'Oh! Unless you weren't planning on going home.' Kaye gazed from Tilly to Jack, the thought belatedly crossing her mind.

'No, no.' Tilly hastily shook her head. 'Of course I'm going home! I just called in to pick up my pashmina. I was practically on my way when you rang the bell. We can leave now if you want.'

'Could we? Would you mind?' Sagging with relief, Kaye said, 'Thanks, it's just that I'm so tired, and I'd love to see Betty properly instead of waving to her through the letterbox.' She summoned a wry smile. 'Everyone in America hates me, but my dog still thinks I'm great.'

They drove back to Beech House and Kaye had her emotional reunion with Betty, prompting yet more tears, but splashy happy ones this time. Then, because it wouldn't be long now before Max and Lou arrived back, they settled down to wait and Kaye opened a bottle of Max's wine.

'Just as well I turned up on Jack's doorstep.' She clinked glasses with Tilly across the kitchen table. 'I think I probably did you a big favour tonight.'

'There's nothing going on between us.' Tilly shook her head in protest.

'You might think that. But Jack may well have had other ideas. And when he wants to be, he can be very persuasive. Not that he usually needs to do much persuading.' Kaye blew kisses at Betty. 'Most of the women around here tend to just fling themselves at him like . . . what's that game where you wear a Velcro suit and throw yourself at a Velcro wall?'

'The Velcro wall game?'

'Whatever. Anyhow, that's what it's like when they do it.'

Tilly flushed slightly; had she done that? If Kaye hadn't arrived, would she have ended up doing the Velcro suit thing and hurling herself at Jack?

'It's like the deli counter at the supermarket,' Kaye went on. 'They all queue up, take their tickets and wait their turn to be served.' She gave a snort of laughter. 'Or serviced.'

Which made Tilly feel *so* much better.

'Never mind.' Kaye leaned forward, patted her arm. 'You may have just had a lucky escape. And didn't I warn you about Jack before? Next time you need to pick up your pashmina from his place, just take along a loudhailer, keep a safe distance from the house and tell him to feed it out through the letterbox.'

Under present circumstances Tilly didn't feel it would be fair to point out the irony of being lectured on the subject of men by someone whose husband of ten years had turned out to be gay. But Kaye was trying to help, and she instinctively liked her.

'Promise?' Kaye waved the wine bottle, ready to top up their glasses.

'Promise.' Mischievously Tilly said, 'He must be pretty good, though.'

'Oh, he is.'

Excuse me?

What?

Tilly opened her mouth to ask if that meant what she thought it meant, but Kaye was busy scraping back her chair, jumping up and tipping Betty off her lap. The beam of headlights swung across the kitchen and gravel crunched under the wheels of the car as it drew to a halt on the driveway. Max and Lou were back.

Opening the front door, Tilly said, 'Well? How did it go?'

'Fantastic.' Max was on a high. 'Bloody brilliant, you should have come with us.'

'Lou?'

Lou rolled her eyes and said dutifully, 'It was fantastic, bloody brilliant.'

'Language,' said Max.

'OK, it was better than having to sit down and read Shakespeare from a book. But only just.'

'Never mind.' Tilly gave her a consoling hug. 'Come on into the kitchen. I've got a surprise for you.'

Lou brightened. 'Did you make marshmallow cake?'

'That's it, I give up. Take her to see a world-class performance by the RSC and the only thing to cheer her up is flaming marshmallow cake.'

'Except I haven't made one,' said Tilly. 'It's better than that.'

At least, she hoped it was good news. Because it had only just occurred to her that if Kaye moved back to Roxborough for good, Max might decide he no longer required the services of a Girl Friday and she could find herself out of a job.

Chapter 22

Eleven o'clock on Saturday morning and Jack was on the doorstep. For a mad moment Tilly fantasised that he'd come to grab her, bundle her back to his house and finish what they had been so tantalisingly close to starting last night before they'd been interrupted.

But no, that would be too much to hope for. Plus, Lou might have something to say about it.

'Yay, you're early!' Skidding up to the front door in her polka-dotted socks, she cannoned into Tilly before Jack had a chance to open his mouth. 'Mum's nearly ready. And I'm coming with you to make sure you don't fob her off with a hovel. I'll go up and tell her you're here.'

'Just sometimes,' Jack remarked as Lou scooted upstairs, 'you wish she had a mute button.'

'She's excited about having her mum back.' Curiously, Tilly said, 'So what's happening?'

He followed her into the kitchen, pinched the still-warm croissant from Lou's plate and added extra butter. 'Kaye rang me an hour ago. She wants a place of her own while she's over here and I've got a couple of properties free at the moment. Easier for her.'

Jack shrugged. 'She can use one until she decides what she wants to do next.'

'Nice of you.'

He half smiled. 'I have my moments. I told you, I can be nice when I want to be.'

He was wearing that aftershave again. Tilly wrestled with staying super-casual but she longed to ask the question that was crashing around inside her head. Any minute now Lou might be back or Max could walk in or Kaye might come rushing downstairs and the opportunity would be—

'Woof!' Betty came trotting into the kitchen with a purposeful air and waited impatiently by the side door.

Oh Betty.

'Want to go out?' Jack started to move towards her but Tilly beat him to it, because if he waited outside for Betty to select a suitable patch of grass and do her wee she'd definitely miss her chance. She hastily unlocked the kitchen door and shooed Betty out, then promptly closed it behind her.

Jack looked surprised. 'She'll be scratching to come back in again in a minute.'

'Can I ask you something?'

He raised an eyebrow. 'Fire away.'

Oh help, and now she couldn't bring herself to say it. It was too much, too personal. Even if it would be a whole lot easier all round to know the answer, particularly now that Kaye was back in Roxborough for the foreseeable future.

She braced herself. 'Are you . . .'

'Am I what?' Jack looked mystified. 'A vegetarian? Fond of flower arranging? In favour of capital punishment?'

Tilly felt her face heat up. What if she'd got completely the wrong end of the stick last night about him and Kaye?

160

'Am I still a virgin? Is that it?' Still guessing away, Jack said cheerfully, 'What did I tell you yesterday? I never discuss my sex life.'

He had indeed said that. Which pretty much meant there was no point in asking the question. Tilly exhaled slowly. The next moment, as if on cue, Betty scratched at the door to be let back in. This time Jack did the honours. Then Lou erupted back into the kitchen and let out a squeak of protest at the sight of her empty plate.

'Who's had my croissant?'

'That was Tilly,' said Jack.

Out of the two vacant properties, a huge unfurnished first-floor flat over in Cirencester and a small but charmingly furnished cottage in Roxborough, Kaye had gone for the cottage.

'I like it,' said Tilly when they went over to see the place on Monday afternoon.

'Small but perfectly formed.' Kaye gazed with satisfaction around the living room. 'Bijou. Compact. But handy for the shops, and close to home. Well,' she amended, 'close to *your* home.'

That you could walk it in ten minutes was a definite bonus now that Kaye had lost confidence in her ability to drive and was refusing to get back behind the wheel.

'You could have stayed with us,' Tilly pointed out. 'Like Max said. And you know he meant it; he wasn't just being polite.'

'And we all know that's true, because Max is never polite.' Grinning, Kaye shook her head. 'It's OK, best not to. I could be around for months. Anyhow, I'll be fine here. Stay separate, stay friends, always the best way.' She seized the suitcase and said, 'Want to give me a hand with this?'

Upstairs in the only bedroom, they took out the bedlinen

borrowed from the airing cupboard at Beech House and made up the double bed.

'Not that I need a double.' Kaye pulled a face as they wrestled with the corners of the dark blue sheet. 'I've been living like a nun for the last two years, and that was before I started murdering small defenceless animals.'

Tilly's mouth went dry. Anyone with manners and an iota of decorum wouldn't dream of asking the question she was about to blurt out, but not knowing the answer was killing her.

'I mean, if I thought I had trouble bagging a man before then, imagine the fun I'm going to have trying to find one now!'

'Can I ask you something really personal?'

Pausing in mid-hospital corner, Kaye regarded her with amusement. 'About my tragically non-existent sex life?'

'Well, kind of. About something you said the other night.' Tilly felt her heart thudding very fast against her ribcage. 'When I made a jokey remark about how, um, Jack must be great in bed.'

Kaye's hair swung to one side as she tilted her head. 'And?'

Oh God, was she offended? Was she going to be as infuriatingly discreet as Jack? Why did people have to *be* discreet when it was so annoying? 'Well, and you said he was.'

'Uh huh.' An enigmatic nod.

Oh well, she'd come this far. Tilly said, 'So does that mean you and Jack . . . ?'

Kaye's eyes sparkled. 'Did it? Slept together? That kind of thing?'

Oh, the shame. Tilly shrugged and said, 'Pretty much. Sorry.'

'No problem. Yes, we did. And he was. Great, I mean. In every way.'

'Gosh.' Now Tilly really didn't know what to say. 'I didn't realise.'

'And now you're thinking what a racy crowd we are down here, wives jumping into bed with their husband's best friends,

162

and you're wondering if we had a relationship.' Half smiling, Kaye abandoned the bed-making and sat down, patting the mattress next to her. 'It's OK, I'd be curious too. And no, it wasn't a relationship. More like therapy. Max and I were no longer a couple. Logically I knew it wasn't my fault but mentally I was at rock bottom. My husband was gay and, let me tell you, that doesn't do wonders for your ego. I lost all my self-confidence. I'd never felt so physically unattractive, so completely undesirable.'

'But—'

'I know it doesn't make sense, but it's how I felt. Like I was such a turn-off Max would rather sleep with a man than me. It was devastating. And poor Max, he felt terrible about it too. It was killing him, seeing me so upset. Then one night I got into a bit of a state – well, quite a lot of a state, actually. And I ended up yelling at him that I was going to go out and pick up a complete stranger and have sex. I just wanted to hurt Max, make him realise how betrayed I felt. Anyway, I followed that up by bursting into tears and saying nobody would want to have sex with me anyway because I was such a hideous turn-off.' Kaye paused, shrugged. 'And a week later, I ended up in bed with Jack.'

Tilly digested this. 'You mean you went out and picked him up, instead of a stranger. You *chose* him.'

'No, we just met up for a drink and a chat, and it went on from there. It was really nice and really natural, the way it happened. But you know something? I've never worked out if it was Max's idea. And neither of them have ever told me.'

'You think Max could have asked Jack to do it?'

'I think it's a possibility. Partly because I don't believe Jack would have gone ahead and done it without Max at least hinting that it might be a good thing. Oh, who knows? Anyway, it happened.' Kaye was unrepentant. 'And it did the trick. Jack was wonderful and he made me feel normal again. He gave me back my self-esteem. I owe him so much for that. Talk about a night you'll never forget.'

Phew. 'But . . . didn't you wish it could have been more?'

'Honestly? No, I didn't. Because Jack and I had been such good friends for so long, it would just never happen. We both knew that. The spark wasn't there, it simply didn't exist. We had fabulous sex, but that was all. And afterwards we were able to go back to being just friends again. Maybe that sounds weird,' said Kaye, 'but it's the truth.'

From the simple shrug of her shoulders Tilly could tell she meant it. Crikey, fancy that.

'And did you ever tell Max?'

Kaye smiled. 'I just said I'd stayed over at Jack's house. Max knew. I didn't need to draw a diagram.'

Doing her best not to visualise the diagram, Tilly quelled a stab of envy. Kaye's might not have been the standard reaction of a woman whose husband announces he's gay, but theirs had been an amicable divorce, so who was to say it hadn't been the right thing to do?

If it works, don't knock it.

And don't knock it till you've tried it.

Except she hadn't had the chance to try it, had she? Because Kaye had turned up the other evening like the celibacy fairy to stop it happening.

Oh well, it was probably for the best.

Chapter 23

Kaye's mobile began to ring as they arrived at Harleston Hall at four o'clock to pick up Lou. The name of the caller flashed up on screen.

'It's my agent,' said Kaye. 'Maybe Charlene's admitted she lied and everyone loves me again. Or Francis Ford Coppola's desperate to have me in his next movie starring alongside George Clooney . . . ooh, maybe Francis isn't sure but George is refusing to do it without me.'

'Yes, it'll definitely be that.'

Oh well, just a thought. Back in the real world, Kaye answered the phone. 'Maggie, hi! Has America stopped sending me to Coventry yet?'

'Is that meant to be some kind of joke?' Maggie was notoriously suspicious of the British sense of humour.

'Sorry. Any news?'

'Charlene's still flogging her story. She's seeing a grief therapist now. And she's hired some pet sculptor to produce a six-foot marble statue of the damn dog.'

A six-foot statue of Babylamb. Scary.

'Any happier news? Like maybe someone wants to give me a job?'

Maggie didn't find this amusing either. Not even a hint of her usual wheezy sixty-a-day chuckle. Then again, when a client suddenly stopped making you money, what was there to laugh about?

'Nobody wants to employ you, Kaye. Just stay over in England for now, keep your head down and try to stay out of trouble. Maybe do a little charity work. Or get yourself snapped coming out of an AA meeting, that might be an idea. But don't go giving any interviews. Keep a low profile.'

'That won't be a problem.' Her level of celebrity over here was far lower than in the States, thank God, and Roxborough wasn't exactly crawling with journalists. 'So . . . um, why did you call?'

'Just to tell you that a delivery arrived here for you yesterday. Some guy sent you flowers. Pretty decent ones, too. About six hundred dollars' worth, at a guess. And a box of chocolates. Godiva, or some such.'

'Godiva chocolates?' Five thousand miles away, Kaye's stomach did a little Pavlovian jig of delight. 'I love Godiva chocolates! Who sent them?' Was it possible that George Clooney had somehow guessed that this was the way to her heart?

'Some nobody guy.' Maggie's tone was dismissive. 'He sent the stuff to cheer you up. So there you go – you still got one fan out there.'

'Unless it's a trick to bump me off and he sprayed the flowers with cyanide. Better not get too close to them,' said Kaye. 'You might keel over.'

'Is that a joke? Ha ha. Anyway, I'm just letting you know. Obviously I took them home, save them from going to waste.'

Oh well, obviously. Flowers were flowers. Kaye said, 'That's fine. But you'll post me the chocolates?'

'What? You kidding me, honey? They're *gone*.'

'You mean you ate them?'

'Oh please, now I know you're kidding me. I threw them straight in the trash.'

Kaye's voice rose. 'But they were Godiva!'

'Honey, they were *carbs*.'

'OK.' Kaye sighed and gazed through the car windscreen as the end-of-school bell rang out. She should have known better than to think Maggie would even allow the chocolates to sit in her office, what with the obvious danger of stray calories escaping and being absorbed into her body through her skin via osmosis. 'Anyway, it's nice that someone's still on my side. I'll have to write and thank him.'

'Don't bother. Really, there's no need. It only encourages these stalker types.'

The first pupils had begun to spill out of the school. Kaye said, 'You threw away his address, didn't you.'

'Oh, *hi* there!' Her whole manner transformed, Maggie exclaimed, 'Take a seat, you look *fabulous* . . . I'll be right with you . . . Kaye, sorry, honey, have to go, Damien's just turned up! Speak soon, bye now . . .'

Dial tone. Hollywood's way of letting you know you weren't important. Damien was Maggie's latest signing, her rising star, evidently on course – if Maggie had her way – to be the next Brad Pitt.

Kaye closed her phone. Oh, for the days when she had been Maggie's favourite client.

Next to her, Tilly said consolingly, 'We'll stop on the way home and buy you a Snickers bar. Who wants Godiva chocolates anyway?'

'Hmm, let me think. You? Me? Lou? *Everyone?*'

'Who sent them?'

167

'We'll never know. One of life's mysteries. There's Lou coming out now . . . ooh, is that Eddie with her?'

Tilly leaned sideways to get a better look. 'Yep, that's him.'

Watching intently as Lou and the boy came down the steps together, Kaye said with pride, 'He's a bit of a looker, isn't he? Rather attractive. I was going to ask you before to take a sneaky picture of him with your camera so I could see what he looked like, but that would have made me the stalker. And imagine the grief if Lou had ever found out . . . oh look, what's happening now?'

For just a second Lou and Eddie had disappeared from view behind a gaggle of boys. Now they reappeared, Eddie brandishing a sheet of paper and Lou making a grab for it. The next moment he was racing across the gravelled driveway, laughing and waving the piece of paper above his head.

'Isn't it sweet?' Tilly grinned as Lou launched herself after him, kicking up sprays of gravel as she sprinted along in his wake. 'All that energy, all those raging hormones.'

Together they watched fondly as Eddie narrowly avoided falling into a yew hedge and Lou caught up with him. In one swift movement she snatched the sheet of paper from his grasp then gave him a hefty shove. Still laughing, Eddie pretended to stagger backwards, clutching his chest. Lou followed up with a don't-mess-with-me punch on the shoulder and stalked off, reducing the paper to shreds en route before stuffing the pieces into a bin.

'That's my girl.' Kaye experienced a burst of satisfaction. 'Don't be a pushover.'

'Then again, if you really fancy a boy, probably best not to push *him* over either.'

'They look so sweet together, though, don't they? Oh, my baby's growing up. How do other mothers cope when this happens? If pretty-boy Eddie breaks Lou's heart, how am I going to stop myself from wanting to break his neck?'

'You're allowed to want to. You just aren't allowed to actually do it,' said Tilly. 'Crikey, who's *that*?'

'Where?'

Wordlessly, Tilly pointed.

'Oh, I *say*.' Having followed the line of her finger, Kaye saw at once what she meant. Together they gazed at the broad-shouldered, tightly muscled vision of sportiness wheeling a racing bike down the drive. His hair was light brown and cropped very short, he was wearing a dark green tracksuit and he exuded health and fitness.

Phew.

'Probably just off for a quick cycle ride up to Scotland and back,' said Tilly, 'before tea.'

The thing was, he really looked as if he might be. As Kaye marvelled at the outline of his thighs, Lou reached the car and flung herself into the back.

'Hi, sweetheart. Who's the chap on the bike?'

Lou rolled her eyes. 'Yes, thanks, I've had a good day at school, got a commendation in maths, sixty-three per cent in my history test and we had chicken Kiev for lunch, my favourite.'

'You know what?' Flapping away the great gusts of garlic fumes, Kaye said, 'I could tell. Is he one of your teachers?'

'Mum, you've come here to pick up your only child, your wonderful talented precious daughter. Not to ogle strange men.'

'We're not ogling, we're just . . . interested.'

'It's Mr Lewis. He teaches French and PE. Please don't tell me you fancy him, that would be *so* embarrassing.'

Mr Lewis, French and PE. Well, that explained the muscles. The name rang a bell now; she'd heard Lou mention him from time to time. In fact . . . 'Didn't you tell me the other week that Miss Endell had a crush on him?'

'Yeah, but it's not as if he'd be interested in her, she's middle-aged. Lots of the mothers fancy Mr Lewis. So do some of the girls in the sixth form,' said Lou. 'But he's already got a girlfriend so they don't have a chance with him either.'

Mr Lewis was making his way up the tree-lined drive now, heading towards them on his bike.

'Hmm, when's the next parents' evening? Don't forget to book me an appointment to see him.'

'Mum! Oh God, he's coming over! Please don't say anything embarrassing . . .'

Having spotted Lou in the back of the car, Mr Lewis braked and drew to a halt beside them. Up close, the blond hairs on his forearms glinted in the weak afternoon sunlight. He indicated that Lou should buzz down her window.

'Louisa, you left your hockey stick on the bench outside the changing rooms. I've put it in the staffroom for safe keeping.' As he spoke, Kaye breathed in the smell of Pears soap; it seemed unfair that in return he was being blasted with garlic.

'Sorry, sir, I forgot. I'll pick it up tomorrow.'

Mr Lewis glanced at Kaye and Tilly, acknowledging them with a brief nod. Then, addressing Lou again, he said, 'You played a good game today. Couple of nice tackles there. Well done.'

'Thanks, sir.'

Thanks sir, your tackle's not bad either. The renegade thought zipped through Kaye's brain. Lou would faint if she could mind-read. Battling to keep a straight face, she caught Tilly's eye and saw that she'd been thinking along those lines too. Oh well, so long as they didn't actually say it out loud.

Mr Lewis rode off, Lou buzzed the window shut and Kaye and Tilly burst out laughing.

'Honestly,' Lou heaved a long-suffering sigh, 'you two are *so* immature.'

'What? What?'

'Just because he said tackle, you've gone all giggly and stupid. And now it's going to be a nightmare for me because next time you meet him you might do it again in front of him like Oliver Benson's mother. Every time she sees Mr Lewis she just can't stop coming out with this ridiculous high-pitched laugh like a hyena on helium. If you do that, I'll just die.'

'I won't, I promise,' said Kaye.

'You're too old for him anyway. He's got a girlfriend called Claudine and she's stunning. Promise me you won't make a show of yourself, Mum.'

'Looks aren't everything,' Kaye teased. 'If he starts racing across the grass waving a sheet of paper, would that count as a sign that he secretly likes me? If he pretends to fall over so I can catch him up and give him a thump, does that mean he's keen?'

'Oh please. Now you're being even more childish. Eddie Marshall-Hicks is a prize prat and I hate him, so don't even go there.'

'Come on, sweetie, you can tell us. There's a definite spark there. Boys and girls don't go chasing each other for no reason.' Entertained by the expression on Lou's face, Kaye said, 'What was it, a love letter?'

'Oh right, of course it was, because I'm bound to be writing love letters to someone I hate. No, Mum, it wasn't a love letter,' said Lou. 'And I promise you, the only time you'll see a spark between me and that prat will be the day I set him on fire.'

Chapter 24

When you were twenty-eight years old and a responsible adult there was no reason whatsoever to feel awkward and embarrassed about visiting your GP and asking to go on the Pill.

No reason *at all*.

The trouble was, Roxborough was a small enough town for people to know who you were and what you'd been getting up to lately. And Dr Harrison had been here forever; he could have heard the gossip about her and be about to deliver a stinging lecture about morals and decency and how it was just as well her mother was no longer around because she would die of shame if she knew what her wicked slut of a daughter was up to, not even married and having sex with a man who'd—

'Erin Morrison,' the receptionist called out, causing Erin to jump and the three-year-old copy of *Cosmopolitan* to slide off her lap. 'Doctor will see you now.'

Was that a note of disapproval in her voice? Erin stood up, aware that not only the receptionist but everyone else in the waiting room was looking at her. God, did they all know too?

Fifteen minutes later the appointment was over. Dr Harrison, bless him, hadn't lectured her at all. Clutching her prescription, Erin left his office feeling a hundred times better.

Until she reached the waiting room and saw who was now seated on the chair she'd been occupying earlier. Even holding the same battered copy of *Cosmopolitan*. Was it too much to hope that she had been reading and taking note of the article: How to Retain Your Dignity When Your Ex Meets Someone Else?

Evidently not. Stella looked up, her lip curling with hatred, and there was a general intake of breath from the rest of the room. Erin half expected the receptionist, like a showdown in a Western, to slam shut the glass partition and disappear under the counter. From the avid expression on the woman's face it was clear that she was up to speed with the situation and had probably given them adjacent appointments on purpose.

Although the chances were that Stella wasn't here to be prescribed the Pill. From the way she was sitting there like a coiled spring quivering with nerves and hatred it was more likely to be horse tranquillisers.

Which was tragic, of course it was. But it *really isn't my fault.*

'Marriage wrecker,' said Stella.

Next to her, an ancient woman put down her knitting and said, 'Eh? Sorry, love, what was that?'

Oh great.

Stella said extra-loudly and extra-clearly, 'That one there, just leaving. She stole my husband, you know.'

'Really?' The ancient woman did a double-take and pointed with a knitting needle. 'What, *her?*'

Erin's face burned as she hurried past them across the waiting room. Just get out, get out, *now.*

'Oof, sorry. Hang on. Christy, get out of the way.' A harassed young mother struggling with a recalcitrant double buggy and a

173

stroppy toddler in a Spiderman suit was trying to squeeze through the doorway, forcing Erin to step aside.

'I know! I couldn't believe it either when I found out!' There was no escaping Stella's voice behind her. 'I'm so much more attractive than she is.'

Oh please, just get out of my way, quick.

'I not Christy,' bellowed the toddler, 'I *Spiderman*.'

Climb up some walls then, instead of blocking the damn doorway.

'I mean, what is she? Nothing! Dumpy and frumpy,' Stella announced with bitterness in her voice. 'Just a desperate, shameless little tramp.'

The harassed young mother gazed at Erin in bemusement. 'Is she talking about you?'

'Yes I am! Don't let her near your husband, she'll probably make off with him too.'

'God, I wish. That'd be too much to hope for.' With a wry grin the young mother steered her stroppy Spiderman into the room, kicked the double buggy into reverse and managed at the second attempt to manoeuvre it through the doorway.

Heart thumping, Erin was finally able to escape.

Two hours later she was wrapping a turquoise and silver Karen Millen skirt in tissue paper when they heard a commotion outside.

'What's that?' The girl buying the skirt frowned and crossed to the window.

Oh God, please no. No no no . . .

'Don't shop in there! The woman's a trollop!'

No no *no no no*.

The girl beckoned Erin over. 'Come and look! Do you know who she is?'

'Yes.' The familiar sensation of nausea set in. Trembling but determined, Erin placed the tissue-wrapped skirt in a Beautiful Clothes bag. This time Stella had gone too far.

Outside on the pavement, acting a lot braver than she felt, she confronted her nemesis.

'You can't do this, Stella.'

'Why can't I? You banned me from your shop, but this isn't your shop, is it? I'm out here on the pavement,' Stella spread her arms wide, 'expressing a personal opinion *that happens to be the truth*, and you can't stop me.'

The woman Stella had been haranguing hurried off, clutching the carrier of clothes she'd been about to bring into the shop.

'This is my business and I'm not going to let you ruin it. If you don't stop, I'll call the police.'

Stella stared at her, her manicured hands clenched at her sides. 'But you've wrecked my life! Why do I have to sit back and take it?'

Erin didn't know what to do. There was no point in phoning Fergus, who was working in Cheltenham today. Besides, hadn't he told Stella over and over again that it hadn't happened that way round? And had Stella taken a blind bit of notice?

'Why can't I hurt you like you've hurt me?' Stella wailed. 'I'm better than you! And I'd *never* steal a married man from his wife!'

There was no getting through to her. Sadly, however, she was getting through to a lot of passers-by who were stopping to watch the drama with interest. Erin was at her wits' end. Could she really call the police or would they laugh at her and tick her off for wasting their time? Should she try a solicitor first? Or how about a hit man to bump Stella off?

'Hey up, what's going on here?'

It was Max Dineen, heading down the street towards them.

Had Tilly told him about the hassle they'd been getting from Stella? Erin braced herself, because he and Stella had been friendly for years. If he joined in with the abuse and started accusing her of being a marriage-wrecking bitch she would die.

Stella turned at the sound of his voice, took one look at Max and promptly burst into tears.

'Bloody hell,' Max exclaimed. 'I'm not that ugly, am I?'

From his laconic tone and the glance he directed at her, Erin knew he was up to speed with the situation.

'Oh Max!' Stella let out a wail of despair. 'I'm so miserable I just want to *die*.'

Erin wasn't proud of the fact that a little voice in her brain was thinking, *now there's a coincidence*, as she watched Stella stumble into Max's arms.

Max's heart sank. Fuck, this was the moment you really wished you hadn't got involved. He didn't mind wading in and breaking up an argument but this was altogether more complicated. Stella was a ranter, not a cryer. Having her burst into noisy sobs on his shoulder was the last thing he'd expected, about as likely as her bouncing down the High Street on a Spacehopper. But she was definitely doing it now. He could feel her tears on his neck, and her fingers digging into his back. She was distraught. And her hair was plastering itself against his face, an unnervingly spooky experience when you considered that it wasn't actually Stella's hair and had probably originally belonged to some ancient Russian peasant.

'Max . . . Max . . . I d-don't know what to d-d-dooo.'

Too late to back out now. Eurgh, what if the hair had belonged to a hairy-chinned seventeen-stone shot-putter called Olga?

'It's OK, it's OK.' Max patted her on the back and pulled a clean handkerchief from his pocket. 'Here, use this.'

Erin was backing away. 'I have to get back. I've left a customer in the shop.'

'Off you go.' He smiled briefly, feeling sorry for her. 'I'll take care of this one.'

Erin shot him a look of passionate relief and hurried back inside. Max in turn glanced around at the ogling bystanders and said, 'Show's over, you can put your knitting away, girls. There's not going to be any bloodshed today.'

'Where are we g-going?' hiccupped Stella as he steered her up the road.

'Your place. You're in no condition to open the shop this afternoon.' Reaching his car, Max pulled open the passenger door. 'Come on, in you get.'

'Oh Max. Thank you. And will you stay with me for a bit? You won't just dump me and drive off?'

Great, because he only had about a million other things to do today. Oh well, too late to worry about that now. Stella wasn't exactly a close friend, but they'd known each other through their complementary businesses for several years and he was fond of her; she was bossy, brash and super-confident. Well, as a rule. She was losing it now. You couldn't help but sympathise.

'I'll come in,' said Max. 'For a bit.'

Back at her modern, super-clean, super-tidy house, Stella opened a bottle of white wine and knocked back the first glass in one go.

Max frowned. 'Is that going to make you feel better?'

'Don't know. I'll tell you when I find out. I'm just in knots, Max. *Knots*.' She shook her head in desperation. 'I wake up in the morning and everything *hurts*. That woman stole my husband.'

She wasn't looking so great, actually. Her face was drawn and the habitual super-polished exterior was missing. This was what jealousy did to you, it demolished your confidence and ate away at your appearance like a maggot invading an apple.

Max said flatly, 'She didn't, you know. You have to believe that.'

'But I'm never *going* to believe it, because I know it's not true.' Stella's jaw was rigid, her mind made up; as far as she was concerned, why else would Fergus leave her? Max knew there was no point in trying to tell her otherwise.

'You just need to get on with your life. Living well is the best revenge.'

'But how *can* I?'

'Bloody hell, by being happy!'

'But the only thing that could make me happy is a baby! That's all I want!'

'So do it.'

Stella was looking at him oddly. She poured herself another glass and jiggled her shoe.

'What?' said Max.

'Would you do it?'

'What? If I was in your shoes?'

'No. I meant would you give me a baby?'

Oh shit. 'You don't mean that.'

'I do! Max, don't you see? It makes perfect sense.' The way she was looking at him, she actually seemed to think it *did* make perfect sense. 'I like you. I always have. You like me. And you're a great dad to Louisa.'

'Plus I'm gay,' said Max.

'Not completely. No, don't start shaking your head! Think about it. We get on well together. I've fancied you for years. Apart from Fergus, you're the only man I could face sleeping with. We could

178

give it a try. Who knows, you might really like it and decide not to be gay any more.'

'Stella, please stop this.'

'If you were really gay, you'd have a boyfriend by now. OK,' Stella blurted out as Max rose to his feet, 'forget the relationship, we can just do the sperm thing instead. Artificial insemination, how about that? And you wouldn't have to pay maintenance or anything. It wouldn't cost you a penny. Don't you see, Max? If I go to a sperm bank, how do I really know what I'm getting? God, they could fob me off with any old leftover rubbish that's coming up to its sell-by date. I'd much rather have a baby and know for sure who the father is. And I'd love it to be you, I really would. You're funny and kind and better looking than bloody Fergus. Picture it, we'd have a beautiful baby . . .'

Max backed away. OK, enough. Apart from anything else, he was picturing the baby and it was sporting spectacles, a full set of extensions and a broad Liverpudlian accent.

'Stella, you aren't thinking straight and you don't mean it. Believe me, you're a great girl and you'll find someone who's right for you, once you get over Fergus. But you have to promise me you'll stop hassling Erin.'

'It makes me feel better,' said Stella.

'Sweetheart, it's not dignified.' At that moment the cat flap rattled and Bing slinked in. Taking advantage of the cat's arrival, Max glanced at his watch and grimaced. 'Look, I'm really sorry but I have to get off now. I'm meeting a new client this afternoon and I can't keep them waiting. Promise me you won't top yourself, OK?'

Stella, who doted on her cat, reached down and scooped Bing into her arms. 'That'd just make it easier for them, wouldn't it? Erin and Fergus.' Stroking Bing and showering kisses on his furry ears, Stella said with some of her old spirit, 'Don't worry, I wouldn't give them the satisfaction.'

'Good girl.' Max nodded with approval.

She smiled and shook back her hair. 'Especially when I've just had my extensions redone. Sod that; they cost me three hundred quid.'

Chapter 25

Jamie Michaels and his fiancée had just moved into a six-bedroomed, eight-bathroomed mock-Tudor mansion in a gated community on the outskirts of Birmingham.

'Me mate recommended you. Cal Cavanagh, yeah? He said you was the business. And as soon as my missus found out you'd done his place, she said we had to have you too.'

'What's good enough for the Cavanaghs is good enough for us,' giggled Tandy. 'And we've got loads of ideas. I can't wait to get started. Can I offer you a drink before we get going? We've got Cristal champagne on ice, if you want. Eighty quid a bottle!'

Tilly kept a straight face, because Max had warned her that any sniggering would get her sacked on the spot. He'd also explained that just because young Premiership footballers had more money than sense, there was no cause to turn your nose up at their ideas. 'They pay good money for our services and it's our job to give them whatever they want. There are interior designers who try and force their version of good taste on to clients who don't share it. I usually get called in to redo the work six months down the line. People are entitled to live with an end product they bloody well like.'

Which was fair enough. Tilly completely agreed with that. And it was just as well, too. Because as they followed Jamie and Tandy over the house, they certainly had some eye-popping ideas.

'I'm thinking of, like, tartan walls in silver and pink metallic hand-painted wallpaper for the dining room. Because when I was little I had a Barbie with a pink and silver tartan dress.' Tandy was tiny, blonde and doll-like herself, bubbling with enthusiasm in a minuscule white skirt and khaki top. She smelled of Chanel No.5 and fake tan, and the ring on her engagement finger was the size of a walnut. 'And you know the chandelier you put in Cal's kitchen? Well, we want one bigger than that. And could you do one of those disco floors that light up, like in *Saturday Night Fever*?'

It was Tilly's job to write down each of their ideas while Max made suggestions as to how they might be adapted, explaining that if the chandelier was any bigger, Jamie would crack his head every time he walked under it, and a disco floor was a fantastic idea but how about having it in the karaoke room rather than the kitchen, because that was where more dancing might take place.

Turquoise and pewter leopard print en-suite bathroom? Tandy crossed her fingers; she evidently had her heart set on this.

Perfect, said Max, he knew just the suppliers. And how about Versace taps?

After two hours the preliminary meeting was over. Tandy threw her arms round Max and cried, 'I love your plans! This is so cool, I can't wait for everything to be done!'

'Hang on,' said Max. 'You haven't had your estimate yet. You might go off me when you find out how much it's going to cost.'

Jamie frowned and rubbed his hand through his spiky bleached hair. 'More than two hundred grand?'

'No.' Max shook his head. 'There's nothing structural. I'll get home and work on the figures, but I'm thinking around one eighty.'

'That's all? Cool. No problem.' His face cleared. 'We're doing a shoot for *Hi!* magazine once it's done, for two hundred. So, quids in!'

Yeek, two hundred thousand for a photo shoot and interview.

'It's going to be a huge party to officially celebrate our engagement.' Having done the maths, Tandy said brightly, 'We'll have twenty grand left over! How about if we get a dear little church built in the garden, for when we get married?'

'Or,' said Max, 'why not get married somewhere really spectacular and have a massive hot tub installed instead.'

'You're brilliant!' Tandy clapped her hands, then hugged Tilly. 'And so are you. You'll both have to come along to the party when everything's finished. All my girlfriends will be wanting to book you when they see what you've done to our house.'

Then the doorbell went and Tandy disappeared upstairs for her weekly session with her nail technician. Jamie showed Max and Tilly out and they made their way across the drive, past the midnight-blue Maserati, the pillarbox-red Porsche and the Barbie-pink 4x4 with the diamanté-studded steering wheel and pink suede upholstered seats.

'She's nineteen,' Tilly marvelled. 'This is where I've been going wrong.'

'Bag yourself a footballer. Become a WAG,' said Max.

Except Tilly knew she didn't have it in her to become high-maintenance; the endless fake tans, trips to the hairdresser and having to get her nails done would drive her nuts. 'I think I'm more of a SAG. Slobby and geriatric.'

'Or how about a DROOP?' Ever helpful, Max grinned as he

unlocked the car and said, 'Dumpy, ropey, 'orrible, ordinary and past it? *Youch.*'

'So sorry,' said Tilly. 'My foot slipped.'

The more you didn't want to bump into someone, sod's law dictated that the more often you would. When Erin paid a visit to the chemist after work, a few days after her last run-in with Mad Stella, she spent a relaxed ten minutes trying out eyeshadows and lipsticks on the back of her hands, blissfully unaware that Stella was in the shop.

Only when she was queuing up at the counter to pay for her sultry beige lipgloss, sparkly bronze eye pencil and oh-so-glamorous packet of panty liners did she find out. Momentarily distracted by the bottles of vitamins promising brighter eyes and clearer skin, she didn't realise the man ahead of her had finished being served. Jolted back to her senses by the woman behind the counter asking, 'Can I help you, love?' Erin opened her mouth to reply when a voice behind her rang out, 'Well, she's having an affair with my husband so she's probably here to stock up on condoms.'

That drawling, sneering, all-too-familiar voice. Erin experienced the swoop of fear that went with it, the rush of blood to her face and the sense of mortification that invariably—

Actually, no, sod it, why *should* she be feeling all these things? Why the bloody hell should *she* stand here and take it? Adrenaline surged up from goodness knows where and Erin slowly turned to lock stares with Stella. Enough with the pussy-footing. She had the attention of everyone in the shop, didn't she? And Stella, with her basket containing a can of Elnett hairspray, paracetamols and a bottle of expensive conditioner *so* thought she had the upper hand.

In a voice every bit as loud and clear as Stella's, Erin said sweetly, 'Condoms? Too right! It's amazing how many we get through.'

'I can't believe I said it.' When Fergus arrived at the flat an hour later, Erin was still shaking.

'So what happened next?'

She shuddered at the memory. 'Stella dropped her basket on the floor – *crash* – and shouted, "I don't know how you can live with yourself." Then she stormed out.'

Fergus folded her into his arms. 'Oh baby, shh. You haven't done anything wrong.'

'Maybe not before. But I have now. I was cruel.' The front of his shirt smelled of washing powder and offices. 'It's like she's dragging me down to her level. I thought retaliating would make me feel better, but now I just hate myself.'

'You mustn't. God, I'm so sorry. You shouldn't have to put up with hassle like this. I'm going to ask my solicitor what we can do.'

'Don't. No.' Shaking her head, Erin pictured more and more people getting involved, the situation spiralling out of control, each bitter exchange being quoted in court and her own spiteful retort returning to haunt her. She couldn't live with the shame. 'Just leave it. We'll emigrate.'

Fergus looked worried. 'Do you want to?'

'No.' She managed a half-smile. 'I just really want it to stop.'

Fergus kissed the top of her head. He said again, 'I'm sorry. I love you.'

'I love you too.' Despite all the horrors, happiness still flooded through her. Giving up her relationship with Fergus simply wasn't an option; he was everything she'd ever dreamed of, from his gentle personality to his easy warmth and innate goodness. Better still, he was attractive without being physically perfect, which had evidently irritated Stella no end but was wonderfully reassuring when you were less than svelte yourself.

Not that she only liked him – loved him – because of that. It was just that not having to suck in your stomach and pretend you were a size twelve was a heart-warming bonus.

'You know, we could go abroad.' As he spoke, Fergus's hand rubbed comforting circles over her back.

'But I like living here. Honestly, I didn't mean it about moving abroad.' Gosh, he knew how to give a sensational back rub. 'And we have these things here – what are they called? Oh yes. Jobs.'

'I was thinking of something less drastic. Look, next fortnight's chaotic at work but I'm pretty sure I can swing a week after that. How about if I book us a holiday? Somewhere hot, my treat.'

Erin twisted round to gaze up at him, unable to speak for a moment.

'Well?' said Fergus. 'We deserve a break, don't we?'

'We do.' She nodded helplessly. What had she done to deserve such a wonderful man? 'We definitely do.'

'Could you get someone to run the shop?'

Possibly, hopefully, maybe . . . maybe not . . . but what the hell, some offers were just too good to turn down.

'If I can't find anyone, I'll close it for the week.' Oh God, a holiday was *so* what she needed right now. 'We can just relax and not worry about who's going to turn up and start causing trouble.' Kissing Fergus's lovely stubbly chin, Erin said, 'I love you. Thank you so much.'

'Right, we're doing it. Name your destination. Marbella, Florence, Paris, Rome. You tell me where, and I'll book everything.'

'Anywhere I like?'

186

'Anywhere.'

'I've always wanted to go to Gdansk.'

'Really?'

It was just another reason to love him. Erin grinned and kissed him again. 'No. But I've definitely always wanted to go to Venice.'

Chapter 26

It was Friday evening and Max was taking Kaye to dinner with old friends in Bristol.

'They're celebrating their wedding anniversary,' Max explained to Tilly as he pulled on his jacket. 'We got married around the same time.'

Kaye was busy checking her tourmaline necklace in the living room mirror. 'Only Paula was lucky. Her husband didn't turn out to be gay.'

'Maybe not, but he's bloody boring when he starts banging on about golf. If he so much as mentions a nine iron,' said Max, 'I swear to God I'll start singing show tunes.'

Kaye said good-humouredly, 'You hate show tunes.'

'I know, but if it gets on Terry's nerves I'll do it. Right there in the restaurant. Up on the table if I have to.'

'Embarrassing Terry is what he lives for,' Kaye told Tilly. 'Right, are we setting off now? Where's Lou?'

'Noooo! Don't go before you've seen me!' Lou, clattering downstairs, landed with a thud in the hallway. 'Right, what about this?'

It was her third outfit change in thirty minutes, in honour of tonight's school disco. Having swapped jeans and a purple T-shirt for slightly different jeans and a blue cropped top, she was now wearing a grey and white striped T-shirt, grey jeans and Converse trainers.

Well, a Year 9 disco was an important event.

'You look lovely, sweetheart.' Kaye looked hopeful. 'But don't you want to wear a nice dress?'

Lou looked appalled. 'Mum, of course I don't want to wear a nice dress! And I don't want to look lovely either. I just want to look like *me*.'

Max said, 'In that case, you definitely look like you. I could pick you out of a police line-up, no problem. That one there, the one with all the red hair and the big spot on her chin, that's my girl.'

'Ha ha, Dad. I don't have any spots. But does my hair look too big?' Crossing to the mirror and grabbing handfuls of curls, Lou said worriedly, 'Should I tie it back?'

'You look just right. Ignore him.' Kaye gave her daughter a hug and a noisy kiss. 'Have a fabulous time tonight. Be good.'

Lou rolled her eyes. 'I'm always good.'

'No getting bladdered,' said Max.

'Dad, this is the Year Nine disco. It's a choice of Pepsi, Diet Pepsi or water.'

'And no snogging.'

'Dad,' Lou wailed. 'Shut *up*.'

'I'm your father. It's my job to say embarrassing stuff. No bad dancing either, OK? If I hear you've been doing any of that hokey-cokey malarkey—'

'OK, stop now. We don't have the hokey-cokey at our discos because we're not *dinosaurs*. And the only person who dances badly in this family is you.'

'Hear, hear.' Kaye threw the car keys over to Max. 'And we're

189

going to be late if we don't set off now. Come on, Methuselah, let's go.'

The timing was a minefield. Lou's disco ran from seven thirty to ten o'clock. But only tragic losers – obviously – were uncool enough to turn up at seven thirty. On the other hand, leave it too late and the evening would be over before you'd had a chance to relax and start enjoying yourself. Oh yes, making the perfect entrance at the exact right time was crucial. Following much frantic texting, the consensus among Lou's friends was that ten past eight was that optimum time.

Which gave Lou long enough to discard her third outfit and instead change into the *first* pair of jeans, an olive green boat-neck T-shirt, silver flip-flops and a plaited green and silver leather belt.

'Perfect.' Solemnly Tilly nodded; bless her, Lou was desperate to impress someone.

'What about the earrings? Too dangly?'

'They're perfect too.'

'No . . . hang on.' Lou turned and galloped back up the stairs. Two minutes later she returned with medium sized sky-blue hoops in her ears. 'Is that better?'

'Fine.' Bemused, Tilly said, 'Don't you have silver hoops?'

'Yes, but then it all might look too coordinated, you know? As if I'm trying too hard.'

'Oh right. In that case, definitely the blue ones.' Tilly just hoped Eddie Marshall-Hicks appreciated all the effort that went into not looking as if you were trying too hard.

Lou checked her watch. 'Is it quarter to eight?'

'Yep. Ready to go?'

Deep breath. 'Do I look all right? Should I wear different shoes?'

'If you change them, your belt won't have anything to go with.'

'Then I'd be completely uncoordinated and that's no good. OK,' Lou made up her mind. 'I'm ready. Let's go.'

The key turned in the ignition and nothing happened.

Tilly tried again. The car still didn't start.

'Are you playing a trick on me?' said Lou.

'No. Hang on, don't panic.' Inwardly panicking, Tilly took the key out and fitted it in again – hopefully *better* this time – then pumped the accelerator and gave it another go.

Still nothing.

Lou said, 'What's wrong with it?'

Tilly flicked the bonnet switch under the dashboard and jumped out of the driver's seat. If she knew what was wrong, she'd be a mechanic, but there was just a smidgen of an outside chance it might be something screamingly obvious, like when you spent ages wondering why the hairdryer wouldn't work then discovered it was because you'd plugged the straighteners in instead.

Except, disappointingly, there were no unplugged hairdryers in the engine. Everything just looked grimy and oily and as incomprehensible as engines always did. With Lou at her side, hopping agitatedly from one flip-flop to the other, she gingerly tugged and poked at a few mysterious tube-type things.

When she tried turning the key again, all she got was grimy oily fingermarks on the steering wheel.

'I'm missing the disco.' Lou began to hyperventilate. 'It's already been going for twenty minutes.'

Making a fashionably late entrance paled into insignificance compared with making no entrance at all.

'Everyone's going to be having fun without me,' Lou wailed.

'OK, go and get the Yellow Pages. Find the number of Bert's company and we'll call him. I'll keep trying here.'

Lou raced into the house and Tilly tried polishing the ignition key with her T-shirt, just in case it made that all-important bit of difference. Well, you never knew, did you? Especially when it came to cars.

When Lou reappeared she was clutching the Yellow Pages in one hand and the cordless phone in the other. 'Hello? Hi, Bert, this is Lou Dineen. Can you come and pick me up from home in, like, thirty seconds?'

Tilly's heart went out to her when Lou's face fell.

'No, that's no good. OK, thanks, bye.' Ending the call and thrusting the Yellow Pages on to Tilly's lap, she said, 'He's picking up a fare in Malmesbury. Can you find another number? Oh God, why does this have to happen to *me*?'

Eight o'clock came and went. The line to the next taxi firm was engaged non-stop and the waiting time for the third was an hour and a half. Lou's friend Nesh had gone away with her parents for the weekend. In desperation Tilly tried calling Erin but there was no reply and her mobile was switched off.

'This is *so* unfair.' In a panic now, Lou began riffling through the Yellow Pages again. 'Does this count as an emergency? Would the police be cross with me if I dialled 999?'

She was joking, but only just. The phone rang in Tilly's lap and she snatched it up, praying it was Erin returning her call. 'Hello?'

It wasn't Erin.

'Hi, it's me.' In the midst of all the panic, it was odd to hear Jack sounding so relaxed. 'I know I've missed Max, but can you pass on the message that the electrician's finishing off at Etloe Road tomorrow morning, so he can get his crew in there after midday.'

'Who's that?' Lou had found another cab number to try and was marking it with her finger.

'Um . . . fine.' Distracted, Tilly said to Lou, 'It's not Erin.'

'Get them off the phone then,' ordered Lou.

'And if you've got a pen handy, I've found a number for a new marble supplier he might be interested in.'

'Say it's a matter of life and death.' Lou gave Tilly a nudge.

'Er . . . I don't have a pen . . .'

'Is everything OK?' said Jack.

'Um . . .' It wasn't easy to concentrate, what with Jack murmuring in her left ear and Lou buzzing like an agitated wasp in her right. 'Sorry, Jack, it's just—'

'JACK?' Lou let out a screech and grabbed the phone, nearly taking Tilly's ear with it. 'Why didn't you SAY? Jack, where are you? The car won't start and we're stuck here and I'm missing my disco . . .'

His Jaguar shot up the drive seven minutes later. Lou catapulted herself into the passenger seat and declared, 'You are my most favourite person in the whole *world*.'

'Thanks so much.' The sight of Jack still caused Tilly's heart to leap into her throat. 'We were desperate.'

'No problem. I'll drop Lou and come back, see if I can figure out what's wrong with the car.'

Tilly stammered, 'Oh, you don't have to. Really. Max can call the garage in the morning and—'

'Excuse me, can we argue about this another time?' Lou shook her head in disbelief. 'In a teeny bit of a hurry here! Can we please *go*?'

Chapter 27

'My hero,' said Tilly, when Jack returned thirty-five minutes later. 'My life wouldn't have been worth living if Lou had missed her big night.' Checking her watch, she added, 'That was quick.'

'I can be speedy when I have to be. And I did have Lou sitting next to me, bellowing, "Faster, faster."'

'Thanks, anyway. And for coming back. Although I don't know how you're going to fix the car, now that it's dark. I can't find a torch anywhere.'

'I don't know how I'm going to fix it either.' Jack grinned as he followed her into the kitchen. 'I'm rubbish at cars. Never mind, we'll leave that to Max. Stick the kettle on. We've got until ten to ten, because Lou wants to be picked up at ten past.'

'You don't have to do it. I can call a cab.'

'Not a problem. Nothing else on this evening anyway. And my rates are very reasonable.'

Was that a provocative remark? Did he expect her to ask how she could repay him?

'Tea or coffee?' said Tilly.

'Coffee, black, one sugar.' He smiled slightly. 'You forget how exciting discos are when you're thirteen. I remember having a crush on a girl called Hayley and wondering how the hell I was going to get her away from her friends so I could kiss her.'

Tilly passed him his coffee and sat down at the kitchen table. 'Did you manage it?'

'Oh yes, I was very suave. I told her the headmaster wanted to see her outside, and that I had to take her.'

'Suave and devious. So, what did she do when you kissed her?'

'Carried on chewing her chewing gum and asked me to buy her a Coke. Actually, that's not true.' Jack paused, remembering. 'She asked me to buy her and her three friends a Coke. Each.'

Tilly started to laugh. 'And did you?'

'No! I told her I didn't have enough money and she said oh well, in that case I couldn't afford her. And then she went back inside.'

'So you haven't always been irresistible to women.' She loved the way he could tell a story against himself.

'God, no. The first few years were disastrous. But you live and learn.'

'Was Hayley pretty?'

'Very. Although obviously I hope she hasn't aged well.'

'All those years ago, and still bitter.' Grinning, Tilly pointed her teaspoon at him. 'You just have to chalk these things up to experience. Like the boy who blabbed to everyone in school that I padded my bra with tissues.'

'Cruel,' said Jack. 'I went out with a girl when I was fifteen and she told all her friends when I tripped up and fell flat on my face outside the cinema.'

Telling stories against yourself was all very well but Tilly couldn't quite bring herself to share the one about wetting herself whilst watching Mr Bean. There was such a thing as too much information.

195

'One boyfriend took me home to meet his mum and I had to pretend to really like this casserole she'd made for dinner. It was awful, full of gristle and arteries and grungly bits.' Tilly shuddered at the memory. 'And after that, his mum made it every time we went to his house. She always said, "Come on in and sit down, pet, I've done your favourite!"'

Jack pointed his own teaspoon back at her. 'Unless she didn't think you were good enough for her precious son and that was her way of getting rid of you.'

'Oh my God, I never thought of that!' Caught in a light bulb moment, Tilly excitedly flapped her hands. 'And I've actually done it too! Years ago I was seeing this guy and I was cooking more and more horrible meals for him and it wasn't until he complained about them that I realised I'd been doing it on purpose!'

Jack raised an eyebrow. 'You mean . . . ?'

'I didn't want to be with him any more, but I didn't want to hurt his feelings either. I'm not like you,' said Tilly, 'I don't like being the one to do the finishing.'

'You leave it to the man to do the dirty work. So you don't have to feel guilty.' He looked amused. 'What happens if they don't want to finish with you, though? If they don't want to let you go?'

She shrugged. 'I just make myself horribler and horribler until they do.'

Jack reached for his coffee. 'And is that what happened with the last one? Max told me you came home from work one day and he'd moved out of your flat.'

Hmm, so did that mean he'd been asking Max about her? Tilly said, 'That's right, he did.'

'Because you'd been horrible to him?'

'I wouldn't call it horrible. I just . . . distanced myself.'

196

'So that's why you weren't devastated when it happened.'

'I suppose.' She took a sip of her coffee. 'He just wasn't . . . The One. God, it's a funny business, isn't it? You can line up ten thousand men and know immediately that nine thousand nine hundred and ninety of them aren't your type. So then you're left with ten who are possibles and you have to narrow it down by a process of elimination. And it can all be going really well, you can think someone's perfect in every way, then they do or say one tiny thing that makes you realise you could never have a relationship with them.'

Jack's smile broadened. 'I've never thought of it like that. So you'd end up rejecting ten thousand men before you found someone you liked. That's kind of picky, isn't it?'

'I don't mean finding someone to just go out on a date with. I'm talking about the one person you'll end up sharing the rest of your life with. And as you get older, you naturally get pickier.' Struggling to explain, Tilly went on, 'When I was at school, all the girls used to imagine being married to the three or four best looking boys in the class. We used to practise writing our new names in our exercise books. Hmm, Nick Castle's quite cute, how does Tilly Castle sound? Or Liam Ferguson with the long eyelashes. Hang on, let's try that for size, Tilly Ferguson . . .' She mimed scribbling her signature with a flourish. 'Hey, that looks great, we should definitely get married!'

Jack said gravely, 'You see, that's the thing about being a boy. We never did that.'

'Well, you don't know what you missed. It was fun! And there were other things you could do to work out how happy you'd be together. You'd write out both your names, one above the other, then cross out all the letters you had in common, then add up the ones that were left and divide the boy's final number into the girl's, and if it made a whole number, you were a perfect match.'

His face was a picture. 'You're kidding. You seriously did *that*?'

'Many, many times.' Oh yes, it was all coming back to her now. 'And if you didn't get the answer you were hoping for, you had to find out what their middle name was, factor that into the equation and start all over again.'

Jack looked dumbstruck. 'Hang on. Girls at school used to ask me my middle name!'

'Now you know why. That's what they were doing. On the bright side,' said Tilly, 'all that endless tinkering around with numbers did wonders for our mental maths.'

Amused, Jack said, 'And do girls still do this?'

'I don't know. I haven't thought about it for years. We'll have to ask Lou.' Tilly grinned. 'I know whose name she'd be doing it with. Eddie Marshall-Hicks.'

'Lou's got a boyfriend?' He sounded shocked.

'Not yet. Ask Lou and she'll tell you she hates him. But we've seen them together at school,' said Tilly. 'There's all this flirty stuff, chasing each other and pretending there's nothing going on. It's so sweet, they obviously fancy each other like mad but can't bring themselves to admit it.'

Jack nodded wisely, then tilted his head to look at her. 'Ever done that?'

Hang on, was this a trick question? Did he mean here? Now? With him?

'God, yes.' Tilly nodded vehemently. 'When I was fifteen I had a huge crush on this boy who used to catch the same bus as me in the morning. He used to look over at me. I used to look at him. This went on for weeks and I knew he liked me. Then he started smiling and saying hello, and every morning I'd practically faint with excitement. I knew nothing about him, but he was my whole world. I imagined us being together forever. We'd get married and have three children, two girls and a boy. And each day I'd start an imaginary conversation with him that would get the ball rolling. But in real life I was sitting there, waiting for *him* to make the first move, because what if I said something first and he snubbed me?' Crikey, where had all this come from? She hadn't even thought about the boy on the bus for years.

'So what happened?'

'Nothing. For months and months he caught the same bus every morning. Then one day he just stopped and I never saw him again.' Tilly shook her head ruefully. 'I like to think he was abducted by aliens. I couldn't believe he'd disappeared like that, without letting me know he was going. In the end I decided his parents had made plans for the family to emigrate and didn't tell him until the last minute, just bundled him on to a plane so he didn't have a chance to say goodbye. But I can't tell you how upset it left me. I was in bits!'

'And you never even knew his name. If that happened in a film, you'd bump into him again.'

'But it didn't, so it won't. Anyway, I learned my lesson. Grasp the nettle. Don't waste opportunities. Never let a chance slip by.'

'Which is how you came to be working for Max, living here in this house. And you're glad you did, aren't you?' He sat back in his chair, dark eyes glittering. 'So it works.'

Distracted by the look he was giving her, Tilly said, 'How about you then, when you were at school? Ever have that thing where you really liked a girl and didn't know how to tell her?'

He tilted his head to one side. 'Because she might have rejected me? Oh yes.'

'Really? Oh, that's so sweet! I wasn't expecting you to say that.'

Jack looked appalled. '*Sweet?*'

'Sorry, but it is. I can't imagine you nervous, even at school.'

'Well, I was.'

'And what happened? After all the flirting, did you finally pluck up the courage to ask her out?'

He nodded solemnly. 'I did. But she explained it probably wouldn't be a good idea, what with her being my maths teacher.'

Tilly just managed to avoid spraying coffee. 'Your teacher! How old was she?'

'Twenty-five. And I was seventeen. So that was that, she turned me down.' Jack paused. 'But three years later she called me up out of the blue and asked if I'd like to meet up for a drink. So it took a while, but I got to go out with her in the end.'

At nine forty-five, leaving Betty asleep in her basket, they set out to pick up Lou.

'I hope she's had a good time.' As they sped along narrow country lanes, Tilly pictured the scene in the school hall. 'What if Eddie asked her to dance? Or what if he didn't? What if the slow music came on and all Lou's friends got asked to dance and Eddie was too shy?' She pulled a face as another thought took hold. 'Or what if he asked some other girl instead? Oh God, poor Lou, and she was just left on her own, propping up the wall, pretending she didn't care . . .'

'OK, that definitely happened to you.'

'Maybe just the once. Or twice. Shut *up*,' Tilly said as he broke into a grin. 'It's a horrible feeling. And boys can be such pigs sometimes, they'll ignore you on purpose just to make you feel worse. We don't know, Lou could be having a completely miserable time, watching everyone else slow-dancing while she's desperately trying not to cry . . . What are you doing?'

Chapter 28

They were still several miles from Harleston Hall and Jack was slowing down. He pulled into an overgrown gateway, stopped the car and switched off the headlights. Had all those cups of coffee proved too much for him? Was he nipping off behind the hedgerows for a caught-short wee? Because if he was, less than ten minutes after leaving Beech House, this could fall into the category of things to put you off a man for good.

Possibly unfair, but true. And maybe disappointing in one way, but probably the best thing all round in the other.

Click. Jack unfastened his seatbelt, then turned to look at her. In the pitch darkness she was just able to make out the angles of his face and the glimmer in his eyes. Why wasn't he speaking? Probably embarrassed; a weak bladder wasn't exactly macho, was it? It wasn't something you'd want to shout about.

To help him out, Tilly said discreetly, 'It's OK, I won't look.'

Pause. 'Excuse me?'

'Are you getting out?'

'Why?'

Oh God, had she offended him now? Was he going to pretend he didn't know what she meant? Why did men have to be so *proud*?

'Look, you're the one who stopped the car. We're supposed to be picking Lou up, remember? Don't be shy,' said Tilly. 'It's nothing to be ashamed of. If you need to go, go.'

Jack laughed and shook his head. 'Is that what you think? Oh dear, talk about cross purposes. The one thing I don't have is an inadequate bladder.'

'Oh. Well . . . good!' Feeling daft now, Tilly said, 'But we still have to get to the school. Lou's going to be wondering where we are.'

'Or she could be having the time of her life and praying we don't turn up too soon to spoil her fun.'

'But—'

'Tilly, I'm not talking about us sitting here for the next two hours playing a game of Monopoly. I just wanted to stop for a couple of minutes. And you've already spent one of them doing your level best to shove me out of the car.'

Indignantly Tilly said, 'I didn't shove you, I was just trying to be helpful.'

Jack's voice changed. 'You'd be more helpful if you'd stop jumping to conclusions.'

Next moment, he'd started the car again, reversed smartly out of the gateway and resumed the journey to Harleston Hall. Before Tilly had a chance to react. If she'd even dared to guess at why else he might have stopped in the first place, her hopes were abruptly dashed. It was like Father Christmas marching back into your bedroom, seizing the sack of presents he'd left for you earlier and making off with them. She felt . . . deflated. And now she'd never know if he'd been about to do what, deep down, she'd kind of been hoping he might do.

They gathered speed, hedgerows on either side whipping past and occasional overgrown branches hitting the sides of the car. In twenty seconds they'd reached the next junction and turned left on to the main Harleston Road. Tilly jumped slightly as a large moth appeared in the beam of the headlights and a split second later ricocheted off the windscreen. Poor moth, not a great end to his evening either. It was five past ten now; they'd be there in less than—

'Sod it.' Jack slammed his foot on the brake. This time, with no gateway in the vicinity, he screeched to a halt in a passing place and switched off the engine. '*This* is why I stopped before.'

He pulled her into his arms and the kiss she'd spent months wondering about happened at last. Father Christmas had returned with her presents after all. Tilly was dizzily aware of his mouth on hers, his fingers stroking the back of her neck, his hair falling forward on to her left cheek . . . God, he was a fantastic kisser, this was like being swept up in a huge wave and carried along on an endless exhilarating roll of joy.

OK, not quite endless. After some time it came to an end. Doing her best not to hyperventilate or appear too over-impressed, Tilly said, 'What was that for?'

'Just curious.' He sounded as if he were smiling. 'Don't tell me you weren't too.'

How was she supposed to breathe normally when her heart was going faster than castanets? How was she meant to speak normally when she was still zinging all over from the feel of his mouth on hers? Did he have that effect on everyone he kissed?

She exhaled slowly. The lit-up clock on the dashboard indicated that it was nearly ten past. 'We have to collect Lou.'

In the darkness, Jack nodded. 'You're absolutely right.'

The disco had finished. A steady stream of cars crawled up the tree-lined drive to Harleston Hall and groups of teenagers hung around outside the school waiting for their lifts. The first person

Tilly recognised was Tom Lewis, not wearing a tracksuit this time, keeping an eye on the gaggles of over-excited pupils and an arm around a strikingly pretty twenty-something brunette.

'There's Lou's PE teacher, over there on the steps.' Tilly pointed him out. 'That must be his girlfriend with him. Lou told us about her. Ooh, and there's Eddie!'

'Which one?'

'Tight black jeans, Jackie Chan T-shirt.' As they watched, Eddie broke away from the group of boys he'd been talking to and loped across to another group of girls. 'There's Lou, behind the girl in the pink skirt. He's going over to her . . . yeek, don't let her see us!'

Since they were stuck in a slow-moving queue of cars, there wasn't a lot Jack could do to hide. Tilly scrunched down in the passenger seat and peered through her fingers; if there was going to be snogging, Lou would just die if she knew they were there watching it happen.

But there wasn't. Eddie said something to Lou, Lou said something back and that was that. Eddie rejoined his friends. Lou tossed her head and looked away, determinedly unconcerned. Oh dear. Tilly's heart went out to her; she hoped they hadn't had a tiff.

Finally they reached the head of the queue. Jack briefly tooted his horn and Lou, spotting them, came over and threw herself on to the back seat. 'Hiya!'

Well, she seemed chirpy enough. Tilly swivelled round. 'Good time?'

'Brilliant. I've had three Pepsis and two packets of crisps.'

Bless. 'Not cheese and onion,' said Tilly, because they were Lou's favourite and how many boys would want to kiss a girl who reeked of cheese and onion crisps?

'They didn't have any. Only ready salted.'

'So, did you dance?'

'Loads!' Animatedly Lou said, 'You should have seen Gemma – she was moonwalking across the dance floor! Then the DJ started playing the music from *Grease* and we were all doing the moves. It was fantastic.'

'The boys were dancing too?' Crikey, things had changed since Tilly's day. Happily she pictured the disco, full of twirling, singing couples, just like in the film. Had Eddie been Lou's Danny Zuko?

'The boys? Dancing to *Grease*? You must be joking!' Lou's tone was disparaging. 'They were superglued to the walls. The boys at our school would rather strip naked and paint themselves pink than do something so uncool.'

'Oh. But how about when the slow dances came on? They must have joined in then.'

Lou gave her a thirteen-year-old's look that signalled Tilly was hopelessly deranged. 'Of course they didn't! A few of the old people danced, that's all. Mr Lewis and his girlfriend. Mrs Thomsett and her husband, who had a beard and *really* looked as if he was hating every minute. That was it. The DJ asked if we wanted another slow song and everyone yelled no, so he played Girls Aloud instead – yay! – and all of us went mental!'

'So no snogging then.' As he said it, Jack caught Tilly's eye.

'Eeurgh, no *way*.'

He grinned. 'Oh well, better luck next time.'

'Yuk, who'd want to snog any of the boys at our school? They're all gross.'

Tilly couldn't resist saying it. 'Even Eddie?'

'Oh, don't start that again. I hate him,' Lou said bluntly. 'He's vile. If I was stranded on a desert island with Eddie Marshall-Hicks, I'd make a canoe out of him.'

Twenty minutes later they arrived back at Beech House.

'Thanks, Jack.' Lou gave him an exuberant hug and peck on the cheek. 'If you hadn't come to the rescue, I'd have missed the whole night.'

They watched her race into the house to greet Betty, who had woken up and was yapping frantically at them from the kitchen window.

Tilly climbed out of the car and said, 'Yes, thanks for helping out.'

He half smiled. 'Don't mention it. My pleasure.'

OK, awkward moment. Having let herself into the house, Lou was now visible in the lit-up window, holding Betty up and waving the dog's front paws at them. Feeling incredibly self-conscious, Tilly said, 'You're welcome to come in for another coffee if you'd like to.'

'Thanks, but I'd better get back. Paperwork to do.'

She nodded. Paperwork, of course that's what it was. Could he still feel the sensation of their mouths meeting for the first time, or was it just her? Oh God, unless the kiss had been a *disappointment* . . . 'Right, fine. Well, thanks again for the lift.'

Lou and Betty were still waving at them. Jack waved back, then paused and turned to look directly at Tilly.

'What?' Well, she had to say something to break the charged silence.

'You asked earlier if I'd ever had that thing where I didn't know how to tell a girl I liked her.'

Tilly's stomach did a triple somersault and stayed suspended in mid-air. 'And you told me about your teacher.'

Jack smiled slightly. 'Well, there's you too.'

Tilly's stomach stayed right up there, showing no sign of coming down. Her mouth bone-dry, she said, 'Oh . . .'

'Sounds like a line, doesn't it?' He looked rueful. 'Like the kind of thing you wouldn't take seriously because I can't possibly mean it, because you don't trust me, because I have a bad reputation and I've probably said it a hundred times before.'

Light-headedness vied with light-stomachedness. True to form, Tilly heard herself say flippantly, 'Only a hundred?'

He shrugged, restarted the car. 'See? But what if I haven't said it before? What if I'm serious?'

Did he seriously expect her to believe he was serious? Was he honestly expecting her to answer that question? Tilly's knuckles whitened as she hung on to the still-open passenger door.

'Well?' said Jack.

Blimey, he did.

'I'd say you had some persuading to do.'

'OK.' A glimmer of a smile. 'That makes sense. Let's see if I can manage persuasive.'

Chapter 29

Erin hadn't seen Kaye since her last visit home at Christmas. Delighted to see her again when Tilly brought her into the shop, she updated Kaye with the story of Scary Stella while Tilly, in the changing room, attempted to battle her way into a lace-up-the-back summer dress that was infinitely covetable but two sizes too small for her.

'Stella. I haven't seen her since I've been back.' Kaye pulled a face. 'You know what? She always used to intimidate me. I went into her shop once and she ended up giving me the phone number of her eyebrow technician. Which made me feel fantastic about my eyebrows, I can tell you.'

'She's still the same. Except more likely to give me the number of the local executioner. Fergus is lovely.' Erin sighed. 'We're so happy together. It's just impossible to really relax and enjoy ourselves when we're forever wondering what Stella might do next.'

'I can't get into this dress,' panted Tilly, inside the cubicle. 'It's too small! This isn't a dress for a human being, it's Barbie-sized.'

'We think she might kidnap Max and force him to have sex with her,' said Kaye with a wicked grin.

'Oh God, don't,' Erin groaned; she hadn't even found out about that until after her run-in with Stella in the chemist's. 'I'm so sorry he got dragged into it.'

'Don't worry about Max, he can look after himself. Ooh, is that a Von Etzdorf?' She flung the sunrise-yellow devoré velvet scarf round her neck. 'And don't feel guilty about Stella either. She treated Fergus like a piece of dog poo for years.' She surveyed herself in the mirror. 'I like this.'

'That colour really suits you.' Erin wasn't angling for a sale; it was the truth.

'Ha, that's something else Stella said to me once: "Poor you, being so pale. I bet you wish you had skin that tanned like mine." Right, I'm going to have this. You know, the brilliant thing about buying secondhand clothes is you never have to feel guilty, because everything's such a bargain.'

'And it's a form of recycling.' Tilly's disembodied voice drifted out to them.

'Are you winning in there?' said Erin.

'No.'

'Here, I've got something you might like. It just came in this morning.' Nipping into the back room, Erin returned with a spaghetti-strapped lilac silk dress with mother-of-pearl beading around the bustline. She passed it over the door of the cubicle. 'Give this a go.'

Tilly emerged two minutes later. The dress flattered her colouring and fitted like a dream. Erin clapped her hands. 'I love my job. You look . . . fab.'

Flushing with pleasure, Tilly said, 'I had a panic yesterday. We were at Jamie Michaels' house and Tandy started asking me what I'd be wearing to their party. Then she took a phone call from one of the other WAGs and I overheard her saying her

209

biggest nightmare would be if anyone turned up wearing High Street.'

'Cheek!' Kaye was indignant. 'That would make me *want* to.'

'I know, but it's not about me, is it? It's Max's business and I don't want to let the side down.'

'I've got so many gorgeous dresses over in the States.' Regretfully Kaye said, 'I may as well sell them all, seeing as it's going to be at least fifty years before anyone invites me to another party.'

Erin felt for her. 'We're in the same boat, aren't we? Both of us blamed for something we didn't do.'

'But you're lucky, at least you've got Fergus. Look at me,' said Kaye. 'My career is in shreds, I'm living in a doll's house and the only male attention I've had since Christmas is from the old bloke with the squint who collects the trolleys at the supermarket.'

'He's not the only one,' Tilly protested. 'There's that fan who sent you chocolates.'

'Which I didn't get to eat. And he lives six thousand miles away. Plus, we've never actually met.' Kaye ticked off each point on her fingers. 'So he doesn't count.'

'Now you're going to make me feel guilty about telling you my happy news.' Reaching under the counter, Erin brought out a holiday brochure. She rolled it up and clonked Tilly on the head to stop her admiring herself in the full-length mirror. 'Hey, are you listening? I'm going away on holiday!'

That caught Tilly's attention. 'What? But you haven't been anywhere for years.'

'I know!' Erin was beaming like a lunatic. 'Fergus is taking me.'

'You always said you couldn't afford to close the shop.'

'I did, but this time I'm going to do it anyway. We need the break. Imagine, a whole week away without having to worry about Scary Stella. And guess where we're going?'

'A muddy caravan site in North Wales.'

'Close. Venice!'

'Oh wow!'

'Now that,' said Kaye, 'is seriously romantic.'

'I know,' Erin said joyfully. 'And it's somewhere I've always wanted to visit. I'm so excited! Look, this is where we're going to be staying, it's a palazzo overlooking the Grand Canal.' Eagerly she showed them the hotel in the brochure. 'Fourteenth century, views of the Rialto Bridge, it's even got a roof garden.'

'That's fantastic.' Tilly squeezed her arm. 'And you deserve it.'

'When Fergus told me, I burst into tears,' said Erin. 'We're going for a week at the end of the month. I can't *wait*.'

'And you're closing the shop?' said Kaye as Tilly disappeared back into the cubicle to change out of her new dress.

Erin nodded. She'd asked Barbara, who had helped her out on occasions in the past, but Barbara was unable to do it this time. 'It's fine. It's only for a week.'

'Because I could always look after it for you. If you want,' Kaye added when she saw the stunned look on Erin's face.

'Are you serious?'

'Why wouldn't I be?'

Erin flapped her hands. 'Sorry, I just wasn't expecting this. I mean, you're a Hollywood actress. It'd be like walking into the post office and Joan Collins selling you a book of stamps.'

'Except Joan still has a career,' Kaye pointed out, 'and I don't. I'm unemployable for the foreseeable future. And it drives me nuts, sitting around doing nothing. I'd love to run your shop for a week, if you think you can trust me.'

'God, are you sure?'

'Absolutely. I like clothes. And it's nice in here, friendly and peaceful.'

'Until you get Stella bursting in, yelling abuse. It's OK,' Erin said hastily, 'she won't do that. I'm the one she's got it in for.'

'Don't worry. Crikey, is that the time? I'm meant to be at the hairdresser's.' As she paid for the Von Etzdorf scarf, Kaye said wryly, 'See? This is what I'm reduced to, filling my empty days with trips to get my roots done and have my eyelashes tinted. How sad is that?'

Tilly's phone began to ring. She rummaged in her bag and answered it.

'Hello, this is Mrs Heron calling from Harleston Hall.'

'Oh! Hi!' Mrs Heron, tall and terrifying, was Lou's headmistress. Tilly unconsciously straightened her shoulders and stood to attention. 'Is everything all right?'

'Louisa isn't unwell. But I'm afraid there has been an . . . incident.' Mrs Heron was choosing her words with care. 'I've been trying to contact Louisa's mother but she isn't answering her phone.'

'Oh, but she's here!' Covering the receiver, Tilly said to Kaye, 'Where's your phone?'

'At home, on charge. Who's that?'

'Mrs Heron.' Belatedly Tilly thrust the mobile into Kaye's hands.

'Hello? This is Lou's mum. What's happened?'

Tilly and Erin watched Kaye's face as she listened intently. Finally she said, 'We're on our way now,' and hung up.

'What kind of an incident?' Tilly's heart was in her mouth.

'She said she'd explain everything when I got there. But it's something to do with Eddie Marshall-Hicks.'

'What?' God, Lou was only thirteen. Surely she hadn't been caught doing something sexual? 'Were they . . . um, kissing?' Would that warrant a phone call from the headmistress?

'I don't know. I don't think so.' Shocked and bemused, Kaye said, 'She said there'd been a fracas.'

A fracas. Well, that didn't sound like a kiss.

'We'd better call Max.' Tilly reached for the mobile but Kaye snatched it away from her.

'No, don't. Mrs Heron said not to. Lou doesn't want him to know.'

Chapter 30

'So much for saying I don't have anything to fill my empty days.' Having called the hairdresser to cancel her appointment, Kaye's imagination was now running riot. 'If that boy has tried anything on with Lou, I'll have him arrested. In fact I'll rip his throat out with my bare hands.'

They reached Harleston Hall in record time. Screeching to a halt outside the entrance, Tilly leapt out of the car and raced after Kaye up the stone steps.

The school secretary was waiting for them in reception. She ushered them through to the head's office and showed them into a high-ceilinged wood-panelled room.

'Oh my God . . . sweetheart, what did he *do* to you?'

Lou's face was pinched and white. Her shirt was torn and splattered with mud and there were holes in her black tights. With a sob, Kaye flew across the room and scooped her out of her chair. 'Oh my baby, don't worry, we're calling the police, that boy's going to suffer for this, he'll wish he'd never been *born*—'

'Mrs Dineen . . . er, Ms McKenna, could you please let me speak?' Astrid Heron, imperious behind her desk, indicated with a tilt of her head that Kaye should take the seat next to Lou. 'I think you need to calm down and listen carefully to—'

'Calm down? CALM DOWN? How can you *say* that?' bellowed Kaye. 'My daughter's been attacked and we're getting the police here this *minute.*'

'Mum, I haven't,' said Lou.

'But . . . but . . .' Kaye gazed wildly from Lou to Mrs Heron to Tilly. 'You said there'd been a fracas.'

Mrs Heron said grimly, 'That is correct. And I'm afraid your daughter was the instigator. She launched a serious physical assault on another pupil and I'm afraid there will be consequences—'

'Hang on, you're telling me my daughter attacked someone else? Lou!' Shaking her head in disbelief, Kaye said, 'Is this true? You were actually *fighting* with another girl? Over Eddie Marshall-Hicks?'

'Oh Mum, no.' Vehemently Lou shook her own head. 'How can you even think that? Of course I wasn't fighting with another girl!'

'Edward Marshall-Hicks is the person she attacked,' said Mrs Heron.

'What?'

'I blacked his eye.' Lou was unrepentant. 'And I *almost* broke his nose.'

Bloody hell. Tilly, watching from her position at the back of the office, heard the pride in Lou's voice.

Kaye's hand had flown to her mouth. 'But why? Why would you do that?'

'Because he deserved it.'

'But . . . I thought you liked him.'

'Mum, I told you I hated him. He's a bastard.'

'*Louisa,*' thundered Mrs Heron. 'Aren't you in enough trouble already? I will *not* tolerate that kind of language in my school.'

'Oh well, I'm probably expelled anyway.' Lou shrugged and

folded her arms. 'In fact, why don't I just clear my locker and leave now?'

'Stop it!' Kaye was beside herself. 'Stop saying things like that and tell me why you did it.'

'OK, you really want to know? Because I have put up and *up* with that brain-dead idiot making pathetic comments and saying horrible stuff and today I decided not to take it any more. I told him to stop.' Lou's voice rose. 'And he didn't, he just laughed. So I *made* him stop. And don't ask me to regret it because I don't. I hate Eddie Marshall-Hicks and today I taught him a lesson. Plus, he deserves everything he got.'

'Oh sweetheart, what's he been saying to you? Has he been making fun of your hair?' Bewildered, Kaye said, 'Is it your freckles?'

Lou bit her lip and said nothing.

'Louisa.' Mrs Heron employed her headmistressy don't-mess-with-me voice. 'We need to know.'

'OK, it's not about my red hair. Or my freckles. Believe it or not, it isn't even about my flat chest, my knobbly knees or my tragic chicken legs. If you *must* know,' Lou said evenly, 'it's to do with having a dad who's gay.'

Kaye asked to see Eddie Marshall-Hicks, who was being kept in a separate room. Tilly stayed behind with Lou while Mrs Heron took Kaye through to another smaller office. As the door opened, she braced herself.

Eddie was standing gazing out of the window. Mr Lewis the PE teacher was sitting on the desk. But now wasn't the time to admire his stupendous physique.

'Hello, I'm Lou's mum.' Kaye hung on to her handbag; somehow shaking hands didn't seem appropriate. 'I've come to see how you are.'

216

Turning, Eddie said, 'I don't know, how do you *think* I am?'

Maybe sarcasm was allowable, given the circumstances. His left eye was almost completely closed, his nose was swollen and there were splashes of blood on the front of his untucked white shirt. He looked as if he'd been set upon by a gang of muggers.

Kaye experienced a secret surge of pride that her skinny thirteen-year-old daughter had managed to wreak such havoc. Calmly she said, 'I'm sorry this happened. But I gather Lou was provoked.'

'She just went mental. Started yelling and screaming. Then she launched herself at me and started throwing punches. It was like being attacked by a wild animal,' Eddie said furiously. 'Look what she did to my face!'

Hooray!

'He's been thoroughly checked out by matron,' Tom Lewis put in. 'His nose isn't broken. There's no permanent damage to the eye.'

'Well, that's good. But I'm sure you can understand why Lou was upset,' said Kaye. 'Apparently you've been making comments about her father for several months.'

Eddie's face reddened and he stuffed his hands in his trouser pockets. 'It was just a bit of fun.'

'To you, maybe. It hurt her. A lot.'

'Oh yeah?' He pointed at his face. '*Snap.*'

The phone began to ring in his pocket at that moment. Eddie checked caller ID and answered it.

'Dad? Uh . . . yeah, I know you're busy. Sorry. The school said I had to call and tell you I was in a fight today.' He paused, listened, then said, 'No, nothing serious. I'm fine. And I didn't start it, right? Mrs Heron just said I had to ask if you wanted to come over and talk about it.' Another pause. 'No, that's OK, you go to your meeting. I'll see you tonight. Bye.' Eddie switched off his phone and mumbled, 'He's got stuff on at work. Anyway, he's cool about it.'

Tom Lewis looked relieved; evidently they'd been worried Eddie's father might roar up, all guns blazing and flanked by lawyers at the first mention of assault. Meanwhile Eddie was torn between embarrassment at having been punched by a girl and the desire to see her punished as a result. But they clearly weren't out of the woods yet. His busy father might well change his mind when he saw the damage that had been done to his formerly handsome son's face.

'She didn't want you to know,' Kaye told Max when he arrived home that evening, 'but I said we had to tell you. Oh Max, she's in a terrible state.'

Max briefly closed his eyes. And he'd thought today had been stressful, what with Jamie Michaels and Tandy faffing about and finally deciding that the lapis lazuli Italian tiles in the downstairs cloakroom were the wrong shade of lapis lazuli.

Now this. He pictured Lou being tormented at school because of him, and thought his heart would break.

Shit. *Shit.* How could he have ever imagined his daughter wouldn't be made to suffer as a result of his own selfishness? His chest tightening, Max left Kaye and Tilly in the living room and made his way upstairs.

'Oh Daddy, I'm sorry.' As soon as Lou saw him, she burst into tears. 'I told them not to tell you.'

Max crossed the room. The great thing about a hug was that the person you were hugging couldn't see if your eyes were misting up. Clasping her tightly, he said, 'Don't you dare apologise. It's my fault.'

'It is not. It's *his* fault. Boys are just so immature. And ignorant.

218

I hate hate *hate* Eddie Marshall-Hicks.' Wiping her wet face furiously with the back of her sleeve, Lou said, 'I know I shouldn't have done it, but you know what? I really wish I'd knocked his teeth out.'

There was a lump in Max's throat. He stroked her bony shoulders. 'You should have said something before.'

'I couldn't tell you. And Mum was over in LA when it started.' Lou shrugged. 'Then after a while you just kind of get used to not saying anything. Boys are horrible, they like to make fun of people. The hilarious thing is, Mum and Tilly both thought I fancied Eddie because they kept seeing us together.' Her lip curled with a mixture of derision and amusement. 'But that was because he was taunting me, saying vile things and being obnoxious. Once they saw me chasing him and ripping up a piece of paper, and they thought it was a love letter. *As if.*'

'What was it?'

'A horrible note he'd stuck on my back. Don't ask me to tell you what it said.'

'Oh sweetheart.' Max exhaled slowly. 'What have I put you through?'

'Dad, this isn't your fault. You're *you.*'

So much for thinking that being honest and open about their situation had worked out well. Max now wished with all his heart he'd simply carried on living a lie. The fact that everyone in Roxborough had been fine about it – to his face, at least – had lulled him into a false sense of security. His big mistake had been believing Lou when she'd told him everyone *she* knew had been fine about it too.

'I'm not ashamed of you.' As if reading his mind, she said fiercely, 'I'm *proud.*'

Oh shit, now she'd stopped crying and he was in danger of

breaking down completely. What had he ever done to deserve a daughter like this?

'Is it just the one guy?' Max's tone was gruff. 'Or more?'

Lou hesitated for a moment. 'More. But Eddie's the worst.'

'What about the girls?'

She shrugged. 'Sometimes they'll laugh at something he says. But they're pretty much OK.'

'Do you want to switch schools?'

'No.' Shaking her head and hugging him, Lou said, 'Who's to say any other school would be different? You're always going to get idiots who are too ignorant to know better.'

'If you ever want to leave, you can. I mean that.'

She pulled a face. 'I might *have* to leave. We don't know yet. I could be out on my ear by next week.'

'I'll make sure that doesn't happen. After what that little bastard's been putting you through? No way. I'm going to meet up with Mrs Heron tomorrow.' Max gazed at Lou intently. 'One way or another, we'll sort this out.'

Chapter 31

The thing about fancying someone rotten was it made you want to make more of an effort with your appearance so when you bumped into them you could at least relax in the knowledge that you were looking great.

Not just with the help of make-up either. Clothes too. Even down to and including the underwear. Tilly knew how completely illogical this was, but still found herself doing it anyway. Instead of just chucking on any old bra and pants, she was choosing, well, not her *best* ones, but the really quite good kind that you wouldn't be embarrassed to be seen in. Similarly, she was wearing nicer clothes, taking more care with her hair and make-up, and had upped her leg-shaving rate from once-a-fortnight-if-you're-lucky to twice a week.

At first she'd tried to pretend it wasn't happening.

Then she admitted it was happening and pretended she was doing it for herself.

When Max noticed and started taking the mickey, she told him it was because she'd felt so scruffy compared with Tandy and all her glossy, high-maintenance WAG friends.

But really Tilly knew it was all for Jack's benefit.

Which just made the fact that she hadn't clapped eyes on him for the last fortnight all the more infuriating. Every day she'd subtly done herself up and every damn day he hadn't *shown* up.

All in all, it had been a total waste of matching underwear and mascara.

She didn't even know where he was. Max was going full steam ahead with the Tandy and Jamie refurb. Maybe Jack was away on holiday somewhere. He could have met and fallen for a girl who was occupying all his time. The more Tilly considered this option, the sicker she felt. Or maybe he was just super-busy building up his property empire . . . yes, that was an easier prospect to handle. Oh God, she was turning into Stella. Was this how the madness took hold, a creeping vine of jealousy stealthily reaching up and up until it tightened around your neck?

'Yeek!' Lou dodged out of the way as Tilly, not concentrating on the task in hand, accidentally sprayed her with the hose.

'Sorry, sorry.' But it was a hot day, the warmest of the year so far, so Tilly wasn't too apologetic. Playfully she sprayed her again. Lou danced sideways, spluttering and squealing then darting out of sight behind the garage.

Amused, Tilly carried on washing and rinsing the car. Any minute now, Lou would race back and attempt to turn the hose on her, but she'd be ready and waiting, and Lou wouldn't get a chance to seize control. Before long, she heard stealthy foot-steps on the gravel behind her and gripped the hose tightly. OK, this was it, this time she was going to really soak her from head to—

'WAAAHHH!' Tilly let out a shriek as a torrent of ice-cold water almost knocked her off her feet. Staggering backwards, she turned and realised, too late, that Lou had flung only half the contents of the bucket at her back. *Whoosh*, the rest of the water

222

hit its target, drenching the front of her T-shirt, her jeans and her hair.

'Right, that's it. You're in big trouble now.' Blinking water out of her eyes and shaking herself like a dog, Tilly turned the nozzle on the hose from medium-fine spray to superjet. Clutching the gun in both hands and taking aim Clint Eastwood style, she prepared to squeeze the trigger. 'You're going to wish you hadn't done that.'

'Help! Child abuse!' Shrieking with laughter as an icy jet hit her in the leg, Lou yelped, 'Someone ring Childline!'

'Do I win?' Tilly aimed at the other leg.

'No way! Look, somebody's coming. Now you're the one in trouble.' Lou pointed exaggeratedly behind Tilly, urging her to turn round. 'It's Esther Rantzen, she's come to arrest you.'

'Yeah yeah.' What did Lou think she was, five years old? 'Of course I'm going to look behind me so you can grab the hose, because I'm *that* gullible.'

Lou, hopping from foot to foot, waved her arms at the imaginary rescuer and cried piteously, 'Help, help!'

Having shaken the water out of her ears, Tilly belatedly heard the sound of wheels on gravel and realised Lou hadn't been bluffing after all. Although it hopefully wasn't Esther Rantzen. Keeping Lou covered, knees bent and arms outstretched as she maintained a firm grip on the gun, Tilly slowly turned her head.

Oh sodding buggering *poo*.

Did other people actually get through their lives without having this kind of thing happen to them?

'Jack, help me, Tilly's being *cruuuuel* . . .'

Tilly blasted one last jet of water at Lou before releasing the trigger. Jack, emerging from his car, came towards them holding his arms aloft in surrender.

Thirteen whole days of mascara, foundation, lipstick, coordinated clothes, nice knickers, leg-razoring and scent squishing. All for nothing. And now this. *Now* he had to turn up.

Nothing like being seen looking your very best.

And this was *nothing* like her very best.

Whereas Jack, it went without saying, was looking tanned and fit and heart-squeezingly gorgeous.

'It's OK. I've stopped being cruel now.' Had he been abroad? He must have been away, to get so tanned. Had he taken anyone with him? Had they had a fantastic time? How about fantastic sex? Oh God, she was doing that Stella thing again. Stop it, stop it, *get a grip*.

'Glad to hear it.' He indicated the Jag. 'You can clean my car next if you like. Max not home yet?'

'He's over at Jamie Michaels' place. They're having a dolphin fountain put in.'

'Right. Well, my chainsaw's buggered so I've come over to borrow his. Do you know if it's in the garage?'

'Yeugh, my trousers feel gross.' Pulling a face and emptying her trainers, Lou said, 'I'm going to get changed.'

When she'd squelched off into the house, Tilly led the way over to the double garage. 'What's the chainsaw for? Chopping up troublesome tenants?'

'Can't say I'm not tempted sometimes,' said Jack. 'That's the downside of being a landlord, they expect you to do all their dirty work for them. I've got a couple of trees to take down and some branches to trim back.'

It was no good, she had to ask. 'Been away on holiday?'

'No. Why, have you missed me?'

'Just wondered. You're tanned.'

'I've been working outside for the last few days, clearing the gardens of people too bone idle to do it themselves. So you were wondering why I hadn't been around? That's encouraging.'

Honestly, did he have to say things like that? Having lifted the garage door, Tilly surveyed the boxes piled against the walls. 'OK, let's look for the chainsaw.'

'In fact, it's what I was hoping,' Jack went on.

What?

'In *fact*,' he amended, 'I stayed away on purpose.'

OK, she couldn't just stand here like a sopping wet village idiot. Her pulse racing, Tilly said, 'Why?'

'To see if it made a difference.'

Her mouth was dry. 'And?'

There was that look again. 'I think we can both guess, can't we?'

Oh God. If he kissed her now, Lou would be bound to reappear, bouncing into the garage like Tigger on springs.

'At least, I know how *I* feel,' said Jack. 'It might be different for you.'

But since he wasn't stupid, he couldn't really think that. The chemistry between them was inescapable; there was a crackling electricity in the air that only a turnip could miss.

Or a thirteen-year-old girl with powerful quick-change skills.

'Honestly, haven't you found it yet?' Lou, now wearing a dry T-shirt and frayed denim shorts, shook her head in disbelief and pointed to the box containing the chainsaw. Tut-tutting, she said, 'It's right there, behind the lawnmower. You're both blind as bats.'

For a split second Jack and Tilly's eyes met, then Jack crossed the garage and lifted out the chainsaw. He turned to Lou and held it up. 'Want me to cut your hair while I'm here?'

'No way. We're going up to Auntie Sarah's wedding this weekend.'

225

Lou darted out of the way as he took a step towards her. 'I don't want to look like a scarecrow.'

'Sarah's wedding? In Scotland?'

Tilly nodded; Sarah was Max's cousin and on Saturday she was getting married in Glasgow. Max, Lou and Kaye were flying up there on Friday afternoon for a weekend of epic celebrations, Glaswegian-style. In honour of the occasion Lou would even be wearing a dress.

Was Jack thinking what she hoped he was thinking?

Happily, yes. When he'd finished putting the chainsaw in the boot of the Jag, he waited until Lou was out of earshot then beckoned Tilly over.

She kept a neutral I-have-*no*-idea-what-you're-about-to-say expression on her face. Well, tried to. Inwardly she felt gorgeous and desirable, like a goddess.

'So, are they leaving you here on your own?'

'Mm.' Goddess-like, Tilly nodded.

'Well, if you don't have any other plans, how about I pick you up on Friday? Around eight?'

This was it. He meant business. Things were going to start happening at last. If Lou hadn't been behind them, finishing cleaning the car, she would have kissed him. She wanted to, so much. Well, not long to wait now. Only two days.

She gave him a tiny, goddessy smile. 'OK.'

'Deal.' Jack smiled too.

He waved to Lou as he drove off. Lou waved back then turned to look at Tilly.

'Don't soak me again.' Tilly raised her hands in surrender.

'I won't. Sorry about your face, by the way.'

'Why? What's wrong with my face?'

Lou shrugged apologetically. 'It's a bit . . . you know.'

Oh bum. Peering into the car's wing mirror at her reflection, Tilly no longer felt like a goddess.

'I didn't mean it to happen,' said Lou. 'I just found the bucket of water under the garden tap. I didn't realise the bottom of it was full of gunk and mud.'

Chapter 32

If Jack hadn't minded her looking like the creature from the black lagoon, the chances were that he wouldn't be too bothered whether she wore her silver-grey top or the navy one.

But it mattered to Tilly. A lot. She wanted to look her best. After so many weeks of prevarication and wondering if she would be making a horrendous mistake, she knew that this evening things were finally going to . . . well, happen.

Her heart did a swallow-dive just thinking about it. But you could only deny your true feelings for so long. Jack knew it too, didn't he? And he had been the one to instigate it. Tonight, everything would change. Their relationship would move to a new level. Now, at last, she truly trusted him. This wasn't yet another of his meaningless flings. There were feelings, real feelings involved. He had finally discovered that time does heal, and that when you meet the next right person it's possible to move on.

OK, too much thinking about it was getting her all jittery with anticipation, and jitters could only result in badly applied mascara. Deliberately clearing her mind and taking deep breaths, Tilly finished towelling her hair dry and said, 'What d'you reckon, Betty? Grey top or blue?'

Betty, lying on the bed with her nose resting on her front paws, raised a bored whiskery eyebrow then lowered it again.

'OK, sorry, not your problem. I'll wear the grey.' Hastily Tilly held the grey top up against herself. 'No, the blue.' Her eye was drawn to the clothes hanging in the wardrobe. 'Or my white shirt.'

Honestly, what a kerfuffle. Was Jack having this much trouble getting himself ready for tonight, or was he jumping into the shower, reaching for the first clean clothes to hand and thinking T-shirt and jeans, that'll do?

Oh well, it was different for girls. They had so many more decisions to make, like dangly earrings or studs, subtle nail polish or bright, flip-flops or proper shoes, bikini-style knickers or thong.

Or no knickers at all . . .

The TV was on, the newsreader was reaching the end of the news, and for the life of him Jack couldn't have named one item on the programme. His eyes had been on the screen, his ears had heard the newsreader's voice and nothing – *nothing* – had permeated his brain. Because all he could think about was tonight. And Tilly. Shit, this was serious.

What's more, she had no idea. How could she know how he felt, how life-changing this evening would be? She couldn't begin to understand what was going on inside him. Jack could hardly believe it himself. When Rose had died, his world had changed forever. It had been like a giant prison door clanging shut. That was what happened when you allowed yourself to fall in love with someone; when they were ripped away from you, the pain and grief were unimaginable.

So he had vowed never to let it happen again, had simply kept that particular door locked. It had been so much easier to act the part of the flirtatious philanderer, to have fun and avoid any form of emotional involvement. OK, so he'd managed to earn himself a fair old reputation along the way, but so what? He'd always been honest from the word go, had never resorted to false pretences.

But now everything was about to change. Because despite his best efforts, Tilly had unlocked that door. And it might be terrifying, but it was also a fantastic feeling, like being sprung from prison after four years.

The tumble-dryer clicked off and Jack opened it, pulling out the warm, no-need-to-iron, dark-green pillow cases, duvet cover and king-sized fitted sheet. If Tilly smelled the fabric conditioner on them, would she think he'd taken it for granted that she'd end up in his bed tonight? Would she be offended at having been regarded as a sure thing? Then again, didn't they both know, deep down, that it *would* happen tonight?

As he carried everything upstairs, Jack wondered what she was doing now. Tilly wasn't the type to flap around, spending ages trying to decide what to wear. She'd probably be out, taking Betty for her walk before heading back to the house, jumping into the shower and quickly changing into a little top and jeans. That was one of the great things about her, she wasn't high-maintenance or vain, like so many of the girls around here.

Right, that was the bed sorted. He stepped back to admire the end result. The bedroom was tidy, everything was clean and the lighting was acceptably discreet. All of a sudden it seemed incredibly important; he wanted Tilly to feel comfortable here, and to approve of the way the room looked. Last Christmas Monica had given him a box of candles in coloured votive glasses and said, 'You could put them on the shelves around your bedroom, there's nothing more romantic than candlelight in a bedroom.'

The candles, needless to say, were still packed away in their gift box in the wardrobe. For a moment Jack wondered if he should get them out. On the one hand he was keen to impress Tilly, but on the other he didn't want her feeling as if she'd just walked into an Austin Powers shag-pad.

OK, give the candles a miss. They were possibly something only a girl could get away with. Briefly pausing in front of the mirror on top of the chest of drawers, Jack checked his hair hadn't dried funny, then crossed to the window to close the curtains. As he reached out to grasp them, his left arm brushed against the blue and silver ceramic bowl on the window ledge. Rose had bought it from a craft shop in Tetbury and painted extra silver stars and polka dots on it herself, pronouncing it perfect for holding bunches of wild flowers. Which, it went without saying, was something else he'd never attempted. Since Rose's death, the bowl had stayed empty. Well, he was a man. Men didn't pick flowers *or* light candles. He moved the bowl closer to the glass then began to close the curtains.

Jack froze as a car turned into his road. Not just any car either; this was a red Audi with number plates he not only recognised, he knew them off by heart. It couldn't be, but it was. For a moment he forgot to breathe, because she'd always had a talent for timing.

Then he gripped the window ledge for support, a great wave of shock and hope and nausea rolling through him as he watched the Audi turn in through the open gates.

Because he wasn't hallucinating.

It was Rose's car.

Chapter 33

This was crazy. Jack shook his head, ordered himself to get a grip. Rose was dead. It might be Rose's car but Rose wasn't the one driving it. *Because she was dead.*

He knew that. It was just the shock of seeing it so unexpectedly. For a split second his brain had been tricked into believing the accident had never happened and Rose was still alive. There had even been time for guilt to kick in, because she would have found out he was about to be unfaithful to her, and blurting out the excuse that he'd thought she was dead *wouldn't* have gone down well with Rose.

Jack took deep breaths, mentally steadying himself. She hadn't come back. Only her car had come back. Following Rose's death he hadn't known what to do with her beloved red Audi. When her parents' rusting old Fiesta had failed its MOT in spectacular fashion, he'd been only too glad to hand it over to them. It had undoubtedly been lovingly washed, polished and valeted on a weekly basis and driven well within the speed limit ever since.

Jesus, though. They'd given him a heart attack. And for them to turn up today of all days, tonight of all nights. It was almost as if Rose had sent them here on purpose.

On the driveway below, the Audi's doors opened. Bryn emerged first, followed by Dilys. They looked older, slower, tireder, worn out with grief. Jack, who hadn't seen them for two years, felt his stomach plummet at the sight of them now.

Maybe they wouldn't stay long.

He was meant to be picking up Tilly in an hour.

Bryn Symonds was now almost seventy, with thin grey hair and a defeated face. Once the life and soul of the village, for thirty years he had owned and run a small hardware shop. With the rise of the megastores, Bryn's business had fallen into difficulties. He had managed to keep it afloat with the help of loyal local customers, but it had been a struggle. Then Rose had died and Bryn had stopped being the life and soul. He gave up the shop and retired.

Dilys had never gone out to work. A proud Welsh housewife, she kept busy polishing windows, cleaning paintwork, scrubbing doorsteps and baking bread. Their little house was immaculate.

And Rose, their beloved only child, had been their whole world.

The doorbell rang as Jack was halfway down the staircase. He crossed the hall and opened the door, dreading what lay ahead and awash with guilt at dreading it.

'Oh Jack.' Dilys took one look at him and dissolved into tears, as she'd taken to doing every time they'd seen each other since the day her daughter had died. He knew why, of course. Because he reminded her of the happy life Rose was supposed to have, the one she should be leading now.

And who could blame her for that? If the accident hadn't happened, Bryn and Dilys would have been proud grandparents, turning up at the house today to visit their daughter and son-in-law, and to shower gifts and affection on their adored three-year-old grandchild. Who knew, maybe he and Rose would have had

233

another baby by now, and Dilys would be in knitting overdrive. Bryn would be building complicated structures out of Lego and painstakingly mending anything that got broken . . . OK, don't think about it, just blank it out and *don't* start trying to imagine what the children might have looked like.

He hugged Dilys, shook hands with Bryn and invited them into the house.

'Oh, thank you, love.' Dilys dabbed at her eyes with an ironed handkerchief as Jack put the cup of tea down in front of her. 'Sorry to land ourselves on you like this. I hope we're not being a nuisance.'

What could he say? 'Of course not. It's great to see you again.'

Another lie, another wave of shame.

'Well, it's been quite a while.' Bryn quietly stirred sugar into his tea.

'I know. I'm sorry.'

'Twenty-three months.'

'I've been pretty busy here.' Jack felt worse and worse.

'It's all right, love. We know. We understand,' said Dilys. 'You've got your work to take care of.'

'And how have things been for you?' He hated even asking the question, already knowing the way the conversation would go.

'Oh well. Not great.' Sorrowfully Dilys shook her neatly permed head. 'We do our best to keep busy, but nothing really seems to help.'

Bryn said, 'Vandals broke into the cemetery and sprayed graffiti all over the gravestones.'

'*What?*'

'Oh Bryn, don't tell him.' Dilys clutched Jack's hand. 'Sorry, love, we weren't going to tell you.'

'But he should know. It's his fiancée's gravestone. Filthy words, they wrote.' Bryn shook his head sorrowfully. 'Broke our hearts, it did.'

'When did this happen? Can it be cleaned off?' Appalled, Jack said, 'Who did it?'

'No one knows. Stupid kids, I imagine. It's all right, we managed to scrub the stone clean.'

'Took him three weeks,' said Dilys. 'All day, every day. But Bryn managed it in the end. Scrubbed his own hands raw too, didn't you, love?'

'I wasn't going to stop until my daughter's headstone was perfect again. And the flowers we planted around it are looking good too.'

Jack nodded, picturing the scene, unable to speak.

'Here, love, you can see for yourself. We've taken some photographs to show you. Although hopefully it won't be long before you can come and see it for yourself, eh?' Dilys took a mini photo album out of her cream leather handbag and passed it over. 'We'd really like that, wouldn't we, Bryn? And you could stay for as long as you l–like . . . oh dear, what did I do with my hanky?'

She was off again, breaking down completely this time. Bryn, doing his best to comfort her, said to Jack, 'We've been going through a tough time, see. It feels like everyone's forgetting about Rose. They used to ask us how we were, and talk about her. But now it's as if they think we should be putting all that behind us. Moving on, like. But they don't understand. We can't put it behind us and we don't want to forget her. And new people are moving into the village who never even knew her – it's like she means nothing to them. Well, I suppose she doesn't. But she means everything in the world to us.'

'That's why we had to come and see you today.' Still tearful, Dilys shook her head and wiped her red-rimmed eyes. 'Because you're the only other person who loves Rose as much as we do.

You're the only other person who understands, because you miss her too. I mean, I know they can't help it, but it's like she's f-fading away, being rubbed out, getting fainter and fainter. And everyone else is just moving on as if she'd never existed.'

Jack escaped from the kitchen and went upstairs. It was eight thirty already and he could no longer even remember whether he'd been meant to pick Tilly up at eight o'clock or nine. Bryn and Dilys Symonds' grief had had that much of an effect on him. What's more, it was catching. At this moment he was riddled with shame and guilt.

Having ensured the bedroom door was firmly shut, he took out his phone. What other choice did he have?

What was going on? Jack had said he'd be here at eight. From not having had the slightest twinge of anxiety that he might not turn up, Tilly was now in knots. Eight o'clock had come and gone and she hadn't been able to stop pacing the kitchen since. All dressed up and nowhere to go. This was like being sixteen again, beginning to realise that the boy you'd fancied for months, who'd said he'd meet you at the bus stop, had stood you up.

Disbelief mingled with misery as, slowly and sickeningly, the hands of the clock slid round to eight thirty. Every few minutes she'd been compelled to check that the phone was still working. By eight thirty-one, she was pinning all her hopes on a car accident. Not too serious, just enough to result in Jack being trapped in his car, unable to reach his mobile. As soon as the firemen managed to cut him free he'd call her, maybe a bit battered and bruised but otherwise unhurt, and he would be *so* apologetic, and she would tell him not to be stupid, he was OK and that was all that mattered, but he'd keep saying he was sorry, even while the paramedics were telling him he had to get off the phone now because they needed to check him over, then she'd hear Jack say to them, 'There's only one person I want to be checked over by, and she's on the other end of this line.'

Bbbbrrrrinnnggg. Back in the real world, the phone on the coffee table rang at last and Tilly launched herself at it like a rugby player. Of course he'd rung, of course he had a genuine excuse, he was probably calling to say he was on his way and would be here in two minutes . . .

'Hello?'

'Hi, it's me. Look, sorry, but I'm not going to be able to make it tonight. Something's come up.'

It was Jack's voice, but it didn't sound like Jack. He was distracted, distant, not himself at all.

'Are you OK?' Tilly's palms were slippery. 'Are you ill?' As she said it, she heard a door opening in the background, a female voice saying apologetically, 'Oh . . . sorry . . .'

'No. I'm fine. Um, I can't talk about it now. Sorry about tonight. I'll call you tomorrow. Bye.'

'Wait—' But it was too late, the phone had already gone dead. She stared at it, trying to imagine what could have happened to cause him to do this.

Except . . .

Except she knew the answer to that, didn't she? It had to be something to do with another woman. Or women, plural. Because let's face it, women were the focus of Jack Lucas's life. He surrounded himself with them, amused himself with them and broke their hearts.

And she'd nearly, *so very nearly* got herself sucked into the madness. Had been on the verge of surrendering herself, joining the harem, making a complete and utter fool of herself. Because

Jack was programmed to hurt the women who passed through his life; it came as automatically to him as breathing. While she'd been busy fantasising that this time it would be different, he'd been metaphorically ticking her name off his to-do list.

Because that was the thing; he wasn't interested in any kind of proper, meaningful relationship. Rose had been his big love and he'd lost her. Since then, he'd immunised himself against the risk of ever letting it happen again. Safety in numbers and all that. Which was fair enough, sensible even. *In theory*. So long as you weren't one of the poor gullible females on the receiving end.

As she had so nearly become.

Oh God, and she'd wanted it to happen *so much*. This hurt.

This was miserable.

Tilly closed her eyes. And if she was miserable now, well, then she'd really had a narrow escape.

Chapter 34

Every time the doorbell rang, Erin's stomach contracted with fear that it could be Scary Stella. When it happened at ten o'clock that evening, she looked at Fergus.

'Oh God. Is that her?'

'Leave it to me.' Fergus rose from the sofa and went downstairs.

He was soon back. 'It's someone slightly less scary.'

'Tilly!' Relief turned to concern. 'God, what's happened? You look awful!'

'You're too kind. I brought wine.' Flopping down on to the sofa and letting out a groan of despair, Tilly passed the bottle to Fergus. 'Big glass for me, please. Oh sorry, have I taken your seat?'

'That's fine.' Erin patted Tilly's arm. The lovely thing about Fergus was, when a friend in need turned up unexpectedly, it wouldn't occur to him to resent the intrusion.

Within seconds they heard the cork being popped out of the bottle. Fergus returned from the kitchen with two brimming glasses.

Tilly took hers. 'Thanks. You're allowed to have some too, you know.'

'I was about to go and pick up the food. We've ordered Indian. Want me to get some for you too, or will you share ours?'

'I'm too churned up to eat.' Tilly took a glug of wine. 'Well, maybe some poppadums. Seeing as I've been stood up.'

Erin said, 'Who by?'

'I've been stupid.'

'Who by?'

'Gullible.'

'WHO BY?'

'It's my own fault. Should've known better.'

'I'll take your wine away if you don't tell me.'

'*Don't.*' Tilly whisked the glass out of reach. 'OK, OK. Jack.'

'Jack *Lucas*?'

'You aren't allowed to say I told you so. I already know that.' Tilly looked over at Fergus, hovering awkwardly in the doorway. 'Big mistake, right?'

'Sorry. Jack's a good bloke, but . . .'

'Maybe not ideal happy ending material.'

Fergus gave her a sympathetic look. 'He does have that reputation.'

'You didn't even tell me!' Erin was stunned. 'I can't believe you didn't tell me!'

'That's because there hasn't been anything to tell. Nothing's . . . you know, happened.' Oh well, no point in being coy. 'It was supposed to happen tonight,' said Tilly. 'But he phoned and cancelled. Just when I was starting to worry that he'd crashed his car. And to think I thought I was different from all the rest. I honestly believed we had a connection.'

The look on Erin's face told her all she needed to know. Every single one of Jack's conquests believed they were different from the rest. His seduction skills were so finely tuned they all thought they had that connection.

'What did he say when he called you tonight?'

'Nothing. That he couldn't make it, that's all. That something had come up. *Tuh*.' Tilly laughed bitterly at the old double entendre. 'He hung up pretty quickly too. Couldn't get off the phone fast enough. And I heard some girl's voice in the background.'

'He might have had a good reason.' But they both knew Erin was only saying it to make her feel better.

'I've just driven past his house. He's at home. The lights are on and there's another car parked on the driveway.'

Fergus said, 'What kind of car?'

'A red one. Anyway, it doesn't matter. I just needed some company. And you two drew the short straw. Bad luck.' Tilly took another swig of wine. 'Now you're stuck with me for the next couple of hours while I bleat on about myself like a big girl's blouse.' She waggled a finger at them both. 'And you can't tell anyone, either. I don't want the whole of Roxborough knowing what a prat I've made of myself. Cross your heart and hope to die. This is classified information.' At that moment her stomach gave a huge rumble of protest. Disgusted with her ability to be simultaneously heartbroken and ravenously hungry, Tilly said, 'OK, better get me a bag of vegetable samosas.'

The headlights lit up the road ahead as Jack drove. Bryn and Dilys had left at eleven thirty. All the emotions he'd thought he'd finally managed to get under control had been churned up again by their visit. When Dilys had gazed around the living room and said in a quavery voice, 'Oh Jack, where are the photos of Rose?' he'd felt like an axe murderer. Attempting to explain why he didn't have any out on display only increased their bafflement and hurt.

Guilt skewered him time and time again as thoughts of Tilly intruded into his brain. There was no way he could tell Dilys and Bryn he'd finally met someone who mattered to him; they would regard it as the worst kind of betrayal of their daughter. And as he listened to them talk on and on about Rose, the old feelings had surged up again until Jack found himself agreeing with them, realising they were right and that the relationship he'd been about to embark on with Tilly would have been very, very wrong.

By the time he'd shown them out of the house, the pain and grief was as fresh as if Rose had just died all over again. Saying goodbye to them, Jack had promised to come and visit her grave soon.

But sleep was beyond him. Exhausted and emotionally wrung out though he was, he couldn't relax. Guilt about having failed Rose fought inside him with guilt about the way he'd treated Tilly tonight. She must be wondering what the hell was going on. He owed her an explanation at least. Even if, just now, he barely understood it himself.

Jack knew he was driving too fast but the road was deserted. As he approached Beech House, he still had no idea what he was going to do. This so wasn't how tonight had been meant to turn out. He'd tried calling her but the phone hadn't been answered, and she deserved more than a phone call anyway. Braking sharply, he swung the car up the drive. Chances were, Tilly wouldn't be too happy with him either.

Shit, life was so much easier when you didn't get emotionally involved.

And after all that Tilly wasn't even here. Having rounded the bend, Jack saw that the top of the drive was empty. Her car was missing. She could be anywhere, and could he blame her?

He swung the Jag round in a circle. Right, so much for that

idea. Maybe it was better that they left it for tonight anyway, given the current state of his brain.

Time to go back home.

'There he is! That's *him*. That's his car!' Tilly let out a shriek of recognition and threw herself sideways.

Fergus, struggling to fend her off, said, 'Don't beep the—'

BEEEEEEP!

'Bastard,' roared Tilly. 'Stop the car!'

They were just driving over the bridge on the Brockley Road. Fergus braked, as did Jack.

'Oh great.' Fergus sounded resigned. 'Now he'll probably throw me into the river.'

But Tilly, emboldened by drink, was already scrambling out of the car. As she approached the top of the bridge, the driver's door of the Jag swung open and Jack stepped out, illuminated by the silvery light of the almost full moon behind him.

The fact that he looked so perfect made it easier for Tilly. How could she ever have imagined they might have a future together?

'Thanks for tonight.' Her voice carried clearly across the distance between them.

Jack shook his head. 'I'm sorry. I said I was sorry. I've just been over to see you, but you weren't there. I tried calling you too.'

'You don't have to apologise. I'm not being sarcastic. I really mean it,' said Tilly. 'Thanks for standing me up tonight, I'm glad you did. And I'm sure you had a lovely time too, with whoever it was who turned up – was it one of your regular harem or an exciting new one? Not that it bothers me.' She held up her hands before he had a chance to speak. 'I'm just curious. Actually, it must have been one of the old gang, because a complete stranger wouldn't just turn up on your doorstep, would they? Although

243

who knows, maybe I'm wrong. Maybe when you're Jack Lucas they do! Still, as long as you had fun, that's the important thing.'

'Hello? Am I allowed to speak?' If he'd been apologetic before, Jack now sounded less so. Evenly he said, 'It was nothing like that.'

'Ha! Yeah, right. I heard her voice, Jack.'

'Rose's parents turned up.'

Oh.

Tilly hated it when this happened, when you were all geared up for a shouting match and the other person said something that stopped you in your tracks. She closed her eyes and felt herself swaying slightly; that was another thing, she'd had too much wine to be able to argue in any coherent fashion.

'You could have told me that earlier, when you rang me.' She felt sorry for Jack and his in-laws, of course she did. But did that automatically mean she had to forgive him? He hadn't even mentioned that they'd been there.

'Maybe.' Jack nodded slightly. 'But I was distracted. Dilys was upset. It's been a hell of a night.'

'Um . . . sorry to interrupt,' Fergus called from the car, 'but this is a narrow road and we're blocking it.'

'OK. I'm coming now.' Tilly turned and headed back towards him.

'It's all right. I'll take you.' Jack looked over at Fergus and said, 'Let me give her a lift.'

Tilly, her back to Jack, shook her head at Fergus.

Fergus said awkwardly, 'Thanks, but that's OK. I'll drop her home.'

'Tilly. I'm sorry about tonight. I'll speak to you tomorrow.'

'No need.'

'There is. We have to talk.' He exhaled with frustration. 'I didn't *want* this to happen tonight.'

244

Tilly climbed back into Fergus's car. 'I know. But it did. I'm not trying to punish you, Jack. I'm doing it to protect myself.'

Some people were lucky; when they woke up with a blistering hangover they were able to sleep it off. They simply turned over and slid back into unconsciousness until it was all over.

It didn't work that way for Tilly. Her hangovers always woke her early and insisted she stayed awake to enjoy every minute. By the time Betty ambled upstairs and pushed the bedroom door open with her nose at seven o'clock, Tilly had already been awake for an hour and a half.

It was so unfair.

And not just the hangover.

Oh God, what a hideous night. Just when you thought your life was heading in one direction, it did a screeching handbrake turn. It was like taking centre stage at the Palladium preparing to sing 'Nessun Dorma' then realising that the orchestra were launching into 'The Birdie Song' instead.

By eleven o'clock the Nurofens had kicked in, Tilly's headache was gone and her mind was made up. When the doorbell rang, she braced herself and went to answer it.

Except it wasn't Jack.

Dave the postman was standing on the doorstep clutching a large flat rectangular parcel. 'All right, love? Hello, Betty!'

'Hi, Dave.' The parcel possibly contained a king-sized box of chocolates, which might cheer her up. 'Present for me?'

Not that it was likely to be.

'Sorry, love.' Having enthusiastically scratched Betty's ears, he straightened back up and handed the parcel over. 'It's for Kaye. They've addressed it care of Max. Sent it all the way from America too.' The fact that letters and parcels could wing their way here from other countries and continents was a source of endless fascination to Dave.

'Thanks.' Taking it from him and giving it an experimental shake, Tilly hoped it wasn't a squashed chihuahua. 'They're all away for the weekend. I'll give it to Kaye when she gets back.' Over Dave's shoulder she saw the Jag heading up the drive. At the sound of wheels on gravel, Dave twisted round too.

When he turned back, he gave Tilly a doubtful look. 'And Max and Kaye are away? Does that mean there's something going on between you two?'

'No.' Honestly, was nosiness part of the job description? 'No, there's nothing going on. At all,' Tilly said firmly.

'Oh right. Just as well.' Lowering his voice, Dave leaned closer. 'Gets sent a lot of Valentine cards, that one does.'

'I'm sure. But not from me.'

Dave made his way back to the post van, nodding and saying hello to Jack as they passed each other. Then he glanced at Betty, who had tolerated having her ears scratched by him but was now racing across the gravel and launching herself joyfully at the new arrival like an over-excited It girl. The last look Dave shot at Tilly spoke volumes; dogs or girls, it didn't matter. They all superglued themselves to Jack.

Chapter 35

'But I said I was sorry.' In the kitchen, Jack frowned. 'I know I let you down last night, but it was for a reason. You can understand how I was feeling, surely? Everything came flooding back and I thought I was betraying Rose. But that was just the guilt. I've had time to sleep on it now, and it doesn't have to be like that. This morning I've really thought things through.' He shook his head reassuringly at Tilly. 'This doesn't have to be the end for us.'

Tilly stood her ground. 'You can't end something that hasn't had a beginning.' Inwardly she was amazed she could sound so strong. Then again, it was a question of having to. Last night she'd been semi-drunk and furious. Today she was sober and resigned, because this was one of the hardest things she'd ever had to do. But she also knew it was for the best. Self-preservation. The relationship might not have properly begun but she'd already become way too emotionally involved. And when an unhappy ending was inevitable, who but a complete masochist would want to carry it on?

'You can't do this.' Jack was clearly finding her attitude hard to believe. 'Bryn and Dilys turned up out of the blue. That wasn't my fault. What was I supposed to do? Chuck them out of the house?'

'They're not the ones who changed my mind. They just gave me time to think. And I think we should forget . . . you know, *that* side of things.' Tilly gestured vaguely to indicate the romantic aspect. 'Let's just be friends, OK? That's what I want.'

Jack continued to stare at her. 'Really?'

Why did there have to be that look in his eyes? She nodded. 'Yes.'

'Why?'

Why? Now that was the killer question. Because last night she had watched the easy interaction between Erin and Fergus, had seen how blissfully happy they were together and had recognised that they truly *unconditionally* loved and trusted each other.

And she'd known then that achieving a relationship like that might just conceivably be within the realms of possibility, but that it would never – *could* never – happen with Jack.

How ironic that Fergus had Stella doing her best to stir up trouble in his new relationship, and now Jack had Rose's parents piling in on her behalf. Even if they didn't realise what they'd done they'd undoubtedly be delighted when they learned of their success.

Tilly felt her heart beating faster and harder; they *had* done her a favour. Because a night or a week or a month with Jack would never be enough and what she really wanted would never happen. Sooner or later he would back off as he always did, leaving her bitter and eaten up with jealousy like Stella. Heartbroken and the laughing stock of the town.

He was still waiting for her to say something.

Tilly gave a tiny shrug. 'Just because.'

'Are you open to persuasion?' said Jack.

'No, no.' She shook her head, simultaneously relieved and utterly desolate. 'I've made up my mind. That's it.'

'Oooh, baby Betsy Boo, how are *you*?' Kaye scooped Betty up into her arms and twirled around. 'Have you been a good girl this weekend?'

'We've both been good girls.' Tilly, who had spent the day virtuously cleaning the house, said, 'How was the wedding?'

'Noisy, boozy, lots of dancing with hairy-legged men in kilts. Those Scots know how to party.'

'And one of them showed me what he was wearing under his kilt,' said Lou.

'God, really? Gross.'

'Yeah, it was pretty gross. Giant pink boxer shorts with blue hearts on.' Lou peered interestedly at the parcel on the kitchen table. 'What's this? Has someone sent me a present?'

'No, it's for your mum.'

'Me? Ooh, I love presents.' Putting Betty down, Kaye came over to have a look. Her face fell when she saw the American stamps. 'Unless it's a pile of legal papers from Denzil and Charlene, suing me till my eyeballs squeak.'

Lou said, 'I'll open it,' and tore into the outer wrapping. She unwound a ream of bubblewrap, finally pulling out a painting in a simple black frame.

'Oh my God, it's a Dinny Jay!' Kaye let out a squeak of disbelief and grabbed the painting from Lou. 'Who sent me this? I *love* Dinny Jay.'

Tilly looked at the painting, A3-sized and packed with quirky detail, depicting ice skaters in Central Park. She'd never heard the name before.

Lou said, 'There's an envelope taped to the back.'

Detaching the envelope, Kaye opened it and began to read the letter aloud.

Dear Miss McKenna,

I remember reading a magazine interview a while back, in which you mentioned your fondness for the work of Dinny Jay. I saw this in a gallery last week and thought you might enjoy it, so I do hope you will accept this small gift from me. I also hope it reaches you safely. Having read in the paper about your move back to the UK, I am sending this via your ex-husband, whose address I found on his website. Don't worry, I'm not a stalker, just someone who wishes you well and wants you to know you aren't universally hated in the States.

Stay well and happy.

Best wishes,

P. Price.

PS. Hope you liked the chocolates and the flowers.

'So he's a stalker.' Tilly grimaced. 'Anyone who has to tell you they aren't a stalker, definitely is one.'

Kaye was gazing adoringly at the painting. 'He might just be a really nice man.'

'How much would that have cost him?'

'I don't know, I'll have to check on the internet. Three or four thousand dollars, something like that.'

'Shouldn't you send it back?'

'Oh God, I don't know. Should I? I love it so much! And I'd hurt his feelings if I did. If you bought someone the perfect present, how would you feel if they chucked it back in your face? I think the best thing to do is graciously accept and write him a really nice letter. At least I've got an address this time. And he lives in New York, so that's OK, that's safe enough.'

Max came in with their cases. 'Until he turns up on your doorstep with an axe.'

'That's all right. I won't be giving him my address, will I?' Kaye hugged the painting to her chest and beamed at him. 'I'll keep using yours.'

Two days to go. *Less* than forty-eight hours, in fact! In forty-six and a half hours they would be boarding their flight and setting off from Bristol airport, bound for Venice, tra-la. And the most needed, most longed-for, most romantic holiday of her life.

Willing today to be over, Erin checked her watch. Two thirty. Three more hours before she could close the shop, head upstairs and get on with her packing. The cases were lying open on the living room floor and she'd spent ages between customers working on her list. She loved making lists, had compiled them since childhood, often writing Get up, and Brush teeth and Eat breakfast for the sheer joy of being able to tick them off and experience that lovely feeling of accomplishment, a good job well done. Lists meant you were on top of the situation, in control. People who didn't make lists had no idea what they were missing. And holiday lists were extra-special, an integral part of the whole heady, thrilling, going-away experience.

Plus it meant you were less likely to arrive at your fabulous fourteenth-century palazzo without your straighteners.

Ooh, heat protection spray, that was something else she needed to add to the list. And she'd better buy a new bottle too; imagine getting there and discovering they didn't sell it in Venice.

The door to the shop flew open and Erin dropped her pen in fright. There, standing in the doorway with a grim, almost robotic look on her face, was Stella. Oh God, this was like those terrible stories you saw in the papers, where the spurned lover went completely ballistic and started murdering people.

'I need to speak to Fergus.' Even Stella's voice sounded odd, like a new one she was in the process of breaking in.

'He's not here.'

'I know he's not here. And his phone's switched off. Where is he?'

Erin didn't dare bend down and pick up the dropped pen. What if Stella took the opportunity to attack her? 'I don't know. Probably with a client.' *OK, say it, say it.* 'Could you leave my shop, please? I don't want you in here.'

'Right, I'll just have to tell you instead.' Stella didn't move. 'I need Fergus to look after Bing. I'm going away, so he needs to pick him up from my house after work today. I'll leave all the food out, and Bing's basket, and—'

'Hang on, Fergus can't do it.' Erin blurted the words out, indignation overcoming fear. 'You'll have to get someone else to look after your cat.'

'He has to do it. There isn't anyone else.'

'Book it into a cattery. That's what they're there for.'

Stella's jaw tightened. 'Bing isn't going into a cattery. He wouldn't like it.' Her eyes flashing, she added icily, 'And he's not an *it*.'

'Well, Fergus still can't look after him. Because he won't be here.' Erin felt her stomach clench. 'We're going away too.'

Ha. *So there.*

Stella stood there looking as if she'd been punched. 'Away?'

'Yes.'

'For how long?'

'A week.' *If* it's any business of yours.

'But I *need* someone to look after Bing.'

252

This was crazy. 'So get one of your friends to do it. Amy,' said Erin.

'Amy's too busy with her new man.' Stella's jaw tensed. 'She couldn't get me off the phone fast enough.'

'Well, how about—'

'Look, there isn't anyone, OK? No one else I can ask. And I *won't* put Bing into a cattery — he couldn't handle it. Where are you going, anyway?'

Oh brilliant, was she planning on asking them to take Bing along with them? Erin said, 'Venice.'

'Venice. How nice.' Stella's voice was as brittle as glass.

'Look, I'm sorry. If we weren't going away, we would have looked after Bing for you.' Crikey, who'd have thought five minutes ago that she'd be saying this and meaning it? But Stella was clearly desperate and in a complete state. Beneath the heavily applied make-up and stylish cream trouser suit she was as tense and nervy as a greyhound.

'Right. OK. Well, tell Fergus I've . . . no, don't bother.' For a second, tears brimmed in Stella's eyes before she turned abruptly away and left the shop.

Erin watched her jump into the car she'd left recklessly parked on double yellows across the road. Next moment it had kangarooed forward, narrowly missing an old lady with a tartan shopping basket on wheels. Then it shot back at an angle, mounted the pavement and went smack bang into a lamp post behind it.

By the time Erin reached her, Stella was hyperventilating and rocking to and fro in the driver's seat, moaning, 'I don't know what to *doooo.*'

'Stella, what's going on? Tell me.'

Stella shook her head wildly. '*Noooo.*'

'You can't drive in this state. You just hit a lamp post.'

'Who's going to look after Bing?'

Erin raised her voice. 'Where are you supposed to be going?'

'Nowhere nice like you.' Covering her face, Stella mumbled something that might have been hotel.

Oh, for God's sake. '*What?* What hotel?'

Stella peeled her hands away and said dully, 'Not hotel. Hospital. I have to go into hospital this afternoon.'

'Why?' Erin stared at her.

'Mind your own business. What difference does it make to you? Off you go to Venice with my husband. Have a wonderful time.'

Erin said, 'Tell me why you're going into hospital.'

'Oh, nothing much. I have cancer, that's all. Could you close the door now please?'

'*What?*'

'Close the door.' Tears were sliding down Stella's face, leaving white trails in her foundation.

'You've got cancer? Really?'

'Really. Cross my heart and hope to—' Stella stopped abruptly, shook her head. 'Anyway, I have to go now.'

'You can't drive like this. You've already dented your bumper.'

'If I dent the car, believe me, it's not the end of the world.'

'But if you knock someone down and kill them, it'll be the end of theirs. Wait here.' To be on the safe side, Erin leaned inside the car, reached across and grabbed the keys. 'I'll take you. Just give me two minutes to lock up the shop.'

Chapter 36

The car was an automatic, thankfully, otherwise Erin would have made as much of a pig's ear of driving it as Stella. As they made their way through Roxborough it crossed her mind that maybe Stella had been lying. What if this was a trap, and she was being lured to Stella's house . . .

Except it wasn't, she knew that. Stella had been telling the truth. God, *cancer*.

'I feel like I'm falling off a cliff in slow motion,' said Stella. 'I think I'm in shock. All the pain and cramps I've been having, I just ignored them for ages. Took more painkillers, drank more wine. I thought the reason I was feeling so awful was because my marriage was over. I mean, it stands to reason, doesn't it? Love hurts. You find out your husband's seeing someone else, so you feel like crap. I only went along to the surgery to see if Dr Harrison would prescribe me some happy pills. But because I'd lost weight he started poking and prodding me. Turn left down here, it's the house by the second lamp post, with the green front door.'

Now that Stella had started, she was like a tap that couldn't be turned off. Erin pulled up at the kerb and they climbed out of the car.

'Then he said how about a scan to be on the safe side, so I had one done on Monday just to shut him up, then this afternoon I went back to Dr Harrison so he could finally give me my Prozac, and that's when he told me. I've got cancer. I mean, it doesn't make any sense, does it? This kind of thing doesn't happen to *me*.' Her hands shaking so badly she couldn't fit her front door key in the lock, Stella said, 'I keep wanting to wake up and have everything back to normal. It's bad enough with the cancer thing, but now you're here too, coming into my house, and that's even more surreal.'

'Here, let me do it.' Taking over, Erin opened the door then stepped aside to allow Stella in first. Stella uttered a loud gulping sob as Bing sauntered over to her, his blue-grey furry body as sinuous as a snake. Scooping him up into her arms, she broke down completely while Bing, his lime-green eyes unconcerned, blinked impassively at Erin, as if to say, 'Oh God, what *now*?'

That was cats for you. No doubt he was tolerating the attention and wondering what was for tea.

An hour later, with Stella's overnight case packed, they set off for the hospital. So much for making lists to keep you in control of a situation. As Erin drove, Stella said, 'I'm scared. So scared. Is it all right to be scared?'

'Anyone would be scared. It's normal.'

'I want my mum.'

'Where is she? Do you want to phone her?'

'She's dead.' Stella wiped her face. 'But I still want her.'

Oh God. A lump formed in Erin's own throat.

'This really isn't supposed to happen, you know? I don't want to have cancer. I want a *baby*.'

Feeling helpless, Erin said, 'But thousands of people have cancer and they beat it. You can still have a baby afterwards. Look at the treatments they have these days, they can cure practically anything!'

'Who's going to look after Bing? He'll wonder where I am.'

'I'll sort something out, I promise.' They'd reached the hospital. Erin followed the signs until they reached the entrance to the block where the wards were situated. She stopped the car and said awkwardly, 'Well, here it is.'

Stella checked her face in the rear-view mirror, wiping away smears of mascara with a tissue. Then, turning to look at Erin, she blurted out even more awkwardly, 'Will you come with me? I don't want to go in on my own.'

The hospital brought back a million memories, very few of them happy. Erin had spent weeks practically living in the chair beside her mother's bed following her initial stroke. Then after that, life had been punctuated by endless return visits to the stroke rehabilitation unit, the physio department, outpatients. Hours of waiting and sitting and desperately trying to stay outwardly cheerful when there was nothing to be cheerful about. Endlessly attempting to conjure up yet more one-sided conversations when you'd completely run out of things to say. Tired magazines, the smell of wee, other patients incapable of speech wailing in frustration, getting trapped in a narrow corridor behind someone struggling along with a Zimmer frame at two metres an hour, the all-pervasive smell of disinfectant and over-cooked vegetables . . .

When Erin's mother had finally died, at least it had meant the interminable hospital visits were over. She'd have been happy never to clap eyes on the place again.

Anyway. Different ward, different staff, different patient now. Only the chairs remained the same. Erin sat on one – moulded

257

plastic, bright orange, bum-numbingly uncomfortable – and a young blonde nurse perched on the other while Stella occupied the bed. The nurse was filling out the information page of Stella's notes in careful loopy handwriting. Verrrry sloooowly indeeeed.

'Now, religion?'

'None,' said Stella.

'OK. Shall we just put C of E then?' It took her thirty seconds to write it. 'That's great. And who's your next of kin?'

Stella was busy rolling and unrolling the edge of the hospital sheet between her fingers. She looked as if she was struggling to hold back tears.

'Mum? Dad?' the nurse prompted helpfully. 'Brother or sister?'

'I don't have any relatives.' As the rolling quickened, Stella glanced over at Erin and said brusquely, 'Can she put you down?'

The little nurse's tone was soothing. 'That's fine. Who *are* you?'

'She's my husband's girlfriend,' said Stella.

'Oh! Well, shouldn't he be your next of kin?'

'I don't know. He doesn't give a stuff about me. And he's rubbish at hospitals anyway.' Shaking her head, Stella said, 'Put Erin's name down. How long am I going to be in for?'

'Ooh well, that's all down to the doctors, isn't it?' The nurse had a cosy, avoid-awkward-questions-at-all-costs manner and a comforting smile. 'Dr Wilson will be along soon to take a look at you.'

Stella's tone was curt. 'And I need some more painkillers.'

'No problem. We'll sort that out for you too.'

Outside the hospital Erin sat on a sunny bench and, knees juddering, tried Fergus's mobile again. This time he answered. 'Hi, angel, how's it going with the packing?' It was so odd to hear his voice sounding cheery and normal. 'Listen, do you have a three-pin adaptor, because I can't find mine—'

258

'Fergus, hang on, something's happened.' Too late, Erin realised she hadn't rehearsed what to say. 'It's about Stella.'

'Oh God, what's she done now? Right, that's it, I've had enough. Where are you?'

'I'm at the hospital.'

'*What?* Jesus, are you hurt? Did she attack you?'

'She's ill, Fergus. She didn't attack me. She's been admitted for tests.'

Clearly baffled, Fergus said, 'OK. But I don't get it, what are *you* doing there?'

Back on the ward, the orange and blue curtains had been drawn around Stella's bed. Then they were pulled back with a flourish and a tall, rather good-looking man emerged, white coat flying. Spotting Erin hovering, he pointed and said, 'Stella's friend?'

Of all the things she'd never imagined hearing herself described as. Erin nodded, dry-mouthed, and he beckoned her to follow him. 'Let's have a quick chat, shall we, while Stella's having her bloods taken. I'm Dr Wilson.'

He led her out of the ward, down a corridor and into a small windowless office lined with textbooks and files. Offered her a seat. Sat down opposite her and said, 'Well, I won't beat about the bush. Your friend Stella is going to need all your support. I'm very sorry, and of course we still have needle biopsies to carry out this afternoon, but from the MRI scan the cancer appears to be significantly advanced. You're going to have to be strong too. I'm so sorry, I know this is a shock for you.'

Erin felt as if she were watching herself on TV. As if she'd somehow inadvertently ended up in an episode of *Casualty*. Now didn't seem an appropriate time to tell him that, actually, she wasn't

Stella's friend at all, and what's more she really needed to get home and finish her holiday packing.

'But you can treat it.' Unable to meet the consultant's gaze, she looked at his long, clever fingers instead.

'We'll check out every option, of course. But I have to warn you that it's not looking good. At all, I'm afraid. The cancer has metastasised. The scan shows evidence of spread to the bowel, the lungs and the liver. It's a very aggressive form.'

Well, someone like Stella was hardly likely to have a shy retiring cancer, were they? Erin took a tissue from the box in front of her on the desk, and wiped her perspiring palms. Horrible, shameful, unworthy thoughts were jostling for pole position in her brain. Because of course she felt desperately sorry for Stella, but Stella in turn had made her life a misery . . . and what about Venice and the fourteenth-century palazzo with the fabulous roof garden and unrivalled views over the Grand Canal?

Oh God. Liver. Bowel. Lungs. *Aggressive*.

She felt sick.

Really, what choice did she have?

'Cancel?' Fergus, who knew how much she'd been looking forward to it, looked at Erin as if she were mad. 'Stella's ill, so you seriously want to cancel *our holiday*?'

They were outside the hospital. Erin clutched his hands; *want* didn't come into it. 'We have to. She's got no one else. I was with her this afternoon when she phoned a couple of her girlfriends. Deedee and Kirsten?'

Fergus's lip curled. 'Right, I know them.'

'Yes, well. They're too busy to come and visit her. Turns out that Deedee's put on a couple of pounds lately so she daren't miss her evening session at the gym. Kirsten's really busy at work and has to supervise the team fitting her new kitchen. And Amy's found herself a new man. So that's nice for her.' It was all Erin had been able to do to stop herself snatching the hospital phone from Stella's thin, French-manicured hand and yelling at the so-called friends to get off their selfish bony backsides and get down here *now*.

'Look, I'm shocked too. But this is our holiday. And Stella's always been vile to you.' Fergus frowned, bemused by her sudden change of attitude; after Erin's phone call, he'd driven straight over to the hospital. His stomach was rumbling and he was shattered. Stella had always been such a drama queen, the chances were that it would turn out to be something minor and easily treatable. He was touched by Erin's concern – crikey, how many women would do what she'd done after the way Stella had treated her? – but there was no need to go this far. 'Look, it's fantastic of you to offer, but it'll be fine. We'll only be away for a week. If she's still in here, we'll come and visit. But you never know, she might not be. She could be back home by then!'

But Erin didn't look relieved. Her face was drawn and pale, her whole body rigid. 'The consultant spoke to me. The cancer's really bad, Fergus.' Her voice cracking, she said, 'It's *everywhere.*'

Chapter 37

Talk about being thrown in at the deep end. What had sounded so simple and straightforward the other day when Erin had run through what she'd need to learn, now seemed alarmingly complicated. With Erin staying at the hospital with Stella, Kaye had found herself thrust into the job a day early and – as it turned out – woefully unprepared. By midday she had already managed to mortally offend a bossy middle-aged woman by not offering as much for her mannish tweed trousers as the woman felt they deserved.

'*How* much? That's not enough!' Her bushy eyebrows had practically quivered with indignation. 'I paid ninety pounds for those!'

In Savile Row, at a guess. The trousers were horrible. Nobody in their right mind would want to buy them. Kaye, watching as the woman stomped out of the shop, realised that Erin must be more skilled in the art of rejection, whereas she belonged more in the Simon Cowell camp. Maybe learning how to be a tad more diplomatic wouldn't go amiss.

God, but it was so hard not to offend people when they were trying on outfits that didn't suit them, or were blind to the faults of their own cast-offs. By lunchtime she had upset four more customers. When Tilly came through the door at one thirty she greeted her with relief.

'Hi! You look fantastic!'

Tilly gave her an odd look. 'I've been using a floor-sander. I'm covered in dust.'

'Oh, but I love your T-shirt! And your jeans fit you so *well*, although with a figure like that, you'd look great in anything! And the colour of your top really sets off your eyes.'

'You're starting to scare me,' said Tilly. 'Is this one of those hidden camera shows?'

Kaye pulled a face. 'I'm practising being nice. Paying compliments. Customers don't like it if they try something on and you tell them it makes them look like a hippo.'

'You have to say it in a nice way. Erin's great at that. She's honest but tactful.'

'Well, I'm not. If anyone else brings in stuff to sell, that's it. From now on, I'm going to tell them to leave it here for Erin to price.'

Tilly exhaled. 'I can't believe she's not going to Venice. Cancelling like that at the last minute.'

Kaye nodded in sympathy and handed her the key to Stella's house. 'I can't believe we're all taking it in turns to look after Scary Stella's cat.' Since Bing was so pampered, it had been decided that he should stay in his own home. Four or five times each day, one of them would drop in to check on him, keep him fed and watered and make sure his litter tray was scrupulously clean. Because Bing was Stella's baby, her number one priority, and keeping him in familiar surroundings was what she'd decreed he'd like best.

Plus, if the litter tray wasn't spotless he'd just go on the carpet.

So Erin had gone ahead and organised it. And when Tilly had dared to suggest – purely hypothetically of course – that with

Stella in hospital they could put Bing into a cattery and she'd be none the wiser, Erin had said, 'Can we just do it, please? The last thing Stella needs is to be worrying about her cat.'

'Right,' said Tilly now, 'I'll get over there and check on Bing. Try not to bring the shop to its knees before five o'clock.' Wagging a finger, she said, 'Remember, honesty and tact.'

Kaye nodded. 'Absolutely. Like, it's lucky your nose is so huge, it really draws attention away from your double chin.'

'That's the way. Perfect.'

An hour later, a tall woman in her sixties came into the shop. She eyed Kaye with surprise. 'You're not the usual lady.'

'I'm the reserve team.'

'But you still know about fashion. I certainly hope so anyway, because I'm useless! Now, two things. I need a new evening dress, nothing frilly or flowery, size fourteen. But I also want to ask your advice.' As she rattled on, the woman plonked a carrier bag on to the counter. 'And I promise you, I feel dreadfully guilty doing this, but we're a bit desperate. You see, my son's mother-in-law gave me this for Christmas. I know it's designer and terribly expensive, because she's got pots of money and she kept banging on about how much it cost. But it's a bit too smart for me to actually use, and one of the big prizes in our charity auction has just fallen through, so I've decided to offer this instead.' She opened the carrier and looked hopefully at Kaye. 'And I wondered if you'd tell me roughly how much it's worth, then we can advertise it as Stunning Hermès Bag, retails at six million pounds. Well, maybe not six million, but a jolly good price anyway!'

Oh Lord. Honesty and tact. Stalling for time, Kaye examined the shoulder strap and tugged at a loose thread.

'Look, I'm sorry, but this isn't a Hermès bag. It's a copy.'

'Oh no! Really? So how much is it worth?'

Kaye shook her head, agonising over having to say it whilst privately marvelling at the woman's inability to tell real from fake. 'Nothing. It's one of those cheap market knock-offs. See the wonky stitching here? And the crooked side pocket. And this isn't leather, it's plastic.'

And it had so nearly been donated to a charity auction too. How awful.

'Right. Well, thanks. Bugger.' The woman heaved a sigh.

'I'm really sorry.'

'Oh, bless you, it isn't your fault. I dare say we'll sort something out. And on the bright side, it means I don't have to feel guilty about giving away a present! Between you and me, I can't stand my son's mother-in-law anyway. She's always boasting about her millions. Ghastly woman. Oh well, let's forget her. We can at least find me a dress for the night.' Stopping and frowning, the woman looked more intently at Kaye. 'I keep thinking we've met before. But we haven't, have we?'

'I don't think so.'

'You're very familiar though. Have you worked in any other shops?'

'Um, no.' Kaye began searching through the evening dress rails, pulling out a stately midnight-blue taffeta. 'Now, how about this one? The colour would really suit—'

'Hotels, then? Restaurants? The thing is, I know your voice too.' The woman shook her head, baffled. 'Please don't take this the wrong way, but . . . I think I've seen you crying.'

'Well, I've been living over in the States for the last few years.'

'We spent a month in Texas last year! Were you there too?'

'No, LA. I'm an actress,' said Kaye.

'Good heavens! *Over the Rainbow*!' The woman gave an excited yelp of recognition. 'We used to watch you on that show – you were the one whose husband ran off with your sister!'

'That's right.' Kaye smiled, because it hadn't occurred to her for one moment that this woman might have been a fan of the show.

'Oh, we loved *Over the Rainbow*. Fancy you being in that, then coming over here!' The woman clapped her hands in delight, not showing the remotest interest in the dress Kaye had picked out for her. 'You know what? This has to be fate!'

Fate. Really? 'Why?'

'Because you're a famous Hollywood actress! And if you wanted to do me a huge favour, you could.'

Kaye eyed her with caution. She only owned one really good designer bag and she loved it with a passion. Charity or no charity, having to hand it over to this woman would break her heart.

Warily she said, 'What kind of favour?'

'Well, the whole reason I'm in such a flap is because this girl's just pulled out of our event. Antonella Beckwith? The singer? Have you heard of her?'

This was a bit like saying the Rolling Stones? They're a band? Ever heard of them? Because Antonella Beckwith was young, super-glamorous and in the last two years had sold about fifty million albums. Kaye nodded, anxiety unfurling in her stomach.

'Well, can't say I know much about her myself. But apparently we were jolly lucky to get her. One of her aunts is a friend of one of our organisers and they set it up. Except now, of course, the event's two weeks away and the wretched girl's gone and cancelled on us. Seems she's been offered something far more high-profile in London, so our little charity's been dropped like a stone. And we've been racking our brains to come up with another celebrity, but everyone we've approached has had other commitments. Which means we're now officially desperate!'

266

'OK, two things. One,' said Kaye, 'I'm not really a celebrity. Not over here anyway. Nobody would know who I am.'

'*I* know who you are! And so does my husband! We'd tell everyone you're a Hollywood star!'

OK, so far, so toe-curlingly embarrassing.

'The other thing is, I had kind of an accident recently and there's been quite a lot of bad press about me.' Kaye grimaced. 'And I'm not working on *Over the Rainbow* any more. They dropped me. That's why I'm living back here now.'

'But don't you see? Perfect!' As she spoke, the woman dug out a business card. 'If people don't know you, they won't know about that either, will they? So it won't be a problem!'

The woman was a whirlwind, an unstoppable force. Examining the card, Kaye saw that her name was Dorothy Summerskill.

'It's a week on Saturday at the Mallen Grange Hotel,' said Dorothy.

OK, this was the moment to look devastated and exclaim apologetically, 'Oh no, a week on Saturday? What a *shame*', and reel off an entirely plausible reason why she couldn't make it. But two things stopped her. She couldn't think of a plausible reason fast enough. And even if she could, she had a feeling Dorothy wouldn't believe her.

'It's for a very good cause,' Dorothy continued persuasively. 'The charity's called Help for Alzheimer's.'

'Oh! I've got a friend who supports them! Jack Lucas.'

'You know Jack? But how marvellous! And he's going to be there, so that makes it even more perfect!'

'OK, I'll do it.' Not that she'd ever had a choice, Kaye realised. Still, it might be fun. And hadn't her agent said she should get involved in charity work in a bid to stop everyone hating her? 'What will I be doing, just opening the evening?'

'Oh yes,' Dorothy nodded blithely, 'that too. But of course the main draw will be the auction.'

Auction? Uh oh, panic. Worried, Kaye said, 'The thing is, I know some people are brilliant at running charity auctions, but I don't think I could do that.'

'Oh, sweetheart, we wouldn't ask you to conduct the auction! You'd be taking Antonella's place as the star lot!'

What?

'The highlight of the evening,' Dorothy continued. 'People will be bidding for a dinner date with you. It'll be fabulous!'

'It won't be fabulous if nobody bids.' Oh God, the woman was deluded; compared with Antonella Beckwith she was going to attract as much excitement as . . . as an *ant*.

'Don't be silly, it'll be fine. Who wouldn't jump at the chance to have dinner with a genuine Hollywood star?'

'You don't even know my name,' Kaye protested.

'Anyway, I promise you won't be embarrassed. Our supporters are wonderfully generous. And it'll be after the meal so they'll have had time to knock back plenty of drinks!' Dorothy beamed, pleased at having the matter settled. 'There, all done. All you have to do now is help me find a dress for the night. And don't look so worried,' she added gaily, taking the midnight-blue taffeta gown from Kaye. 'It'll be fun!'

Chapter 38

Stella had slipped from shock into flat-out denial. Erin knew the doctor had spoken to her about the results of the needle biopsies but Stella had decided she didn't want to be ill and had shied away from any mention of prognosis. Instead she insisted on talking about future holidays, whilst sitting up in bed applying copious amounts of make-up. In less than a week, the changes in her physical appearance were pronounced. Watching it happen day by day was horrifying and having to pretend you hadn't noticed harder still. Erin braced herself each time she entered the ward; it was like one of those time-lapse photography sequences, speeded up. When Stella had first mentioned the word cancer, Erin had envisaged an illness lasting years and years. This, though, was in a different league. Stella's skin had turned greenish-yellow, her eyes had become sunken and she was losing weight practically by the hour. Her movements were slowed too, curtailed by pain, but still she insisted upon redoing her lipstick, piling on more eyeshadow and liberally dusting her face and chest with bronzer.

The doctor had spoken to Erin again, spelling out to her what she didn't want to hear either.

'I'm sorry, but it's about as bad as it gets. We can control the pain but I'm afraid the cancer isn't treatable. I did broach the subject, but Stella didn't want to hear it. Her husband does need to be aware of this, though.' He shot Erin a brief, sympathetic smile. 'It's nice that you and Stella get along so well.'

Meaning that she was practically Stella's only visitor. Erin didn't tell him the truth.

'And we'll be keeping her here,' the consultant added. 'It's not worth moving her to a hospice. We're talking a matter of days now.'

Not even weeks. *Days.* Erin closed her eyes; she'd had no idea cancer could be this quick.

'You missed a bit.' Stella's tone was querulous.

On her deathbed and dissatisfied with the way her nails were being painted. Erin, redoing the edge of the nail, said, 'Sorry.'

'I want to look my best for Max. Why isn't he here yet?'

'Probably trying to find somewhere to park. It's a nightmare sometimes.'

The doors to the ward crashed open. 'There you are,' said Stella. 'You're late.'

Max arrived at the bedside; if he was shocked by the change in Stella's appearance since his last visit, he covered it well. 'Still stroppy after all these years. Bloody hell, woman, can't you give me a break? Some of us have work to do, WAGs to fight with.' He bent and gave her a hug. 'Tandy's got into the power of crystals – she's set her heart on having an eight-foot blue crystal pyramid in the hall. Anyway, how are you feeling?'

'Like shit. I hate this place. And Erin's completely mucking up my nails.' Raising her face for a kiss, Stella said, 'Do I look all right?'

'You look fab. I suppose you've been flirting with all the doctors.'

'Maybe. Except they're all obsessed with completely grim body

270

functions.' Stella pouted and rearranged her hair. 'I mean, it's all very well getting flirty and batting your eyelashes, but then they go and spoil it all by asking if you've opened your bowels today.'

'I hate it when that happens,' said Max. 'Really kills the moment. Here, I brought you some mags.'

'Thanks. I've already seen that one. And that one.'

Max shook his head. 'I wish I hadn't bothered. Did nobody ever tell you it's polite, when someone gives you something, to at least pretend to be pleased?'

Stella managed a smile, her bleached teeth bizarrely white against the muddy brownish-yellow of her complexion. 'Like you'd know about being polite. Sorry. I haven't read the rest of them.' Fumbling for one of the glossies, she studied the cover. 'Did you choose this one on purpose?'

'No. Why?' Max looked at Erin, clearly thinking what she was thinking: God, don't say there was a piece in there on things to do when you've only got a week to live.

Stella pointed a still-wet burgundy fingernail at the words 'Biological Clock Clanging? Phone a Gay Friend!' 'Thought this might be your way of telling me you've changed your mind.'

'No.'

'But you might.'

'No I bloody won't,' said Max.

'Not now, obviously. But when I'm better.' Stella gazed intently at him. 'I want a baby, Max. *Please.*'

Erin stared at him. Max shook his head. 'I know you do, but it's not going to be with me. Sorry, you'll have to get some other sucker to do it.'

'Fine then. I will.' Summoning up another brief smile, Stella said, 'Wouldn't want any child of mine inheriting a nose like *that*, anyway.'

271

Max stayed for another forty minutes, swapping insults, regaling them with Roxborough gossip and eating not only the contents of Stella's fruit bowl but half a dozen of the biscuits belonging to the woman in the next bed.

When he left, Stella watched him go then sank back against her pillows with a sigh. 'He's great, isn't he?'

'Hmm.' Erin shrugged and semi-nodded, privately outraged by Max's earlier behaviour. God, would it have killed him to *pretend* that—

'He's made me feel so much better.'

Oh cheers. Max breezes in and makes all the difference in the world, while some of us cancel our holidays and spend practically the whole week here; how absolutely fantastic that one quick visit from him should help so much.

'I feel silly even saying this, but at least I know now that I'm definitely not dying.'

'*What?*'

'Oh well, you know.' Sheepishly Stella said, 'When you feel this rough and people keep being nice to you, it kind of crosses your mind. And that's pretty bloody terrifying, right? But if I was dying, Max would have gone along with anything I said, wouldn't he? He'd have humoured me, promised me as many babies as I want. Pass me one of those.' She gestured weakly at the box of tissues as tears slid down her cheeks. 'But he didn't. He told me to get stuffed. So that means I'm all right.'

'Well, good.' Erin didn't know what else to say.

'God, it's such a relief! All I have to do now is get my strength up so they can make a start on the treatment. So, when are you and Fergus planning on getting married?'

Erin was having trouble keeping up with this conversation. 'We haven't even talked about it. You aren't divorced yet.'

'That won't take long. We can get it sorted. I don't care about Fergus any more, you can have him. I just want you to promise me one thing.'

Oh help, what now? 'Promise you what?'

'That you'll invite me to the wedding. So I can turn up looking absolutely fantastic, in a truly great outfit. I'll be thin and classy and gorgeous,' said Stella, 'and everyone will wonder why Fergus ever divorced me.'

'You know something?' said Erin. 'I have the strangest feeling your invitation's going to get lost in the post.'

'Don't worry, I'll gatecrash.' Stella winced with pain, then her smile of satisfaction broadened. 'Ha, stealing the show at your ex-husband's wedding. How cool is that?'

Chapter 39

'Guess what I've been doing all day?' Tilly burst into the shop and flung her arms above her head. 'You'll never guess!'

Kaye, who had been carefully de-bobbling a Brora cashmere sweater, eyed Tilly with her arms in the air and said, 'Pretending to be an orang-utan? Swinging from high branches? Ooh, I know, learning to be a trapeze artist!'

'Any of those would have been so much more fun. I've been glueing Swarovski crystals to a midnight-blue ceiling. A thousand square feet of ceiling. Fifteen thousand Swarovski crystals. My hands are covered in glue and all the feeling's gone from my fingers.' Wincing as she lowered her arms, Tilly said, 'And I had the completely brilliant idea of rollering glue over the whole ceiling then just flinging handfuls of crystals at it, but Max wouldn't let me.'

'He's an evil slave-driver.'

'Tell me about it. Oh, and you have to see the Alzheimer charity's website.' Tilly reached past her and waggled the mouse to bring the computer's screen to life. 'Jack called Max earlier and told him to take a look.'

'Oh my *God*,' Kaye wailed when she reached the charity's home page. Tilly, who had already seen it on Max's laptop, gave her arm a sympathetic squeeze.

Beneath the headline NEWSFLASH! NEWSFLASH! came the announcement: 'Due to unforeseen circumstances Antonella Beckwith has had to pull out of our charity auction. However we are thrilled and *delighted* to inform everyone that her place will now be taken by a true celebrity, the sensational and much-loved award-winning Hollywood superstar, KAYE McKENNA!!!'

'Oh God,' Kaye let out a groan and covered her face. 'That is *soooo* embarrassing.'

'It's not too bad.' Well, sometimes you just had to lie.

'It is. It's like a million people turning up at Wembley for a Madonna concert, then you walking out on stage and telling them they've got you instead.'

'Wouldn't that be fantastic, though?' Enthusiastically Tilly said, 'It's always been my secret dream to sing at Wembley.'

'Except you wouldn't get a chance, because the audience would rip you limb from limb before you even opened your mouth. And that's what it's going to be like for me.' Kaye banged the heel of her hand against her forehead. 'Furious old people, feeling cheated and booing me off the stage, throwing their false teeth at me — and I bet Max thinks it's hilarious.'

'Just a bit.'

'I can't believe Dorothy stitched me up like this. She asked me if I'd won any Emmys or Oscars and I said the only award I'd ever won was when I was seven, for the carrying-the-jelly-on-a-plate race.'

'Well, it's for charity. People won't mind.'

'They might not mind, but who's going to bid to spend a couple of hours with me?' Gesturing around the shop, Kaye said helplessly, 'If they wanted to, they could come and sit in

275

here for free. All they'd have to do is give me a hand with the de-bobbling.'

The door opened and a couple of women Tilly vaguely recognised came into the shop. Well-groomed and in their early thirties, she'd seen them somewhere before. In the Lazy Fox, probably. They were chattering away together. Tilly watched as Kaye prepared her easy welcoming smile and waited for the potential customers to smile and acknowledge her in return.

Well, that didn't happen. Ignoring both of them, the two women began flicking through the rails. Kaye shrugged slightly and turned back to the computer. Tilly checked her watch; she should be heading over to Harleston to pick Lou up from school.

'. . . I mean, can you believe it? I know she's always been a tart, but not knowing who the father of your kid is, God, that's just *tacky*.'

'Ha, though, I bet we can guess which one she's hoping it is.'

Tilly exchanged a glance with Kaye; honestly, they might as well be wearing an invisibility cloak. Still, it had its own entertainment value. As Erin had remarked in the past, working in a shop was great if you wanted to eavesdrop.

'Well, if it's Andrew's,' said the taller, blonder woman, 'it's going to be born with weird little stumpy legs.'

'And if it's Rupert's,' the brunette grimaced, 'God help it! It'll have a bald head, hairs sprouting out of its pointy ears and come out wearing mustard-coloured corduroys!'

They both snorted with laughter at this. Tart or otherwise, Tilly felt sorry for whoever they were mocking. Tapping her watch, she said in an undertone to Kaye, 'I'd better be making a move . . .'

'Ha, no wonder she's worried. At least she knows it won't look like a gargoyle if it's Jack's. I suppose we should all keep our fingers crossed, for the kid's sake if nothing else. Now, what about the buttons on this shirt? Do they make it look too officey?'

Tilly's stomach disappeared. One minute her insides had been there. The next, they were just gone. Like in *Tom and Jerry* when Tom hangs in thin air for a bit before crashing to the ground. She looked over at Kaye, who was staring at the women, equally stunned.

'Those shoulders look a bit square. And I'm not sure about the collar. If it's Rupert's,' giggled the brunette, 'it might come out doing that laugh of his, like a hyena on helium.'

Who were they talking about? *Who?*

'And if it's Andrew's, it'll be wearing vile stripey socks.'

Tilly closed her eyes. Please let it be some other Jack.

'God, she must be desperate for it to be Jack's. Ooh, look at this!' Triumphantly the woman pulled out a grey crepe bias-cut dress. 'Ghost!'

Tilly felt as if she'd seen one. Her heart was pounding and she felt sick.

'Plus,' said the blonde, 'at least he has a decent surname. Imagine if she married Rupert!'

'I never even thought of that. God, how *awful*,' squealed the other woman. 'She'd be Amy Pratt!'

Amy, oh God no. Tilly still vividly remembered being interrogated by skinny, stiletto-heeled Amy in the pub on the night of Declan's birthday. She'd been besotted with Jack then. And now she was pregnant with what could turn out to be his baby. How could Jack have been so reckless?

Except that was a rhetorical question, wasn't it? Because the answer was that he was a man, and when it came to sex they didn't bother to consider the possible consequences. Tilly felt light-headed and, to her horror, just the tiniest bit jealous.

'So what does Amy's new bloke make of it all?' The blonde was still carefully examining the Ghost dress.

'Haven't you heard? He's legged it. Dropped her like a stone. You know, you could wear your gold Kurt Geigers with that.'

'So she's going to be chasing after all three of them.'

'Poor sods. I bet they're wishing they'd kept it in their trousers now.'

'Um, excuse me.' Frowning, Kaye said, 'Is this Jack Lucas you're talking about?'

The two women turned to look at her, eyebrows raised as far as Botox would allow. The blonde said, 'That's right. Do you know him?'

Kaye was visibly dismayed. 'Yes I do. *Very* well.'

'Ohhhh.' The brunette gave a slow, knowing nod. 'You're another one. Well, the law of averages says it had to happen one day. I mean, I know it's his own fault, but you can't help feeling sorry for him.'

Tilly's mouth was dry. There was a one in three chance that Jack had casually impregnated Amy and the news had knocked her sideways.

The other woman shook her head. 'And you know what Amy's like when it comes to money. She'll be praying that baby's Jack's. If he's the father she'll have that lawyer of hers working overtime, pushing for every last penny she can get.'

Chapter 40

Fergus shifted uncomfortably on the bright orange hospital chair. The sight of his estranged wife, shrunken and discoloured and growing visibly weaker by the day, filled him with a mixture of emotions he could barely define. Years ago, he had loved Stella enough to marry her. But theirs had never been the kind of easy, natural relationship he now had with Erin. Stella's towering ego, her high self-regard and endless capacity for criticising others had succeeded in wearing that love away. But now, seeing her like this was really churning him up; he felt guilty and ashamed of himself and resentful and . . . oh God, guilty again because if she hadn't put her physical symptoms down to the fact that her husband had just left her, she might have gone to the doctor months earlier, in time for the cancer to be caught before it had spread . . .

'Come on, come on, you're supposed to be making polite conversation.' Even now, Stella was able to mock him.

And it was true; he was an estate agent, a salesman. The art of chatting about anything under the sun was something he should be good at, normally *was* good at. But here, in this hospital, he was finding it hard, almost impossible. He didn't know how Erin did it. Erin, of all people, the one Stella had been most vile to.

Incredibly, though, she had put all that behind her. Day in and day out, for hours at a time, she stayed here and kept Stella company, talking easily about the hospital staff, their favourite doctors and nurses, the other patients, clothes, TV, schooldays – anything and everything.

'You look like someone in deep trouble, waiting to see their bank manager,' said Stella.

Fergus made an effort to cheer up. But that was exactly how he felt. Checking the clock on the wall, he saw that it was almost three. Erin would be here soon, thank God. And he could get back to work. Looking at Stella he wondered if she knew, deep down, that she was dying. And if she did, what did it feel like? There were so many questions he wanted to ask her, but couldn't. God, who could have imagined that something like this would happen?

Sarkily Stella said, 'We could always play I-Spy.'

More guilt. He was being a lousy hospital visitor. 'Do you want to?'

She rolled her eyes. '*No.*'

'Erin'll be here soon.'

'Thank God for that. She's a damn sight better company than you are. Mind you, a bedpan would be better company.'

'Sorry.'

'I like Erin, you know. She's nice.'

Fergus slowly nodded. At last.

'I'm coming to your wedding, did she tell you?' Stella half smiled. 'When it gets to that bit where the vicar asks if anyone knows of any reason why you shouldn't marry, I'm going to stand up and say yes, because you wear women's underwear in bed.'

It was Fergus's turn to smile. It wasn't true, but he could certainly imagine Stella standing up and saying it. Except she wouldn't get the chance, would she? Because by then she'd be – oh God, no, no, don't let him cry . . .

But it overtook him without warning, a great tidal wave of emotion, and with a loud honking noise like a startled goose, Fergus buried his face in both hands and broke down completely. He sobbed and sobbed, unable to control himself, and the woman in the bed opposite sent her husband over with a box of man-sized tissues.

Finally he got himself back on an even keel. He wiped his face, noisily blew his nose and looked up to see Stella lying back against her pillows, impassively watching him.

'Sorry.' Fergus shook his head, embarrassed by the outburst. 'I don't know where that came from.'

Did Stella know she was dying? Or, if she hadn't before, had he just given the game away?

She slid her skinny arm across the bed and clasped his hand in hers. Her skin was dry and papery and too big for the bones beneath it.

'It's all right, I know why you're crying.' With a ghost of a smile Stella said, 'You've just realised you're stuck with Erin now. And you wish you were still with me.'

And, being Stella, it was impossible to know whether this was a joke or if she meant it.

Fergus, who had no intention of finding out, checked his watch again and said, 'She'll be here in a minute. I'll go and find someone to help, then we'll get you into a chair.'

Between them, he and the cheerful nurse managed to transfer Stella from the bed into a wheelchair. She grimaced and winced with pain but didn't complain. Finally, with the bag from her intravenous drip swinging from its hook above her head, she was ready to go.

This, another of Erin's ideas, was the highlight of Stella's day. Fergus wheeled her out of the ward and down the long corridor until they reached the main entrance. Outside the building, smokers congregated in the sunshine. Seated on a bench opposite, beneath a chestnut tree, Erin was waiting for them.

This time it was Stella's eyes that filled with tears. Fergus parked her in front of the bench and Erin opened the front of the carrying case next to her. Bing snaked out, yowling impatiently, and stepped across on to Stella's bony, blanket-covered lap.

'Oh Bing, my baby.' Stella lovingly stroked him and Bing, regarding her with his usual baleful expression, submitted himself to her kisses. He tolerated the attention like a truculent teenager being forced to visit his whiskery incontinent granny.

At least he stayed put, didn't try to run off. Erin watched as Stella cradled her cat and murmured endearments into his ear. Bringing Bing along to see her had really lifted Stella's spirits and given her something to look forward to each day, even if persuading Bing into his carrying case and having to endure his outraged commentary of miaows and yowls during the car journeys were enough to test anyone's patience.

'It's all right, baby, Mummy'll be home soon.' Stella kissed his front paws. 'Are you missing me, hmm?'

'He had a tin of salmon last night.' Well, *had* was putting it optimistically. When Erin had put the bowl on the floor, Bing had given her his most disdainful Gordon-Ramsay-served-rank-food-by-some-useless-amateur look and stalked off. Still, most of it had gone by this morning.

'He prefers smoked salmon, chopped up into pieces an inch square. Oh sweetheart, did they try and make you eat nasty old tinned? My poor baby, they're so *mean* to you.'

Erin didn't take offence; gratitude would have been too much to hope for. She sat back and idly watched the comings and goings outside the entrance to the hospital, then turned to follow the progress of a boy on crutches making his way towards the gates.

Hang on. Who was that, heading up the road past him?

Wasn't that . . . ?

Crikey, it *was*.

'Stella.'

'Oh, look at your beautiful whiskers, they're so *silky*.'

'Stella.' Erin gave the side of the wheelchair a gentle nudge. 'Looks like you've got another visitor.'

'What?'

'Someone's come to see you.' *At last*, but better late than never. Pleased for Stella, Erin pointed the visitor out to her. Amy, wearing a daffodil-yellow V-necked top, cream jeans and high-heeled sandals, was making her way up the road towards them.

Stella smiled, visibly relieved to see her friend at long last.

Amy grew closer. Recognising first Erin, then Fergus, she nodded briefly in acknowledgement.

Then carried on walking by.

Boggling, they stared after her as she click-clacked past and approached the glass sliding doors of the building's main entrance.

'*Amy*,' Fergus called out, stopping her in her tracks. When she turned, he said redundantly, 'We're over here!'

Mystified, Amy looked at him, then at Erin. Finally her gaze went to Stella in the wheelchair and her expression altered, changed to one of horror as recognition dawned. Belatedly Erin realised that Amy hadn't come here to visit Stella; the thought that she might bump into her today hadn't so much as crossed her mind.

'Stella? How *are* you?' Staying where she was, Amy waved across the distance between them as if greeting a casual friend on Ladies' Day at Ascot. 'How nice to see you! You're looking . . . um . . .'

'Stunning,' Stella murmured drily. 'I know.'

'Gosh, I'd love to stop and chat, but I'm late for my appointment! Having my first scan.' Amy beamed with excitement.

'Erin mentioned you were pregnant,' said Stella. She paused. 'Congratulations.'

'Thanks! Well, I'd better rush, don't want to keep the doctor waiting. Wish me luck,' trilled Amy. 'See you around!'

They watched in silence as Amy teetered in through the glass doors.

Stella carried on stroking Bing. Finally she spoke. 'That poor baby. Fancy not even knowing who the father is. D'you think the scan will be able to see if it's got Rupert's ears?'

Chapter 41

For once the school car park was alive with activity at seven in the morning. Max pulled into a space and hauled Lou's turquoise case off the back seat of the car.

She threw her arms around him, kissed him on both cheeks and gave him an extra hug for luck, a habit they'd got into when she'd been a toddler and one he hoped she'd never break. When you counted up how many extra hugs he'd had over the years, they probably amounted to – God, tens of thousands. And he wouldn't have missed out on them for the world.

'Thanks for bringing me this early.' Lou's curls tickled his nose. 'Love you. Bye, Dad.'

'Hang on a sec.' Releasing her, Max strode round to the back of the car and clicked open the boot.

'Why? What's in there?' Lou's puzzled frown deepened as he pulled out a second case. 'What's going on? Who's that for?'

The coach was already filling up with pupils and teachers; in ten minutes it would be setting off on its journey to Paris.

'Me,' said Max.

'Why? You're not coming.'

'I am.'

285

'Oh Dad, no!' Lou looked panicky and upset, and Max knew why. His heart went out to her.

'Hey, it's OK. It'll be fine.'

'It won't be fine! Eddie Marshall-Hicks is going on the trip, and his friend Baz . . . they might *say* things . . .'

'If they try it, I'll crack their heads together and push them off the Eiffel Tower. Well,' Max amended, 'I would if I was allowed to.'

Parents and children were swarming around them. Lou was already glancing apprehensively at each arriving car, clearly unhappy with the situation. 'Dad, they're vile. This is going to be awful.'

Which just went to prove that, contrary to what she might have promised him, the snide remarks *hadn't* stopped.

'Sweetheart, do you think I can't handle a couple of spoiled brats? Coming along on the trip was my idea, after Mrs Heron and I had our chat. She was all for it.'

'So you set this up weeks ago, and it didn't even occur to you to tell me?' Lou said plaintively, 'Dad, this is *my* school trip.'

'That's why we didn't tell you. You'd have begged me not to come along.'

'I'm begging you *now*.'

'Too late. We're here. Oh, don't look at me like that.' Max prayed he hadn't made a terrible mistake. 'I'm not doing this to punish you. Mrs Heron thinks it's a great idea.'

Lou's eyes narrowed. 'Well, she would, wouldn't she? You aren't *her* dad.'

But there was nothing she was able to do about it; he'd presented her with a fait accompli. Over the course of the next fifteen minutes, forty children and forty-four assorted items of luggage were installed on the coach. Astrid Heron turned up to see everyone off. Finally, she stood at the front of the coach, facing her over-excited pupils, and gave a brief headmistressy speech.

'Now, you already know Miss Endell and Mr Lewis, so just let me introduce our two volunteer parent helpers. Mrs Trent, mother of Sophie.'

Next to Max, a beaming Fenella Trent leapt to her sensibly shod feet, waved enthusiastically and trilled, 'Hello, everyone!'

'And Louisa's father, Mr Dineen.'

OK, he definitely wasn't going to beam or wave. Max rose to his feet, gazed at the sea of faces and said, 'Hi there, you can call me Max.'

It didn't take a genius to work out where Eddie and his side-kick were sitting. Everyone on the bus heard the sniggers at the back and the loudly whispered, 'Or we could call you Poof.'

Outraged, Mrs Heron barked, 'Who said that?'

'It's OK.' Max stopped her with a brief smile; hadn't they already agreed to let him handle this in his own way? Addressing the back of the bus he said pleasantly, 'You *could* call me that, but you might not like what I'd call you in return.'

Astrid Heron was now looking as if she might be regretting her decision. 'Right. Well. Have a wonderful trip, all of you. And remember, you're representing Harleston Hall, so behave your-selves! Do us proud! *À bientôt! Bon chance! Au revoir!*'

They got shot of her at last, and the coach trundled down the tree-lined, sun-dappled driveway. Max sat back and wondered if *behave yourselves* applied to him too. If the ferry crossing was rough and the opportunity presented itself, would it be so very wrong to tip Eddie and his sniggering sidekick over the rail and into the Channel?

Next to him, Fenella adjusted her pink Alice band and said gaily, 'Well, we're off! This is going to be fun, isn't it!'

'Let's hope so.'

She leaned towards him slightly and lowered her voice. 'What was all that about, just now? I didn't quite catch it.'

'A couple of the boys were having a dig at me,' said Max. 'Because I'm gay.'

Fenella's eyebrows nearly collided with her Alice band. 'Are you joking?'

'No.'

'But . . . but you're Louisa's father!'

Max shrugged slightly. 'Still gay.'

Having evidently led an extremely sheltered life, Fenella flushed and shrank away from him. 'Well, I . . . I had no idea . . . good grief!'

'I know. Shocking, isn't it?' said Max.

God, keeping an eye on forty over-excited thirteen- and four-teen-year-olds was knackering. Following an afternoon of sight-seeing – the Eiffel Tower, the Louvre, the Arc de Triomphe – they'd all eaten dinner at tables outside a vast pizza restaurant. *(Pizza? Mais naturellement!)* Now they were chatting and switching seats and eyeing up other groups of teenagers in the vicinity. Some of the boys were kicking screwed-up balls of foil around, dribbling them between the tables and showing off their skills.

Max drank his black coffee and watched Josie Endell's body language as she chatted animatedly to Tom Lewis. On to her second glass of wine now – *quel daring!* – she was leaning forward and arching her back in order to expose another inch of cleavage, using her hands a lot to illustrate whatever she was saying, and being slightly – daringly – flirtatious. To illustrate a point, she touched his arm. Each time she laughed, she flicked back her hair.

Oh yes, the classic mating ritual of the bright-eyed, flicky-haired history teacher. No doubt about it, Miss Endell was not-so-secretly smitten with Mr Lewis.

And she wasn't the only one. Amused, Max observed the scene playing out before him. Adolescent girls flitted around Tom Lewis like moths, asking him questions, making jokey comments and generally practising their fledgling flirting skills in the most harmless way, on someone who was attractive but safe.

'Sir? Could you look after my Zen for me?'

The other thing that was interesting was watching the interaction between the—

'Sir?'

'Oh, sorry.' Belatedly Max turned to the left. 'Didn't know you meant me. No one's ever called me sir before. Yes, I'll take care of it.' He slipped the Zen into his jacket pocket. 'But it might be easier if you called me Max.'

'OK, sir – Max.' The girl giggled.

'Now that sounds good. Sir Max. I like it.' He nodded. 'How are you getting on, anyway? Having fun?'

'Oh yes, Paris is dead cool. I liked seeing the Mona Lisa this afternoon. I saw a TV programme about Leonardo da Vinci once and he did so many brilliant things.'

One of the balls of foil had just been kicked under Max's chair. Eddie Marshall-Hicks, deftly hooking it out with his foot, gave a snort and said with derision, 'Leonardo da Vinci was *gay*.'

The girl rolled her eyes. 'Eddie, you are such a div.'

He feigned innocence. 'But he was! I'm just *saying*.'

'That's right. He was a genius,' said Max. 'One of the most multi-talented people who ever lived.'

As Eddie dribbled the makeshift ball back to the game on the pavement, he said under his breath, 'And a shirt-lifter.'

The girl shook her head in disgust. 'Sorry about him, sir . . . Max. He's really immature.'

'You know what? I'd noticed.'

'It was so great, that time when Lou punched him. Anyway, we're not all like Eddie. I think you're OK.'

Max grinned. 'And guess what? You're absolutely right.'

When the girl had rejoined her friends, Tom Lewis raised a hand to stop Josie Endell in mid-flirt and said to Max, 'Are you all right? Want me to have a word with him?'

'No thanks, I'm fine.' Max shook his head briefly and signalled to the pretty waitress for another coffee. Bringing it, her gaze slid with sultry appreciation over the PE teacher's solid, super-trained body. Tom Lewis, wearing an open-necked khaki shirt and black jeans, exuded virility and fitness to a terrifying degree that women clearly found irresistible.

'*Non, merci.*' Tom shook his sleek head when she asked if he'd like anything too, and Josie Endell, possibly without even realising it, gave the waitress a possessive hands-off-he's-mine smile.

Max finished stirring sugar into his coffee. Was it Superman who was the one with the X-ray vision, who could look at people and see right through their clothes? Because this was how he felt right now, being the only one who knew without a shadow of a doubt that Josie was wasting her time.

No two ways about it. Gaydar was a wonderful thing.

Chapter 42

Climbing on to the coach the next morning, Max could almost sympathise with the children. When you were thirteen or fourteen and there was a Disneyland in the vicinity, it wasn't easy to get excited about the fact that you were having to visit the Palace of Versailles instead.

Oh well, that was school trips for you. Whoever said they were supposed to be fun? And this one was about to get worse for Eddie Marshall-Hicks.

'Right, I'm sitting back here today. You,' Max indicated Baz, 'can move up to the front and show Mrs Trent what a charming conversationalist you can be.'

'Eh?' Mouth gormlessly open, Baz gazed up at him.

'And I'm going to sit right here, next to Poison Eddie.'

Eddie bristled. 'What? Why? I don't want you sitting next to me!'

'Sorry, this is your punishment for all those witty comments yesterday. And I'm the parent helper so you have to do as I say.'

The girl from last night, whose name he now knew to be Saskia, crowed, 'Yay, Sir Max! Way to go!'

Baz and Eddie looked at each other in disgust. Like an irritated gorilla, Baz hauled himself out of his seat and clumped up to the front of the coach. Fenella had a treat in store.

Out of the corner of his eye, Max glimpsed Lou's anxious face over the top of the row of seats ahead of him. She could cope with Eddie in her own way but wasn't at all happy about her father – the root of all the trouble – wading in and getting involved.

Max ignored her and sat down. If he'd had a plan to win Eddie round with his warmth, wit and generally irresistible personality, well, he now knew that wasn't going to work. Especially not in three days.

So, Plan B was definitely preferable. But Plan B relied rather heavily on divine intervention, involving as it did some kind of terrible accident requiring Eddie to find himself in mortal danger and Max, swooping heroically to the rescue, to save his life.

And the chances of that happening, it had to be said, were slim.

Which meant he was going to have to go with Plan C. Max wasn't proud of himself, but sometimes you just had to make the best use you could of what you had. The tactics might be underhand, but if they worked, well, who gave a toss?

Eddie, meanwhile, had ostentatiously shifted across in his seat until he was hunched against the window.

'So, looking forward to Versailles?'

Could an eyebrow sneer? Eddie's appeared to be managing it. 'No.'

'It's pretty spectacular, you know.'

'If chandeliers and mirrors and fancy curtains are your thing.' Turning to stare pointedly out of the window, Eddie said, 'They're not mine.'

'Well, that's my job. Did Lou tell you I'm an interior designer?'

Eddie snorted. 'What a surprise.'

'Yes, well. It's not a bad career. You get to meet some interesting people.'

'What, like Lawrence Llewellyn-Bowen?'

Max shrugged and unfolded yesterday's newspaper. As the coach rolled out of the hotel's courtyard he made a start on the crossword.

Twenty silent minutes later, he took out his mobile and rang home.

'Tilly? Hi, sweetheart, it's me. Listen, did the lads finish tiling that bathroom floor last night?'

'They finished at ten o'clock,' said Tilly. 'How's everything going with you?'

'Oh, fine. We're all getting on together really well.' Max grinned. 'Everyone loves me to bits.'

Next to him, Eddie heaved a sigh of you're-so-funny irritation.

'Now I know you're lying,' Tilly said cheerfully.

'Thanks. Anyway, about the bathroom. Jamie's happy with it, is he?' Lowering his voice slightly, Max went on, 'And Tandy?'

Eddie abruptly stopped picking at the loose threads on the knee of his ripped jeans.

'They're over the moon. When Tandy saw it, she cried.'

'Tandy cried? God, that girl's soft in the head. When she sees the bill for the finished job, that's when she'll want to start crying.'

'Except they've covered their costs, remember?'

Max chuckled. 'God bless *Hi!* magazine. Anyway, we'll be at Versailles in a minute, so I'll leave you to it. Give me a call if there are any problems.'

'God, poor you, I can't think of anything more boring.'

Max said, 'I know. Don't tell Jamie, he'll be as sick as a parrot. OK, speak to you later. Bye.'

He put away his phone. Eddie carried on gazing out of the window, his profile as chiselled and perfect as a Rodin statue.

Max returned his attention to the crossword. Bloody stupid crosswords, he hated the damn things. What were they *for*, exactly? What was the point of using up precious brain cells, just so you could fit stupid letters into squares? And speaking of stupid and pointless, was Eddie *ever* going to say anything or was he just going to keep staring out of that damn—

'So, what was that about then?'

Yee-ha! Bait taken!

'Hmm? Sorry?' Max glanced up from the paper, peered at him over the rim of his spectacles. 'Oh, just keeping in touch with my assistant. Making sure the clients are happy.'

'Right.' Eddie gave a dismissive shrug in agreement. But this time you could almost feel the curiosity burning through his Led Zeppelin T-shirt. 'So . . . who are they, then?'

Because that was the great thing about Jamie and Tandy. Their names, together, were recognisable. They were all set to be the new Posh and Becks, the new Wayne and Coleen – well, they were if Tandy got her way.

'I'm not meant to talk about my clients.' Max hesitated then said reluctantly, 'It's just a footballer and his girlfriend.'

Eddie was staring at him now. 'Jamie Michaels and his girl-friend? Serious, is that who you're working for?'

'Sshh. Don't tell everyone.'

'Bloody hell. And you've actually met them? Like, properly?'

'Of course I've met them.'

'But, Jamie Michaels isn't . . . you know, *gay*.'

'No, he isn't.' Max marvelled at the workings of a fourteen-year-old's mind. 'I did his friend's house last year, and his friend recommended me to Jamie and Tandy.'

'Who was his friend?'

'Colin, was it?' Frowning as if trying to remember, Max said, 'No, Cal, that's the one. Cal Cavanagh.'

Eddie sat bolt upright and shouted, 'You are joking! Cal *Cavanagh*!'

'Will you keep your voice down?'

'But . . . but he's, like, the most genius footballer on the planet.'

'Is he? I don't know a lot about football. Lucky old Cal.'

Eddie's eyes narrowed. He was visibly hyperventilating. 'Is this a wind-up?'

Max shrugged and said, 'Why would it be a wind-up?'

Finally convinced, Eddie leaned his head against the padded velour seat back. 'That is so amazing. You have no idea. Cal Cavanagh and Jamie Michaels play for the best team in the world and you actually *know* them. Any minute now, your phone could ring and it could be them on the other end. That's the team I support, you know. Ever since I was a little kid. I was wearing the shirt yesterday.'

Max knew that, although it had taken a while to twig. He hadn't been lying about football not being his thing.

'I can't believe it,' Eddie went on. 'All this time and Lou never said anything.'

'She's not interested in football either.'

'So, Cal Cavanagh. Does he live in, like, a huge mansion?'

Max nodded. 'Pretty huge. Electric gates. Eight bedrooms, nine bathrooms, a snooker room and an indoor pool with the names Cal and Nicole spelled out in gold tiles on the bottom of the pool.' They were reaching the entrance to the park of Versailles now.

'Cal and *Nicole*?' Eddie's eyes widened. 'But they broke up six months ago. He chucked her!'

Max nodded briefly. 'I know. I told him those gold tiles were a mistake.'

On Saturday evening they ate outside in the courtyard of the hotel. An almost-full moon hung in a clear starry sky and the scents of bougainvillea, garlic and Gauloises mingled with those of Year 9, Harleston Hall – a rather less exotic blend of adolescents and overheated trainers.

As the children let off steam, playing pétanque against teams of French teenagers, Max and Fenella Trent sat at a long trestle table with Tom Lewis and Josie Endell. The conversation had been about Versailles for long enough. Topping up his and Josie's wine glasses, Max had finally managed to swing it around – via Sophia Coppola's lush version of *Marie Antoinette* – to favourite films.

'*It's a Wonderful Life*!' Fenella's glossy hair swung from side to side as she excitedly clapped her hands. Bloody hell, and she was only on orange juice. 'Ooh, *Follow the Fleet*! Or *Top Hat*! Anything with Fred Astaire and Ginger Rogers!' Clasping her chest in ecstasy, she cried, 'I could watch them *forever*.'

Blimey, how old was she? Ninety?

'I won't be inviting you out to the pictures, then.' In his easy, laconic way, Tom Lewis leaned back on his chair and counted off on his fingers. 'OK, top three. *Terminator. Gladiator. Rambo*.'

Josie Endell gave him a playful thump on the arm. 'You and your testosterone. Honestly, you are such a *boy*.'

For a split second Max caught Tom's eye and something unspoken passed between them. Tom knew that he knew. The silent acknowledgement was there. Then the moment passed and Tom shrugged. 'What's wrong with that? They're the kind of films I like to watch.'

'Audrey Hepburn!' squealed Fenella.

Max kept a straight face. 'Was she in *Rambo*?'

'No, silly! *Breakfast at Tiffany's*!'

Josie said comfortably, 'Boys like boys' films, girls go for girly ones. My favourites are *Love, Actually* and *When Harry Met Sally*. Can't beat a good old romantic comedy.' Dimpling, she addressed Tom. 'And I bet Claudine's the same, isn't she?'

Claudine, that was it. Max recalled Lou telling him about Mr Lewis's seriously attractive girlfriend. The question was, did Claudine know her boyfriend was gay?

'God, yes, all that girly stuff.' Tom took a glug of lager and wiped the condensation from his hand on to his jeans. 'She watches her films while I'm out training. I watch mine while she's buying handbags or getting her hair done. There's only one film we both like, and that's *The Great Escape*.' He looked at Max and said cheerfully, 'How about you?'

'Well, I'm afraid I'm a bit of a purist when it comes to the cinema. Black and white with subtitles for me. Fassbinder,' said Max. 'Wenders, Almodóvar, Truffaut.' He paused, nodding in a thoughtful, intellectual way. 'But I suppose if I'm forced to narrow it down, I'd have to say my top three would be *Borat*, *Mr Bean* and *ET*.'

Tom grinned. Josie clutched at Tom's wrist and shrieked with laughter. Eddie and Baz, who had been hovering a short distance away, moved closer. Fenella gave Max a sympathetic look. 'And they're all outsiders seeking acceptance, aren't they? Is that why they're your favourite films, because you identify with the lead characters?'

'No, they're my favourite films because they make me laugh,' said Max. 'Same as you liking *Breakfast at Tiffany's* doesn't mean you secretly want to become a prostitute.'

Sniggering under their breath, Eddie and Baz casually pulled up a couple of chairs and joined them at the table. '*Mr Bean*'s funny,' Eddie ventured. 'He's hilarious. Have you seen the one where he's a spy?'

'I like that one too.' Max nodded.

Baz said eagerly, 'And *Alien*, sir? Where they're on a space-ship in outer space and this, like, *alien* bursts out of this guy's stomach?'

'Goodness me!' Clearly shocked, Fenella said, 'I can't believe your parents allow you to watch films like that.'

Eddie said defensively, 'It's brilliant.'

'The sequel's even better,' said Max.

'Well, *really*,' Fenella huffed.

'They're fourteen years old,' Max told her. 'Kids these days watch this stuff.'

'My Sophie doesn't! I don't let her! We only watch educational programmes on TV.'

Which could go some way towards explaining why prim, cosseted little Sophie always seemed to be hovering miserably on the sidelines watching the rest of the children having fun. Heroically Max didn't say this aloud. Instead, turning back to Eddie and Baz, he said, 'How about Bruce Lee? Ever seen any of his films?'

'Yeah! Bruce Lee, brilliant!' Eddie struck a pose and began to yowl like a cat.

'I've got all of them on DVD. In fact, *Enter the Dragon* may have to go into my all-time top three.'

'Three's not going to be enough.' Tom shook his head. 'We haven't even started on James Bond yet.'

'James Bond's all right.' Max intercepted Eddie's grimace. 'But I prefer *Shrek*.'

298

'*Shrek is* cool.' Vigorously nodding in agreement, Eddie said, 'Uh, sir? You know you know footballers? Well, do you know any, like, famous film stars as well?'

Max glanced across the table at Tom. There it was again, that complicit flicker of connection. He thought for a moment then shrugged. 'I suppose maybe one or two.'

Chapter 43

'Oooh, I need a wee, I'm *scared*.' Kaye was bleating with fear as they pulled up in the taxi outside the hotel.

Tilly didn't blame her. If she was the one being auctioned off for charity she'd be petrified. But, since this was what friends were for, she said consolingly, 'It'll be great, everyone'll be bidding for you. Dorothy won't let them *not* bid.'

'Yeah, right.' Kaye remained unconvinced. 'It's going to be embarrassing. God, why couldn't I be Beyoncé or Helen Mirren or someone men drool over?'

'Hey, relax. We're just going to have fun.' Bundling her out of the cab, Tilly said, 'And it's all in a good cause, isn't it? Even if you only raise fifty quid for the charity, that's still fifty quid more than they'd have had without you.'

Kaye let out a wail of anguish. 'Fifty quid!'

'OK, that was just an example. You'll get loads more than that, you know you will.'

'But that's the thing, I *don't* know. Oh God, at this rate I'm going to be bidding for myself.'

Inside the hotel, the buzzy atmosphere embraced them. Vaguely familiar faces from the ball were dotted around. Tilly spotted

Dorothy and Harold, and carted Kaye over to them. Having greeted her effusively, they then dragged Kaye off – looking like a baby seal about to be clubbed to death – to meet and greet potential bidders.

Poor Kaye.

'She'll be all right,' said a voice behind her.

Tilly's heart did a dolphin leap in her chest. Turning, she stopped feeling sorry for Kaye and felt sorry for herself instead. She'd known Jack would be here tonight, had been bracing herself for the moment when she'd see him again, and he'd still managed to catch her off guard.

Jack was in the business of breaking hearts. He was damaged, scarred by grief and incapable of giving himself fully to anyone. Irresistible he might be, but she'd made her decision. She was going to resist him because it was the only way. The irony of the situation didn't escape her; never having been able to bring herself to reject anyone once she'd gone off them, she had been forced to reject Jack, who'd meant more to her than any man before.

Still, that was self-preservation for you. It might hurt like hell but it was undoubtedly the right thing to do. Jack Lucas wasn't someone you could trust, he was anti-commitment, he was trouble in every way you could think of.

And if you needed any more evidence of that, well, just look at Amy.

If he could wear a bell around his neck, that would be a big help too.

And now he was waiting for her to say something. Damn, what was it they'd been talking about? Oh yes, Kaye.

'She's terrified,' said Tilly.

'Watch her.' Moving to her side, Jack nodded over as Dorothy

Summerskill began introducing Kaye to a boisterous group of men. 'She'll click into actress mode any second now. Ha, there, see it?'

And he was right. Kaye had pressed the switch and metaphorically lit up. To the casual onlooker she was confident, dazzling, completely at ease as she laughed and chatted and effortlessly won over a group of complete strangers.

'Neat trick,' Tilly marvelled. 'And inside, she's jelly.'

'It's called putting on a front.'

Tilly swallowed. What did he think she was doing right now? She summoned a breezy smile. 'Don't tell me you're here on your own tonight.'

Jack shook his head. 'My partner's been held up. She'll be along later. See the big guy with the white hair?' He indicated the men clustered around Kaye. 'That's Mitchell Masters. He owns half the nightclubs this side of London. Seriously loaded.'

Maybe, but he still had a Santa-sized stomach. Without thinking, Tilly said jokily, 'He looks a bit pregnant.'

Oops.

'Don't worry.' Jack sounded amused. 'I'm sure he isn't.'

He took a swallow of his drink, seemingly unconcerned by her faux pas. Did he think she hadn't heard the news? Oh help, now she'd started she couldn't stop. Tilly blurted out, 'So, what's happening with Amy, then?'

Jack surveyed her steadily. 'Now I hear she *is* pregnant.'

'And have you talked to her?'

He shrugged. 'No.'

'But you could be the father!' Baffled by his not-my-problem attitude, Tilly's voice inadvertently rose. 'She's twelve weeks pregnant! That's when you slept with her. What if she's having your baby?'

A passing couple turned to look at them. Jack murmured, 'Sure you don't want a megaphone?'

Oh God, she was turning into a shrew. With an effort Tilly controlled herself. 'But she could be. Doesn't that even bother you?'

Jack certainly didn't look bothered. 'I hear she slept with a couple of other guys too. I doubt the baby's mine.'

How could he *be* like this?

'You mean you used contraception so you think you're out of the frame? Nothing's one hundred per cent effective,' said Tilly. 'Except castration.'

He looked amused. 'Ouch.'

'It's not *funny*,' she protested. 'What'll you do if it does turn out to be yours? Will you marry Amy?'

Jack tilted an eyebrow. 'I think we can safely say no to that question.'

'Will you live with her?'

He shook his head.

Did he not realise how upsetting she found his attitude? If she'd been the one in Amy's position, he'd be rejecting *her* now. In desperation, Tilly said, 'Will you even *see* the baby?'

Jack raised his hands. 'Do you seriously think I'm that much of a bastard? Because I'm really not. OK, I'll make you a promise. If it turns out that I'm the father, I will absolutely see the baby and support it financially. Scout's honour.'

As if that was all that mattered. Still upset, Tilly said, 'Money isn't everything.'

Jack grinned. 'If you asked Kaye that question right now, I think you'd find she might disagree.'

The main business of the evening got started after dinner. It was a jolly, unstuffy affair, accompanied by much cajoling, blackmail

303

and laughter. The first, smaller items up for auction were an eclectic bunch – dinner for six at an Indian restaurant, a signed football shirt, a hand-knitted sweater featuring the cartoon character of your choice.

'Come on, Mitchell, show us what you're made of!' Dorothy Summerskill, up on the stage with the auctioneer, was in full flow.

Mitchell Masters obediently sat back and stuck his hand in the air, bidding two hundred pounds and securing the item in question. When he discovered he'd just acquired a month's membership of a health and fitness club, he let out a shout of dismay and had to knock back a double brandy to get over the terrible shock.

But meanness clearly wasn't one of his faults. Minutes later he was off again, bidding generously for salsa lessons.

'And you could do with them too,' Dorothy heckled from the stage. 'Don't forget, we've all witnessed your so-called dancing skills.'

'The cheek of it, woman. I'll have you know my hokey-cokey's second to none.'

'Oh God,' Kaye whispered to Tilly when he won the salsa lessons. 'Can't he stop spending his money now? He won't have any left for me.'

The next few lots were auctioned. Kaye grew more and more jittery. Tilly had just popped an after-dinner mint into her mouth when Jack appeared at their table.

'How are you doing?' He rested a hand on Kaye's bare shoulder, causing Tilly's skin to tingle as she envisaged how it felt.

'I may look calm from the waist up. But under this table I'm digging an escape tunnel.'

He gave her shoulder a consoling squeeze. 'Max just called from France. He's told me to bid for you if no one else does.'

Kaye said gloomily, 'Better than nothing, I suppose.'

'Hey, you'll be fine. I'd have done it anyway. Jesus, what was *that*?'

The loud CRAACK was Tilly's after-dinner mint breaking in half as she bit down on it. 'Nothing, just my mint. Did your guest turn up?'

'Oh yes, she's here. Why, were you worried about me?' Amused, Jack said, 'Did you think I might have been stood up?'

Tilly turned away, kicking herself for having asked. Even more annoyingly, when Jack returned to his own table at the very back of the room, she discovered it was impossible to see who this evening's companion was. Unless she clambered on to a chair and peered over everyone's heads, and he'd be bound to spot her doing that.

'Oh God, please don't let this happen to me,' squeaked Kaye as, up on the stage, the auctioneer struggled to get a starting bid for lunch with a local author. The poor author, blinking like an owl in her droopy purple dress, was looking petrified.

'Come along, ladies and gentlemen, this is your chance to meet a real live author in the flesh! Marjorie's written a wonderful book about old English churchyards! She'll even throw in a signed copy! Now then, who'll offer me thirty pounds?'

Clearly unable to bear another moment of the woman's agony, Kaye yelled out, 'Me!'

Tilly's mouth was dry. Thirty pounds, that was just too tragic. It looked like a pity bid. If nobody else joined in, the poor woman would feel totally humiliated.

'We have a bid of thirty pounds.' The auctioneer looked relieved but still not happy. 'Do I hear forty?'

Oh hell. Tilly stuck her hand in the air. The look of abject relief and gratitude on Marjorie's face was worth it.

Chapter 44

'Here we go,' crowed the auctioneer. 'Well done to the lady at the front in pink. Great start. Now, do I hear fifty?'

'Yep.' A male voice at the back of the room. Possibly belonging to Jack.

'Excellent! Sixty?'

Tilly found herself nodding rapidly. For some reason she couldn't begin to explain, it suddenly seemed vital to win something away from Jack, who made such a point of always getting whatever he wanted.

'Sixty I have. Seventy?'

'Yes.' It was definitely Jack; all the little hairs on the back of her arms had gone up in recognition.

'Eighty?'

'*Yes!*'

'Ninety?' The auctioneer was on a roll now.

Pause. Jack drawled, 'Yep.'

'One *hundred*.' Triumphantly the auctioneer turned his attention back to Tilly. 'Do I hear one hundred pounds?'

Tilly began to hyperventilate; one hundred pounds was actually a lot of money, especially when it was your own. Her heart might be hell bent on beating Jack but her head was having a complete panic attack. What was she thinking of?

Nothing that made any sense, that was for sure. Having absolutely intended to shake her head and concede defeat, she found herself nodding it instead.

'One hundred pounds,' the auctioneer bellowed in triumph. 'Excellent!'

Oh, for crying out loud, what had she done? This was ridiculous. She really couldn't afford that much. If Jack didn't make another bid, she was going to have to write out a cheque that would actually send her overdrawn—

'Two hundred pounds.' Jack's voice carried all the way from the back of the room, his exasperation plain for all to hear.

Oh, thank God for that. Tilly felt like a landed fish miraculously unhooked and set free. She shook her head at the auctioneer, took a gulp of wine and exhaled with relief. If Jack needed to win that badly, he was welcome to it.

There were no further bids. With Marjorie by this time practically weeping with relief, the auctioneer tapped his gavel and moved on to Lot 15.

'Oh God, it's me after this.' Pushing back her chair, Kaye said, 'I need another wee.'

As soon as she'd left, Jack appeared and slid on to the empty chair. 'Thanks a lot.'

'What?' Indignantly Tilly said, 'You won it, didn't you? You got what you wanted.'

'I was trying to help you out. Why did you bid?'

'Because I felt sorry for the woman!'

'And could you afford forty pounds?'

'Not really.'

'Exactly. So my bid was to get you off the hook.' Jack shook his head. 'You weren't supposed to keep going.'

'Oh.' Realisation dawned. 'Bum. I thought you just wanted to beat me.'

'I did. But in a good way, because Max happened to mention on the phone that you're broke. I was trying to help you out.'

'Right. Sorry.' And she'd ended up costing him two hundred pounds.

'I can't believe you kept going up,' said Jack.

'I didn't want you to win.'

'Well, you owe me.' He tapped the back of her hand. 'In fact, you can do me a favour.'

The possibilities were endless. Tilly eyed him warily. 'What kind of favour?'

'Go out to lunch with the author.'

'That's really kind of you. But I couldn't possibly.'

'Why not?'

'I don't want to! She wrote a book about English churchyards! I'd die of boredom.'

'But I don't want to have lunch with her either,' said Jack.

'Too bad. You bid for her and you won.'

'But—'

'It's your own fault. You can't back out now. Oh look, she's so thrilled. She's waving at you!'

'Who's waving at him?' Back from the loo, Kaye prodded Jack out of her seat.

'Marjorie. Over at the side of the stage.' Tilly nodded and they watched the elderly lady author gesticulating wildly and blowing ecstatic kisses at Jack.

'You've pulled,' said Kaye.

'Hmm, looks as if I'm going to get my money's worth.' He winked at them both. 'Better get back to my table before my date gets jealous.'

Tilly couldn't help herself. 'And when you do go out to lunch with Mrs Churchyard, try not to get her pregnant.'

'I'll do my best,' said Jack.

The next lot was sold, then it was Kaye's turn. Dorothy gave her the most tremendous build-up then invited her on to the stage and led the applause. A couple of tables away from Tilly, Mitchell Masters stuck his sausagey fingers into his mouth and gave an ear-splitting wolf-whistle. This was promising. From the stage, Kaye shot him a grateful smile.

Behind Tilly, a woman grumbled, 'Kaye who? I've never heard of her.' Which made Tilly itch to throw a coffee spoon at her head, but she controlled herself and just applauded extra loudly instead.

Again Kaye hid her nervousness as the auctioneer launched into his spiel. Thankfully there was no tumbleweed moment this time before bidding got started. Mitchell Masters kicked off proceedings, a couple of other people joined in, then at three hundred pounds Tilly heard Jack make his bid from the back of the room.

'Four hundred!' cried Mitchell.

Tilly relaxed. There, Kaye could stop worrying now. Four hundred pounds was a perfectly respectable amount; she wasn't going to be publicly humiliated and laughed off the stage.

'Five? Do we have five hundred? *Yes*,' cried the auctioneer, pointing to the back of the room. 'Thank you, sir. We have five hundred pounds.'

Blimey, Jack was giving it some, clearly intent on boosting Mitchell's bid.

'Six,' bellowed Mitchell.

'Seven at the back,' confirmed the auctioneer as people began to whoop with delight.

'And she's worth every penny,' Dorothy chimed in.

'Eight.' Mitchell paused then shook his head and yelled, 'No, dammit! Make it a thousand!'

Tilly exhaled. You had to admire Jack's nerve. He had achieved what he'd set out to do. Now he could relax and—

'Twelve hundred,' announced the auctioneer, pointing his gavel at Jack.

'Fifteen hundred,' roared Mitchell.

'Eighteen,' countered the auctioneer.

Gordon Bennett, what was Jack playing at? Up on the stage, Kaye was visibly stunned. Unable to contain herself, Tilly jumped up and peered over the heads of the applauding diners. She located Jack just as Mitchell said loudly, 'Two grand!'

Jack spotted her looking at him. From the stage, the auctioneer was saying, 'Gentleman at the back? Do I have two thousand two hundred?'

Tilly gazed in disbelief at Jack. Jack shrugged in return, signalling bafflement. Then she saw an elderly man standing behind him nod and raise a gnarled hand at the auctioneer. The man was in his eighties, clutching a can of beer, wearing a baggy grey cardigan and a pair of slippers. Oh God, no wonder Kaye was looking appalled. Who the hell was he? What if he were some drink-addled homeless guy who'd happened to wander in off the street?

'Two thousand two hundred!'

'Two five,' bellowed Mitchell, who clearly hated to be outdone.

'Three thousand pounds!'

'Four!'

'Five thousand!' roared the auctioneer. 'We have five thousand pounds at the back of the room!'

'Oh, sod it.' Mitchell shook his head, heaved a sigh and knocked back the contents of his refilled brandy glass. 'I give up. I'm out.'

And that was it. Ancient cardigan man had won. Everyone in the room cheered and applauded wildly, and Tilly expected the victor to make his way on to the stage to be introduced to Kaye.

Instead, following a brief exchange with one of the organisers, he slid out through the double doors and disappeared. The organiser came to the front and spoke to Kaye and Dorothy. Moments later, Kaye rejoined Tilly at their table.

'Oh my God!' Tilly topped up both their glasses. 'Who was he? Was he just mucking around? Where's he *gone*?'

'OK, the woman who owns this hotel? He's her dad.'

'He's ancient! Oh well, at least you know he won't make a pass at you.' Tilly had a horrible thought. 'At least you hope he won't.'

'He's not the one I'll be going out with. He was just bidding on behalf of someone else.'

'Seriously? Who?'

Kaye was still trembling and hyperventilating from the ordeal. 'Someone who couldn't be here tonight.'

'No!' Tilly was stunned. 'Max bid five thousand pounds?'

'Someone who couldn't be here tonight because he lives in New York. His name's Price,' said Kaye. 'Parker Price.'

Hang on. That name rang a distant bell. Price . . . Price . . .

'Oh my God!' Tilly jerked upright and slopped wine down her front. 'The stalker!'

Numbly Kaye nodded. 'I know.'

'Who is he?' Jack had reappeared with his guest in tow. It was Monica, her sparkly turquoise eyeshadow exactly matching her Mae West-style Spandex dress.

'The chap who's been sending her stuff.' Tilly shook her head

311

at Kaye. 'Well, he can't expect you to fly over to New York to have dinner with him. That's just stupid.'

'He doesn't. He'll come over here. We just have to fix a date.'

'But . . . but he's your stalker! He could be deranged! No, no.' Vigorously Tilly shook her head. 'You can't meet him.'

'I have to. He's paid all that money. I still can't believe he found out about this thing here tonight . . . it's just so bizarre . . .'

'It was advertised on the internet, wasn't it?' Ever-practical Monica in her throaty, sexy voice said, 'He'll have had your name on Google Alert, love. They can track your every move.'

Jack frowned. 'Did you write and thank him for that painting he sent you?'

'Of course I did. I was really polite and grateful. But I swear I didn't encourage him.' Kaye twisted her fingers in agitation. 'I never imagined for a second that he'd go and do something like this.'

'Don't take this the wrong way, love. But you want to be careful,' said Monica. 'He's paying five grand to go out with you. If you ask me, that means he's got to be some kind of maniac.'

Chapter 45

It was now eleven fifteen and Lou couldn't sleep. Everyone had been sent up to their rooms at ten thirty but the adults had stayed downstairs in the bar. Making up her mind, she crept out of bed so as not to wake Nesh, quickly pulled on a T-shirt and jeans and quietly let herself out of the room.

The bar downstairs was still busy but she couldn't see Max anywhere. Or Mr Lewis. Only Miss Endell and Mrs Trent were still there, sitting at a small table being chatted up by a couple of middle-aged Frenchmen. Which was totally gross for a start. Miss Endell looked as if she was enjoying herself while Mrs Trent was clutching her orange juice tightly to her chest. Wondering if her father and Mr Lewis might have gone out to another bar, Lou hovered in the doorway for a few seconds then made her way over to the table.

'. . . Gosh no, they're not our husbands, heaven forbid!' Sophie Trent's mother sounded scandalised at the very idea. 'We're just here on a school trip. I'm a parent helper! The one with the glasses is *gay*!'

'And I'm not married to the other one. Yet.' Giggling and clearly having sunk a fair few glasses of wine, Miss Endell winked –

yeurch, actually *winked* – at the Frenchmen. 'But I'm working on it! He's got a girlfriend at the moment, but I reckon I can see her off, no problem!'

Which was hilarious and *so* not going to happen, seeing as Mr Lewis's girlfriend Claudine was way prettier than Miss Endell.

'Ahem.' Spotting Lou, Mrs Trent coughed and said loudly, 'Hello, Louisa, you should be upstairs asleep.'

Lou kept a straight face. Ha, how embarrassing for Miss Endell was this?

'Sorry, I wanted to talk to my dad. I thought he'd be in here with you.'

Miss Endell fumbled to do up the button that had mysteriously come unfastened on her shirt.

'He went upstairs . . . ooh, about twenty minutes ago. With Mr Lewis,' said Mrs Trent. 'They were both tired. I expect your father's fast asleep by now. As should you be, my girl.'

As should you be. Seriously, only Mrs Trent could come out with a sentence like that. And she was wagging a finger at her as if she was six.

'OK, I'll go up.' Lou thanked her lucky stars she wasn't Mrs Trent's daughter.

'Straight to bed now.' Wine might be spilling out of Miss Endell's tilted glass but she was enunciating with care. 'Straight to sleep. See you in the morning.'

'Yes, miss.' Except I won't have a stonking hangover, Lou thought gleefully, and you will.

Anyway, of course her dad wouldn't be asleep. It was only half past eleven and he never went to bed before midnight. Heading back upstairs, Lou reached the third floor and made her way along the silent, thickly carpeted corridor. She counted the doors on the left. Room 303, that was Mr Lewis's. Next was 305, Miss

Endell's. Then 307, lucky enough to be occupied by Mrs Trent. Finally she came to 309, her dad's room.

Lou knocked on the door. She had to see him.

No reply. Surely he hadn't fallen asleep so early? She tried knocking again. 'Dad? It's me.'

Finally the door opened. Max said, 'Hi, sweetie, what's up? Everything all right?'

'Fine, thanks.' Lou followed him into the bedroom. Her dad finished brushing his teeth in the bathroom then came back through. He'd been reading in bed. She picked up the battered paperback and said, 'This any good?'

'A damn sight better than sitting downstairs in the bar with Fenella and Josie.' He shuddered as he climbed back under the covers. 'I had to get out of there.'

'I know, I just saw them. Miss Endell's getting trolleyed and chatting up Frenchmen. But that's not why I'm here.' Lou bounced on to the bed on her knees.

'Ouch! Don't tell me, you're here to shatter all the bones in my foot.'

'Wimp. Eddie caught up with me on the stairs as we were coming up to bed.'

Max eyed her carefully. 'And?'

'He gave me a little shove in the back. Just like old times. So I swung round to give him an earful and push him down the stairs, but he dodged out of the way.'

'That little shit,' seethed Max.

'Hang on, and then he said, "Hey, give me a break, I was only going to say something." So I said, "What, twerp-head?" And he looked at me as if he was really offended, and said, "I just wanted to tell you that I've been talking to your old man. Quite a lot, actually. You know what? Your dad's pretty cool."'

Max adjusted his spectacles. 'He said that?'

'He really did.' Breaking into a grin, Lou lunged forward and gave him a hug. 'Honestly, you have no idea. It's like P Diddy saying he loves . . . God, I don't know, Dot Cotton!'

'Oh great. So now you're comparing me with a chain-smoking, raddled old bat.'

'You know what I mean. I couldn't believe I was hearing it. He said you were a good laugh too.'

'Damn cheek. I *am* a good laugh.'

'Anyway, he likes you.'

'That's because I'm very likeable,' said Max.

'Hmm. The funny thing is, he seems to think you're best friends with all sorts of famous people.'

'Cal Cavanagh. Jamie and Tandy.' Her father shrugged modestly.

Lou raised an eyebrow. 'Not to mention Johnny Depp.'

He tweaked a strand of her hair. 'Probably best not to mention Johnny Depp then.'

'Dad! You *lied*. That's naughty!'

'Hey, so what?' Flashing his unrepentant smile, Max said, 'How's he ever going to find out? If the kid's shallow enough to be impressed by something like that, I'm shallow enough to say it.'

The coach rumbled back up the driveway of Harleston Hall at ten o'clock on Sunday night. Forty exhausted but happy children piled off to be met by their parents. In the darkness everyone milled around waiting for their cases to be unloaded. Max, helping to lift them out of the luggage compartments, found his own and passed it to Lou.

'Here.' He chucked her the car keys; she was shattered and it was starting to rain. 'Put mine in the boot and wait in the car. We'll soon be done here.'

316

Lou nodded, yawned widely and wandered off into the darkness, the case on wheels trundling along behind her. Next to Max, Tom Lewis hauled out a dark green case and said, 'She'll be asleep before you get home.'

'That one's mine.' Eddie squeezed past Tom and reached for the green case. 'Thanks, sir.' Then, turning, he said, 'Bye, Max. See you. Good trip, wasn't it?'

Max nodded, straight-faced. 'Great trip. Bye, Eddie.'

'And if you ever need a hand with . . . you know, if you're really busy on a job and you could do with someone to help out, give me a call.'

Max said gravely, 'Thanks, I'll remember that. Is your lift here?'

'Yep.' Pleased with himself, Eddie extended the handle on his case and carted it off.

'Well done.' Tom Lewis smiled slightly. 'You did it.'

'I cheated.' Max slid out a blue case with silver tinsel wrapped around the handle and glanced after Eddie. The boy had now reached a gleaming Mercedes and was being hugged by his mother while his father manhandled the case into the boot of the car.

'Oh well. If it does the trick.' Tom frowned at a black Nike rucksack. 'This one doesn't have a name tag on it.'

One of the girls hovering next to the pile of offloaded cases said, 'That's Eddie's bag. Sir, can you reach mine for me? It's that tartan one right at the back.'

'I'll see if I can catch him.' Grabbing the rucksack, Max started across the car park. The Mercedes had been fired up and its headlights were on, but he saw Eddie spot him from the back seat. Next moment, the driver's door opened and the boy's father strode over to meet him.

'Hi there. Thanks so much. Ted Marshall-Hicks.' The tone was jovial, the handshake very firm. Eddie's father had a clipped, upper-class voice and an impressive moustache. 'We've just been hearing all about you! Your daughter was the one who blacked my son's eye, I gather.'

Max nodded in agreement. 'That's my girl.'

'Good for her, eh? Never does a lad any harm to be taught a lesson by a member of the opposite sex.' He took the Nike bag from Max and went on cheerily, 'Anyway, all over now. Sounds like my boy's seen the error of his ways. All part of growing up, hmm?'

'I'm sure,' said Max.

'Good man. And in case you were wondering, he didn't get his former views from me, oh no.' Ted Marshall-Hicks shook his head like a great bear then lowered his voice a notch. 'Of course, got the wife and kids now, but back in my boarding school days, all boys together, we did our share of experimenting! Lots of fun after lights out, know what I mean? Happy days! Anyhow, best get off home now. Good to meet you.' He shook Max's hand again with burly enthusiasm, then turned and strode back to his car.

In the back seat, Eddie waved at him.

Max automatically raised a hand in return as the Mercedes moved off down the drive.

Well, well. Max smiled slightly as he made his way back to the coach. Talk about getting things arse-backwards. During his own schooldays he'd done all his experimenting with girls.

Chapter 46

The moment Tilly clapped eyes on Max on Wednesday morning, she knew what it was.

As a rule he was up disgustingly early, showered and immaculately dressed and ready to go. Today, coming downstairs in his towelling robe, he looked as if he'd been on a bender for a week.

Although if she were to say that aloud . . . well, she might choose to phrase it differently.

'I hate to say I told you so,' Tilly lied.

He shuffled across to the nearest chair and sat down with a groan. 'But you're going to.'

'But it's your own fault! I can't believe you thought it wouldn't happen!' Tilly softened. 'Oh God, you look awful. Is it really bad?'

Max nodded, his skin green-tinged and pallid. 'I'm going to sue that bloody takeaway.'

'Well, you can't do that. It's not their fault you left it out all night and finished it up the next morning.'

'I don't like to see food going to waste. And it tasted all right.' He heaved a sigh and clutched his stomach. 'God, my muscles hurt. Do you know how many times I've thrown up?'

'I don't *want* to know, thanks. I'm just wondering how we're going to manage today. I can't do Jamie and Tandy's on my own.'

'I know, I know. You take Lou to school and I'll sort something out.' Max reached across the kitchen table for his mobile and rose wearily to his feet.

Right on cue, Lou burst into the kitchen and recoiled at the sight of him. 'Eeuw, Dad, you're all green!'

'I love you too.'

'Is this the Szechuan chicken?'

Max nodded. 'Possibly.'

'Oh Daddy, poor you! But we did say it'd make you ill.'

'Yes. Thanks for pointing that out. Again.'

'And you did keep saying it'd be fine. That means we were right,' Lou persisted, 'and you were wrong.'

'You know what?' Max aimed a feeble swipe at her and missed. 'I could always have you adopted.'

By the time Tilly returned from dropping Lou at school, Max had made the necessary arrangements.

'The schedule's too tight to cancel. So I gave Jack a call. He's on his way over.'

Just what she needed. Now Max wasn't the only one feeling sick. But under the circumstances she didn't have a lot of choice.

Jack arrived ten minutes later. Max opened his design portfolio and ran through the list of jobs needing to be completed.

'No problem. We'll take care of that.' Having checked through the detailed plans, Jack tucked the portfolio under one arm.

'Thanks,' Max croaked.

'I like coming to the rescue, saving the day.'

'Yeah, right. You just want to have a nose around Jamie Michaels' house.'

Jack grinned. 'That too. Do you know, you're actually turning greener.'

'Oh Christ, here we go again.' Shooing them out, Max said with a groan, 'Bugger off, both of you. Leave me to be ill in peace.'

As they were loading everything they needed into the back of Jack's van, his phone rang. Tilly was forced to stand by and listen as some female did her best to persuade him to go out with her tomorrow night. Gently but firmly, Jack turned her down.

'See?' He put the phone back in his pocket, his tone self-mocking. 'I can say no when I want to.'

'It's a miracle.'

'And how about last Saturday night? Admit it,' Jack went on, 'you were expecting me to turn up with someone a bit different, weren't you? But I didn't. Monica said it sounded like a fun night so I invited her along, and we—'

'Actually, can we not do this?' Stepping back, Tilly held up her hands. 'We have to work together for today and that's fine, but could we please stick to talking about work, because I really really don't want to hear about your social life.'

'But—'

'No, I mean it. Sorry.' She smiled apologetically to soften the blow. 'But you have to promise, or I'm not getting in the van.'

Taken aback, Jack said, 'Not even—'

'Not even nothing. I'm serious.' Tilly stood her ground, nodding slightly to show she meant business. She *did* mean business; being in his company was hard enough without having to worry about him getting personal.

Jack gazed at her for several seconds. She didn't flinch. Finally he shrugged and said, 'Fine.'

★   ★   ★

The first sign that something was up was the level of activity outside the front gates.

'Are there usually this many paparazzi?' said Jack as they steered their way past the assembled throng.

'No.' Recognising Tilly and the van, the security guard opened the gates and let them through.

'Hi there! What's going on today then?' Tilly asked chattily when Tandy opened the door. Then she saw Tandy's swollen, pink-rimmed eyelids and clapped a hand to her mouth. 'Oh my God, what's *happened*?'

'The engagement's off. Jamie's been shagging some hideous slapper. Come on in.' Tandy gazed dully past her at Jack, busy unloading the platinum-plated wall sculptures from the back of the van. 'Who's that?'

'Jack Lucas. Max has food poisoning. God, I can't believe that about Jamie. Is he here?'

Miserably, Tandy shook her head. Fresh tears sprang out. 'He left last night. I said I never wanted to see him again. I can't believe you didn't know. Cup of tea?'

Tilly followed her into the vast kitchen where the central island was awash with today's newspapers. Tandy's face, happy and smiling, beamed up from each of them. The real Tandy, tiny and make-up free, huddled inside her fluorescent pink sweatshirt and wiped her face with an overlong sleeve.

'Oh, look at you.' Desperately sorry for her, Tilly enveloped her in a hug. 'What a bastard. You don't deserve this.'

'I know. And she's, like, not even pretty, that's the thing. Just some desperate little tart who works as a pole-dancer and thinks she's so great. It's just . . . oh God, it's so *humiliating*.'

Tilly patted her birdlike shoulders. And to think she'd envied Tandy for having managed to meet and fall in love with Jamie.

322

At just nineteen, she'd been living what she'd thought was her dream, and now it was all over.

'How could he *dooo* this to *meee*?' Tandy wailed. 'I just want to *screeeeam*!'

Ouch. Bit close to the eardrum, that.

'Of course you do.' Tilly inched away, aware of Jack waiting in the doorway. Turning, she said, 'The wall sculptures are for the master bedroom. Turn left at the top of the stairs and it's the fourth door on the right.'

'Hi. Sorry to hear about Jamie.' Addressing Tandy, Jack said, 'Does this mean the party on Friday is cancelled?'

God, talk about insensitive. Tilly glared at him in disbelief; as if the party was any of his concern anyway.

'Of course it's cancelled.' Tandy eyed him stonily. 'It was going to be an engagement party.' She held up her left hand, bereft of rings. 'And I'm not engaged any more, am I?'

Definitely no party then. Tilly felt sorry for Tandy but also a teeny bit sorry for herself. So much for buying that new dress, doing herself up to the nines and mingling with celebrities; her one and only chance to appear in *Hi!* was now well and truly scuppered.

Jack, meanwhile, was shaking his head. 'So . . . excuse me, but Max did mention that a magazine was buying the rights to the party, and that the payment for that was covering Max's bill.'

'Riiiight.' Tandy nodded slowly.

'So no party means no money from the magazine. Now I really don't mean to be rude,' said Jack, 'but could that cause a problem?'

Tilly winced. She hadn't thought of that.

'The party's cancelled.' Tandy lifted her tiny pointed chin. 'But I'm still doing sixteen pages for the magazine, so don't worry about Max getting paid. In fact my agent's negotiated an increase in my fee.'

Tilly was taken aback. 'What, just for photos of the house?'

The look Tandy gave her was filled with pity. She held up a skinny hand and began counting off on her fingers.

'For a start, it'll be an exclusive. My heartbreak at Jamie's betrayal. I thought we were so happy together, living the fairytale dream, but now he's done this terrible thing and I'm *grief-stricken* and *devastated*.' She paused, thinking for a moment. 'And I thought I was pregnant and I was so happy because all we ever wanted was a baby, but when I found out about this other girl I had a tragic miscarriage.'

'Hang on.' Stunned, Tilly said, 'You had a miscarriage *yesterday*? Shouldn't you be in hospital?'

'Why?'

'Because after a miscarriage, don't women have to have a D&C?'

Defensively Tandy said, 'I thought I *might* have been pregnant. My period was a day late. Anyhow, I'm never going to get over it. And this all happened after I'd worked so hard to create our dream home, so they'll take loads of photos of me around the house. So it all still has to be perfect.'

'In that case, we'd better get on with what we came here to do.' Jack hefted the wall sculptures into his arms and headed up the stairs.

When he was out of earshot, Tilly said consolingly, 'I know it feels like the end of the world now, but you'll get over this, I promise. You'll meet someone else and be happy again.'

'I won't.' Vehemently Tandy shook her head.

'You *will*.'

'I won't, because I don't *want* to meet anyone else.'

'Oh, you think that now, but just give yourself time,' said Tilly, 'and you'll change your mind, that's guaranteed.'

Tandy gave her an odd little look. 'No, you don't get it. I mean I won't need to meet anyone else because me and Jamie'll be back together next week.'

'Excuse me?'

'He played away. He got caught. I could kill him for what he's done.' Tandy took a deep breath then exhaled noisily. 'But he doesn't want us to break up. It's not like he's in love with this other girl. She threw herself at him, that's all.'

Tilly shook her head. 'You're going to forgive him?'

'Oh, don't look at me like that! Don't you see? I *have* to forgive him! Because what happens to me if I don't?'

'But—'

'Without Jamie I'll be just another ex-WAG.' Tandy's eyes glittered with tears. 'I'd have to go back and live with my mum. And she'd make me get a job. And everyone would be sniggering at me behind my back, and what if I couldn't get myself another footballer? What if I had to settle for some boring bloke who works in Comet and drives a . . . a clapped-out *Ford Fiesta*?'

Tilly was stunned. 'But if you stay with Jamie, wouldn't you always be wondering if he's going to do it again?'

'I don't know.' Tandy shrugged. 'I suppose. But that's the price you have to pay.'

'And Jamie would know he could do anything, sleep with anyone he wants, and you'd put up with it.'

'It's not just me, though. It's what all the girls do.'

Tilly's voice rose. '*I* wouldn't!'

'I don't mean girls like you,' Tandy retaliated. 'I mean girls like *me*, who go out with Premiership footballers. It's just the way it goes. We kick up a fuss when they do it, but then we forgive them. Because if we don't, there's plenty more queuing up to take our place.'

325

'And you honestly think it's worth it?' said Tilly.

Tandy shook her head at her as if she were five. 'Look at this house. Look at my shoe collection. I live with Jamie Michaels and millions of girls wish they were me. I'm living the dream, aren't I?'

Having opened her mouth to protest, Tilly promptly closed it again. Jack had come back downstairs and was shooting her a warning look from the doorway.

'Yes.' She gave up. Tandy knew the bargain she'd made with herself and, deep down, she knew it was wrong. 'Anyway, I'd better get to work.'

Jack carried the rest of the sculptures upstairs and they started organising them on the walls. After working together for ten minutes he said, 'I heard a saying once: if you marry for money, you end up earning every penny.'

'Hmm.' Tilly was still inwardly seething at the injustice of it all, at Jamie's inability to keep it in his pants and Tandy's reasoning in letting him get away with it, almost as if it were expected . . .

'Are you cross with her?'

'I wouldn't call it cross.' She reached up and held one of the large intricate sculptures firmly in place while Jack, behind her, drilled one of the fastening screws into the wall. 'I'd call it furious.'

He laughed and she felt his warm breath on her neck. 'Thought so.'

'Jamie's going to break her heart.' Super-aware of his proximity, Tilly supported the second section of the sculpture. 'I mean, he's broken it already and he'll just keep on breaking it, over and over again.'

'For what it's worth, I agree with you.' Jack's hand brushed against her arm as he prepared to drill in the next screw. 'I'm on your side.'

'Tuh.'

'I was always faithful to Rose.'

'Well, you would say that,' said Tilly, possibly unfairly.

Zzzzzzzrrrrrggghhh went the electric drill, twisting the screw into the wall.

'Because it's true.' Jack's mouth was now perilously close to her ear.

'Fine. I believe you.' Taking extreme care to avoid any physical contact, Tilly released her hold on the sculpture and slid away from her position between Jack's body and the wall. 'There, can we get on with the rest of the jobs now? There's loads to do and I have to pick Lou up from school at four.'

Chapter 47

The end was near. The curtains were now kept permanently drawn around the bed and Stella was drifting in and out of sleep. For the last forty-eight hours she'd been like a clock whose batteries were wearing out. For Erin, sitting by the bed stroking her hand, the periods of silence were lasting longer and longer. All around them the chatter of nurses and visitors and the clanking of trolleys carried on regardless, but inside their curtained-off cubicle there was just the slow rasping of Stella's breath and the intermittent clunk-hiss of the electronic pump dispensing morphine through the line into her arm.

When she stirred and mumbled something unintelligible, Erin leaned closer and said, 'Sorry?'

Stella opened her eyes, the whites yellow and the eyelids heavy. 'I'm not scared.'

'Good.' A lump expanded in Erin's throat. Yesterday, for the first time, Stella had admitted, 'I know this is it. I just don't want to say it.'

Now Stella murmured, 'Nothing hurts. That's good, isn't it? I feel kind of floaty.'

'It's OK. You're doing fine.' Erin gave her hand a gentle squeeze.

'Shame I'll have to miss the funeral.' Stella managed a ghost of a smile and her voice grew stronger. 'Hearing people say nice things about me. Even if they don't mean it.'

Since there was really no answer to that, Erin just carried on stroking her hand.

'No black,' said Stella after a while.

'Sorry?'

'I don't want anyone wearing black at my funeral. Make sure you tell them that. Bright colours only.'

'OK.' Erin nodded. 'Bright cheerful colours.'

'Ha, my so-called friends won't be cheerful. The only reason they go to funerals is to look thin and beautiful in black. Serve those bitches right.'

Hiss-clunk went the electronic drip.

'And make sure Bing's all right.' Stella's eyes began to close.

'I will.'

'Promise.' Her voice had weakened.

'Absolutely promise.'

'. . . Good . . . home.'

Good home? What did that mean? Was Stella saying she wanted her, Erin, to give Bing a good home? Or that she understood how difficult it would be for Erin to keep him, so would she please make sure Bing went to a good home with someone else?

'What was that?'

No reply.

Erin leaned closer, gave Stella's hand a little shake. 'Stella? Do you want me to find someone to give Bing a good home?'

Nothing. Stella's breathing was slow and even. She wasn't going to get an answer out of her just now. She'd have to wait until Stella woke up then raise the subject again and keep her fingers crossed that it was the latter answer.

After an hour Stella opened her eyes, gazed blankly at the ceiling then closed them again before Erin could ask the all-important question. One of the nurses, popping in to check on her shortly afterwards, rested a hand on Erin's shoulder and said discreetly, 'You might want to give Fergus a call. It won't be long now.'

Erin's heart gave a leap of panic. 'What? But there's something I need to ask Stella!'

'I think you should get him in.'

'Yes, but what about my question? It's really important.'

The nurse nodded sympathetically but didn't give in. 'Don't worry about that. Now, do you want to phone him or shall I?'

Fergus arrived forty minutes later, his grey suit smelling of the outside world where life carried on regardless. Stella's breathing was very slow now. During thunderstorms Erin always counted the number of seconds between each flash of lightning and the subsequent rumble of thunder to calculate how far away the storm was. Now she found herself doing the same between each delayed rasping breath. There was a terrible sense of inevitability about it . . . nine . . . ten . . . eleven . . .

Stella's chest rose and fell.

'Is it going to happen?' whispered Fergus.

Erin nodded sadly.

'Oh God.' He pulled up a chair, sat down. 'She's not in any pain, is she?'

Erin shook her head, then jumped as someone on the other side of the curtain yelled, 'I hate you, I hate you so much, just GET OUT OF MY LIFE!'

330

The woman in the next bed said through the curtain, 'Whoops, sorry,' and hastily turned down the volume on her TV.

Ten . . . eleven . . . twelve . . . Erin held her own breath as she counted, determined not to be put off by the two *EastEnders* actresses arguing furiously less than six feet from where Stella lay.

'Oh God . . .' Fergus was staring at Stella's motionless chest.

Fourteen . . . fifteen . . . sixteen . . .

Erin carried on stroking Stella's hand. She stopped counting at thirty and tidied a strand of hair away from Stella's marble–smooth forehead. It had happened. It was done. Stella was no longer here with them.

Where had she gone?

It was strange, not knowing the answer.

Hiss-clunk went the electronic pump, despatching its hit of morphine into a body that no longer needed it.

Answering the phone, Tilly said cheerfully, 'Hello, you, how's it going?'

Erin picked at the flakes of peeling green paint on the corridor wall in front of her. 'Stella's gone.'

'*Oh.*' Tilly's voice dropped at once. 'Oh Erin. I'm sorry.'

Erin felt the aching lump in her throat. For a moment neither of them spoke but she knew they were both acknowledging the irony of those last two words. But Tilly had meant them and she, Erin, was grateful for the condolence. Swallowing the lump, she said, 'It was peaceful at the end. She wasn't in any pain.'

'Well, that's good. Is Fergus with you?'

'Yes. He's upset too.'

'Oh, sweetheart. She was lucky to have you with her. I'll tell Max, shall I? And let other people know.'

'Thanks. That'd be good.' Tears began to slide down Erin's face as she leaned against the wall. 'Is it strange to say I'm going to miss her?'

'Sshh. Of course not.' At the other end of the phone, Tilly said soothingly, 'It's not strange at all.'

Chapter 48

'Remember before the auction last week when I thought I was scared?'

'Because you were worried no one would bid for you,' said Tilly.

'And now that they have, I'm *more* scared. This is fifty times worse.' Kaye's eyes darted around the hotel, her fingers agitatedly twiddling the fringed ends of her silk scarf. 'I feel like I'm about to do the world's highest bungee jump.'

'Look, it's going to be fine. We're all here, aren't we? Nothing can happen.'

'I feel sick. And I need a wee.'

'You're completely safe.' Tilly gave Max a meaningful look; it was all thanks to his Anthony-Perkins-in-*Psycho* impressions that Kaye was such a gibbering wreck.

'Off to the loo? Check he isn't hiding behind the door.'

'Dad, shut up,' said Lou. 'You're not helping.'

It was ten to eight and the four of them were in the bar of the White Angel, a busy restaurant in Tetbury with a good reputation for food. Max had arranged everything, chosen the venue and decided the time. Parker Price was due to arrive at eight o'clock. While he and Kaye were eating dinner, the rest of them would be seated at a nearby table keeping a discreet eye on them, ready to intervene at a moment's notice if Kaye's biggest fan did or said anything that might give them cause for concern.

At that moment, Max's mobile rang. He checked caller ID and said, 'It's him.'

Kaye's eyes widened. They all listened to Max's side of the ensuing conversation, which comprised a series of Rights, OKs, Fine, no problems and If you're sures. Finally he said, 'Bye then,' and hung up.

'Is he going to be late?' Lou was indignant.

'He's not coming.'

'*What*?' Tilly sat up. 'Why not?'

'Just doesn't feel it's right.' Max shrugged. 'So he's decided not to turn up. Fine by me.'

'Are you serious?' Kaye's voice rose. 'It's not fine at all! I've been . . . oh my God, I've just been stood up by a stalker!'

'I thought you'd be thrilled,' said Max.

'Well I'm *not*. Here, give me that phone.' Snatching it from him, Kaye jabbed at the buttons. 'Hello? Hello? Is that you? Yes of course it's me! Oh, well spotted, Einstein, I *am* upset, how *dare* you do this?'

Lou wondered if Kaye had gone mad. She watched as Kaye listened to Parker Price's explanation.

'No, I *don't* appreciate it. I've never been so insulted in my life! Where are you now?' Pause. 'Well, get yourself over here this minute. You paid to have this dinner with me and that's what you're damn well going to do.'

They all thought she was off her rocker but Kaye didn't care. After hyping herself up to meet the man and enduring all that stomach-churning anxiety, not going through with it would have been a complete *waste*.

Parker Price didn't look like a fanatic. He looked perfectly normal. His hair was dark with a few silvery threads around the temples. He was in his early forties, lightly tanned, with warm grey eyes and the beginnings of a double chin. His teeth were good, he had nice hands and he was wearing a well-tailored charcoal-grey suit.

The moment she'd clapped eyes on him, Kaye's nerves had melted away. Calmness descended. There was nothing to be worried about. Across the room, Max and Tilly and Lou were watching like hawks but here at her table she was in control.

'So tell me why you tried to cancel.'

Parker Price grimaced. 'God, I'm sorry. I can't believe you were so cross on the phone.'

'I can't believe you came all this way over from the States and suddenly decided to pull out at the last minute. I mean, why would you do that? It's just bizarre.'

'OK, I'm going to level with you. I was in the hotel this evening getting ready to come here and really, *really* looking forward to meeting you. Then all of a sudden it hit me.' Parker shook his head and said wryly, 'I wondered how you'd be feeling about meeting me, and realised you'd probably be scared witless.' He paused. 'Was I right?'

'Well, maybe. Maybe not scared *witless*,' said Kaye. 'Call it . . . wary.'

'Now you're just being polite. As you would have been tonight, on the surface. But let's face it, I could have been a complete psychopath. I still might be, for all you know.'

'You're not.' Kaye's confidence was absolute.

'I know I'm not.' He smiled. 'But you don't. And the fact that

335

I bid five thousand pounds to have dinner with you has to be a worry. Anyhow, that's why I suddenly decided I couldn't see you. I couldn't bear the thought of you sitting opposite me, wishing you could be anywhere else and hating every minute. The money didn't matter. I just wanted to let you off the hook, because anything would be better than knowing you were frightened of me.'

'I'm not frightened any more,' said Kaye. 'I promise.'

'Glad to hear it. And thanks for not letting me cancel.' He relaxed visibly in his chair. 'It's really good to meet you.'

'Very nice to meet you too.' Kaye couldn't begin to describe the way she was feeling about this gentle, sensitive man; all she knew was that he was someone she would trust with her life.

'We're being watched,' said Parker.

'I know. Sorry about that.'

'Your security team. We could invite them to join us if you want. The waiters would rearrange the tables if we ask nicely, so we're all sitting together.'

'No thanks, they're fine where they are.' Kaye didn't want Max and Lou constantly interrupting, asking questions, spoiling the evening. 'I can't tell you how much I love that painting you sent, by the way. It's hanging up in my living room. So kind of you to think of me.'

'My pleasure. You'd been through a rotten time. Trial by tabloid. I just wanted to cheer you up,' said Parker.

'You shouldn't have spent that much.'

He shrugged. 'Money isn't too much of an issue. As you may have gathered. Anyway, I'm glad you're enjoying the painting.'

He had the nicest eyes, warm and sparkly and crinkling at the corners each time he smiled. Kaye, who didn't make a habit of asking impertinent questions, said, 'How'd you get so rich?' Well,

336

she wanted to know. Googling Parker's name hadn't come up with anything helpful. She really hoped he'd earned his money rather than inherited it.

'I'm an architect. Not very exciting, but we have a successful practice. P. K. Price, over on Hudson Street.' Taking out his wallet, he removed a business card. 'Residential, corporate, big buildings, small buildings, anything you like. Just say the word and we'll design it.'

'And nobody minded you taking time off work to come over here?'

'Mind? They were delighted to be rid of me. No, it was fine. I've just finished a big project so I was due a break.'

He seemed so normal, yet what he'd done definitely came under the heading of unusual. Kaye said bluntly, 'How much would you have bid up to, at the auction?' God, she couldn't believe she was coming out with these questions.

And the best thing was, he was answering them.

'Twenty thousand. Dollars,' he added hastily as her eyes widened. 'Ten thousand pounds, that was what I told the old guy over the phone. Which was pretty nerve-wracking, but I had to give him some kind of limit. No offence, but I couldn't risk him getting back to me, saying he'd had to go up to half a million to get you.'

'I'm definitely not worth half a million.' Kaye shook her head. 'I can't believe you thought I was worth ten grand.' She looked at him, completely unafraid now, and said, 'Why am I? Why did you come all this way?'

The waitress had brought them their menus ten minutes ago and they hadn't even looked at them yet. Parker said steadily, 'I can't tell you why. It'd sound . . .' He stopped, shook his head. 'No, sorry, I can't tell you why.'

Kaye liked it that he couldn't tell her. He wasn't exactly blushing but he looked as if he might be on the verge of it. Spotting the waitress hovering at a discreet distance, she said, 'We're holding up the kitchen. Let's decide what we're going to eat. Are you hungry?'

'Not really.' His smile was wry.

Kaye's eyes danced. 'Nor me.'

Chapter 49

'Look at them.' It was ten thirty and Max was getting fed up. 'They haven't stopped yakking all night. Bloody hell, he's getting his money's worth, isn't he?'

'Dad, calm down. He paid a *lot*.'

'But it's late and you have to go to school in the morning.'

'I know,' said Lou, 'but it's only double geography first thing. Everyone sleeps through that.'

'Here comes the cavalry,' said Parker. 'Riding to your rescue. Looks like my time's up.'

Glancing at her watch, Kaye couldn't believe it was eleven o'clock. And here came Max, determinedly heading across the almost deserted restaurant. 'It's OK, I'll deal with him.'

'Hi there. Good evening. We have to go now,' Max said without preamble.

'That's fine. You go. I'm going to stay on for a bit longer.'

'No no no.' He shook his head. 'You can't do that.'

'Yes I can.' Kaye signalled with her eyes that everything was fine. 'We're having a lovely evening and I don't want to leave yet. I'll catch a taxi home when I'm ready.'

'No you *won't*,' said Max, 'because we arranged to come here and keep an eye on you, and leaving you on your own with a stranger who could be a complete *freak* – no offence – would be a crazy thing to do.'

'But that was before we met him. And Parker isn't a freak, so you don't have to worry any more!'

Parker raised a hand. 'Hey, it's OK. He's right. We've had a great evening but now we should call it a night.'

Kaye felt like a teenager being picked up early from the disco by her dad. She heaved a sigh and said to Max, 'Just give us two minutes.'

'Fine. Two minutes.' Max shot her an are-you-mad? look in return. 'No more.'

As soon as he was out of earshot Kaye said, 'Sorry about my ex-husband. Tact was never his strong point.'

'He's looking out for you. That's a good thing.'

She gazed at Parker, whose features were becoming more wonderfully familiar by the minute. They'd talked about their childhoods, holidays, old schoolfriends, embarrassing experiences, food dislikes, bizarre Christmas presents received, favourite films and least favourite chat-up lines, darting endlessly from one subject to the next because there was simply so much to say. And still so very much to learn. Was this how it felt when you met your soulmate?

Without even stopping to think about it, Kaye blurted out, 'So anyway, are we seeing each other again?'

Parker's whole face lit up. 'Are you just being polite?'

'No, not at all.'

He relaxed visibly. 'I'd love that.'

'Tomorrow night?'

'Hmm.' Smiling, Parker pretended to reach into his jacket pocket. 'I'll have to check my diary, see if I'm free.'

'At bloody last,' said Max when Parker left the restaurant and Kaye joined them at the bar. 'Job done. Let's go. I thought we'd have been out of here by ten o'clock.'

'What was he like?' Tilly was curious.

Kaye could feel herself glowing. 'Really, really nice.' How could she begin to explain the way she was feeling without making them think she was off her rocker? Then again, who cared what they thought? 'In fact, he still is nice. I'm seeing him again tomorrow night.'

'Over my dead body,' snorted Max.

'OK.' Pointing two fingers at him, she fired. 'Bang, you're dead.'

'That's what you'll be when he does it to you. Jesus Christ, don't you get it?' Max was incredulous. 'You have no idea who this man is. All you know is that he's sent you stuff, practically stalked you and paid a crazy amount of money to cross the Atlantic and have dinner with you. So tell me, how normal does that sound, eh?'

Kaye shrugged. 'I'm still meeting up with him tomorrow night. You don't have to tag along.'

'Of course I do! Somebody has to! Bloody hell, I don't believe this is *happening*,' bellowed Max.

Me neither, Kaye thought joyfully, but it is.

Isn't it great?

There were some things you really didn't expect to see on your way to work at seven forty-five on a Thursday morning, and Jack Lucas holding a wailing half-naked baby at arm's length was one of them.

Tilly, having pulled into the filling station for petrol, queued behind a white van and observed the goings-on with a mixture of emotions. Jack's car was parked at one of the pumps and a red Fiat stood with its doors flung open in the valeting bay. A toddler was screaming in his car seat, his harassed mother attempting to calm him with a carton of Ribena. That task completed, she turned her attention back to the younger baby, peeling the sodden white Babygro carefully down over its frantically kicking legs so as not to splash baby sick over Jack's polo shirt. Mission finally accomplished, she dropped the Babygro into a carrier bag. The nappy-clad baby, still being held under the arms by Jack, promptly threw up again, missing Jack's jeans by a whisker. Handing it over to the mother, he went over to his car and re-emerged with a pack of tissues which the woman gratefully took from him.

The white van drove off. Tilly moved up and began filling her car with petrol. Further along the row of pumps, Jack was now doing the same. Having mopped clean her bawling infant and stuffed it back into its babyseat, the mother effusively thanked Jack – her knight in shining armour – before driving off.

Tilly was torn. Half of her acknowledged that he'd done a good thing. The other half simmered with frustration because it was genuinely beyond her how he could be so thoughtful one minute and so selfish the next.

Nodding across at her, Jack called out cheerily, 'Morning!'

'Morning.' Conflicting emotions continued to tussle inside Tilly's chest. In his sand-coloured polo shirt, faded Levi's and desert boots he was looking . . . God, pretty damn fit. His dark hair glistened in the morning sunlight and as he handled the fuel nozzle she could see the way the muscles moved beneath the gleaming tanned skin of his forearm. Put it this way, if you were to make a YouTube clip of Jack filling his car with petrol, you'd want to watch it over and over again. Physically he was perfect. Which only made the other side of him that much more of a let-down.

'See my narrow escape back there with the incredible puking baby?'

Oh, for crying out loud, was he deliberately goading her now? 'Yes I did. What a complete hero you are. Then again, who's to say it wasn't one of yours anyway?'

'Actually it wasn't.' He sounded amused. 'I'd never seen the woman before in my life.'

'Oh well then, you can cross her off your list. But have you even been in touch with Amy yet?'

Jack's smile faded. 'No.'

The look of utter disinterest on his face said it all.

'So you'll go out of your way to be nice to the baby of a complete stranger, but you couldn't care less about one that could be your own flesh and blood.' Tilly's tank was full of petrol now and she clunked the nozzle noisily back into its holster. 'Don't you see how cruel that is? I just don't know how you can live with yourself.'

Jack shook his head; now she'd really annoyed him. Well, good. Someone had to say it.

'OK, let me just tell you something. The reason I haven't spoken to Amy is because I'm not the father of that baby of hers.'

'But—'

'And I know that for a fact because I haven't slept with her.'

Tilly stopped dead. What? *What?*

Was he serious?

She looked at Jack. 'You mean . . . you haven't *had sex* with her?'

The older woman at the next pump was listening avidly.

'That's another way of putting it,' said Jack.

'What, *never*?'

'Never.'

'But . . . but, she said you had!'

He shrugged, turned away.

Tilly was incredulous. 'Why would she say that if it wasn't true?'

'Who knows?' bawled the man in the Volvo behind her. 'Bloody women, law unto themselves, they drive us all bloody nuts. And you're another one.' He jabbed an irate finger at Tilly. 'Standing there, yakking away without a care in the world while the rest of us sit here in the queue waiting for you to SHIFT YOUR BLOODY CAR!'

Eek. Tilly glanced round and saw that he was right. Blushing, she hopped into the car and moved it over to one of the parking spaces. Back at the pumps, Jack was hanging up his nozzle and twisting the petrol cap back into place. Tilly headed on into the station shop to pay for her petrol, expecting him to follow her so she could continue the interrogation. Ten seconds later, through the window, she saw his Jag disappearing up the road.

Tilly let out a squeak of surprise, prompting the cashier to raise an eyebrow and look up.

'Someone just drove off without paying,' Tilly bleated.

The cashier looked bored. 'That's because they were in the Express lane, love. You put your credit card in before you start.'

Oh.

Right.

So a fleet of police cars weren't about to be sent out to catch Jack and haul him back. That was a real shame.

What had happened between him and Amy anyway? Why had they both lied about it? Tilly couldn't begin to imagine, but one thing was for certain.

She had to find out.

Chapter 50

When she'd come down from London to work for Max, how could she ever have imagined that part of her job description would be chaperone-cum-gooseberry?

'I've got an appointment with Matt and Lizzie Blake over in Bath tonight,' Max had said earlier. 'You'll have to keep an eye on Kaye.'

'OK.' Tilly shrugged. Well, there were worse ways to spend an evening. 'Lou? Want to come along and keep me company?'

'If you don't mind me getting expelled.' Lou pulled a face. 'I got a detention today for not paying attention in geography and tonight I've got my French essay to do, plus history and a mountain of maths. Calculus, *yeeurgh*.' Hopefully, she added, 'Unless you want to write a letter to my form tutor saying I couldn't do any of it because I *had* to come out with you.'

Which was how Tilly came to be sitting, like a right Nellie No-mates, all on her own at a table in the garden of the Horseshoe Inn on the outskirts of Roxborough. Well, not completely on her own. She had Betty with her. But adorable though Betty was, when it came to sparkling conversation she was no Dawn French.

At the other end of the garden, Kaye and her stalker were

engrossed in conversation, laughing together and generally having a brilliant time. In addition, a dozen or so wooden tables were occupied by customers enjoying a warm summer evening outside a picturesque Cotswold pub. They all looked as if they were having fun too. Then again, they weren't stuck with a companion who'd spent the last hour snuffling around in the grass for bits of old crisps.

Ten minutes later, Jack emerged from the pub and Tilly's heart lolloped into overdrive. As he stood surveying the scene, Betty abandoned her crisp hunt and raced over to her hero, greeting him like an ecstatic groupie.

See? Even Betty was under his spell.

But Tilly was glad he'd turned up. Max must have told him she'd be here on her own and Jack had come over to keep her company. Which meant she could quiz him and find out what had really gone on between him and Amy. She was longing – *longing* – to know.

Jack came over with Betty bouncing around his feet.

'Hi.' Tilly beamed. 'Let me guess, Max rang you.'

Jack nodded. 'He did.'

'Betty, leave Jack alone. Let him sit down.' Eagerly, Tilly moved her glass of orange juice, the empty crisp packet and her handbag out of the way.

'I can't stop.' Shaking his head, he said, 'I've got new tenants moving into the Farrow Road flat this evening. Said I'd meet them there in thirty minutes.'

What? She had to shield her eyes from the sun that was setting behind him. 'So why did you come?'

Jack tilted an eyebrow. 'Because Max asked me to. It's OK, I'm pretty good on first impressions. Five minutes'll be enough to check him out, see what I think.'

So, not here for her benefit then. Now how stupid did she look? Scooping Betty up on to her lap, Tilly watched Jack head over to where Kaye and the stalker were sitting. He greeted Kaye with a kiss, shook Parker by the hand and joined their table.

'I'm off.' Four minutes had passed and Jack was back.

'One thing before you go.' Tilly blurted the question out; it had been driving her nuts all day. 'Because there's something I *really* don't understand. Why would Amy say she'd slept with you if she hadn't?'

He shook his head, smiled slightly. 'I don't know.'

Which meant he *did*.

'And if it's true that you didn't sleep with her, why didn't you tell me *that* before, instead of letting me carry on thinking you had?'

'OK, now listen to me.' Jack regarded her steadily. 'What did I tell you months ago? I said I never discussed my sex life. Never have, never will. Because I have certain standards.' His eyes glittered. 'If you and I were to . . . have any kind of relationship, would you be happy to know that I was off telling everyone all about it? Regaling them with all the details? Well, would you?'

Tilly flushed and shook her head. 'No.'

'No, you wouldn't. And neither would any girl. So I respect that and say nothing.' Pause. 'I shouldn't have told you about Amy this morning, but this baby business was getting out of hand. So there, that's your answer. Happy now?'

Well, that told her. Feeling thoroughly chastened – and frustratingly none the wiser – Tilly brushed away a hovering insect and murmured, 'Yes.'

'Good.' Jack pulled his car keys out of his pocket, ready to leave. With a wink he added, 'Who knew I had morals? Tell me you aren't secretly impressed.'

After chastising her like that? Not a chance. Ignoring this, Tilly said, 'What's the verdict on Kaye's stalker?'

'Seems OK. Not obviously howling at the moon. Kaye's keen.'

'Just a bit.'

'Right, I'm off.' He bent down to ruffle Betty's ears. Betty promptly rolled over, squirming with delight and shamelessly waggling her legs in the air.

'Bye then.' Tilly put on a brave face. God, you really knew you were in trouble when you wished you could swap places with a dog.

To say that Kaye was keen on Parker Price was an understatement. She was besotted. When he'd said his goodbyes and left the Horseshoe at closing time, you could tell she was longing for him to kiss her. Possibly if Tilly hadn't been there, he would have. But a chaperone wouldn't be doing her job if she were to allow *that* to happen so she hadn't discreetly waited around the corner, but had stayed put instead.

Then Parker's taxi had taken him back to his hotel and Tilly and Kaye walked with Betty the short distance into the centre of Roxborough.

Well, Tilly and Betty walked. Kaye was probably floating along a couple of inches above the pavement. And keeping her attention was like trying to get a kitten to read a book.

'He's just lovely, isn't he? You do like him, don't you? Honestly, I can't remember the last time I felt this comfortable with a man, it's like we've known each other for *years* . . .'

'Excuse me.' Tilly's tone was accusing. 'Did you just skip?'

'Sorry?'

'Skip. You know.' She pointed at Kaye's scarlet-sandalled feet. 'Oh my God. You did, didn't you? You actually physically *skipped*.'

And instead of looking guilty and ashamed and issuing an imme-
diate flat-out denial, Kaye grinned and shook back her hair. 'Well,
maybe I can't help it. That's how he makes me feel!'

'You still have to be sensible.' Tilly felt duty-bound to say it.
She was a chaperone, after all.

'I know, I know. I am!' Kaye gleefully executed another skip
and followed it up with a twirl.

'Can I ask you something?'

'About Parker? Anything!'

'No, about Jack.'

Kaye stopped twirling. 'What did Jack say about him?'

'Nothing. I mean, he said he seems fine.'

'Can you believe Max, sending him along to cross-examine
Parker?'

'This thing about Jack.' Tilly tried again. 'It isn't anything to do
with Parker. Listen, remember after you and Max broke up?'

Kaye wrinkled her nose. 'What about it?'

'You told me you'd slept with Jack.'

'Ye-es.'

'Well, did you really?'

'Sorry?' Kaye sounded puzzled. 'Did I really what?'

'Sleep with Jack.'

'Of course I slept with Jack.' Incredulously Kaye said, 'Why
would I say I had if I hadn't?'

Well, exactly. *Exactly.* And there was no question of not believing
Kaye. The thing was, she believed Jack too. Tilly pulled Betty away
from a discarded chocolate wrapper and waited for Kaye to ask
why she was so interested.

'So anyway, listen to this. Parker came over here for a week's
holiday but he's going to see if he can stretch it to a fortnight,
isn't that *fantastic*?'

So much for curiosity. Kaye evidently had far more important things on her mind. Tilly smiled at her and said, 'Great.'

Max was already back from his meeting in Bath, frying eggs and bacon and slathering brown sauce on bread. He waved his spatula in greeting and said, 'Lou's gone up to bed. How did it go with the stalker?'

'Fine. She's seeing him again tomorrow. But she doesn't want a chaperone this time. She says she's a big girl now, you're not her dad and you have to let her and Parker go out together on their own some time.'

'OK.'

'Really?' Tilly was astounded; she hadn't expected him to give in so easily.

Max shrugged. 'They can go out together. Not stay in.'

'Well, that's a start. Kaye'll be pleased.' Marvelling at his change of heart, she said, 'Is there enough bacon for me and Betty too?'

'Yep.' As he flipped the rashers Max's phone began to ring on the kitchen table. 'See who that is, will you?'

Tilly peered over at the screen. 'It's Kaye. Shall I answer?'

Was he struggling to keep a straight face? 'Be my guest.'

'Is Max there with you? Oh my God, you won't believe what he's done,' Kaye shouted over the phone. 'Tell him he's a complete bastard!'

'You're a complete bastard,' Tilly dutifully reported. 'Why, what's he done?'

'Only gone and phoned up Parker's offices and interrogated everyone who works there! I'm so *embarrassed*,' shrieked Kaye. 'What are they going to *think*?' He's already had calls from two of his fellow architects, his secretary and his office cleaner. He's never going to live this down – they're going to tease him about it until the day he dies.'

'OK.' Seizing the phone, Max said laconically, 'I can hear you squealing away, but I happen to think it was the sensible thing to do. I could have called them up and heard them say, "Parker's girl-friends? Oh, it's the strangest thing, after a week or so they always seem to vanish off the face of the earth . . . oh yeah, now you come to mention it, there *is* a funny smell coming from under the floorboards in his apartment."'

Max's New York accent was spot on. Hiding a smile, Tilly took over frying the bacon. Now it was her turn to hear Kaye's outraged tinny squawks.

'No,' Max switched back to his normal voice, 'as it turns out, they didn't say that. They told me he was a nice normal guy, everyone likes him, no history whatsoever of chopping women up into small chunks.' Pause, tinny squawk. 'Well, I thought you'd be happy to hear it.' Pause, tinny squawk. 'Look, I just want you to be safe and I'm sure Parker can appreciate that. None of them had anything bad to say about him at all . . . yeah, yeah, I know, unlike me. And Jack says he seems OK too. So now that we know all this, I'm happy to let you go out with him tomorrow night on your own.' Pause, brief tinny squawk. 'Well, charming.'

'What did she say?' Tilly busily piled rashers of crispy bacon on to the lined-up slices of bread.

'She just called me something *very* rude.' Max pulled a sorrowful face at Betty, whose only concern was that there might not be enough bacon for her too. 'And then she hung up. I potentially saved her life and this is the thanks I get.'

Chapter 51

Tilly studied the order of service in her hands and felt guiltily void of emotion. It felt faintly fraudulent, attending the funeral of someone you'd only known briefly and hadn't even liked very much.

Oh God, and even that was an exaggeration. She had barely known Stella and hadn't liked her at all. But Erin had begged her to come along today and she hadn't had the heart to say no. Petrified that the turnout would be pitiful, Erin had been badgering practically everyone Stella had ever met in her determination to ensure that the church would be reasonably full.

And thank goodness – for Erin's sake if not Stella's – it was. Over a hundred people had turned up. Potential disaster had been averted. The so-called friends who hadn't visited Stella in the hospital were all here today. Either their consciences had been well and truly pricked by Erin or the opportunity to look glamorous in black was simply too good to pass up. The request to wear bright colours had been ignored by most of the women; black was *so* much more slimming and stylish.

Tilly, furtively gazing around the church as they waited for the service to begin, recognised Stella's fellow shopkeepers amongst the assembled congregation, mixed in with several of her neighbours and various familiar faces from the Lazy Fox. Staff from Fergus's estate agency were here too, including his secretary Jeannie whom she knew for a fact had never got on with Stella.

And there, towards the back of the church, was still-thin but visibly pregnant Amy, wearing dark glasses (perhaps she thought she was in Hollywood) and an elegant black velvet wrap-around dress. Tilly still hadn't been able to get her head around the Amy conundrum. Had Jack got her stupendously drunk? Had she woken up the next morning with a cracking headache and amnesia, only to be told by Jack that they'd done the dreaded deed *when in fact they hadn't?*

Had he hypnotised her into somehow believing she'd had wild sex with him?

Tilly gulped. Oh dear, now she was imagining wild sex with Jack, which had to be totally inappropriate at a funeral . . . *Stop it this instant . . .*

Hearing her strangled intake of breath, Max gave her a nudge and murmured, 'You all right?'

She nodded, her mouth dry. Sunshine was streaming in through the church's west-facing stained-glass windows, casting rainbows of coloured light on to the congregation. She forced herself to exhale slowly, then breathed in the mingled churchy scents of dust and sun-warmed polished wood and ancient Cotswold stone. And speak of the devil, here was Jack coming into the church now. Tilly did her best to look as if she wasn't looking.

Then again, was there really any need when everyone else was?

Nodding at people he knew – but not at Amy, she noted – Jack made his way up the aisle then joined Declan from the Fox in a pew on the right. He was wearing a dark grey suit, white shirt and black tie. Just the sight of him was enough to set off the usual reaction. Tilly wondered if it would ever stop. Life would be so much simpler, it really would. It couldn't be good for you, feeling like this about another human being and not allowing yourself to do anything about it.

OK, breathe. Breathe. Of course it hurt but wasn't keeping your distance safer in the long run? It indisputably was. And breathe again. This way was a million times less painful than the alternative.

Anyway, never mind that now. The vicar was readying himself to begin the service. Here came Fergus and Erin, the last to enter the church, moving slowly together up the aisle like the very opposite of a wedding. Fergus, ironically, a widower now too. And Erin, being brave but biting her lower lip at the sight of Stella's coffin. When they'd seated themselves in the front pew, the vicar cleared his throat and signalled to the organist to stop playing.

It was time to say goodbye to Stella Welch.

There was a good turnout at the Fox afterwards, thanks to the funeral having taken place at three o'clock. By the time it was over, nobody felt the need to rush back to work; far easier to soften the blow of mortality with a few drinks instead. And it was a jolt, to think that someone you knew had died before reaching forty. God, forty was nothing at all. Suddenly you realised it was no longer safe to assume that one day you'd be a pensioner. Anything could happen to anyone at any time. The prospect induced an atmosphere of almost wartime recklessness and Tilly, observing from the sidelines, saw Stella's single female friends visibly step up their efforts to flirt with the available males. An exotic-looking girl with waist-length black hair was currently monopolising Jack. Fergus's fellow estate agents were being targeted too. Even Declan, hard at work behind the bar, found himself the subject of attention. Everyone was drinking that bit more rapidly than usual. Well, why not?

As one of the barmaids approached with an open bottle of Moet, Tilly stuck out her glass for a refill. Kaye had volunteered to pick Lou up from school today, so it was allowed. She found her gaze sliding over towards Jack again.

'All right, sweetheart? Penny for them.'

Tilly turned, smiled at Fergus and decided on balance not to tell him what had been occupying her thoughts. 'Just thinking that Stella would be pleased with all this.'

'She would.' Fergus nodded in agreement. 'Most of it's thanks to Erin, getting everyone here today. She's been amazing.'

'Of course she's amazing. She's my best friend.' Tilly gazed fondly at Erin, across the room talking to a portly white-haired woman in her sixties. 'You're lucky to have her.'

'She feels guilty. We both do. No more warring solicitors, no expensive messy divorce. We can just get married now, whenever we want. And I *do* want, but Erin says we can't because it would look bad. She won't even discuss it, says she's not going to have people calling us Charles and Camilla . . . Oh hello, yes, so good of you to come . . .'

Fergus had been buttonholed by the man who ran the antiques market a couple of doors up from Stella's shop. Slipping tactfully away, Tilly made her way over to Erin.

'Well, if Fergus isn't going to be moving back into the house, I do hope it'll go to a nice family. We don't want any rowdy teenagers crashing around on skateboards.' The hectoring tone belonged to one of Stella's neighbours. Tilly recalled hearing her over the fence while she'd been taking her turn at feeding Bing.

Erin was nodding, looking slightly trapped and anxious. 'I'll tell Fergus. I'm sure he'll do his best.'

'And what about the cat? Who's having Bing?'

Flustered, Erin said, 'Um . . . well, we're probably going to be—'

'Stella wanted him to go to a good home,' Tilly leapt in. 'It was her last wish.'

'Really?' The woman's chins quivered. 'Well, the reason I asked was because if you don't have a home lined up, I wouldn't mind taking him.'

Since Erin was hesitating, Tilly said quickly, 'That would be fantastic, brilliant. Wouldn't it, Erin? The perfect answer. Just what Stella would have wanted.'

When the woman had moved on, Tilly murmured triumphantly, 'There you go. Sorted.'

Erin was worried. 'But what if that wasn't what Stella wanted? What if she was trying to say she wanted *me* to give Bing a good home?'

'You just have.'

'Oh, you know what I mean!'

'You don't want a cat living with you.' Least of all Bing, who had that perpetual belittling Jeremy Paxman air about him.

'I know, but if it was what Stella wanted, maybe I should try to—'

'No.' Tilly shook her head very firmly at her. 'No, no, *no*. Listen to me. You've done enough for Stella. Ten times more than enough. You did more for her than she deserved, and now you can stop. Let someone else take care of Bing.'

Slowly, like a leaf unfurling, Erin's shoulders sagged with relief. 'OK. I will. Thanks.'

'You don't have to feel guilty.'

'I know. Logically I know that.' Erin managed a wry smile, took a sip of wine. 'I just can't help it. Because I'm still here and Stella isn't, and I'm going to be living the life she wanted to live.'

Marrying someone you love, having babies, watching them grow up and go on to have children of their own, staying married till death do you part . . . well, that was the fairytale existence for millions of people but how often did it actually happen? There were no guarantees. Look at Max and Kaye, Jamie Michaels and Tandy, and what about Jack and Rose?

Tilly's gaze was drawn helplessly across the room. The exotic-looking girl was still busily flirting away, flicking her long hair like a pony. 'Who's that talking to Jack?'

'Oh, Stella used to belong to a fitness club in Cheltenham. I went over there on Wednesday night and told everyone the funeral was today. I think she teaches Ashtanga yoga.'

Hmm. Bendy, then.

Still watching them, Erin said with amusement, 'So it looks like Jack's got his evening entertainment sorted out.'

She was undoubtedly right. Tilly determinedly didn't envisage the acrobatic and wildly improbable positions a yoga teacher might be capable of conjuring up. Then her attention was caught by the conversation taking place to the right of them, between a curvaceous blonde in an emerald-green summer dress and a reed-thin brunette in black.

'. . . I mean, I know it's not the done thing to speak ill of the dead, but she could be pretty intimidating sometimes,' the blonde confided.

Her friend said, 'You're not kidding. She scared the living daylights out of me.'

Erin gave Tilly a tiny nudge, letting her know she was listening too.

'Stella told me I should sue the surgeon who left me with a nose like this.' The brunette shook her head. 'I said I hadn't had a nose job. So *she* said wasn't it about time I got one?'

'But if you tried to tell her she was being mean, she'd be really surprised.' The curvy blonde nodded in agreement. 'As far as she was concerned, she was just being honest. She was so *confident*, wasn't she?'

'I'll tell you something else,' the brunette confided. 'My Auntie Jean always does my hair for me. She cuts and colours it in her kitchen. But when Stella asked me where I'd had it done, I knew she'd laugh if I told her that. So I said Toni and Guy.'

Tilly grinned at Erin. Had Stella really been that intimidating?

'Well, guess what I did,' countered the blonde. 'She wanted me to go along with her to that new health spa in Cirencester last year. I mean, you can just picture it, Stella looking amazing in a bikini, me and my cellulite wibbling around in my swimsuit, Stella pointing out my rolls of fat and telling me I should do something about them. Yeurgh, no thanks! So I said I couldn't go because I had to visit my granny in hospital in Dundee. But then Stella didn't go to the spa, which meant I had to hide in the house all weekend because I couldn't risk her finding out I was still here.'

'Nightmare,' agreed the brunette.

'You're telling me. Then afterwards Stella asked me how my gran was and I couldn't remember whether I'd said she'd had a stroke or a heart attack, so I had to pretend she'd had both. I mean, God, can you imagine? The wicked lies I was telling! And talk about tempting fate. How would I have felt if my gran *had* had a stroke?'

'Awful.' The brunette shook her head in sympathy. 'Still, I suppose it was nice of Stella to ask after her.' Then she perked up. 'Ooh look, Declan's bringing out more of those smoked salmon thingies, let's grab some before they go.'

They rushed off. Tilly frowned, feeling as if she was standing in the middle of a supermarket having forgotten something vital.

She cast about in her mind, searching for a clue to jog her memory . . .

'What's wrong?' said Erin.

'I don't know.' It was like waking up and trying to cling on to a dream as it slithered away. If she could just concentrate hard and catch it before it evaporated completely . . . nearly there, *nearly there* . . .

And then it came to her. The connection she'd been struggling to make. Not a definite answer to her question, but a possible explanation so bizarre yet so feasible that it might . . . *might* . . . just be true.

My God. Could it be?

Erin was staring at her. 'Tilly? What is it?'

'OK, I need you to do me a favour.' The beginnings of a plan were ricocheting like a trapped fly inside Tilly's head. She checked out the gathering of mourners – yes, there was Deedee, there was Kirsten, there was thingummy with the red hair who was another one. 'When I tell you, don't ask any questions, just follow me and go along with everything I say.'

'Why?'

'Because I've had an idea.'

'About what?'

'Wait and see.' Tilly knocked back her drink for Dutch courage. 'But if it doesn't work I'm going to look a complete berk.'

'Fine. Just so long as it doesn't involve taking our clothes off,' said Erin.

Chapter 52

They didn't have long to wait. After twenty minutes Deedee and her red-headed friend went off together to the loo.

'Here we go,' Tilly murmured, nudging Erin in the same direction. She deliberately didn't look over at Jack and Max, standing by the bar. If she was wrong about this, she'd be laughed out of town.

The cubicles were both engaged by the time Tilly and Erin got there. Unzipping her bag and taking out her make-up, Tilly said, 'The thing is, I've got a confession to make. I don't know why I lied to you, I just felt so embarrassed.'

The great thing about Erin was she knew her so well; throw her a ball and she'd catch it. 'So now you're going to tell me the truth? Go ahead, then. I'm listening.'

Tilly rattled through her make-up, choosing and uncapping a lipstick. 'You know I went out with Jack last week.' As she said it, she shook her head.

Grinning at her in the mirror, Erin played along and said, 'Ye-es.'

'And you know I said the sex was fantastic.'

Erin pulled an Omygod face. 'Ye-es.'

'Well, I was lying.'

'*What?* You mean it was awful?'

'No, no, I mean there was no sex. We didn't sleep together. I'm sorry.' Miming disbelief, Tilly mouthed, *Why?*

'I don't get it!' Erin rose effortlessly to the occasion. 'Why would you *lie* about something like that?'

'Oh God, why do you think? Jack's so gorgeous, he's been out with hundreds of girls and he *always* sleeps with them. The thing is, we had a really nice evening together, I thought it was going to happen,' Tilly wailed, 'and it just didn't! He dropped me home, gave me a kiss and said goodnight! I'd never been so humiliated in my life! I mean, to be the only one he wasn't interested in, how gutting is that? Total rejection!' Pause. 'So there, I'm sorry, but I was just so ashamed. That's why I lied.'

There was silence then. Poor Erin, still utterly in the dark, searched Tilly's face for clues as to how she was meant to react but Tilly shook her head and pressed a finger to her lips.

Wait.

Wait.

Oh God, had she just made a hideous mistake?

Then they heard the sound of flushing and the first cubicle door slowly swung open to reveal the redhead. Moments later, Deedee emerged from the one next to it. They glanced sheepishly first at each other, then at Tilly. Tilly held her breath.

'OK,' Deedee blurted out, 'you're not the only one it didn't happen to.'

The redhead clapped a hand to her mouth and let out a shriek of disbelief. 'WHAT? Are you serious? *I* was just going to say that!'

Yesssss. Bingo. Exhaling slowly, Tilly sent up a prayer of thanks for the tongue-loosening properties of Moet.

Deedee and the redhead stared at each other.

'You too?'

'Me too! I thought I was the only one! I felt like a complete *troll . . .*' Starting to laugh incredulously, the redhead exclaimed, 'But I couldn't admit it, could I? So I just pretended it had happened . . .'

'And everyone else has always said he's spectacular in bed, so I said it too.' Deedee shook her head.

'Which means he's less likely to call you a liar,' Tilly pointed out.

'Hang on a second.' Bemused, Erin surveyed them. 'Are you sure you're all talking about the same person here?'

'Of course we are. Jack Lucas.' Deedee's eyes were like saucers. 'Oh my God, this is unbelievable. There's three of us here and we've all had the same thing happen!'

'There's four. Not you,' Tilly added as Erin looked astonished. 'Amy. She didn't sleep with him either.'

'Do you know what? I feel *soooo* much better,' squealed the redhead as the door opened and someone else came into the loos. 'Kirsten! Listen to this! You know we've all had sex with Jack? Well, we were lying! None of us have!'

From the look in Kirsten's heavily mascaraed blue eyes they knew at once. Guilt mingled with relief as she said, 'Oh, thank God. I thought there was something horribly wrong with me.'

Then they were all gabbling away at once. Shrieks of laughter bounced off the tiled walls. Erin looked at Tilly and whispered, 'How did you know?'

'I didn't, not for sure. But I knew Amy hadn't slept with him.' In the mirror above the sink, Tilly saw that her cheeks were flushed. 'Then we heard those girls talking about how intimidated they'd been by Stella, and how they'd lied to her about

363

their hairdresser and their granny, and I suddenly thought *what if . . .?*'

'And you were right. God.' Erin thought it over then said puzzledly, 'Does this mean Jack's . . . gay?'

She'd said it quietly but not quietly enough. Kirsten swung round and squealed, 'That's it! Of course he's gay! That explains *everything*.'

Deedee was triumphant. 'Ha, no wonder he gets on so well with Max Dineen.'

Eek, this was getting out of hand. Tilly could only imagine Jack's reaction when he heard who had unwittingly outed him. She said hastily, 'He's not gay. He definitely slept with a friend of mine.' Better not say the friend was Kaye, whose track record when it came to telling hetero from homo wasn't exactly stellar.

But the problem that had been niggling at her for months had been solved at last. Thanks to women's insecurities and their determination to keep up with the Joneses, Jack had acquired a reputation as a legendary seducer and he had done nothing to disabuse the general public of this notion.

Well, why would he? The rumours they'd been spreading about his bedroom skills were great.

'I'm back.' Kaye approached Max at the bar. 'I've dropped Lou at the house and fed her. I said you'd be home in an hour or two.'

'Fine. And where are you off to?' Max raised an eyebrow, noting the change of clothes, the perfume, the redone make-up.

'Parker's on his way over in a taxi. He's picking me up and we're going to have dinner at the Hinton Grange.'

'Maybe I should come along. Just to be on the safe side.'

'Max, there's no need. The Hinton Grange *is* safe.'

He considered this. 'OK, but stay on your guard. If you're

worried about anything, call me. Or yell for help. And whatever you do, don't let him book a room.'

Kaye nodded obediently. 'Don't worry, I won't.'

'Good.' Max knocked back his brandy.

'OK if I book one myself?' Ha, the look on his face. 'Joke,' said Kaye.

'No joking matter. "Hollywood Actress Slaughtered by Stalker." How about that for an epitaph?'

'You're right. I'll be sensible. No room-booking, no risk-taking. But I'm telling you,' said Kaye, 'he's not like that. He's a nice man.'

'Who *bid* for you.' Max's steel-framed spectacles glinted in the light from above the bar. 'I'm just saying, it's not the normal way to go about starting a relationship.'

'Sshh. He's here. Right, we're off.'

'Hey there.' Parker greeted Max from the doorway as Kaye hurried over to greet him.

'Have a good time,' said Max. He nodded at her. 'Straight home afterwards.'

She rolled her eyes. 'Yes, *Dad*.'

In the taxi, Parker leaned forward and addressed the driver. 'Right, we're going to the Hinton Grange, it's—'

'Straight down to the end of this street,' Kaye interrupted, 'then turn left.'

The taxi driver obeyed. Having turned left, he set off along the road.

'This is fine,' said Kaye. 'Just pull up here by the post box.'

Parker looked at her. 'This is your cottage, isn't it? Have you forgotten something?'

God, he was lovely. So lovely that she wasn't even nervous, and that was a first. 'No. I've decided something.'

'Like what?'

'I've decided I'm not hungry. I don't want to go to the Hinton Grange.'

His face fell. 'You don't?'

She leaned towards him, touched his cheek, 'Oh, don't look like that. I'm not abandoning you. I don't want you to go to the Hinton Grange either.'

The taxi drove off and Kaye led Parker by the hand into her tiny cottage. First she pointed out the painting he'd bought her, hanging on the wall in the living room. Then she took him upstairs.

'Are you sure about this?' He searched her face as she stood in front of him.

'You know what?' Kaye punctuated her words with kisses. 'I've never been more sure of anything in my life.'

Afterwards she lay back against the pillows gazing up at the ceiling. A tear slid out of her eye down to her ear.

'Oh my God. You're crying.'

'Sorry.'

'Was I that awful?'

She half smiled, because only a man who knew for sure he wasn't awful would ever ask a question like that. 'I think I've just made the biggest mistake of my life.'

Parker gently wiped her other eye. 'Hey, shh. How can what we just did be a mistake?'

'Because you're only here for a few more days. Then you have to go back to the States.' Gazing at him, Kaye felt bereft already. 'And I know I shouldn't be saying this, but I can't help it.'

'You know something?' He was holding her, stroking her face. 'Can I tell you something? I love you.'

She clung to him and burst into tears. 'I love you too.'

Parker rested his forehead against hers and said drily, 'Your ex-husband isn't going to be thrilled.'

'I don't care. I can't believe this is happening to me. I'm just happy it has.' Kaye closed her eyes as he kissed her again. 'I'm so glad you bid for me. Imagine if you hadn't!'

'OK, now I'm going to tell you something else. I couldn't before,' said Parker. 'You'd have been scared to death. But now that all this has happened, I'll say it. Forty-five years ago, in New York, my father was doing a bit of Christmas shopping. He was making his way through Bloomingdales when he happened to see a girl in a red coat. She was chatting and laughing with the staff in the hat department as she tried on hats in front of the mirror. And there and then, my father knew this was the girl he wanted to marry. It was love at first sight.'

'Oh my God, I already love this story! Did he just march up to her and—'

'Sshh, no, he was still wondering how to make his approach when the girl turned and left. So of course he followed her, all the way out of the store on to Lexington Avenue, but it was really busy out on the streets and the crowds meant he lost sight of her. She'd gone, vanished into thin air. My father couldn't believe it. This was his future wife and he'd found and lost her again in the space of five minutes.'

Kaye couldn't bear it. She'd thought it was going to be a story with a happy ending and instead it was turning into one of lost opportunities and regret. 'So he never saw her again? That's—'

'Will you stop interrupting and let me tell you the rest?' Amused by her impatience, Parker said, 'My father did the only thing he could do and went back to the millinery department. The girl had been chatting away to the women who worked there; he figured if she was a regular customer she might have an account with the store and they could maybe be persuaded to tell him her name. So he asked them and found out that she wasn't a regular customer. She didn't have an account either.' He paused. 'But she did work at Bloomingdales, upstairs in the ladies' fashion department.'

'Oh!' Kaye clutched her chest with relief. 'I *do* love this story after all!'

'That day was her afternoon off. Well, my father didn't sleep that night. He went back the next morning and trawled through the fashion department until he found her. Then it got a bit complicated because she thought he was wanting to buy a dress for his girlfriend, but in the end he came clean and told her why he was there. Leaving out the love-at-first-sight bit, of course. But he asked her to meet him for a coffee after work, and she liked the look of him so she accepted. Her name was Nancy, he discovered. She lived with her family in Brooklyn and she was twenty-one years old.'

Now Kaye understood why he was telling her this. 'Nancy's your mother.'

'She is. They're still together, still ridiculously happy all these years later. But my father always told me the same thing would happen to me one day, that I'd see a girl and that would be it. Love at first sight.' He took a deep breath. 'And guess what? He was right. It did happen. I saw this beautiful woman and knew she was everything I'd ever wanted.'

Tears were threatening again. But they were happy tears. Just to be on the safe side, Kaye said hopefully, 'Was it me?'

'Yes it was. Except you weren't standing there in front of me when it happened. You were on TV. Which was inconvenient to say the least.' Parker's tone was dry. 'Love at first sight in the real world is wonderfully romantic. But when it's happened through a TV screen, it makes you a stalker.'

'Michael Caine did it. He saw Shakira on TV and tracked her down, and they've been married forever.'

'Well, that could be because he was Michael Caine. When you're a world-famous actor you can get away with all sorts. It's not quite the same when you're an unknown New York architect.' Smiling, Parker said, 'Anyway, can I just say that meeting you in person hasn't been a let-down. If I thought I loved you before, I know I *really* love you now.'

Was this one of the very best moments of her life? Absolutely. 'And if I had a choice between you and Michael Caine, I'd choose you. In fact,' said Kaye, 'if I had a choice between you and *anyone* else, it'd still be you.' She wriggled closer and kissed him on the nose. 'And the story about your parents is wonderful. But I still don't know what's going to happen to us.' Frustratedly she said, 'Bloody sodding Atlantic ocean.'

Parker held her and stroked her hair. 'Hey, we'll work something out. Don't think about it now.'

Chapter 53

'I'm sorry, I just feel lousy. This is no fun for you, is it?' Having coughed and sneezed her way through the last hour in the Fox, Erin shook her head apologetically and said, 'Should we just call it a night?'

Tilly felt sorry for both Erin and herself. After all the stress of the past few weeks, Erin had succumbed to a virus and would clearly prefer to be at home in bed. Which wasn't her fault, but it was still disappointing when you'd been looking forward to a girly evening out together on your Friday night off. Lou was spending the weekend at Nesh's house to help Nesh celebrate her fourteenth birthday. Max was at home working on a complex proposal for a hotel refurb. When she'd left the house she'd told him to expect her back around midnight.

Well, it was going to be more like nine o'clock. Talk about rock and roll.

In fact it was nine thirty by the time she arrived back at Beech House after first walking Erin back home then queuing up at the takeaway for chips and curry sauce. Plus an extra portion of chips for Max and Betty to share, because if she didn't they'd pinch half of hers and that drove her insane.

There were bats flitting and darting around the house at warp speed. Never able to convince herself that they were harmless and smart enough not to get themselves tangled up in her hair, Tilly leapt out of the car and made a dash across the gravel. Clutching the bags of chips to her chest she unlocked the front door and – *oof.*

The bicycle that had been propped against the wall clattered to the floor, nearly taking her with it. Stumbling and letting out a shriek of surprise, Tilly thought three things in quick succession:

First, what a stupid place to leave a bike.

Second, who would have cycled here at half past nine on a Friday night?

Third . . . *crikey, bloody hell, surely not.*

Then a door opened upstairs and Max appeared at the top of the staircase in his dressing gown.

'God, I'm sorry.' Tilly wished she could evaporate on the spot.

'Well, at least it's only you.' Max looked relieved. 'You said midnight.'

'Erin was ill. I'm really sorry . . . I'll go out again . . .'

Max shook his head. 'It's OK. He was just leaving anyway. Um, we'll be down in a minute.'

Mortified, she waited in the kitchen. True to his word, Max came downstairs less than three minutes later, followed by a clearly embarrassed Tom Lewis.

'Well, this is awkward.' Max came straight to the point. 'Look, can we just be honest here? This is the first time. I thought we'd be undisturbed. Tom's leaving Harleston Hall at the end of term. He's moving up to teach at a school in Dundee in September. For his sake I hope we can trust you to keep this . . . tonight . . . to yourself.'

371

Tilly flushed. As if she would broadcast it. 'Of course I will. I won't say a word to anyone, least of all Lou.'

'Thanks,' said Tom. 'Right, well, I'll be off. Bye. Don't worry, I'll see myself out.'

'I hope your bike's all right.' It was a toss-up which of them was blushing more, Tom or herself.

'I'm sure it'll be fine.' With a brief smile he was gone.

'Oh God, I'm so sorry,' Tilly groaned again when the front door had closed behind him.

'Hey, he was leaving anyway. He turned up ten minutes after you left to meet Erin.'

So at least they'd had an hour and a half together before she'd turned up to ruin everything. 'I can't believe he's gay. Oh God, Lou *told* me he'd broken up with Claudine. Is that why? Did she find out?'

Max shook his head. 'Claudine never was his girlfriend. Just his flatmate. She helped out when Tom had to produce a partner.'

Even these days the pressure was still on for a lot of people to conceal their sexuality. Tilly thought of all the school mothers pointlessly lusting over and flirting with their children's superfit teacher.

'Oh Max. And now he's moving to Scotland. Do you really like him?'

He shrugged. 'What's not to like? But we both knew nothing could ever develop. Poor Lou, it was traumatic enough when she thought her mother might make a play for him.'

He had a point. As a feeble attempt at a peace offering, Tilly handed over one of the steaming parcels of chips. 'Here, these are for you and Betty.' Another thought struck her. 'Poor Kaye too. She really did fancy Tom.'

'I know. Let's not tell her, eh?'

'Probably best. Everyone she's attracted to turns out to bat for the other side. Oh God . . .' Seized by an even horribler thought, Tilly exclaimed, 'Don't say Parker's gay too.'

Max grinned and ate a chip. 'Don't worry, some of us have better gaydar than my ex-wife. Parker's definitely straight.'

Saturday night, and it was Tilly's turn to be alone in the house with just Betty for company. Max had caught the train up to London to meet with the owners of the West Kensington hotel he'd been hired to revamp, and would be back tomorrow lunchtime. Lou was continuing her weekend sleepover at Nesh's and Kaye had whisked Parker off to Oxford for sightseeing and shopping and a night to remember in the stunning presidential suite at the Randolph.

Well, allegedly stunning. Not that Tilly had ever been lucky enough to check the place out for herself. Still, there were worse ways to spend a Saturday night than at home on a comfortable sofa, with a widescreen TV in front of you and a cute dog on your lap. Outside, rain was bucketing down and gusts of wind were rattling the branches of the beech trees.

Whereas inside it was warm and dry and one of her all-time favourite films was about to start on TV.

With impeccable timing Betty stretched, jumped off her lap and trotted over to the living-room door. She turned and gave Tilly a meaningful look.

'Fine, but you have to be quick.' Unfolding her legs, she went over to let Betty through. The trouble with dogs was they didn't appreciate how much you hated to miss the first few minutes of a film while they snuffled around the garden in search of the perfect place to pee. As she opened the kitchen door a smattering of rain hit Tilly in the face. 'Yeuch, I'll wait here. No hanging about out there, OK?' Hopefully with weather like this Betty would do whatever she had to do and shoot back inside, pronto.

The little dog obediently slipped past her into the darkness of the back garden.

'Faster than a speeding bullet,' Tilly called after her.

Afterwards she wondered if saying that had somehow tempted fate. One second all you could hear was the wind and the rain. The next, a volley of high-pitched barks rang out, there were sounds of a furious scuffle and Betty shot across the grass, closely followed by a fox. Letting out a shout of alarm, Tilly glimpsed the fox's long bushy tail as it chased after Betty, *faster than a speeding bullet*, down the lawn and into the depths of the bushes at the end of the garden.

Oh God, *Betty* . . .

Tilly raced barefoot after them but they were gone, over the drystone wall and vanishing into the woods beyond. Panting and panicking, she yelled out Betty's name over and over again. Last week a big old dog fox had managed to tunnel into the chicken coop over at Barton's Farm and had left sixteen chickens dead. Poor Esme Barton had been inconsolable. Foxes were nasty creatures who killed for the fun of it, and Betty was only small, a third of the size of the one that had just scared her half to death and chased her over the wall.

Did foxes slaughter dogs too? Tilly's heart thump-thumped against her ribcage. She hadn't heard of such a thing happening. Then again, she was such a townie she just didn't know.

And it had to happen while Max was away. She raced back into the house, dragged on a pair of wellies and found a torch in the kitchen drawer. It didn't work. After hunting high and low she discovered Lou's Game Boy and with shaking fingers transferred the batteries from it to the torch. Right, leave the back door open in case Betty came home while she was out searching for her . . . oh please, please don't let the fox have ripped her to pieces . . .

Twenty minutes later Tilly was back again, soaked to the skin and hoarse from shouting Betty's name. Her throat was burning, she was dripping water all over the kitchen floor and Betty still wasn't home. This was serious. Sick with worry and gasping for breath, she glugged down a mug of water and reached for the phone. There was no question that she needed help, but who to call? Ruin Nesh's birthday party by phoning Lou? Contact Max who was a hundred miles away? Kaye at the Randolph in Oxford? Or how about Erin, except she was still laid low with her virus . . .

OK, she knew what she had to do. Tilly scrolled through the names stored on the phone until she reached the only one she could feasibly call. Erin might be ill but Fergus wasn't. He'd come over and help. Except Betty didn't know Fergus; if she were terrified and hiding or lying injured somewhere and heard a stranger shouting her name, would she creep out of the undergrowth and go to them?

She might not, and they couldn't afford to take that risk. Whereas there was someone else Betty was so besotted with that she'd crawl over broken glass to reach him. Not unlike most of the single females in Roxborough.

'Jack?' Tilly's voice cracked with emotion as he answered the phone. Rain dripped off her nose and she brushed it away with a shaking hand. 'I'm really sorry, but Betty's missing. Can you help me?'

She didn't ask what she'd interrupted, what he'd been doing at ten o'clock on a Saturday night, and Jack didn't tell her. Nor did he waste any time. Having arrived less than eight minutes after her phone call, he listened grimly to Tilly's description of the fox chasing Betty out of the garden, and from his car fetched a far more powerful torch than her weedy one. 'Right, we'll start in the woods and spread out after that. Got your mobile on you?'

Tilly nodded and patted her jacket pocket.

'OK.' Putting up the collar of his Barbour, Jack said, 'Let's go.'

He was so strong and dependable. In a situation like this, when you were desperately in need of help, nobody did it better than Jack.

Chapter 54

By midnight Tilly's hopes were fading fast. The rain was still hammering down, she'd never been wetter in her life and the wind was howling like a wolf through the trees. There was still no sign of Betty. They'd been searching and calling for her non-stop and would surely have found her by now if she were alive.

Oh God, it didn't bear thinking about. Lou would be devastated . . . they all would. Blundering on through the darkness Tilly tried not to imagine how Betty might have suffered – sharp teeth sinking into her neck, blood spurting out, flesh being ripped—

Phone ringing in her pocket. Fearing the worst, she scrabbled with the pocket flap and braced herself. In her mind's eye Jack was crouching in the rain over an inert, lifeless body. She let it ring twice more, suffused with cowardice, postponing the moment when she'd have to hear him tell her that Betty was dead.

'Yes?'

'I've got her. She's safe.'

The words reverberated through her brain. For a moment she wasn't sure she'd heard him right. Through chattering teeth, Tilly said, 'Is she alive?'

'Alive and kicking and very muddy.' Jack sounded as if he were smiling. 'Come on, meet you back at the house.'

Tilly ran all the way. Jack and Betty arrived two minutes later.

'Oh Betty, *look* at you.' Bursting into tears of relief, she held out her arms but Betty, predictably, preferred to stay in Jack's. 'Where have you *been*?'

'She was trapped in a rabbit hole. Must've been running away from the fox when she fell down it, then couldn't manage to scramble up again. I called her name and heard this tiny bark,' said Jack. 'The grass was muffling the sound. Then I had to reach right down, grab hold of her front paws and haul her out. It was like helping a cow to give birth to a calf.'

'Oh sweetie, how horrid for you.' Tilly lovingly stroked the little dog's ears; she was covered from head to foot in slimy mud. 'We need to get you into the bath.'

Jack's mouth twitched. 'Thanks.'

'Not you.' Tilly paused. 'But thank goodness you came over. Betty would have died if you hadn't found her. You saved her life.' The moment the words were out of her mouth, she realised their significance. God, the irony of it. Rose had saved her parents' dog's life too and had died in the process.

Jack didn't comment on this, thankfully. He simply glanced at her and said instead, 'I'll give you a hand.'

Upstairs in the bedroom they scrubbed and shampooed Betty between them in the roll-top bath. Less than keen on being sprayed with the shower attachment, Betty put up something of a squirmy struggle but after twenty minutes she was clean again. Jack wrapped her in a bath towel and gently patted her dry. Betty, exhausted by her exertions, was fast asleep within seconds.

Downstairs, he lowered a gently snoring Betty into her basket. Catching a glimpse of herself reflected in the kitchen window,

Tilly marvelled at Jack's ability to look glistening and irresistible when wet, whilst she resembled a bedraggled refugee. Not that it mattered. She was past the stage of doing herself up for him.

'Well, thanks again.' Now the drama was behind them she thrust Jack's Barbour at him, anxious to see him gone. 'I hope we didn't wreck your evening.'

He took the waxed jacket from her. 'So I'm leaving now, am I? I've outlived my usefulness and you're kicking me out.'

Yes. Because this isn't easy for me, you know.

Aloud, Tilly said, 'It's late. You must want to get home.' Hastily, before he could say he was in no hurry, she added, 'I'm shattered.' And faked a yawn for good measure.

The look Jack gave her signalled that he recognised a fake when he saw one. 'Tilly.' He shook his head slightly. 'Why are you still giving me such a hard time?'

Oh God. 'I'm not, I'm just tired.' Moving towards the door, she opened it. *Please leave, please leave.*

Jack followed her to the door, then turned and placed a hand on the back of her neck. He bent his head, drawing her to him, and kissed her.

It felt like coming home. The feel of his mouth on hers, warm and dry, was simultaneously the most perfect experience of her life and the most agonising. It was all too much to handle, because her body wanted him but her brain was yelling that she couldn't – *absolutely couldn't* – let it happen. Her whole life she'd held back a part of herself for this reason. Fear of hurt meant she'd needed to be the one in control of any relationship, and up until now she'd achieved that. Loss of control was just too scary to contemplate, particularly when it involved someone who could have anyone they wanted, because why on earth, out of all the women in the world, would they choose you? Even now, while her heart

379

was thumping crazily away and adrenaline was causing her whole body to tingle and fizz, she knew the subsequent untold misery would far outweigh the fleeting moments of joy.

His hand sliding up from her neck to the back of her head, his other arm around her waist, Jack murmured, 'See? I'm not so bad, am I?'

Tilly closed her eyes. It would be so easy to agree. She was balancing on a high-wire, teetering this way and that. The tiniest slip and she would be falling helplessly to the ground. And that wouldn't be something you'd easily recover from.

Come on, weigh it up. One night, maybe a couple of nights, maybe even a whole week with Jack. Versus months and years of gut-churning misery and regret. Because that was how it would feel and it was exactly what would happen.

'I want you to go.'

There was that look again, the fractionally raised eyebrow that signalled he knew better. 'Really?'

'Yes, really.' Tilly put a hand against his chest and moved back. She forced herself to stay calm.

'Why?'

'Because it's what I want.'

Jack surveyed her steadily. 'OK, I don't get this. You hated it when you thought I'd slept with a million girls. And now you know I haven't. I thought you'd have been happy about that.' He shook his head in disbelief. 'God, I thought you'd be delighted.'

She swallowed; understandably, it hadn't taken long for *that* irresistible snippet of gossip to become common knowledge and make its way back to him. 'But it's not just that side of things, is it?' Obviously it had been nicer in one way to discover that he hadn't shagged his way completely indiscriminately around Roxborough, but it wasn't the chief factor. Tilly said, 'There's trust and commitment. I know I could never trust you, and *you* know you have a problem with commitment. Well, we both know that. And after what happened to Rose, I don't blame you. But at the same time, I don't want to get involved with someone when I know it's never going to work out.'

'Who says it won't? It might.' He smiled persuasively, evidently intent on not taking no for an answer. 'I really think it would. The way I feel about you . . . well, it's different. Look, I'm not very good at saying this stuff, but I really think there's something special going on here. And I think you know it too.'

Which was *exactly* the kind of thing you'd expect a man who didn't take no for an answer to say.

'I think you want me to believe you mean that. And it's still not going to happen.'

Exasperated, Jack spread his hands. 'What can I do to make you change your mind?'

It was actually really sad. Tilly shook her head. 'Nothing.'

'One night. One date. Just say yes and I'll prove to you I'm not lying. Pick a day,' said Jack. 'Any day.'

'A date? Well, I *could* say tomorrow evening . . .'

'Fine. Right.' He nodded, his still-wet hair falling into his eyes. 'Tomorrow.'

'But I *won't* say it,' Tilly continued, 'because there wouldn't be any point in getting ready or actually expecting it to happen, because you probably wouldn't turn up.'

Jack exhaled audibly. 'That happened *once*. I didn't know Rose's parents were going to knock on my door, did I?'

OK, that had been well below the belt. She was being unfair now. But that had been the night she'd realised she couldn't cope with the agony of being rejected by him. It would break her in half.

381

'Right, let's just say I'm not interested in becoming another name to add to your list of conquests. Whether you've slept with them or not,' Tilly added, because the sex was actually irrelevant. Either way they were still conquests.

'You wouldn't be.'

'You say that now. But look at your track record.'

'So I can't win.' His eyes glittering, Jack said evenly, 'You're the one I want, but you don't trust me because you're convinced I'm incapable of maintaining a normal, happy, committed relationship. So the only way I could possibly change your mind about me would be by having a normal, happy, committed relationship with someone else.'

Yes, she *knew* it was deeply ironic. In a weird way though, it was also true.

'That would do the trick, would it?' Jack persisted. 'That'd make you happy?'

Tilly's mouth was dry. The thought of it made her feel sick, but what could she say?

'Fine. I'll do that then.' Having called her bluff, Jack moved over to the door. He stood there, an unreadable expression in his dark eyes, waiting for her to change her mind.

Don't give in, *don't give in*. Whatever you do, don't speak.

But she had to.

'Jack . . .' Her voice broke.

'Yes?'

Tilly cleared her aching throat. 'Thank you for finding Betty.'

Jack looked at her. Then he turned the handle, let himself out and – *click* – closed the door behind him.

Chapter 55

Unable to get to sleep, Kaye lay in Parker's arms and gazed up at the bedroom ceiling. In four days he would be flying home to New York and she couldn't bear the thought of being parted from him. In just this short space of time he had become . . . God, practically *part* of her. For three years she'd been single and lonely. Now she'd found someone who made her feel whole again and everything would be perfect if only he hadn't been inconsiderate enough to live an entire continent away.

Why couldn't life be simple? When she'd lived and worked in LA, why couldn't she have fallen for a fellow actor? Or since moving back here, why couldn't someone local have caught her eye, a strapping Cotswolds farmer, say, or a nice hunky plumber?

But no, that would have been far too easy. And besides, neither of them would have been Parker. Smiling and turning her head, Kaye watched him sleeping peacefully beside her, not snoring at all, thank goodness, just breathing easily and—

'Shit, what's *that*?' Jerking awake and sitting bolt upright, Parker clutched his chest as an unearthly wailing noise filled the bedroom.

Oh great, just as she met the love of her life, she managed to finish him off with a heart attack.

'It's OK, sorry, sorry, that's my phone.' Snatching it up from the bedside table, Kaye marvelled at her own stupidity in having allowed her daughter to choose a new ringtone. She'd asked for something gentle and Lou had selected some thrash-metal rocker screaming AAAANNSWER MEEEEEE! at the top of his lungs.

'Kaye?'

'Who's this?' Kaye frowned, unable to place the voice.

'Kaye, honey, it's Macy!'

Macy Ventura, one of her co-stars on *Over the Rainbow*. Kaye let out a groan and fell back against the pillows. Five times married Macy, not even bothering to think of the time difference, calling to regale her with all the latest twists and turns in her roller-coaster, never-knowingly-uneventful love life.

'Macy, it's one o'clock in the morning. Everyone's asleep here.' She rubbed Parker's arm by way of mute apology.

Macy, who had no such scruples, shouted, 'Never mind about that! Guess what I have right here in my hand?'

This seriously didn't bear thinking about. 'Macy, just tell me.'

'Oh baby, brace yourself.' Now Kaye *really* hoped Macy was addressing her. 'I am holding something that's gonna rock your world. You are gonna *love* this. In fact, I'd say—'

'Just say it before I hang up,' Kaye ordered.

'OK, here we go. I have a little tape in my hand, containing CCTV footage of you running over Babylamb. Or rather *accidentally* running over him.'

'What?'

'It's all there on the tape, clear as day. You're heading slowly down the drive, the dog shoots out from nowhere, you brake as hard as you can but it's too late, there's no way you could avoid him.'

'I know that.' Kaye sat up, her heart racing. 'I meant how did you get a tape of it? There *was* no CCTV footage, that camera wasn't switched on when it happened.'

'Ah, that's where you're wrong.' Triumphantly Macy said, 'The camera was working just fine. Charlene saw the accident happen from her bedroom window. First thing she did was tell Antonio, one of the security guys, to take out the tape and destroy it.'

Kaye closed her eyes. 'Why would he do that?'

'Hey, this is Charlene we're talking about! She was schtupping him, wasn't she! Plus, she threatened to sack him if he didn't. So he took the tape and told her it was sorted.'

'Charlene was sleeping with this security guy? But she was furious with me because she thought I was flirting with Denzil!' Kaye was outraged; honestly, talk about hypocritical.

'Yeah, well, she was feeling neglected because Denzil had stopped sleeping with her. She was also convinced this meant he was getting it somewhere else. Which it turns out he was,' Macy continued. 'And now he's divorcing Charlene so he can marry his one and only true love. So Charlene's moved out, the security guy no longer has to worry about losing his job, and what with him being a good Catholic and all, his conscience has been kind of troubling him. So he confesses everything to the new love of Denzil's life and she knows at once exactly what she has to do about it. She has to get right on the phone to Kaye McKenna and let her know she's about to be completely exonerated.'

'Well, she hasn't called yet.' Kaye was indignant. 'When did all this happen? Does she know how to reach me? Can you make sure she has my number?'

'Oh, baby, you really don't have your brain in gear, do you? She has your number,' Macy said cheerily, 'and she has called you. In fact, she's doing it right now.'

'You *what*?'

'Oh, well done, you've caught on at last. Isn't it just the most fabulous news? The new love of Denzil's life is me!'

Tilly gulped down a cup of coffee with one hand and ironed Lou's PE kit with the other. It was eight o'clock in the morning, Kaye and Parker had turned up on the doorstep half an hour ago and Kaye was still fizzing like a bucket of bicarb.

'. . . so no wonder Charlene was twitchy and paranoid! The whole time she thought Denzil was seeing me, he was with Macy.'

'So he's a cheating bastard who let you take the rap.' Max was singularly unimpressed. 'If I saw him, I'd break his nose.'

'Yes, but he believed Charlene when she said I'd run Babylamb over on purpose. He feels incredibly guilty now he knows the truth. I spoke to him this morning and he's so sorry. And he's already got his publicist on to it. They're releasing the CCTV tape to the news stations. I'm innocent and everyone's going to know about it.' Kaye hugged Lou, sitting next to her. 'They're all going to be so sorry they were mean to me!'

'You can sue them,' Lou chimed in, 'for millions.'

'Tell them what else Denzil said,' Parker prompted.

'He wants me back on the show.' Kaye beamed and helped herself to Max's toast. 'The writers are already working on it. I'm not going to drown after all. Everyone's going to think I died in the water, but it's going to turn out that I was rescued at the last minute by my long-lost half-brother who's a priest! And Denzil's quadrupling my salary. It's all going to be fantastic publicity for the new series. Can you believe it? They're desperate to have me back!'

Tilly switched off the iron and folded Lou's PE kit, glancing at Parker as she did so. He was doing his best to look pleased but she could sense his concern that he might be on the verge of losing Kaye back to her old Hollywood life.

'Well, I think they've got a damn cheek and you should tell them to get stuffed.' Unlike Parker, Max didn't bother to hide his feelings. 'They hung you out to dry! I don't know why you aren't furious with the lot of them.'

Kaye smiled and shook her head. 'I know, but it's over now. And how can I blame Macy and Denzil? God, I still can't believe they're together. She's already been married and divorced five times.'

'It's not just them, though, is it?' Max shrugged. 'It's the whole Hollywood machine. They turned on you like a pack of wolves. If you go back, it's like you're forgiving them. I'd tell them to fuck off.'

'Dad. Language.'

'Lou.' Max tapped his watch. 'School.'

'OK, two things,' said Kaye. 'First, I'm an actress. Hollywood is where I work and telling Hollywood to fuck off would be cutting off my nose to spite my face.'

'Mum! Honestly, we're going to have to set up a swear-box.'

'And second.' As she spoke, Kaye reached for Parker's hand. 'If the rest of America hadn't hated me, this wonderful man wouldn't have sent me flowers and chocolates to cheer me up. Even if I never actually got to see them. And if I hadn't been back here I wouldn't have been a prize in an auction, would I?' Eyes shining, she went on, 'Basically, if none of the awful stuff had happened, I believe Parker and I would never have met. So how can I be angry? This is the happiest I've been in years.'

'Oh Mum. That's really sweet.' Lou hugged her then jumped up, went over to Parker and hugged him too. 'And I never thought you were a mad stalker, I promise.'

Visibly touched, Parker said, 'Well, thanks.'

'I did.' Max refilled Parker's coffee cup. 'But I'm prepared to admit I was wrong.'

'So what's going to happen?' Lou's eyes were bright. 'What'll happen with you and Parker if you go back to Hollywood? Will he move over there too?'

Eek. Out of the mouths of thirteen-year-olds. From the look of things, Lou was voicing the question neither Kaye nor Parker had yet dared to ask. Reaching for the car keys, Tilly said, 'Come on, get your bag, you don't want to be late for school.'

Lou wrinkled her nose. 'Actually I do. And this is kind of a special occasion, isn't it? America is about to stop hating my mother. I'm sure I'm allowed to be a little bit late. So what'll you do?' Fixing her gaze on Parker, she said, 'Give up your business in New York and move in with Mum?'

Kaye said hastily, 'Sweetheart, it's too soon to be thinking about that!'

'I don't see why.' Lou began buttering another slice of toast. 'You just said this is the happiest you've been for years. And Parker's crazy about you, that's pretty obvious. So you want to be together, don't you?'

'Well . . . we need to, um, talk about it . . .'

'Mum, you're blushing! Listen, you've found someone lovely at last—'

'Thanks a lot,' said Max.

'Oh Dad, you know what I mean. Lovely and not gay.' Lou turned back to Kaye. 'So you have to decide how you're going to organise things in future.'

Tilly experienced a pang of envy. For Lou, because everything was so straightforward in her world, a dilemma was simply something to be solved. And for Kaye too, because she was in love with

388

a man who loved her in return and, despite their unpromising start, she could see that once the hiccups were ironed out they had a happy future together.

'Sweetheart, give us time. There's lots to discuss.' Kaye was still blushing.

When it came to persistence, Lou could give any Turkish rug-seller a run for his money. 'But you can't be a proper couple if you're living thousands of miles apart.'

'School,' Tilly announced, expertly tipping Lou off her chair. Because Parker might not be saying anything, but from the look in his eyes you didn't have to be a mind-reader to know that he wasn't remotely keen on the idea of having to leave New York.

The next couple of days were completely crazy. The high-quality CCTV clip aired on American TV, America fell in love with Kaye McKenna all over again and Charlene Weintraub, trans-formed in the blink of an eye into the Wicked Witch, slunk off into rehab.

Kaye barely had a moment to breathe. Journalists and reporters descended on Roxborough and the phone didn't stop ringing. Interviews and photo shoots took hours. It was lovely to have been exonerated but all she really wanted was to be with Parker, whose time over here was running out fast.

On the evening of the second day, Kaye switched off her phone and they holed up together in his hotel room.

'Denzil's putting on the pressure. He's desperate for me to sign that new contract. And he's upped the offer again.'

Parker stroked her hair. 'Well, that's good, isn't it? It's what you wanted.'

'I know.' Kaye nodded in half-hearted agreement. But she wanted Parker more. Finally plucking up the courage to ask the question that had been zapping around her brain for the last forty-eight hours, she took a deep breath. 'Would you move to LA?'

There, done. She'd said it.

'Listen to me.' Parker, who'd been so incredibly patient during all the recent madness, gave her the kind of look she'd been dreading. 'I love you. You mean the world to me. But I can't just abandon my company. It wouldn't be fair on my staff, or to my clients. I can't let them down. And I definitely couldn't move in with you and not work. I'd look like a complete parasite. People would think I was . . . worthless.'

A lump expanded in Kaye's throat. He was absolutely right, and no one knew better than she did how vituperative the Hollywood gossip machine could be.

'I'm sorry.' Parker hugged her. 'Thank you for asking me. But I guess it's that male pride thing. I built up a successful business and I'm proud of it. But we can still see each other, can't we? We'll make it work out. New York to LA is only a six-hour flight.'

It sounded reasonable when he said it like that, but it was only six hours in theory. What with getting to and from the airport, queuing through security and the various hold-ups that always seemed to plague her like a swarm of mosquitoes, it would be more like ten. Kaye gazed out of the window at the rolling hills, the orange-violet sky and the slowly setting sun. And she'd never been one of those people who enjoyed flying anyway. When you factored in Parker's working hours and her own gruellingly hectic filming schedule, how much time would they end up spending together really?

Not nearly long enough to be able to call it a proper relationship, that was for sure.

Chapter 56

'Sweetheart, listen. I need to know how you feel about it and I want you to be completely honest.'

'Oh Mum, look at you being all worried.' Vigorously shaking her head, Lou said fondly, 'I'm *fine*. You've got your job back and that's brilliant. With the amount they're offering, you'd be mad to turn it down.'

Kaye was still wracked with guilt. 'I know, I know. It's just been so lovely being back here and seeing you every day.'

'But I can still come over during the holidays.' Unlike Kaye, Lou adored flying. 'If you go back to the States, we'll still be in touch, won't we? Just like we did before! Mum, I'm happy here with Tilly and Dad.' Her face suddenly turning three shades pinker, Lou added casually, 'And I think I'm kind of getting a boyfriend, so I wouldn't want to leave anyway.'

'Sweetie, really?' Hugging her, Kaye was overcome with emotion. 'That's fantastic. Is it someone nice?'

'No, he's completely vile.' Lou smiled and rolled her eyes. 'It's Cormac.'

'Oh, he's in your class.' Vaguely able to picture him, Kaye said, 'Fair hair, quite athletic?'

'Captain of the football team.' Lou looked proud. 'He's really nice. Although it's not like we're going *out* out together. We just text a lot, and sit next to each other at lunch. But it makes going to school more fun. So stop panicking and wondering if I'm going to mind if you move back to the States, because I promise you I won't. I'm more worried about how you and Parker are going to sort yourselves out.'

Kaye said wryly, 'Me too.'

'I really like him, Mum.'

'Me too.'

'You'll have to persuade him to change his mind about leaving New York.'

What had she done to deserve a daughter like this? Stroking Lou's face, Kaye said, 'I know, sweetie. I'm still working on that bit.'

There were seven of them gathered in the drawing room at Beech House, eight if you counted Betty, and having Jack in the vicinity was making Tilly nervous. The nerves, in turn, were making her ravenous. Hovering beside the French windows leading out on to the garden, she snapped yet another breadstick into quarters and trawled the first quarter through the bowl of guacamole on the table beside her. Concentrating on the different dips was easier than looking over at Jack. She'd been taking them in turns. Chilli cheese next, then salsa, then mayonnaise . . .

'Phew, you *reek* of garlic.' Lou flapped her hands in protest.

OK, garlic mayonnaise. You knew you'd exceeded your garlic limit when you could no longer taste it.

'These are great.' Tilly pointed her breadstick at the tray of dips. 'You should try some.'

'Yeurgh, no thanks, I've got to go to school tomorrow. Don't want to frighten Cormac off.'

'Well, here comes Erin. She's not scared of a bit of garlic.'

Erin wrinkled her nose. 'Actually, you are a bit strong.'

'Oh well, who cares?' Holding out her arms to Betty, Tilly said, 'Come over here, sweetie, you still love me, don't you?' Prompting Betty to bounce up to her, wince with horror and promptly screech into reverse.

'I feel like I've got leprosy.' She began to regret monopolising the dips; probably just as well she didn't have a love life to put in jeopardy. 'Anyway, how's the house sale going?'

'Pretty good. Fergus is showing another two couples round it this afternoon.' Erin grimaced slightly; this was a subject with which she wasn't completely at ease. When Fergus and Stella had split up, Fergus had moved into a rented flat. As Stella's husband, the house they had bought together was now his. In a year or so, when he and Erin felt it would be appropriate to marry, they would buy a new house in Roxborough.

'OK, here we go, I'm going to say a few words.' Clapping her hands, Kaye captured everyone's attention.

Max said, 'Only a few? That'll be a first.'

'As you know, Parker and I are leaving tomorrow.' Holding out a hand, Kaye gestured for Parker to come and stand beside her. 'And I'm going to miss you all terribly. Well, some more than others.' She looked pointedly at Max, then grinned and took a deep breath. 'Anyway, the thing is, I've come to a decision. I'm not going to renew my contract with *Over the Rainbow*. I won't even be moving back to LA. Because I've decided I'd far rather go to New York.' Turning to watch the look of disbelief spreading across Parker's face – he'd clearly had no idea she'd been about to say this – she added, 'If this man here is sure he doesn't mind.'

393

Unable to speak for a moment, Parker shook his head help-lessly.

'And I'm just warning you,' Kaye told him, 'now would be a seriously bad time to tell me you have a wife waiting at home for you to go back.'

Unable to resist it, Max chimed in, 'Or a husband.'

Parker was gripping Kaye's hands. 'Are you sure? Really?'

'Oh please, what's more important? Working on some stupid, meaningless, so-called glamorous soap? Or being with someone who means the world to you?' Tears glittered in Kaye's eyes. 'I mean, hopefully I'll be offered something in New York, maybe theatre work for a change. But who knows if that'll happen? Either way, I've been lucky enough to find a wonderful man. I'm not going to be stupid enough to risk losing him.'

To her absolute horror Tilly realised she was on the verge of crying too. Hastily she rubbed her hot cheeks and stuffed another mayonnaise-loaded breadstick into her mouth, because it was phys-ically impossible to simultaneously eat and cry. Kaye and Parker were hugging each other now, wrapped up in a haze of joy that was all-consuming. Of course Kaye was doing the right thing; it was blindingly obvious. A happy relationship was worth more than ten dazzling careers.

Aware that she was being watched, Tilly glanced up and saw, across the room, Jack's gaze on her. God, she must be hormonal at the moment; perilously close to bursting into tears but hampered by her mouthful of food, she almost sprayed breadstick across the carpet. Inhaling instead, she ended up coughing and spluttering and being vigorously whacked on the back by Erin.

Which never helped.

'Are you all right?'

Tilly nodded, coughed, swallowed and wiped her streaming eyes.

'Isn't that romantic about Kaye and Parker?'

'Yes.' Oh God, and now Jack and Max were coming over; clutching her neck by way of apology, Tilly croaked, 'Crumbs . . . windpipe . . .' and dodged past them on her way out of the room.

Upstairs in the cool marble bathroom she cleared her throat and used a tissue to clean away the flecks of mascara under her eyes. Not wanting to head back down just yet, she picked up the magazines Lou had left on the floor after her bath this morning. Emblazoned across the cover of *Hi!* magazine were the words 'STOP PRESS!! He Broke My Heart But I Forgive Him!' above a posed shot of Tandy and Jamie. Tandy's petal-pink mouth was turned up at the corners in a sad-but-hopeful smile whilst Jamie looked handsome and suitably penitent in a shirt that exactly matched her lipstick.

Tilly had already read the interview inside; as she'd turned the glossy pages she'd been torn between feeling sorry for Tandy and wanting to shake some sense into her. To be with Jamie she was prepared to be hurt and humiliated. And Jamie, realising he could get away with being unfaithful, would do it again and again. Overwhelmed with sadness, Tilly smoothed the wrinkled cover and placed the handful of magazines on the window ledge.

She opened the bathroom door and came face to face with Jack. Oh God, how was this fair?

'I came to see if you were all right.' He studied her. 'Everything OK?'

Damn, why hadn't she thought to brush her teeth? To blast him with eye-watering garlic breath or to hide it, keep her mouth clamped shut and just nod?

Tilly nodded.

'Sure?' Jack gave her a shrewd look.

She held her breath and nodded again. 'Mmm hmm.'

'So . . . have you changed your mind about me yet?'

Tilly's teeth were tightly clenched to stop any stray deadly fumes from leaking out. She shook her head.

'OK, listen to me.' His tone altered, became matter-of-fact. 'The trouble with you is, you think you know best. But just this once, I happen to know you're wrong. And chasing after a girl who gives me a hard time really isn't my thing, but the reason I haven't given up on you before now is because I *know* I'm right. So, seriously, what do I have to do to make you realise that too?' Jack spread his hands. 'You just tell me what it is and I'll do it.'

Oh no, not more tears, *please no.* Tilly rolled her eyes, desperate to siphon them back down to wherever they'd come from. By some kind of miracle, it actually worked. She even remembered to keep her mouth closed. Only when she'd edged far enough away and was already halfway down the staircase did she open it enough to say, 'Please don't, Jack.'

Because this was hurting, actually *physically hurting*, more than she could ever have imagined. And she couldn't cope with the pressure of it any more.

If Jack could be a commitment-phobe, so could she.

'Where's Jack?' said Erin twenty minutes later.

'Had to shoot off, see a tenant or something.' Max shrugged and refilled their glasses as a phone beeped somewhere in the room. 'Mind you, he's been a miserable bugger today. No idea what's wrong with him. Woman trouble, maybe.' A thought occurred to him. 'Could be something to do with that pretty physio who's moved into the Fallon Road place. You've seen her bombing around in her white MG, haven't you? Long blond hair, looks like Claudia Schiffer.'

Tilly's stomach lurched. Was that where he'd gone? Would the two of them start a—

'Oh noooo!' Beside her, Lou was gazing in dismay at her mobile. 'I don't *believe* it.'

'What's that, a text from Cormac?' Max tried to peer at the screen but Lou whisked it away with practised thirteen-year-old dexterity. 'Has he dumped you?'

'Shut up, Dad. No he hasn't. It's about Mr Lewis. He's just told everyone he's leaving at the end of this term!'

Erin said, 'Who's Mr Lewis?'

'He teaches French and PE. Everyone really likes him.' Lou, who had been allowed the afternoon off for Kaye's leaving party, frantically scrolled through the rest of the message from Cormac. 'He's got a job at another school up in Scotland. Oh, that's such a pain, he's so cool. He broke up with his girlfriend just recently. That could be why he's decided to move away, to get over it and make a fresh start. Mum?' Lou called Kaye and Parker across. 'You'll never guess what! Mr Lewis is leaving! He's moving up to Dundee! And you fancied him, remember?' She pulled a comical face. 'Although I'm not sure you'd have been his type.'

'Or he might not have been mine. There's such a thing as being over-sporty.' Kaye, who had never caught the LA fitness bug, entwined her fingers with Parker's. Beaming with happiness she said, 'Anyway, I've got someone else now. And this one's definitely my type.'

Chapter 57

'Right, back to work.' Draining his coffee, Max rose to his feet and collected up the files on the table in front of him. 'I'm meeting the Petersons in Malmesbury then heading on over to Bristol. I need you to get hold of those bloody electricians and tell them we need polished chrome sockets in the Rowell Street flat, not brushed chrome. And the curtains need picking up too.' His steel-framed glasses glinted as he tilted his head to one side. 'Can I tell you something? You look like crap.'

'Gosh, thanks.' Tilly forced a smile. *Tell me something I don't know.*

'And you still smell of garlic.'

She knew that too. Brushing her teeth twice last night and three times so far this morning had been an exercise in futility; all it had done was make her gums sore and give the evil garlick-yness a fresh minty edge. Which was rather like adding a fetching pink lace trim to a decontamination suit.

'In fact,' said Max, 'just breathe on the electricians. That'll do the trick.'

'You know how to make a girl feel good about herself.' Actually, a decontamination suit could be the answer she was looking for;

if she zipped herself up inside it, she could hide both her face and her breath from the world.

'Sorry, pet. You just look as if you haven't slept well.'

'I didn't.' She'd spent half the night miserably tossing and turning, and the other half watching the sun come up. The fact that it had been the most beautiful June morning had only served to emphasise her own unhappiness. By seven o'clock the earlier horizontal layers of low-lying mist had dispersed, the air was zingily clear and the sky was a cloudless cerulean blue. Birds had been singing in the trees. Somewhere overhead, Kaye and Parker were on their way to New York and a whole new life together.

Whereas she, Tilly, was stuck here with her increasingly hard to handle old one.

'You and Kaye really hit it off, didn't you? We'll all miss having her around. Didn't expect you to be taking it worse than Lou, though. Was she OK when you dropped her off at school?'

'Fine. Cheery as anything.' Tilly smiled slightly at the memory of Lou casually asking to be dropped off at the school gates so that she and Cormac could walk up the tree-lined drive together. 'She's already excited about going to visit Kaye and Parker in New York.'

'Good. OK, I'm off. Oh, hang on, nearly forgot.' Rummaging in the top left kitchen drawer, Max picked out a key. 'I was supposed to give this to Jack yesterday; it's the master for Devonshire Road. Can you drop it off at his place before you do anything else?'

Jack's place. She really wasn't up to seeing him today. 'Can't you do it?'

'It's on your way. I'm heading in the opposite direction. Are you *ill*?' Max surveyed her with concern.

Tilly's shoulders sagged. Of course she wasn't ill. Feeling guilty, she shook her head. 'No.'

'He's not at home, I tried ringing him earlier. So all you have to do is shove it through the letterbox. God only knows where he is.' Max's tone was laconic. 'His mobile's switched off too.'

Which was more information, frankly, than Tilly needed to hear, but what else did she expect? Still, at least it meant she wouldn't have to face him. Reaching for the key, she said, 'OK, I'll drop it off.'

Max left, taking Betty along with him to the dog-loving Petersons in Malmesbury. Tilly stuffed the Devonshire Road key into the back pocket of her cut-off jeans, slid her feet back into her silver flip-flops and headed out to the car. Swing past Jack's house first, then over to Rowell Street in Cheltenham to give the electricians hell.

The gates were shut and the driveway was empty. Thankful that Jack was still out, Tilly hopped out of the car and pushed open the right-hand gate. It might only be nine thirty but the sun was already hot and her white vest was sticking to her back. She reached the front door and let the key fall through the letterbox. Right, done. Electricians next. *Oh God*.

Sod's law dictated that of course it was Jack's car pulling up outside the gates. As she watched, frozen into immobility on the doorstep, he emerged from the driver's seat, opened both gates wide then climbed back in and drove through them. Since the gap between car and gateposts was too narrow to navigate without a struggle, Tilly's only means of escape now was over the six-foot wall. And for a moment she was tempted.

But no, she mustn't. She wasn't a burglar. Nor was she gymnastic enough to be confident of reaching the pavement with both ankles intact.

Instead she hovered by the front door, waiting for the Jag to move past the gateposts, thereby enabling her to squeeze through and reach the safety of her own car.

But Jack left it where it was, effectively blocking her in. By accident or design? Tilly's pulse was hammering away in her throat like an ominous jungle beat.

'Here to see me?' For the second time he climbed out of the car. He was wearing yesterday's clothes, dark grey trousers and a blue and white striped shirt. There was stubble on his chin too. He hadn't shaved. What did that tell you?

'I just dropped off the master key for Devonshire Road. Max forgot to give it to you yesterday.' Edging sideways in a wide arc around him, Tilly said, 'Actually, if you could move your car, I need to get over to Cheltenham.'

'I don't bite,' said Jack.

'I know that! I'm just in a hurry, that's all!' He was twelve feet away but even out here in the open air she was conscious of the garlic. How far were the hideous fumes capable of wafting?

Jack rubbed the flat of his hand over his stubbly jaw and looked down at the ground. Then he raised his gaze, fixed it on Tilly and said, 'I've only just got home.'

'I spotted that.' The annoying thing was, when Jack was rumpled and sleep-deprived, he still managed to look as sexy as hell.

'Aren't you going to ask me where I've been?'

He might as well ask if she'd like to stab herself in the eye with a fork. Tilly did her best to sound as if she couldn't care less. 'I don't know. Where were you?' *Please don't let him start rattling on about a girl who looks like Claudia Schiffer.*

Jack stayed where he was, standing with his hands in his pockets. 'I was with Rose's mother.' He kept his tone level. 'And her father.'

Which wasn't what she'd been expecting to hear at all. Completely wrong-footed, Tilly said, *'Oh.'*

'I drove over to Wales yesterday afternoon. I needed to see them.' Jack's gaze was unwavering. 'Because you don't trust me. You refuse to believe what I say when I tell you how I feel about you. And I suppose I can't blame you, what with my track record. But then yesterday, when you couldn't even bring yourself to speak to me, well, I realised I had to prove to you that I was serious. So I went to see Bryn and Dilys.' He paused, a muscle going in his jaw. 'And we visited Rose's grave together. Then they asked me to stay to dinner. And after dinner I told them that I'd met this girl . . .'

Tilly felt as if the ground had been whisked away, tablecloth-style. Her feet were still there but she no longer knew how they were managing to hold her up.

'And I didn't know how they'd react.' Jack shook his head. 'The last thing I wanted to do was upset them, you know? But they were amazing. Dilys said she was so happy for me, and they'd been waiting for this to happen. Bryn said they were proud of me, and that Rose would have wanted me to meet someone else.'

Now the ground felt as if it were tilting underfoot. Tilly's head was spinning and perspiration was trickling down her spine.

'So that was when it got a bit awkward and I had to explain to them that things weren't exactly going full steam ahead,' said Jack. 'But they were on my side. Bryn told me if I needed one, he'd write me a reference. You know, they're an incredible couple. They asked a million questions about you. We were still talking at one o'clock in the morning – that's how I ended up staying the night.' He paused, his eyes glittering in the sunlight. 'And they agree with me. They think you and Rose would have got on like a house on fire.'

Tilly couldn't speak. She took a step backwards, into the shade of the mulberry tree. That was better, not so hot.

402

'And I've just driven back from there this morning. With Bryn and Dilys's blessing.' Tilting his head fractionally in the direction of the car, Jack said, 'Not to mention half a baked gammon wrapped in foil, a dozen Welsh cakes and a loaf of bara brith. So, is that enough to convince you I'm serious?'

Tilly closed her eyes for a moment. She wanted to believe him, of course she did. But who was to say Jack wouldn't change his mind next week? What if he was just getting carried away because she was the box he hadn't yet ticked?

When she opened her eyes again, Jack was approaching. Oh God . . . Stepping back in a panic, she bounced off the trunk of the tree.

'Still not convinced, then.' Shaking his head, Jack said, 'Dilys did wonder if that'd be enough. Fine, we'll move on to Plan B.'

'No!' Tilly darted sideways and covered her mouth in terror as he moved towards her. 'Please no . . .'

'Oh come on, I'm not that bloody scary.' He frowned in disbelief.

'It's not that.' Deeply ashamed, Tilly hung her head and muttered, 'It's the garlic.'

'What? I can't hear you. Talk properly.'

She tried to say it out of the corner of her mouth. 'I have garlic breath.'

'You don't.' He was in the vicinity now. Less than eighteen inches from her face. Definitely inside the danger zone. 'I can't smell anything.'

'I do. Max told me this morning. And I had to drive Lou to school with all the windows open. I can even taste it myself.' Her skin prickled with shame. 'It's really bad.'

Jack began to smile. 'Lucky I had dinner last night with Dilys

403

and Bryn, then. Lamb studded with garlic. Served with Dauphinoise potatoes because she knew they were my favourite.' He took another step closer and said, 'Do I smell of it as well?'

Despite everything, Tilly smiled too. 'No idea. Can't tell.'

So that was it. Fumes-wise, they were immune to each other. Neat trick.

For several seconds they stood there together under the tree, gazing into each other's eyes. Tilly waited for Jack to kiss her. Frustratingly, it didn't happen.

Finally she said, 'Is this Plan B?'

'No. Plan B was going to be me asking you to marry me.'

OK, now the ground had definitely disappeared beneath her feet. Tilly's fingers grasped the rough bark of the tree trunk.

'Don't you think that would prove to you that I'm serious?' said Jack.

Oh God, this had to be some kind of drug-induced hallucination. Had someone slipped something into yesterday's mayonnaise dip? Shakily Tilly said, 'This is crazy.'

'No? Not good enough? Ah, you *still* don't trust me, because I could say it today, then next week call it all off. Fair point.' Jack's eyes began to crinkle at the corners. 'That moves us along to Plan C.'

'What's Plan C?' gulped Tilly as he prised her fingers off the tree trunk and clasped her left hand firmly in his right one. Expecting him to lead her into the house, she was taken by surprise when he headed out through the front gates instead. With the Jag still rakishly parked in the way, it was a tight squeeze getting past it. Jack pointed his keys at the car and zapped the locks shut. As he hauled her after him down the street, Tilly said breathlessly, 'Where are we going?'

'Wait and see.' Jack waved at the middle-aged man pruning his roses in the garden next door. 'Morning, Ted, this is the girl I've just asked to marry me.'

What?

Ted looked equally astounded. 'Really? Well, um, excellent. Well done, lad.'

'Oh my God, oh my God,' squeaked Tilly as they made their way down the street.

'Morning, Mrs Ellis, how are you?' Cheerily greeting an elderly lady walking her Pekingese, Jack said, 'This is Tilly, my future wife, touch wood!'

'Jack!' Mrs Ellis stopped dead in her tracks, almost garrotting her dog. 'Good heavens, how marvellous. I had no idea!'

'Is this Plan C?' Tilly demanded as they approached the High Street.

'Not yet.' Leading her across the road, Jack called out to a couple of teenage boys on bikes, 'Hey, guess what? I've just asked this girl to marry me!'

The teenagers turned and gave them a big-deal look. The taller of the two sneered and said, 'Loser.'

Tilly shook her head. 'OK, you have to stop this. You're going to end up getting arrested.'

'There's Declan! Hey, Declan!' Bellowing across the road, Jack yelled, 'Meet my future wife!'

Declan did a double-take, then waggled an imaginary glass at Tilly, cringing behind Jack. 'How many's he had, love?'

'No, I haven't been drinking. I've just come to my senses. Come on,' Jack squeezed Tilly's hand and dragged her on, 'keep up.'

Erin's shop next. He barged in, startling Erin and a curvaceous brunette who was in the process of trying on a strapless cerise ballgown.

'Jack! Long time no *see*,' cried the brunette, clearly thrilled to see him. 'How've you *been*?'

'Never better. Just asked Tilly to marry me.'

'Sorry?' Erin's mouth dropped open in disbelief.

The brunette's gasp was audible. She stared at him as if he'd sprouted an extra head. 'You're getting married?'

'Well, she hasn't said yes yet.' Jack flashed a grin. 'Wish me luck. Nice dress,' he added over his shoulder as he whisked Tilly out of the shop. 'Right, on with Plan C.'

'I'm meant to be working.' God, where was he taking her now? Her mind in a whirl, Tilly said breathlessly, 'I'm going to be in so much trouble with Max.'

'Leave Max to me.' Jack stopped as they reached Montgomery's the jewellers, and rang the bell to be let in.

The fact that you had to ring a bell in order to be let in was the reason Tilly had never been inside Roxborough's smartest jewellery shop. As the possibility of why they were here began to sink in, she hung back. 'Jack, stop it, this is mad.'

The buzzer went, the door opened and Jack said, 'It's Plan C. I want you and everyone else to know I'm serious. And I'm warning you . . .'

'What?'

'There is no Plan D.'

Inside the shop, expertly angled pools of light illuminated the polished cabinets of both antique and modern fine jewellery. The topaz carpets were plush and velvety, the walls were oak-panelled and if Tilly and Jack's combined eye-watering breath was a hideous intrusion upon this rarefied atmosphere, Martin Montgomery was far too much of a gentleman to show it.

Twenty minutes later, by a process of elimination and without once even letting her glimpse how much any of them cost, Martin Montgomery had succeeded in narrowing the choice of rings to two. Coloured stones had been discarded. Multiple stones had been discarded. Yellow gold had been cast aside in favour of platinum. The two remaining solitaire diamonds, both stunning and shooting out glittery rainbow sparks of light, were so beautiful Tilly could barely breathe. One was square and princess cut, the other oval and cushion cut. The square one was her favourite – the shape of the ring and the setting made it more unusual – but the diamond was bigger. Which meant she had to choose the smaller one because just the thought of how many thousands of pounds each of these rings must cost was enough to bring on a panic attack.

No wonder there were elegant gold chairs beside the counters – so that customers catching sight of the price tags had something to crash down on when they came over all faint.

Tilly looked at Martin Montgomery. 'If he changes his mind next week and brings the ring back, will you give him a full refund?'

Startled, Martin Montgomery said, 'Er . . .'

'I'm not going to change my mind.' Jack held up the two rings. 'Come on, which one do you prefer?'

The big square one, obviously. The shape of the setting suited her hand. It was the most beautiful ring she'd ever seen in her life. 'I like the oval one best.'

Jack raised an eyebrow. 'Are you sure?'

'Absolutely.' Oh God, disappointment welled up. Which was completely ridiculous, because the oval one was the second most beautiful ring she'd ever seen in her life.

'Not just saying that because you think it's cheaper?'

Tilly shook her head. 'No.'

'Because it isn't, you know.'

It wasn't? Adrenaline shot through her entire body. She turned to Martin Montgomery. 'Is that true?'

The jeweller smiled slightly and nodded. 'You see, when the clarity and the colour are taken into account, *this* ring is actually of higher—'

'OK!' Cutting him off before he could start burbling on all over again about colour, cut and clarity, Tilly grabbed the square-cut diamond and said joyfully, 'I'll have this one then!'

'Not just saying that because it's cheaper?' Jack's mouth was twitching at the corners.

'No! I love it!'

'Good. Me too. That's it then, Martin. This is the one we'll have.'

As Jack took the ring from her and slid it slowly and deliberately on to the third finger of her left hand, Tilly felt her eyes fill with tears. Because she now knew he was serious. He really, really meant it.

Martin Montgomery diplomatically busied himself putting the oval diamond back in the window. Jack drew Tilly to him and kissed her on the mouth. God, he was good at that.

In her ear, he murmured, 'So has Plan C done the trick?'

'You know what?' Tilly shook her head, hardly able to believe it herself. 'It really has.'

He broke into a wicked smile. 'I'm going to take you home now.'

Tilly quivered in anticipation. 'You haven't paid for the ring yet.'

She waited a discreet distance away while Jack took a card from his wallet and the transaction was completed. Then she jumped out of her skin as her mobile began to trill.

'Oops. It's Max.' Even holding the phone was an excuse to admire the ring miraculously glittering away on her hand.

'Here, let me.' Jack took control, said, 'Hi Max' and pressed speaker-phone.

'What's going on?' Max's voice registered suspicion. 'Why are you answering Tilly's phone?'

'She's here with me now. I've just asked her to marry me.' Jack's amused gaze went to the ring on Tilly's hand. 'And she's more or less said yes.'

Silence. Tilly's mouth was bone dry. She waited for Max to roar with laughter and come out with some mucky retort.

Instead, having digested this information, he said, 'Is she the one?'

Jack gave Tilly's hand a reassuring squeeze. 'Yes, she is.'

'Thought so,' said Max. 'Put her on.'

Still trembling, Tilly took the phone. 'Hi, Max.'

'Is this a wind-up?'

'No. It's been a bit of a weird morning.'

'You're telling me. So it's serious between you and Jack?'

She saw Jack nodding. 'Yes.'

'Christ, I can't keep up with this. The whole world's gone mad. Are you still working for me?'

'Yes!' Though obviously not at this minute.

'Where are you?' demanded Max.

'Um, in Montgomery's the jewellers.'

'So you haven't been in touch with the electricians?'

Tilly winced. Oops. 'Sorry, Max.'

'Max?' Jack stepped in. 'I love Tilly. I'm hoping she loves me, although she hasn't actually said as much yet. This is a pretty special day for us. So basically, bugger the electricians.'

'OK, tell Tilly I'll deal with them myself.' After a pause, Max said, 'So it's finally happened, then?'

Jack squeezed Tilly's hand and gave her a look that melted her insides. He nodded and smiled. 'It's finally happened.'

'Well, it's about time too. And trust me, it really must be love if you've just asked her to marry you.' Max sounded both impressed and amused. 'Because that girl absolutely reeks of garlic.'

**This book is to be returned on or before
the last date stamped below.**